A. Conan Doyle 著

梅紹武 屠珍 譯

SHERLOCK HOLMES ADVENTURES

福爾摩斯七大奇案

商務印書館

本書譯文由上海世紀出版股份有限公司譯文出版社授權使用

書　　名：*Sherlock Holmes Adventures* 福爾摩斯七大奇案
作　　者：A. Conan Doyle
插　　圖：Sidney Paget
譯　　者：梅紹武　屠珍
責任編輯：張朗欣　黃家麗
封面設計：楊愛文
出　　版：商務印書館（香港）有限公司
　　　　　香港筲箕灣耀興道 3 號東滙廣場 8 樓
　　　　　http://www.commercialpress.com.hk
發　　行：香港聯合書刊物流有限公司
　　　　　香港新界大埔汀麗路 36 號中華商務印刷大廈 3 字樓
印　　刷：中華商務彩色印刷有限公司
　　　　　香港新界大埔汀麗路 36 號中華商務印刷大廈
版　　次：2019 年 1 月第 1 版第 3 次印刷
　　　　　© 2015 商務印書館（香港）有限公司
　　　　　ISBN 978 962 07 0392 8
　　　　　Printed in Hong Kong

Publisher's Note 出版説明

　　大名鼎鼎的福爾摩斯雖無案不歡，卻會對平平無奇的案件嗤之以鼻。他接手調查的離奇案件，或許成功，或許失敗，都經過一番迂迴曲折才解開案中之謎。無論是謀殺案還是盜竊案，兇手都經過精心策劃，非常人能破解，是為此書的"奇"。

　　初、中級英語程度讀者使用本書時，先閱讀英文原文，如遇到理解障礙，則參照中譯作為輔助。在英文原文結束之前或附註解，標註古英語、非現代詞彙拼寫形式及語法；同樣，在譯文結束之前或附註解，以幫助讀者理解原文故事背景。如有餘力，讀者可在閱讀原文部份段落後，查閱相應中譯，觀察同樣詞句在雙語中不同的表達。

　　神探福爾摩斯究竟敗在誰手上？是甚麼令福爾摩斯徘徊生死邊緣？由《波希米亞醜聞案》到《紫銅櫸》七個精選故事，讀者可藉此機會訓練偵探頭腦，享受破案的樂趣，亦不忘享受文字的饗宴。

商務印書館 (香港) 有限公司

編輯出版部

Contents 目錄

A Scandal in Bohemia

To Sherlock Holmes she is always *the* woman. I have seldom heard him mention her under any other name. In his eyes she eclipses and predominates the whole of her sex. It was not that he felt any emotion akin to love for Irene Adler. All emotions, and that one particularly, were abhorrent to his cold, precise, but admirably balanced mind. He was, I take it, the most perfect reasoning and observing machine that the world has seen: but, as a lover, he would have placed himself in a false position. He never spoke of the softer passions, save with a gibe and a sneer. They were admirable things for the observer—excellent for drawing the veil from men's motives and actions. But for the trained reasoner to admit such intrusions into his own delicate and finely adjusted temperament was to introduce a distracting factor which might throw a doubt upon all his mental results. Grit in a sensitive instrument, or a crack in one of his own high-power lenses, would not be more disturbing than a strong emotion in a nature such as his. And yet there was but one woman to him, and that woman was the late Irene Adler, of dubious and questionable memory.

I had seen little of Holmes lately. My marriage had drifted us away from each other. My own complete happiness, and the home-centred interests which rise up around the man who first finds himself master of his own establishment, were sufficient to absorb all my attention; while Holmes, who loathed every form of society with his whole Bohemian soul, remained in our lodgings in Baker Street, buried among his old books, and alternating from week to week between cocaine and ambition, the drowsiness of the drug, and the fierce energy of his own keen nature. He was still, as ever, deeply attracted by the study of crime, and occupied his immense faculties and extraordinary powers of observation in following out those clues, and clearing up those mysteries, which had been abandoned as hopeless by the official police. From time to time I heard some vague account of his doings: of his summons to Odessa in the case of the Trepoff murder, of his clearing up of the singular tragedy of the Atkinson brothers at Trincomalee, and finally of the mission which he had accomplished so delicately and successfully for the reigning family of Holland. Beyond these signs of his activity, however, which I merely shared with all the readers of the daily press, I knew little of my former friend and companion.

One night—it was on the 20th of March, 1888—I was return-ing from a journey to a patient (for I had now returned to civil practice), when my way led me through Baker Street. As I passed the well-remembered door, which must always be associated in my mind with my wooing, and with the dark incidents of the Study in Scarlet, I was seized with a keen desire to see Holmes again, and to know how he was employing his extraordinary powers.

His rooms were brilliantly lit, and, even as I looked up, I saw his tall spare figure pass twice in a dark silhouette against the blind. He was pacing the room swiftly, eagerly, with his head sunk upon his chest, and his hands clasped behind him. To me, who knew his every mood and habit, his attitude and manner told their own story. He was at work again. He had risen out of his drug-created dreams, and was hot upon the scent of some new problem. I rang the bell, and was shown up to the chamber which had formerly been in part my own.

His manner was not effusive. It seldom was; but he was glad, I think, to see me. With hardly a word spoken, but with a kindly eye, he waved me to an armchair, threw across his case of cigars, and indicated a spirit case and a gasogene in the corner. Then he stood before the fire, and looked me over in his singular introspective fashion.

'Wedlock suits you,' he remarked. 'I think, Watson, that you have put on seven and a half pounds since I saw you.'

'Seven,' I answered.

'Indeed, I should have thought a little more. Just a trifle more, I fancy, Watson. And in practice again, I observe. You did not tell me that you intended to go into harness.'

'Then, how do you know?'

'I see it, I deduce it. How do I know that you have been getting yourself very wet lately, and that you have a most clumsy and careless servant girl?'

'My dear Holmes,' said I, 'this is too much. You would certainly have been burned had you lived a few centuries ago. It is true that I had a country walk on Thursday and came home in a dreadful mess; but, as I have changed my clothes, I can't imagine how you deduced it. As to Mary Jane, she is incorrigible, and my wife has given her notice, but there again, I fail to see how you work it out.'

He chuckled to himself and rubbed his long nervous hands together.

'It is simplicity itself,' said he; 'my eyes tell me that on the inside of your left shoe, just where the firelight strikes it, the leather is scored by six almost parallel cuts. Obviously they have been caused by someone who has very carelessly scraped round the edges of the sole in order to remove crusted mud from it. Hence, you see, my double deduction that you had been out in vile weather, and that you had a particularly malignant boot-slitting specimen of the London slavey. As to your practice, if a gentleman walks into my rooms smelling of iodoform, with a black mark of nitrate of silver upon his right forefinger, and a bulge on the right side of his top hat to show where he has secreted his stethoscope,

I must be dull indeed if I do not pronounce him to be an active member of the medical profession.'

I could not help laughing at the ease with which he explained his process of deduction. 'When I hear you give your reasons,' I remarked, 'the thing always appears to me to be so ridiculously simple that I could easily do it myself, though at each successive instance of your reasoning I am baffled, until you explain your process. And yet I believe that my eyes are as good as yours.'

'Quite so,' he answered, lighting a cigarette, and throwing himself down into an armchair. 'You see, but you do not observe. The distinction is clear. For example, you have frequently seen the steps which lead up from the hall to this room.'

'Frequently.'

'How often?'

'Well, some hundreds of times.'

'Then how many are there?'

'How many! I don't know.'

'Quite so! You have not observed. And yet you have seen. That is just my point. Now, I know that there are seventeen steps, because I have both seen and observed. By the way, since you are interested in these little problems, and since you are good enough to chronicle one or two of my trifling experiences, you may be interested in this.' He threw over a sheet of thick, pink-tinted note-paper[1] which had been lying open upon the table. 'It came by the last post,' said he. 'Read it aloud.'

The note was undated, and without either signature or address.

'There will call upon you tonight, at a quarter to eight o'clock,' it said, 'a gentleman who desires to consult you upon a matter of the very deepest moment. Your recent services to one of the Royal

Houses of Europe have shown that you are one who may safely be trusted with matters which are of an importance which can hardly be exaggerated. This account of you we have from all quarters received. Be in your chamber then at that hour, and do not take it amiss if your visitor wear a mask.'

'This is indeed a mystery,' I remarked. 'What do you imagine that it means?'

'I have no data yet. It is a capital mistake to theorize before one has data. Insensibly one begins to twist facts to suit theories, instead of theories to suit facts. But the note itself. What do you deduce from it?'

I carefully examined the writing, and the paper upon which it was written.

'The man who wrote it was presumably well-to-do,' I remarked, endeavouring to imitate my companion's processes. 'Such paper could not be bought under half a crown a packet. It is peculiarly strong and stiff.'

'Peculiar—that is the very word,' said Holmes. 'It is not an English paper at all. Hold it up to the light.'

I did so, and saw a large E with a small g, a P, and a large G with a small t woven into the texture of the paper.

'What do you make of that?' asked Holmes.

'The name of the maker, no doubt; or his monogram, rather.'

'Not at all. The G with the small t stands for 'Gesellschaft,' which is the German for 'Company.' It is a customary contraction like our 'Co.' P, of course, stands for 'Papier.' Now for the Eg. Let us glance at our Continental Gazetteer.' He took down a heavy brown volume from his shelves. 'Eglow, Eglonitz—here we are, Egria. It is in a German-speaking country—in Bohemia, not far from Carlsbad. 'Remarkable as being the scene of the death of Wallenstein, and for its numerous glass factories and paper mills.' Ha, ha, my boy, what do you make of that?' His eyes sparkled, and he sent up a great blue triumphant cloud from his cigarette.

'The paper was made in Bohemia,' I said.

'Precisely. And the man who wrote the note is a German. Do you note the peculiar construction of the sentence—'This account of you we have from all quarters received.' A Frenchman or Russian could not have written that. It is the German who is so uncourteous to his verbs. It only remains, therefore, to discover what is wanted by this German who writes upon Bohemian paper, and prefers wearing a mask to showing his face. And here he comes, if I am not mistaken, to resolve all our doubts.'

As he spoke there was the sharp sound of horses' hoofs and grating wheels against the kerb, followed by a sharp pull at the bell. Holmes whistled.

'A pair by the sound,' said he. 'Yes,' he continued, glancing out of the window. 'A nice little brougham and a pair of beauties. A hundred and fifty guineas apiece. There's money in this case, Watson, if there is nothing else.'

'I think that I had better go, Holmes.'

'Not a bit, Doctor. Stay where you are. I am lost without my Boswell. And this promises to be interesting. It would be a pity to miss it.'

'But your client—'

'Never mind him. I may want your help, and so may he. Here he comes. Sit down in that armchair, Doctor, and give us your best attention.'

A slow and heavy step, which had been heard upon the stairs and in the passage, paused immediately outside the door. Then there was a loud and authoritative tap.

'Come in!' said Holmes.

A man entered who could hardly have been less than six feet six inches in height, with the chest and limbs of a Hercules. His dress was rich with a richness which would, in England, be looked upon as akin to bad taste. Heavy bands of astrakhan were slashed across the sleeves and fronts of his double-breasted coat, while the deep blue cloak which was thrown over his shoulders was lined with flame-coloured silk, and secured at the neck with a brooch which consisted of a single flaming beryl. Boots which extended half-way up his calves, and which were trimmed at the tops with a rich brown fur, completed the impression of barbaric opulence

which was suggested by his whole appearance. He carried a broad-brimmed hat in his hand, while he wore across the upper part of his face, extending down past the cheek-bones[2], a black vizard mask, which he had apparently adjusted that very moment, for his hand was still raised to it as he entered. From the lower part of the face he appeared to be a man of strong character, with a thick, hanging lip, and a long, straight chin, suggestive of resolution pushed to the length of obstinacy.

'You had my note?' he asked, with a deep, harsh voice and a strongly marked German accent. 'I told you that I would call.' He looked from one to the other of us, as if uncertain which to address.

'Pray take a seat,' said Holmes. 'This is my friend and colleague, Dr Watson, who is occasionally good enough to help me in my cases. Whom have I the honour to address?'

'You may address me as the Count Von Kramm, a Bohemian nobleman. I understand that this gentleman, your friend, is a man of honour and discretion, whom I may trust with a matter of the most extreme importance. If not, I should much prefer to communicate with you alone.'

I rose to go, but Holmes caught me by the wrist and pushed me back into my chair. 'It is both, or none,' said he. 'You may say before this gentleman anything which you may say to me.'

The Count shrugged his broad shoulders. 'Then I must begin,' said he, 'by binding you both to absolute secrecy for two years, at the end of that time the matter will be of no importance. At present it is not too much to say that it is of such weight it may have an influence upon European history.'

'I promise,' said Holmes.

'And I.'

'You will excuse this mask,' continued our strange visitor. 'The august person who employs me wishes his agent to be unknown to you, and I may confess at once that the title by which I have just called myself is not exactly my own.'

'I was aware of it,' said Holmes dryly.

'The circumstances are of great delicacy, and every precaution has to be taken to quench what might grow to be an immense scandal and seriously compromise one of the reigning families of Europe. To speak plainly, the matter implicates the great House of Ormstein, hereditary kings of Bohemia.'

'I was also aware of that,' murmured Holmes, settling himself down in his armchair, and closing his eyes.

Our visitor glanced with some apparent surprise at the languid, lounging figure of the man who had been no doubt depicted to him as the most incisive reasoned, and most energetic agent in Europe. Holmes slowly reopened his eyes and looked impatiently at his gigantic client.

'If your Majesty would condescend to state your case,' he remarked, 'I should be better able to advise you.'

The man sprang from his chair, and paced up and down the room in uncontrollable agitation. Then, with a gesture of desperation, he tore the mask from his face and hurled it upon the ground. 'You are right,' he cried; 'I am the King. Why should I attempt to conceal it?'

'Why, indeed?' murmured Holmes. 'Your Majesty had not spoken before I was aware that I was addressing Wilhelm Gott-

sreich Sigismond von Ormstein, Grand Duke of Cassel-Falstein, and hereditary King of Bohemia.'

'But you can understand,' said our strange visitor, sitting down once more and passing his hand over his high, white forehead, 'you can understand that I am not accustomed to doing such business in my own person. Yet the matter was so delicate that I could not confide it to an agent without putting myself in his power. I have come *incognito* from Prague for the purpose of consulting you.'

'Then, pray consult,' said Holmes, shutting his eyes once more.

'The facts are briefly these: Some five years ago, during a lengthy visit to Warsaw, I made the acquaintance of the well-known adventuress Irene Adler. The name is no doubt familiar to you.'

'Kindly look her up in my index, Doctor,' murmured Holmes, without opening his eyes. For many years he had adopted a system of docketing all paragraphs concerning men and things, so that it was difficult to name a subject or a person on which he could not at once furnish information. In this case I found her biography sandwiched in between that of a Hebrew rabbi and that of a staff-commander who had written a monograph upon the deep-sea fishes.

'Let me see,' said Holmes. 'Hum! Born in New Jersey in the year 1858. Contralto—hum! La Scala, hum! Prima donna Imperial Opera of Warsaw—Yes! Retired from operatic stage—ha! Living in London—quite so! Your Majesty, as I understand, became entangled with this young person, wrote her some compromising letters, and is now desirous of getting those letters back.'

'Precisely so. But how—'

'Was there a secret marriage?'

'None.'

'No legal papers or certificates?'

'None.'

'Then I fail to follow your Majesty. If this young person should produce her letters for blackmailing or other purposes, how is she to prove their authenticity?'

'There is the writing.'

'Pooh, pooh! Forgery.'

'My private note paper.'

'Stolen.'

'My own seal.'

'Imitated.'

'My photograph.'

'Bought.'

'We were both in the photograph.'

'Oh, dear! That is very bad! Your Majesty has indeed committed an indiscretion.'

'I was mad—insane.'

'You have compromised yourself seriously.'

'I was only Crown Prince then. I was young. I am but thirty now.'

'It must be recovered.'

'We have tried and failed.'

'Your Majesty must pay. It must be bought.'

'She will not sell.'

'Stolen, then.'

'Five attempts have been made. Twice burglars in my pay ransacked her house. Once we diverted her luggage when she travelled. Twice she has been waylaid. There has been no result.'

'No sign of it?'

'Absolutely none.'

Holmes laughed. 'It is quite a pretty little problem,' said he.

'But a very serious one to me,' returned the King, reproachfully.

'Very, indeed. And what does she propose to do with the photograph?'

'To ruin me.'

'But how?'

'I am about to be married.'

'So I have heard.'

'To Clotilde Lothman von Saxe-Meningen, second daughter of the King of Scandinavia. You may know the strict principles of her family. She is herself the very soul of delicacy. A shadow of a doubt as to my conduct would bring the matter to an end.'

'And Irene Adler?'

'Threatens to send them the photograph. And she will do it. I know that she will do it. You do not know her, but she has a soul of steel. She has the face of the most beautiful of women, and the mind of the most resolute of men. Rather than I should marry another woman, there are no lengths to which she would not go— none.'

'You are sure that she has not sent it yet?'

'I am sure.'

'And why?'

'Because she has said that she would send it on the day when the betrothal was publicly proclaimed. That will be next Monday.'

'Oh, then we have three days yet,' said Holmes, with a yawn. 'That is very fortunate, as I have one or two matters of importance to look into just at present. Your Majesty will, of course, stay in

London for the present?'

'Certainly. You will find me at the Langham, under the name of the Count Von Kramm.'

'Then I shall drop you a line to let you know how we progress.'

'Pray do so. I shall be all anxiety.'

'Then, as to money?'

'You have *carte blanche*.'

'Absolutely?'

'I tell you that I would give one of the provinces of my kingdom to have that photograph.'

'And for present expenses?'

The King took a heavy chamois leather bag from under his cloak, and laid it on the table.

'There are three hundred pounds in gold, and seven hundred in notes,' he said.

Holmes scribbled a receipt upon a sheet of his notebook and handed it to him.

'And Mademoiselle's address?' he asked.

'Is Briony Lodge, Serpentine Avenue, St John's Wood.'

Holmes took a note of it. 'One other question,' said he. 'Was the photograph a cabinet?'

'It was.'

'Then, good night, Your Majesty, and I trust that we shall soon have some good news for you. And good night, Watson,' he added, as the wheels of the royal brougham rolled down the street. 'If you will be good enough to call tomorrow afternoon, at three o'clock I should like to chat this little matter over with you.'

At three o'clock precisely I was at Baker Street, but Holmes had not yet returned. The landlady informed me that he had left the house shortly after eight o'clock in the morning. I sat down beside the fire, however, with the intention of awaiting him, however long he might be. I was already deeply interested in his inquiry, for, though it was surrounded by none of the grim and strange features which were associated with the two crimes which I have already recorded, still, the nature of the case and the exalted station of his client gave it a character of its own. Indeed, apart from the nature of the investigation which my friend had on hand, there was something in his masterly grasp of a situation, and his keen, incisive reasoning, which made it a pleasure to me to study his system of work, and to follow the quick, subtle methods by which he disentangled the most inextricable mysteries. So accustomed was I to his invariable success that the very possibility of his failing had ceased to enter into my head.

It was close upon four before the door opened, and a drunken-looking groom, ill-kempt and side-whiskered with an inflamed face and disreputable clothes, walked into the room. Accustomed

as I was to my friend's amazing powers in the use of disguises, I had to look three times before I was certain that it was indeed he. With a nod he vanished into the bedroom, whence he emerged in five minutes tweed-suited and respectable, as of old. Putting his hands into his pockets, he stretched out his legs in front of the fire, and laughed heartily for some minutes.

'Well, really!' he cried, and then he choked; and laughed again until he was obliged to lie back, limp and helpless, in the chair.

'What is it?'

'It's quite too funny. I am sure you could never guess how I employed my morning, or what I ended by doing.'

'I can't imagine. I suppose that you have been watching the habits, and perhaps the house, of Miss Irene Adler.'

'Quite so; but the sequel was rather unusual. I will tell you, however. I left the house a little after eight o'clock this morning, in the character of a groom out of work. There is a wonderful sympathy and freemasonry among horsey men. Be one of them, and you will know all that there is to know. I soon found Briony Lodge. It is a bijou villa, with a garden at the back, but built out in front right up to the road, two stories. Chubb lock to the door. Large sitting-room on the right side, well furnished, with long windows almost to the floor, and those preposterous English window fasteners which a child could open. Behind there was nothing remarkable, save that the passage window could be reached from the top of the coach-house. I walked round it and examined it closely from every point of view, but without noting anything else of interest.

'I then lounged down the street, and found, as I expected, that there was a mews in a lane which runs down by one wall of the garden. I lent the ostlers a hand in rubbing down their horses, and received in exchange twopence, a glass of half-and-half, two fills of shag tobacco and as much information as I could desire about Miss Adler, to say nothing of half a dozen other people in the neighbourhood in whom I was not in the least interested, but whose biographies I was compelled to listen to.'

'And what of Irene Adler?' I asked.

'Oh, she has turned all the men's heads down in that part. She is the daintiest thing under a bonnet on this planet. So say the Serpentine Mews, to a man. She lives quietly, sings at concerts, drives out at five every day, and returns at seven sharp for dinner. Seldom goes out at other times, except when she sings. Has only one male visitor, but a good deal of him. He is dark, handsome, and dashing; never calls less than once a day, and often twice. He is a Mr Godfrey Norton, of the Inner Temple. See the advantages of a cabman as a confidant. They had driven him home a dozen times from Serpentine Mews, and knew all about him. When I had listened to all they had to tell, I began to walk up and down near Briony Lodge once more, and to think over my plan of campaign.

'This Godfrey Norton was evidently an important factor in the matter. He was a lawyer. That sounded ominous. What was the relation between them, and what the object of his repeated visits? Was she his client, his friend, or his mistress? If the former, she had probably transferred the photograph to his keeping. If the latter, it was less likely. On the issue of this question depended whether I should continue my work at Briony Lodge, or turn my attention to the gentleman's chambers in the Temple. It was a delicate point, and it widened the field of my inquiry. I fear that I bore you with these details, but I have to let you see my little difficulties, if you are to understand the situation.'

'I am following you closely,' I answered.

'I was still balancing the matter in my mind when a hansom cab drove up to Briony Lodge, and a gentleman sprang out. He was a remarkably handsome man, dark, aquiline, and moustached— evidently the man of whom I had heard. He appeared to be in a great hurry, shouted to the cabman to wait, and brushed past the maid who opened the door with the air of a man who was thoroughly at home.

'He was in the house about half an hour, and I could catch glimpses of him, in the windows of the sitting-room, pacing up and down, talking excitedly and waving his arms. Of her I could see nothing. Presently he emerged, looking even more flurried than before. As he stepped up to the cab, he pulled a gold watch from his pocket and looked at it earnestly, 'Drive like the devil,' he shouted, 'first to Gross & Hankey's in Regent Street, and then to the Church of St Monica in the Edgeware Road. Half a guinea if you do it in twenty minutes!'

'Away they went, and I was just wondering whether I should not do well to follow them, when up the lane came a neat little landau, the coachman with his coat only half-buttoned, and his tie under his ear, while all the tags of his harness were sticking out of the buckles. It hadn't pulled up before she shot out of the hall door and into it. I only caught a glimpse of her at the moment, but she was a lovely woman, with a face that a man might die for.

' "The Church of St Monica, John," she cried, "and half a sovereign if you reach it in twenty minutes."

'This was quite too good to lose, Watson. I was just balancing whether I should run for it, or whether I should perch behind her landau, when a cab came through the street. The driver looked twice at such a shabby fare; but I jumped in before he could object. 'The Church of St Monica,' said I, 'and half a sovereign if you reach it in twenty minutes.' It was twenty-five minutes to twelve, and of course it was clear enough what was in the wind.

'My cabby drove fast. I don't think I ever drove faster, but the others were there before us. The cab and the landau with their steaming horses were in front of the door when I arrived. I paid the man and hurried into the church. There was not a soul there save the two whom I had followed, and a surpliced clergyman, who seemed to be expostulating with them. They were all three standing in a knot in front of the altar. I lounged up the side aisle like any other idler who has dropped into a church. Suddenly, to my surprise, the three at the altar faced round to me, and Godfrey Norton came running as hard as he could towards me.

' "Thank God!" he cried. "You'll do. Come! Come!"

' "What then?" I asked.

' "Come, man, come, only three minutes, or it won't be legal."

'I was half dragged up to the altar, and before I knew where I was I found myself mumbling responses which were whispered in my ear, and vouching for things of which I knew nothing, and generally assisting in the secure tying up of Irene Adler, spinster, to Godfrey Norton, bachelor. It was all done in an instant, and there was the gentleman thanking me on the one side and the lady on the other, while the clergyman beamed on me in front. It was the most preposterous position in which I ever found myself in my life, and it was the thought of it that started me laughing just now. It seems that there had been some informality about their license, that the clergyman absolutely refused to marry them without a

witness of some sort, and that my lucky appearance saved the bridegroom from having to sally out into the streets in search of a best man. The bride gave me a sovereign, and I mean to wear it on my watch-chain in memory of the occasion.'

'This is a very unexpected turn of affairs,' said I; 'and what then?'

'Well, I found my plans very seriously menaced. It looked as if the pair might take an immediate departure, and so necessitate very prompt and energetic measures on my part. At the church door, however, they separated, he driving back to the Temple, and she to her own house. 'I shall drive out in the park at five as usual,' she said as she left him. I heard no more. They drove away in different directions, and I went off to make my own arrangements.'

'Which are?'

'Some cold beef and a glass of beer,' he answered, ringing the bell. 'I have been too busy to think of food, and I am likely to be busier still this evening. By the way, Doctor, I shall want your co-operation.'

'I shall be delighted.'

'You don't mind breaking the law?'

'Not in the least.'

'Nor running a chance of arrest?'

'Not in a good cause.'

'Oh, the cause is excellent!'

'Then I am your man.'

'I was sure that I might rely on you.'

'But what is it you wish?'

'When Mrs Turner has brought in the tray I will make it clear to you. Now,' he said, as he turned hungrily on the simple fare that our landlady had provided, 'I must discuss it while I eat, for I have not much time. It is nearly five now. In two hours we must be on the scene of action. Miss Irene, or Madame, rather, returns from her drive at seven. We must be at Briony Lodge to meet her.'

'And what then?'

'You must leave that to me. I have already arranged what is to occur. There is only one point on which I must insist. You must not interfere, come what may. You understand?'

'I am to be neutral?'

'To do nothing whatever. There will probably be some small unpleasantness. Do not join in it. It will end in my being conveyed into the house. Four or five minutes afterwards the sitting-room window will open. You are to station yourself close to that open window.'

'Yes.'

'You are to watch me, for I will be visible to you.'

'Yes.'

'And when I raise my hand—so—you will throw into the room what I give you to throw, and will, at the same time, raise the cry of fire. You quite follow me?'

'Entirely.'

'It is nothing very formidable,' he said, taking a long cigar-shaped roll from his pocket. 'It is an ordinary plumber's smoke-rocket, fitted with a cap at either end to make it self-lighting. Your task is confined to that. When you raise your cry of fire, it will be taken up by quite a number of people. You may then walk to the end of the street, and I will rejoin you in ten minutes. I hope that I have made myself clear?'

'I am to remain neutral, to get near the window, to watch you, and at the signal to throw in this object, then to raise the cry of fire, and to wait you at the corner of the street.'

'Precisely.'

'Then you may entirely rely on me.'

'That is excellent. I think perhaps, it is almost time that I prepare for the new role I have to play.'

He disappeared into his bedroom, and returned in a few minutes in the character of an amiable and simple-minded Nonconformist clergyman. His broad black hat, his baggy trousers, his white tie, his sympathetic smile, and general look of peering and benevolent curiosity were such as Mr John Hare alone could have equalled. It was not merely that Holmes changed his costume. His expression, his manner, his very soul seemed to vary with every fresh part that he assumed. The stage lost a fine actor, even as science lost an acute reasoner, when he became a specialist in crime.

It was a quarter past six when we left Baker Street, and it still wanted ten minutes to the hour when we found ourselves in Serpentine Avenue. It was already dusk, and the lamps were just being lighted as we paced up and down in front of Briony Lodge, waiting for the coming of its occupant. The house was just such as I had pictured it from Sherlock Holmes' succinct description, but the locality appeared to be less private than I expected. On the contrary, for a small street in a quiet neighbourhood, it was remarkably animated. There was a group of shabbily-dressed men smoking and laughing in a corner, a scissors-grinder with his wheel, two guardsmen who were flirting with a nurse-girl, and several well-dressed young men who were lounging up and down with cigars in their mouths.

'You see,' remarked Holmes, as we paced to and fro in front of the house, 'this marriage rather simplifies matters. The photograph becomes a double-edged weapon now. The chances are that she would be as averse to its being seen by Mr Godfrey Norton, as our client is to its coming to the eyes of his princess. Now the question is—Where[3] are we to find the photograph?'

'Where, indeed?'

'It is most unlikely that she carries it about with her. It is cabinet size. Too large for easy concealment about a woman's dress. She knows that the King is capable of having her waylaid and searched. Two attempts of the sort have already been made. We may take it then that she does not carry it about with her.'

'Where, then?'

'Her banker or her lawyer. There is that double possibility. But I am inclined to think neither. Women are naturally secretive, and they like to do their own secreting. Why should she hand it over to anyone else? She could trust her own guardianship, but she could not tell what indirect or political influence might be brought to bear upon a businessman. Besides, remember that she had resolved to use it within a few days. It must be where she can lay her hands upon it. It must be in her own house.'

'But it has twice been burgled.'

'Pshaw! They did not know how to look.'

'But how will you look?'

'I will not look.'

'What then?'

'I will get her to show me.'

'But she will refuse.'

'She will not be able to. But I hear the rumble of wheels. It is her carriage. Now carry out my orders to the letter.'

As he spoke the gleam of the sidelights of a carriage came

round the curve of the avenue. It was a smart little landau which rattled up to the door of Briony Lodge. As it pulled up, one of the loafing men at the corner dashed forward to open the door in the hope of earning a copper, but was elbowed away by another loafer who had rushed up with the same intention. A fierce quarrel broke out, which was increased by the two guardsmen, who took sides with one of the loungers, and by the scissors-grinder, who was equally hot upon the other side. A blow was struck, and in an instant the lady, who had stepped from her carriage, was the centre of a little knot of flushed and struggling men who struck savagely at each other with their fists and sticks. Holmes dashed into the crowd to protect the lady; but, just as he reached her, he gave a cry and dropped to the ground, with the blood running freely down his face. At his fall the guardsmen took to their heels in one direction and the loungers in the other, while a number of better

dressed people, who had watched the scuffle without taking part in it, crowded in to help the lady and to attend to the injured man. Irene Adler, as I will still call her, had hurried up the steps; but she stood at the top with her superb figure outlined against the lights of the hall, looking back into the street.

'Is the poor gentleman much hurt?' she asked.

'He is dead,' cried several voices.

'No, no, there's life in him,' shouted another. 'But he'll be gone before you can get him to hospital.'

'He's a brave fellow,' said a woman. 'They would have had the lady's purse and watch if it hadn't been for him. They were a gang, and a rough one, too. Ah, he's breathing now.'

'He can't lie in the street. May we bring him in, marm[4]?'

'Surely. Bring him into the sitting-room. There is a comfortable sofa. This way, please!'

Slowly and solemnly he was borne into Briony Lodge, and laid out in the principal room, while I still observed the proceedings from my post by the window. The lamps had been lit, but the blinds had not been drawn, so that I could see Holmes as he lay upon the couch. I do not know whether he was seized with compunction at that moment for the part he was playing, but I know that I never felt more heartily ashamed of myself in my life than when I saw the beautiful creature against whom I was conspiring, or the grace and kindliness with which she waited upon the injured man. And yet it would be the blackest treachery to Holmes to draw back now from the part which he had entrusted to me. I hardened my heart and took the smoke rocket from under my ulster. After all, I thought, we are not injuring her. We are but preventing her from injuring another.

Holmes had sat up upon the couch, and I saw him motion like a man who is in need of air. A maid rushed across and threw open the window. At the same instant I saw him raise his hand, and at the signal I tossed my rocket into the room with a cry of 'Fire' The word was no sooner out of my mouth than the whole crowd of spectators, well dressed and ill—gentlemen, ostlers, and servant maids—joined in a general shriek of 'Fire!' Thick clouds of smoke curled through the room and out at the open window. I caught a glimpse of rushing figures, and a moment later the voice of Holmes from within, assuring them that it was a false alarm. Slipping through the shouting crowd I made my way to the corner of the street, and in ten minutes was rejoiced to find my friend's arm in mine, and to get away from the scene of the uproar. He walked swiftly and in silence for some few minutes, until we had turned down one of the quiet streets which lead towards the Edgware Road.

'You did it very nicely, Doctor,' he remarked. 'Nothing could have been better. It is all right.'

'You have the photograph?'

'I know where it is.'

'And how did you find out?'

'She showed me, as I told you she would.'

'I am still in the dark.'

'I do not wish to make a mystery,' said he, laughing. 'The matter was perfectly simple. You, of course, saw that everyone in the street was an accomplice. They were all engaged for the evening.'

'I guessed as much.'

'Then, when the row broke out, I had a little moist red paint in the palm of my hand. I rushed forward, fell down, clapped my hand to my face, and became a piteous spectacle. It is an old trick.'

'That also I could fathom.'

'Then they carried me in. She was bound to have me in. What else could she do? And into her sitting-room which was the very room which I suspected. It lay between that and her bedroom, and I was determined to see which. They laid me on a couch, I motioned for air, they were compelled to open the window and you had your chance.'

'How did that help you?'

'It was all-important. When a woman thinks that her house is on fire, her instinct is at once to rush to the thing which she values most. It is a perfectly overpowering impulse, and I have more than once taken advantage of it. In the case of the Darlington Substitution Scandal it was of use to me, and also in the Arnsworth Castle business. A married woman grabs at her baby—an unmarried one reaches for her jewel box. Now it was clear to me that our lady of today had nothing in the house more precious to her than what we are in quest of. She would rush to secure it. The alarm of fire was admirably done. The smoke and shouting was enough to shake nerves of steel. She responded beautifully. The photograph is in a recess behind a sliding panel just above the right bell-pull. She was there in an instant, and I caught a glimpse of it as she half drew it out. When I cried out that it was a false alarm, she replaced it, glanced at the rocket, rushed from the room, and I have not seen her since. I rose, and, making my excuses, escaped from the house. I hesitated whether to attempt to secure the photograph at once; but the coachman had come in, and as he was watching me narrowly, it seemed safer to wait. A little over-precipitance may ruin all.'

'And now?' I asked.

'Our quest is practically finished. I shall call with the King tomorrow, and with you, if you care to come with us. We will be shown into the sitting-room to wait for the lady, but it is probable that when she comes she may find neither us nor the photograph. It might be a satisfaction to His Majesty to regain it with his own hands.'

'And when will you call?'

'At eight in the morning. She will not be up, so that we shall have a clear field. Besides, we must be prompt, for this marriage may mean a complete change in her life and habits. I must wire to the King without delay.'

We had reached Baker Street, and had stopped at the door. He was searching his pockets for the key, when someone passing said:

'Good night, Mister Sherlock Holmes.'

There were several people on the pavement at the time, but the greeting appeared to come from a slim youth in an ulster who had hurried by.

'I've heard that voice before,' said Holmes, staring down the dimly lit street. 'Now, I wonder who the deuce that could have been.'

I slept at Baker Street that night, and we were engaged upon our toast and coffee in the morning when the King of Bohemia rushed into the room.

'You have really got it!' he cried, grasping Sherlock Holmes by either shoulder, and looking eagerly into his face.

'Not yet.'

'But you have hopes?'

'I have hopes.'

'Then, come. I am all impatience to be gone.'

'We must have a cab.'

'No, my brougham is waiting.'

'Then that will simplify matters.'

We descended, and started off once more for Briony Lodge.

'Irene Adler is married,' remarked Holmes.

'Married! When?'

'Yesterday.'

'But to whom?'

'To an English lawyer named Norton.'

'But she could not love him?'

'I am in hopes that she does.'

'And why in hopes?'

'Because it would spare Your Majesty all fear of future annoyance. If the lady loves her husband, she does not love Your Majesty.

If she does not love Your Majesty, there is no reason why she should interfere with Your Majesty's plan.'

'It is true. And yet—! Well! I wish she had been of my own station! What a queen she would have made!' He relapsed into a moody silence which was not broken until we drew up in Serpentine Avenue.

The door of Briony Lodge was open, and an elderly woman stood upon the steps. She watched us with a sardonic eye as we stepped from the brougham.

'Mr Sherlock Holmes, I believe?' said she.

'I am Mr Holmes,' answered my companion, looking at her with a questioning and rather startled gaze.

'Indeed! My mistress told me that you were likely to call. She left this morning with her husband, by the 5:15 train from Charing Cross, for the Continent.'

'What!' Sherlock Holmes staggered back, white with chagrin and surprise. 'Do you mean that she has left England?'

'Never to return.'

'And the papers?' asked the King hoarsely. 'All is lost.'

'We shall see.' He pushed past the servant, and rushed into the drawing-room[5], followed by the King and myself. The furniture was scattered about in every direction, with dismantled shelves, and open drawers, as if the lady had hurriedly ransacked them before her flight. Holmes rushed at the bell-pull, tore back a small sliding shutter, and, plunging in his hand, pulled out a photograph and a letter. The photograph was of Irene Adler herself in evening dress, the letter was superscribed to 'Sherlock Holmes, Esq. To be left till called for.' My friend tore it open and we all three read it together. It was dated at midnight of the preceding night, and ran in this way:

My Dear Mr Sherlock Holmes,

You really did it very well. You took me in completely. Until after the alarm of fire, I had not a suspicion. But then, when I found how I had betrayed myself, I began to think. I had been warned against you months ago. I had been told that if the King employed an agent, it would certainly be you. And your address had been given me. Yet, with all this, you made me reveal what you wanted to know. Even after I became suspicious, I found it hard to think evil of such a dear, kind old clergyman. But, you know, I have been trained as an actress myself. Male costume is nothing new to me. I often take advantage of the freedom which it gives. I sent John, the coachman, to watch you, ran upstairs, got into my walking clothes, as I call them, and came down just as you departed.

'Well, I followed you to your door and so made sure that I was really an object of interest to the celebrated Mr Sherlock Holmes. Then I, rather imprudently, wished you good night, and started for the Temple to see my husband.

'We both thought the best resource was flight when pursued by so formidable an antagonist; so you will find the nest empty when you call tomorrow. As to the photograph, your client may rest in peace. I love and am loved by a better man than he. The King may do what he will without hindrance from one whom he has cruelly wronged. I keep it only to safeguard myself,

and to preserve a weapon which will always secure me from any steps which he might take in the future. I leave a photograph which he might care to possess; and I remain, dear Mr Sherlock Holmes, very truly yours,

IRENE NORTON, née ADLER

'What a woman—oh, what a woman!' cried the King of Bohemia, when we had all three read this epistle. 'Did I not tell you how quick and resolute she was? Would she not have made an admirable queen? Is it not a pity that she was not on my level?'

'From what I have seen of the lady, she seems, indeed, to be on a very different level to Your Majesty,' said Holmes, coldly. 'I am sorry that I have not been able to bring Your Majesty's business to a more successful conclusion.'

'On the contrary, my dear sir,' cried the King; 'Nothing could be more successful. I know that her word is inviolate. The photograph is now as safe as if it were in the fire.'

'I am glad to hear Your Majesty say so.'

'I am immensely indebted to you. Pray tell me in what way I can reward you. This ring—' He slipped an emerald snake ring from his finger and held it out upon the palm of his hand.

'Your Majesty has something which I should value even more highly,' said Holmes.

'You have but to name it.'

'This photograph!'

The King stared at him in amazement.

'Irene's photograph!' he cried. 'Certainly, if you wish it.'

'I thank Your Majesty. Then there is no more to be done in the matter. I have the honour to wish you a very good morning.' He bowed, and, turning away without observing the hand which the King had stretched out to him, he set off in my company for his chambers.

And that was how a great scandal threatened to affect the kingdom of Bohemia, and how the best plans of Mr Sherlock Holmes were beaten by a woman's wit. He used to make merry over the cleverness of women, but I have not heard him do it of late. And when he speaks of Irene Adler, or when he refers to her photograph, it is always under the honourable title of *the* woman.

2.

The Red-Headed League

I had called upon my friend, Mr Sherlock Holmes, one day in the autumn of last year, and found him in deep conversation with a very stout, florid-faced, elderly gentleman, with fiery red hair. With an apology for my intrusion, I was about to withdraw, when Holmes pulled me abruptly into the room and closed the door behind me.

'You could not possibly have come at a better time, my dear Watson,' he said cordially.

'I was afraid that you were engaged.'

'So I am. Very much so.'

'Then I can wait in the next room.'

'Not at all. This gentleman, Mr Wilson, has been my partner and helper in many of my most successful cases, and I have no doubt that he will be of the utmost use to me in yours also.'

The stout gentleman half rose from his chair, and gave a bob of greeting, with a quick little questioning glance from his small fat-encircled eyes.

'Try the settee,' said Holmes, relapsing into his armchair and putting his fingertips together, as was his custom when in judicial moods. 'I know, my dear Watson, that you share my love of all that is bizarre and outside the conventions and humdrum routine of everyday life. You have shown your relish for it by the enthusiasm which has prompted you to chronicle, and, if you will excuse my saying so, somewhat to embellish so many of my own little adventures.'

'Your cases have indeed been of the greatest interest to me,' I observed.

'You will remember that I remarked the other day, just before we went into the very simple problem presented by Miss Mary Sutherland, that for strange effects and extraordinary combinations we must go to life itself, which is always far more daring than any effort of the imagination.'

'A proposition which I took the liberty of doubting.'

'You did, Doctor, but none the less you must come round to my view, for otherwise I shall keep on piling fact upon fact on you, until your reason breaks down under them and acknowledges me to be right. Now, Mr Jabez Wilson here has been good enough to call upon me this morning, and to begin a narrative which promises to be one of the most singular which I have listened to for some time. You have heard me remark that the strangest and most unique things are very often connected not with the larger but with the smaller crimes, and occasionally, indeed, where there is room for doubt whether any positive crime has been committed. As far as I have heard, it is impossible for me to say whether the present case is an instance of crime or not, but the course of events is certainly among the most singular that I have ever listened to. Perhaps, Mr Wilson, you would have the great kindness to recommence your narrative. I ask you not merely because my friend Dr Watson has not heard the opening part, but also because the peculiar nature of the story makes me anxious to have every possible detail from your lips. As a rule, when I have heard some slight indication of the course of events I am able to guide myself by the thousands of other similar cases which occur to my memory. In the present instance I am forced to admit that the facts are, to the best of my belief, unique.'

The portly client puffed out his chest with an appearance of some little pride, and pulled a dirty and wrinkled newspaper from the inside pocket of his greatcoat. As he glanced down the advertisement column, with his head thrust forward, and the paper flattened out upon his knee, I took a good look at the man, and endeavoured after the fashion of my companion to read the indications which might be presented by his dress or appearance.

I did not gain very much, however, by my inspection. Our visitor bore every mark of being an average commonplace British tradesman, obese, pompous, and slow. He wore rather baggy grey shepherd's check trousers, a not over-clean black frock-coat, unbuttoned in the front, and a drab waistcoat with a heavy brassy Albert chain, and a square pierced bit of metal dangling down as an ornament. A frayed top-hat[6], and a faded brown overcoat with a wrinkled velvet collar lay upon a chair beside him. Altogether, look as I would, there was nothing remarkable about the man save his blazing red head, and the expression of extreme chagrin and discontent upon his features.

Sherlock Holmes' quick eye took in my occupation, and he

shook his head with a smile as he noticed my questioning glances. 'Beyond the obvious facts that he has at some time done manual labour, that he takes snuff, that he is a Freemason, that he has been in China, and that he has done a considerable amount of writing lately, I can deduce nothing else.'

Mr Jabez Wilson started up in his chair, with his forefinger upon the paper, but his eyes upon my companion.

'How, in the name of good fortune, did you know that, Mr Holmes?' he asked. 'How did you know, for example, that I did manual labour? It's as true as gospel, for I began as a ship's carpenter.'

'Your hands, my dear sir. Your right hand is quite a size larger than your left. You have worked with it, and the muscles are more developed.'

'Well, the snuff, then, and the Freemasonry?'

'I won't insult your intelligence by telling you how I read that, especially as, rather against the strict rules of your order, you use an arc and compass breastpin.'

'Ah, of course, I forgot that. But the writing?'

'What else can be indicated by that right cuff so very shiny for five inches, and the left one with the smooth patch near the elbow where you rest it upon the desk.'

'Well, but China?'

'The fish which you have tattooed immediately above your right wrist could only have been done in China. I have made a small study of tattoo marks, and have even contributed to the literature of the subject. That trick of staining the fishes' scales of a delicate pink is quite peculiar to China. When, in addition, I see a Chinese coin hanging from your watch-chain, the matter becomes even more simple[7].'

Mr Jabez Wilson laughed heavily. 'Well, I never!' said he. 'I thought at first that you had done something clever, but I see that there was nothing in it after all.'

'I begin to think, Watson,' said Holmes, 'that I make a mistake in explaining. *'Omne ignotum pro magnifico,'* you know, and my poor little reputation, such as it is, will suffer shipwreck if I am so candid. Can you not find the advertisement, Mr Wilson?'

'Yes, I have got it now,' he answered with his thick red finger planted halfway down the column. 'Here it is. This is what began it all. You just read it for yourself, sir.'

I took the paper from him and read as follows:

To the Red-Headed League

On account of the bequest of the late Ezekiah Hopkins of Lebanon, Penn., U. S. A., there is now another vacancy open which entitles a member of the

*League to a salary of four pounds a week for purely
nominal services. All red-headed men who are sound
in body and mind, and above the age of twenty-one
years, are eligible. Apply in person on Monday, at eleven
o' clock, to Duncan Ross, at the offices of the League, 7
Pope's Court, Fleet Street.'*

'What on earth does this mean?' I ejaculated, after I had twice
read over the extraordinary announcement.

Holmes chuckled, and wriggled in his chair, as was his habit
when in high spirits. 'It is a little off the beaten track, isn't it?' said
he. 'And now, Mr Wilson, off you go at scratch, and tell us all about
yourself, your household, and the effect which this advertisement
had upon your fortunes. You will first make a note, Doctor, of the
paper and the date.'

'It is *The Morning Chronicle*, of April 27, 1890. Just two months
ago.'

'Very good. Now, Mr Wilson?'

'Well, it is just as I have been telling you, Mr Sherlock Holmes,' said Jabez Wilson, mopping his forehead; 'I have a small pawnbroker's business at Coburg Square, near the City. It's not a very large affair, and of late years it has not done more than just give me a living. I used to be able to keep two assistants, but now I only keep one; and I would have a job to pay him, but that he is willing to come for half wages, so as to learn the business.'

'What is the name of this obliging youth?' asked Sherlock Holmes.

'His name is Vincent Spaulding, and he's not such a youth either. It's hard to say his age. I should not wish a smarter assistant, Mr Holmes; and I know very well that he could better himself, and earn twice what I am able to give him. But, after all, if he is satisfied, why should I put ideas in his head?'

'Why, indeed? You seem most fortunate in having an employee who comes under the full market price. It is not a common experience among employers in this age. I don't know that your assistant is not as remarkable as your advertisement.'

'Oh, he has his faults, too,' said Mr Wilson. 'Never was such a fellow for photography. Snapping away with a camera when he ought to be improving his mind, and then diving down into the cellar like a rabbit into its hole to develop his pictures. That is his main fault, but on the whole, he's a good worker. There's no vice in him.'

'He is still with you, I presume?'

'Yes, sir. He and a girl of fourteen, who does a bit of simple cooking, and keeps the place clean—that's all I have in the house, for I am a widower, and never had any family. We live very quietly, sir, the three of us; and we keep a roof over our heads and pay our debts, if we do nothing more.

'The first thing that put us out was that advertisement. Spaulding, he came down into the office just this day eight weeks with this very paper in his hand, and he says:

' "I wish to the Lord, Mr Wilson, that I was a red-headed man."

' "Why that?" I asked.

' "Why" says he, "here's another vacancy on the League of the Red-headed Men. It's worth quite a little fortune to any man who gets it, and I understand that there are more vacancies than there are men, so that the trustees are at their wits' end what to do with the money. If my hair would only change colour, here's a nice little crib all ready for me to step into."

' "Why, what is it, then?" I asked. You see, Mr Holmes, I am a very stay-at-home man, and as my business came to me instead of my having to go to it, I was often weeks on end without putting my foot over the door-mat. In that way I didn't know much of what was going on outside, and I was always glad of a bit of news.

' "Have you never heard of the League of the Red-headed Men?" he asked, with his eyes open.

' "Never."

' "Why, I wonder at that, for you are eligible yourself for one of the vacancies."

' "And what are they worth?" I asked.

' "Oh, merely a couple of hundred a year, but the work is slight, and it need not interfere very much with one's other occupations."

'Well, you can easily think that that made me prick up my ears, for the business has not been over good for some years, and an extra couple of hundred would have been very handy.

' "Tell me all about it," said I.

' "Well," said he, showing me the advertisement, "you can see for yourself that the League has a vacancy, and there is the address where you should apply for particulars. As far as I can make out,

the League was founded by an American millionaire, Ezekiah Hopkins, who was very peculiar in his ways. He was himself red-headed, and he had a great sympathy for all red-headed men; so, when he died, it was found that he had left his enormous fortune in the hands of trustees, with instructions to apply the interest to the providing of easy berths to men whose hair is of that colour. From all I hear it is splendid pay, and very little to do.'

' "But," said I, "there would be millions of red-headed men who would apply."

' "Not so many as you might think," he answered. "You see it is really confined to Londoners, and to grown men. This American had started from London when he was young, and he wanted to do the old town a good turn. Then, again, I have heard it is no use your applying if your hair is light red, or dark red, or anything but real, bright, blazing, fiery red. Now, if you cared to apply, Mr Wilson, you would just walk in; but perhaps it would hardly be worth your while to put yourself out of the way for the sake of a few hundred pounds."

'Now, it is a fact, gentlemen, as you may see for yourselves, that my hair is of a very full and rich tint, so that it seemed to me that, if there was to be any competition in the matter, I stood as good a chance as any man that I had ever met. Vincent Spaulding seemed to know so much about it that I thought he might prove useful, so I just ordered him to put up the shutters for the day, and to come right away with me. He was very willing to have a holiday, so we shut the business up, and started off for the address that was given us in the advertisement.

'I never hope to see such a sight as that again, Mr Holmes. From north, south, east, and west every man who had a shade of red in his hair had tramped into the City to answer the advertisement. Fleet Street was choked with red-headed folk, and Pope's Court looked like a coster's orange barrow. I should not have thought there were so many in the whole country as were brought together by that single advertisement. Every shade of colour they were—straw, lemon, orange, brick, Irish-setter, liver, clay; but, as Spaulding said, there were not many who had the real vivid flame-coloured tint. When I saw how many were waiting I would have given it up in despair; but Spaulding would not hear of it. How he did it I could not imagine, but he pushed and pulled and butted until he got me through the crowd, and right up to the steps which led to the office. There was a double stream upon the stair, some going up in hope, and some coming back dejected; but we wedged in as well as we could, and soon found ourselves in the office.'

'Your experience has been a most entertaining one,' remarked Holmes, as his client paused and refreshed his memory with a huge pinch of snuff. 'Pray continue your very interesting statement.'

'There was nothing in the office but a couple of wooden chairs and a deal table, behind which sat a small man, with a head that was even redder than mine. He said a few words to each candidate as he came up, and then he always managed to find some fault in them which would disqualify them. Getting a vacancy did not seem to be such a very easy matter after all. However, when our turn came, the little man was much more favourable to me than to any of the others, and he closed the door as we entered, so that he might have a private word with us.

' "This is Mr Jabez Wilson," said my assistant, "and he is willing to fill a vacancy in the League."

' "And he is admirably suited for it," the other answered. "He has every requirement. I cannot recall when I have seen anything so fine." He took a step backwards, cocked his head on one side, and gazed at my hair until I felt quite bashful. Then suddenly he plunged forward, wrung my hand, and congratulated me warmly on my success.

' "It would be injustice to hesitate," said he. "You will, however, I am sure, excuse me for taking an obvious precaution." With that he seized my hair in both his hands, and tugged until I yelled with the pain. "There is water in your eyes," said he, as he released me. "I perceive that all is as it should be. But we have to be careful, for we have twice been deceived by wigs and once by paint. I could tell you tales of cobbler's wax which would disgust you with human nature." He stepped over to the window, and shouted through it at the top of his voice that the vacancy was filled. A groan of disappointment came up from below, and the folk all trooped away in different directions, until there was not a red head to be seen except my own and that of the manager.

' "My name," said he, "is Mr Duncan Ross, and I am myself one of the pensioners upon the fund left by our noble benefactor. Are you a married man, Mr Wilson? Have you a family?"

'I answered that I had not.

'His face fell immediately.

' "Dear me!" he said gravely, "that is very serious indeed! I am sorry to hear you say that. The fund was, of course, for the propagation and spread of the red-heads as well as for their maintenance. It is exceedingly unfortunate that you should be a bachelor."

'My face lengthened at this, Mr Holmes, for I thought that I was not to have the vacancy after all; but after thinking it over for a few minutes, he said that it would be all right.

' "In the case of another," said he, "the objection might be fatal, but we must stretch a point in favour of a man with such a head of hair as yours. When shall you be able to enter upon your new duties?"

' "Well, it is a little awkward, for I have a business already," said I.

' "Oh, never mind about that, Mr Wilson!" said Vincent Spaulding. "I shall be able to look after that for you."

' "What would be the hours?" I asked.

' "Ten to two."

'Now a pawnbroker's business is mostly done of an evening, Mr Holmes, especially Thursday and Friday evening, which is just before pay-day; so it would suit me very well to earn a little in the mornings. Besides, I knew that my assistant was a good man, and that he would see to anything that turned up.

' "That would suit me very well," said I. "And the pay?"

' "Is four pounds a week."

' "And the work?"

' "Is purely nominal."

' "What do you call purely nominal?"

' "Well, you have to be in the office, or at least in the building, the whole time. If you leave, you forfeit your whole position for ever. The will is very clear upon that point. You don't comply with the conditions if you budge from the office during that time."

' "It's only four hours a day, and I should not think of leaving," said I.

' "No excuse will avail," said Mr Duncan Ross, "neither sickness, nor business, nor anything else. There you must stay, or you lose your billet."

' "And the work?"

' "Is to copy out the *Encyclopaedia Britannica*. There is the first volume of it in that press. You must find your own ink, pens, and blotting-paper, but we provide this table and chair. Will you be ready tomorrow?"

' "Certainly," I answered.

' "Then good-bye, Mr Jabez Wilson, and let me congratulate you once more on the important position which you have been fortunate enough to gain." He bowed me out of the room, and I went home with my assistant, hardly knowing what to say or do, I was so pleased at my own good fortune.

'Well, I thought over the matter all day, and by evening I was in low spirits again; for I had quite persuaded myself that the whole affair must be some great hoax or fraud, though what its object might be I could not imagine. It seemed altogether past belief that anyone could make such a will, or that they would pay such a sum for doing anything so simple as copying out the *Encyclopaedia Britannica*. Vincent Spaulding did what he could to cheer me up, but by bedtime I had reasoned myself out of the whole thing. However, in the morning I determined to have a look at it anyhow, so I bought a penny bottle of ink, and with a quill pen, and seven sheets of foolscap paper, I started off for Pope's Court.

'Well, to my surprise and delight everything was as right as possible. The table was set out ready for me, and Mr Duncan Ross was there to see that I got fairly to work. He started me off upon the letter A, and then he left me; but he would drop in from time to time to see that all was right with me. At two o'clock he bade me good day, complimented me upon the amount that I had written, and locked the door of the office after me.

'This went on day after day, Mr Holmes, and on Saturday the manager came in and planked down four golden sovereigns for my week's work. It was the same next week, and the same the week after. Every morning I was there at ten, and every afternoon I left at two. By degrees Mr Duncan Ross took to coming in only once of a morning, and then, after a time, he did not come in at all. Still, of course, I never dared to leave the room for an instant, for I was not sure when he might come, and the billet was such a good one, and suited me so well, that I would not risk the loss of it.

'Eight weeks passed away like this, and I had written about Abbots, and Archery, and Armour, and Architecture, and Attica, and hoped with diligence that I might get on to the B's before very long. It cost me something in foolscap, and I had pretty nearly filled a shelf with my writings. And then suddenly the whole business came to an end.'

'To an end?'

'Yes, sir. And no later than this morning. I went to my work as usual at ten o'clock, but the door was shut and locked, with a little square of cardboard hammered on to the middle of the panel with a tack. Here it is, and you can read for yourself.'

He held up a piece of white cardboard, about the size of a sheet of note-paper. It read in this fashion:

THE RED-HEADED LEAGUE
IS DISSOLVED.
OCT. 9, 1890

Sherlock Holmes and I surveyed this curt announcement and the rueful face behind it, until the comical side of the affair so completely over-topped every other consideration that we both burst out into a roar of laughter.

'I cannot see that there is anything very funny,' cried our client, flushing up to the roots of his flaming head. 'If you can do nothing better than laugh at me, I can go elsewhere.'

'No, no,' cried Holmes, shoving him back into the chair from which he had half risen. 'I really wouldn't miss your case for the world. It is most refreshingly unusual. But there is, if you will excuse my saying so, something just a little funny about it. Pray what steps did you take when you found the card upon the door?'

'I was staggered, sir. I did not know what to do. Then I called at the offices round, but none of them seemed to know anything about it. Finally, I went to the landlord, who is an accountant living on the ground floor, and I asked him if he could tell me what had become of the Red-Headed League. He said that he had never heard of any such body. Then I asked him who Mr Duncan Ross was. He answered that the name was new to him.

' "Well," said I, "the gentleman at No. 4."

' "What, the red-headed man?"

' "Yes."

' "Oh," said he, "his name was William Morris. He was a solicitor, and was using my room as a temporary convenience until his new premises were ready. He moved out yesterday."

' "Where could I find him?"

' "Oh, at his new offices. He did tell me the address. Yes, 17 King Edward Street, near St Paul's."

'I started off, Mr Holmes, but when I got to that address it was a manufactory of artificial knee-caps, and no one in it had ever heard of either Mr William Morris or Mr Duncan Ross.'

'And what did you do then?' asked Holmes.

'I went home to Saxe-Coburg Square, and I took the advice of my assistant. But he could not help me in any way. He could only say that if I waited I should hear by post. But that was not quite good enough, Mr Holmes. I did not wish to lose such a place without a struggle, so, as I had heard that you were good enough to give advice to poor folk who were in need of it, I came right away to you.'

'And you did very wisely,' said Holmes. 'Your case is an exceedingly remarkable one, and I shall be happy to look into it. From what you have told me I think that it is possible that graver issues hang from it than might at first sight appear.'

'Grave enough!' said Mr Jabez Wilson. 'Why, I have lost four pounds a week.'

'As far as you are personally concerned,' remarked Holmes, 'I do not see that you have any grievance against this extraordinary league. On the contrary, you are, as I understand, richer by thirty pounds, to say nothing of the minute knowledge which you have gained on every subject which comes under the letter A. You have lost nothing by them.'

'No, sir. But I want to find out about them, and who they are, and what their object was in playing this prank—if it was a prank—upon me. It was a pretty expensive joke for them, for it cost them two-and-thirty pounds.'

'We shall endeavour to clear up these points for you. And, first, one or two questions, Mr Wilson. This assistant of yours who first called your attention to the advertisement—how long had he been with you?'

'About a month then.'

'How did he come?'

'In answer to an advertisement.'

'Was he the only applicant?'

'No, I had a dozen.'

'Why did you pick him?'

'Because he was handy, and would come cheap.'

'At half wages, in fact.'

'Yes.'

'What is he like, this Vincent Spaulding?'

'Small, stout-built, very quick in his ways, no hair on his face, though he's not short of thirty. Has a white splash of acid upon his forehead.'

Holmes sat up in his chair in considerable excitement. 'I

thought as much,' said he. 'Have you ever observed that his ears are pierced for ear-rings[8]?'

'Yes, sir. He told me that a gipsy had done it for him when he was a lad.'

'Hum!' said Holmes, sinking back in deep thought. 'He is still with you?'

'Oh, yes, sir; I have only just left him.'

'And has your business been attended to in your absence?'

'Nothing to complain of, sir. There's never very much to do of a morning.'

'That will do, Mr Wilson. I shall be happy to give you an opinion upon the subject in the course of a day or two. Today is Saturday, and I hope that by Monday we may come to a conclusion.'

'Well, Watson,' said Holmes, when our visitor had left us, 'what do you make of it all?'

'I make nothing of it,' I answered frankly. 'It is a most mysterious business.'

'As a rule,' said Holmes, 'the more bizarre a thing is the less mysterious it proves to be. It is your commonplace, featureless crimes which are really puzzling, just as a commonplace face is the most difficult to identify. But I must be prompt over this matter.'

'What are you going to do, then?' I asked.

'To smoke,' he answered. 'It is quite a three-pipe problem, and I beg that you won't speak to me for fifty minutes.' He curled himself up in his chair, with his thin knees drawn up to his hawk-like nose, and there he sat with his eyes closed and his black clay pipe thrusting out like the bill of some strange bird. I had come to the conclusion that he had dropped asleep, and indeed was

nodding myself, when he suddenly sprang out of his chair with the gesture of a man who has made up his mind and put his pipe down upon the mantelpiece.

'Sarasate plays at the St James's Hall this afternoon,' he remarked. 'What do you think, Watson? Could your patients spare you for a few hours?'

'I have nothing to do today. My practice is never very absorbing.'

'Then put on your hat and come. I am going through the City first, and we can have some lunch on the way. I observe that there is a good deal of German music on the programme which is rather more to my taste than Italian or French. It is introspective, and I want to introspect. Come along!'

We travelled by the Underground as far as Aldersgate; and a short walk took us to Saxe-Coburg Square, the scene of the singular story which we had listened to in the morning. It was a pokey, little, shabby-genteel place, where four lines of dingy two-storied brick houses looked out into a small railed-in enclosure, where a lawn of weedy grass and a few clumps of faded laurel bushes made a hard fight against a smoke-laden and uncongenial atmosphere. Three gilt balls and a brown board with 'JABEZ WILSON' in white letters upon a corner house, announced the place where our red-headed client carried on his business. Sherlock Holmes stopped in front of it with his head on one side and looked it all over, with his eyes shining brightly between puckered lids. Then he walked slowly up the street and then down again to the corner, still looking keenly at the houses. Finally he returned to the pawnbroker's, and, having thumped vigorously upon the pavement with his stick two or three times, he went up to the door and knocked. It was instantly opened by a bright-looking, clean-shaven young fellow, who asked him to step in.

'Thank you,' said Holmes, 'I only wished to ask you how you would go from here to the Strand.'

'Third right, fourth left,' answered the assistant promptly, closing the door.

'Smart fellow, that,' observed Holmes as we walked away. 'He is, in my judgment, the fourth smartest man in London, and for daring I am not sure that he has not a claim to be third. I have known something of him before.'

'Evidently,' said I, 'Mr Wilson's assistant counts for a good deal in this mystery of the Red-headed League. I am sure that you inquired your way merely in order that you might see him.'

'Not him.'

'What then?'

'The knees of his trousers.'

'And what did you see?'

'What I expected to see.'

'Why did you beat the pavement?'

'My dear doctor, this is a time for observation, not for talk. We are spies in an enemy's country. We know something of Saxe-Coburg Square. Let us now explore the parts which lie behind it.'

The road in which we found ourselves as we turned round the corner from the retired Saxe-Coburg Square presented as great a contrast to it as the front of a picture does to the back. It was one of the main arteries which conveyed the traffic of the City to the north and west. The roadway was blocked with the immense stream of commerce flowing in a double tide inwards and outwards, while the footpaths were black with the hurrying swarm of pedestrians. It was difficult to realize as we looked at the line of fine shops and stately business premises that they really abutted on the other side upon the faded and stagnant square which we had just quitted.

'Let me see,' said Holmes, standing at the corner, and glancing along the line, 'I should like just to remember the order of the houses here. It is a hobby of mine to have an exact knowledge of London. There is Mortimer's, the tobacconist, the little newspaper shop, the Coburg branch of the City and Suburban Bank, the Vegetarian Restaurant, and McFarlane's carriage-building depot. That carries us right on to the other block. And now, Doctor, we've done our work, so it's time we had some play. A sandwich and a cup of coffee, and then off to violin land, where all is sweetness and delicacy and harmony, and there are no red-headed clients to vex us with their conundrums.'

My friend was an enthusiastic musician being himself not only a very capable performer, but a composer of no ordinary merit. All the afternoon he sat in the stalls wrapped in the most perfect happiness, gently waving his long thin fingers in time to the music, while his gently smiling face and his languid, dreamy eyes were as unlike those of Holmes the sleuth-hound, Holmes the relentless, keen-witted, ready-handed criminal agent, as it was possible to conceive. In his singular character the dual nature alternately asserted itself and his extreme exactness and astuteness represented, as I have often thought, the reaction against the poetic and contemplative mood which occasionally predominated in him. The swing of his nature took him from extreme languor to devouring energy; and, as I knew well, he was never so truly formidable as when, for days on end, he had been lounging in his armchair amid his improvisations and his black-letter editions. Then it was that the lust of the chase would suddenly come upon him, and that his brilliant reasoning power would rise to the level of intuition, until those who were unacquainted with his methods would look askance at him as on a man whose knowledge was not that of other mortals. When I saw him that afternoon so enwrapped in the music at St James's Hall I felt that an evil time might be coming upon those whom he had set himself to hunt down.

'You want to go home, no doubt, Doctor,' he remarked, as we emerged.

'Yes, it would be as well.'

'And I have some business to do which will take some hours. This business at Coburg Square is serious.'

'Why serious?'

'A considerable crime is in contemplation. I have every reason to believe that we shall be in time to stop it. But today being

Saturday rather complicates matters. I shall want your help to-night.'

'At what time?'

'Ten will be early enough.'

'I shall be at Baker Street at ten.'

'Very well. And, I say, Doctor! there[9] may be some little danger, so kindly put your army revolver in your pocket.' He waved his hand, turned on his heel, and disappeared in an instant among the crowd.

I trust that I am not more dense[10] than my neighbours, but I was always oppressed with a sense of my own stupidity in my dealings with Sherlock Holmes. Here I had heard what he had heard, I had seen what he had seen, and yet from his words it was evident that he saw clearly not only what had happened, but what was about to happen, while to me the whole business was still confused and grotesque. As I drove home to my house in Kensington I thought over it all, from the extraordinary story of the red-headed copier of the *Encyclopaedia* down to the visit to Saxe-Coburg Square, and the ominous words with which he had parted from me. What was this nocturnal expedition, and why should I go armed? Where were we going, and what were we to do? I had the hint from Holmes that this smooth-faced pawnbroker's assistant was a formidable man—a man who might play a deep game. I tried to puzzle it out, but gave it up in despair, and set the matter aside until night should bring an explanation.

It was a quarter-past[11] nine when I started from home and made my way across the Park, and so through Oxford Street to Baker Street. Two hansoms were standing at the door, and as I entered the passage, I heard the sound of voices from above. On entering his room, I found Holmes in animated conversation with two men, one of whom I recognized as Peter Jones, the official police agent, while the other was a long, thin, sad-faced man, with a very shiny hat and oppressively respectable frock-coat.

'Ha! Our party is complete,' said Holmes, buttoning up his pea-jacket, and taking his heavy hunting crop from the rack. 'Watson, I think you know Mr Jones, of Scotland Yard? Let me introduce you to Mr Merryweather, who is to be our companion in tonight's adventure.'

'We're hunting in couples again, Doctor, you see,' said Jones in his consequential way. 'Our friend here is a wonderful man for starting a chase. All he wants is an old dog to help him to do the running down.'

'I hope a wild goose may not prove to be the end of our chase,' observed Mr Merryweather gloomily.

'You may place considerable confidence in Mr Holmes, sir,' said the police agent loftily. 'He has his own little methods, which are, if he won't mind my saying so, just a little too theoretical and fantastic, but he has the makings of a detective in him. It is not too much to say that once or twice, as in that business of the Sholto murder and the Agra treasure, he has been more nearly correct than the official force.'

'Oh, if you say so, Mr Jones, it is all right!' said the stranger, with deference. 'Still, I confess that I miss my rubber. It is the first Saturday night for seven-and-twenty years that I have not had my rubber.'

'I think you will find,' said Sherlock Holmes, 'that you will play for a higher stake tonight than you have ever done yet, and that the play will be more exciting. For you, Mr Merryweather, the stake will be some thirty thousand pounds; and for you, Jones, it will be the man upon whom you wish to lay your hands.'

'John Clay, the murderer, thief, smasher, and forger. He's a young man, Mr Merryweather, but he is at the head of his profession, and I would rather have my bracelets on him than on any criminal in London. He's a remarkable man, is young John Clay. His grandfather was a Royal Duke, and he himself has been to Eton and Oxford. His brain is as cunning as his fingers, and though we meet signs of him at every turn, we never know where to find the man himself. He'll crack a crib in Scotland one week, and be raising money to build an orphanage in Cornwall the next. I've been on his track for years, and have never set eyes on him yet.'

'I hope that I may have the pleasure of introducing you tonight. I've had one or two little turns also with Mr John Clay, and I agree with you that he is at the head of his profession. It is past ten, however, and quite time that we started. If you two will take the first hansom, Watson and I will follow in the second.'

Sherlock Holmes was not very communicative during the long drive, and lay back in the cab humming the tunes which he had heard in the afternoon. We rattled through an endless labyrinth of gas-lit streets until we emerged into Farrington Street.

'We are close there now,' my friend remarked. 'This fellow Merryweather is a bank director and personally interested in the matter. I thought it as well to have Jones with us also. He is not a bad fellow, though an absolute imbecile in his profession. He has one positive virtue. He is as brave as a bulldog, and as tenacious as a lobster if he gets his claws upon anyone. Here we are, and they are waiting for us.'

We had reached the same crowded thoroughfare in which we had found ourselves in the morning. Our cabs were dismissed, and, following the guidance of Mr Merryweather, we passed down a narrow passage, and through a side door, which he opened for us. Within there was a small corridor, which ended in a very massive iron gate. This also was opened, and led down a flight of winding stone steps, which terminated at another formidable gate. Mr Merryweather stopped to light a lantern, and then conducted us down a dark, earth-smelling passage, and so, after opening a third door, into a huge vault or cellar, which was piled all round with crates and massive boxes.

'You are not very vulnerable from above,' Holmes remarked, as he held up the lantern and gazed about him.

'Nor from below,' said Mr Merryweather, striking his stick

upon the flags which lined the floor. 'Why, dear me, it sounds quite hollow!' he remarked, looking up in surprise.

'I must really ask you to be a little more quiet[12]!' said Holmes severely. 'You have already imperilled the whole success of our expedition. Might I beg that you would have the goodness to sit down upon one of those boxes, and not to interfere?'

The solemn Mr Merryweather perched himself upon a crate, with a very injured expression upon his face, while Holmes fell upon his knees upon the floor, and, with the lantern and a magnifying lens, began to examine minutely the cracks between the stones. A few seconds sufficed to satisfy him for he sprang to his feet again, and put his glass in his pocket.

'We have at least an hour before us,' he remarked, 'for they can hardly take any steps until the good pawnbroker is safely in bed. Then they will not lose a minute, for the sooner they do their work the longer time they will have for their escape. We are at present, Doctor—as no doubt you have divined—in the cellar of the City branch of one of the principal London banks. Mr Merryweather is the chairman of directors, and he will explain to you that there are reasons why the more daring criminals of London should take a considerable interest in this cellar at present.'

'It is our French gold,' whispered the director. 'We have had several warnings that an attempt might be made upon it.'

'Your French gold?'

'Yes. We had occasion some months ago to strengthen our resources, and borrowed, for that purpose, thirty thousand napoleons from the Bank of France. It has become known that we have never had occasion to unpack the money, and that it is still lying in our cellar. The crate upon which I sit contains two thousand napoleons packed between layers of lead foil. Our reserve of bullion is much larger at present than is usually kept in a single branch office, and the directors have had misgivings upon the subject.'

'Which were very well justified,' observed Holmes. 'And now it is time that we arranged our little plans. I expect that within an hour matters will come to a head. In the meantime Mr Merryweather, we must put the screen over that dark lantern.'

'And sit in the dark?'

'I am afraid so. I had brought a pack of cards in my pocket, and I thought that, as we were a *partie carrée*, you might have your rubber after all. But I see that the enemy's preparations have gone so far that we cannot risk the presence of a light. And, first of all, we must choose our positions. These are daring men, and though we shall take them at a disadvantage they may do us some harm, unless we are careful. I shall stand behind this crate, and do you conceal yourselves behind those. Then, when I flash a light upon them, close in swiftly. If they fire, Watson, have no compunction about shooting them down.'

I placed my revolver, cocked, upon the top of the wooden case behind which I crouched. Holmes shot the slide across the front of his lantern, and left us in pitch darkness—such an absolute darkness as I have never before experienced. The smell of hot metal remained to assure us that the light was still there, ready to flash out at a moment's notice. To me, with my nerves worked up to a pitch of expectancy, there was something depressing and subduing in the sudden gloom, and in the cold, dank air of the vault.

'They have but one retreat,' whispered Holmes. 'That is back through the house into Saxe-Coburg Square. I hope that you have done what I asked you, Jones?'

'I have an inspector and two officers waiting at the front door.'

'Then we have stopped all the holes. And now we must be silent and wait.'

What a time it seemed! From comparing notes afterwards it was but an hour and a quarter, yet it appeared to me that the night must have almost gone, and the dawn be breaking above us. My limbs were weary and stiff, for I feared to change my position, yet my nerves were worked up to the highest pitch of tension, and my hearing was so acute that I could not only hear the gentle breathing of my companions, but I could distinguish the deeper, heavier in-breath of the bulky Jones from the thin, sighing note of the bank director. From my position I could look over the case in the direction of the floor. Suddenly my eyes caught the glint of a light.

At first it was but a lurid spark upon the stone pavement. Then it lengthened out until it became a yellow line, and then, without any warning or sound, a gash seemed to open and a hand appeared, a white, almost womanly hand, which felt about in the centre of the little area of light. For a minute or more the hand, with its writhing fingers, protruded out of the floor. Then it was withdrawn as suddenly as it appeared, and all was dark again save the single lurid spark, which marked a chink between the stones.

Its disappearance, however, was but momentary. With a rending, tearing sound, one of the broad, white stones turned over upon its side and left a square gaping hole through which streamed the light of a lantern. Over the edge there peeped a clean-cut, boyish face, which looked keenly about it, and then, with a hand on either side of the aperture, drew itself shoulder high and waist high until one knee rested upon the edge. In another instant he stood at the side of the hole, and was hauling after him a companion, lithe and small like himself, with a pale face and a shock of very red hair.

'It's all clear,' he whispered. 'Have you the chisel and the bags. Great Scott! Jump, Archie, jump, and I'll swing for it!'

Sherlock Holmes had sprung out and seized the intruder by the collar. The other dived down the hole, and I heard the sound of rending cloth as Jones clutched at his skirts. The light flashed upon the barrel of a revolver, but Holmes' hunting-crop came down on the man's wrist, and the pistol clinked upon the stone floor.

'It's no use, John Clay,' said Holmes blandly. 'You have no chance at all.'

'So I see,' the other answered with the utmost coolness. 'I fancy that my pal is all right, though I see you have got his coat-tails.'

'There are three men waiting for him at the door,' said Holmes.

'Oh, indeed. You seem to have done the thing very completely. I must compliment you.'

'And I you,' Holmes answered. 'Your red-headed idea was very new and effective.'

'You'll see your pal again presently,' said Jones. 'He's quicker at climbing down holes than I am. Just hold out while I fix the derbies.'

'I beg that you will not touch me with your filthy hands,' remarked our prisoner, as the handcuffs clattered upon his wrists. 'You may not be aware that I have royal blood in my veins. Have the goodness also when you address me always to say "sir" and "please". '

'All right,' said Jones with a stare and a snigger. 'Well, would you please, sir, march upstairs, where we can get a cab to carry your Highness to the police station.'

'That is better,' said John Clay serenely. He made a sweeping bow to the three of us and walked quietly off in the custody of the detective.

'Really, Mr Holmes,' said Mr Merryweather as we followed them from the cellar, 'I do not know how the bank can thank you or repay you. There is no doubt that you have detected and defeated in the most complete manner one of the most determined attempts at bank robbery that have ever come within my experience.'

'I have had one or two little scores of my own to settle with Mr John Clay,' said Holmes. 'I have been at some small expense over this matter, which I shall expect the bank to refund, but beyond that I am amply repaid by having had an experience which is in many ways unique, and by hearing the very remarkable narrative of the Red-headed League.'

'You see, Watson,' he explained in the early hours of the morning, as we sat over a glass of whisky-and-soda in Baker Street, 'it was perfectly obvious from the first that the only possible object of this rather fantastic business of the advertisement of the League, and the copying of the *Encyclopaedia*, must be to get this not over-bright pawnbroker out of the way for a number of hours every day. It was a curious way of managing it, but really it would be difficult to suggest a better. The method was no doubt suggested to Clay's ingenious mind by the colour of his accomplice's hair. The four pounds a week was a lure which must draw him, and what was it to them, who were playing for thousands? They put in the advertisement; one rogue has the temporary office, the other rogue incites the man to apply for it, and together they manage to secure his absence every morning in the week. From the time that I heard of the assistant having come for half-wages, it was obvious to me that he had some strong motive for securing the situation.'

'But how could you guess what the motive was?'

'Had there been women in the house, I should have suspected a mere vulgar intrigue. That, however, was out of the question. The man's business was a small one, and there was nothing in his house which could account for such elaborate preparations and such an expenditure as they were at. It must then be something out of the house. What could it be? I thought of the assistant's fondness for photography, and his trick of vanishing into the cellar. The cellar! There was the end of this tangled clue. Then I made inquiries as to this mysterious assistant, and found that I had to deal with one of the coolest and most daring criminals in London. He was doing something in the cellar—something which took many hours a day for months on end. What could it be, once more? I could think of nothing save that he was running a tunnel to some other building.

'So far I had got when we went to visit the scene of action. I surprised you by beating upon the pavement with my stick. I was ascertaining whether the cellar stretched out in front or behind. It was not in front. Then I rang the bell, and, as I hoped, the assistant answered it. We have had some skirmishes, but we had never set eyes upon each other before. I hardly looked at his face. His knees were what I wished to see. You must yourself have remarked how worn, wrinkled and stained they were. They spoke of those hours of burrowing. The only remaining point was what they were burrowing for. I walked round the corner, saw the City and Suburban Bank abutted on our friend's premises, and felt that I had solved my problem. When you drove home after the concert I called upon Scotland Yard, and upon the chairman of the bank directors, with the result that you have seen.'

'And how could you tell that they would make their attempt tonight?' I asked.

'Well, when they closed their League offices that was a sign that they cared no longer about Mr Jabez Wilson's presence; in other words, that they had completed their tunnel. But it was essential that they should use it soon, as it might be discovered, or the bullion might be removed. Saturday would suit them better than any other day, as it would give them two days for their escape. For all these reasons I expected them to come tonight.'

'You reasoned it out beautifully,' I exclaimed in unfeigned admiration. 'It is so long a chain, and yet every link rings true.'

'It saved me from ennui,' he answered, yawning. 'Alas! I already feel it closing in upon me! My life is spent in one long effort to escape from the commonplaces of existence. These little problems help me to do so.'

'And you are a benefactor of the race,' said I.

He shrugged his shoulders. 'Well, perhaps, after all, it is of some little use,' he remarked. ' "*L'homme c'est rien—l'oeuvre c'est tout*," as Gustave Flaubert wrote to George Sand.'

3.

The Five Orange Pips

When I glance over my notes and records of the Sherlock Holmes cases between the years '82 and '90, I am faced by so many which present strange and interesting features, that it is no easy matter to know which to choose and which to leave. Some, however, have already gained publicity through the papers, and others have not offered a field for those peculiar qualities which my friend possessed in so high a degree, and which it is the object of these papers to illustrate. Some, too, have baffled his analytical skill, and would be, as narratives, beginnings without an ending, while others have been but partially cleared up, and have their explanations founded rather upon conjecture and surmise than on that absolute logical proof which was so dear to him. There is, however, one of these last which was so remarkable in its details and so startling in its results that I am tempted to give some account of it, in spite of the fact that there are points in connection with it which never have been, and probably never will be, entirely cleared up.

The year '87 furnished us with a long series of cases of greater or less interest, of which I retain the records. Among my headings under this one twelve months, I find an account of the adventure of the Paradol Chamber, of the Amateur Mendicant Society, who held a luxurious club in the lower vault of a furniture warehouse, of the facts connected with the loss of the British barque *Sophy Anderson*, of the singular adventures of the Grice Patersons in the island of Uffa, and finally of the Camberwell poisoning case. In the latter, as may be remembered, Sherlock Holmes was able, by winding up the dead man's watch, to prove that it had been wound up two hours ago, and that therefore the deceased had gone to bed within that time—a deduction which was of the greatest importance in clearing up the case. All these I may sketch out at some future date, but none of them present such singular features as the strange train of circumstances which I have now taken up my pen to describe.

It was in the latter days of September, and the equinoctial gales had set in with exceptional violence. All day the wind had screamed and the rain had beaten against the windows, so that even here in the heart of great, hand-made London we were forced to raise our minds for the instant from the routine of life, and to recognize the presence of those great elemental forces which shriek at mankind through the bars of his civilization, like untamed beasts in a cage. As evening drew in the storm grew louder and louder, and the wind cried and sobbed like a child in the chimney. Sherlock Holmes sat moodily at one side of the fireplace cross-indexing his records of crime, whilst I at the other was deep in one of Clark Russell's fine sea stories, until the howl of the gale from without seemed to blend with the text, and the splash of the rain to lengthen out into the long swash of the sea waves. My wife was on a visit to her aunt's, and for a few days I was a dweller once more in my old quarters at Baker Street.

'Why,' said I, glancing up at my companion, 'that was surely the bell? Who could come tonight? Some friend of yours, perhaps?'

'Except yourself I have none,' he answered. 'I do not encourage visitors.'

'A client, then?'

'If so, it is a serious case. Nothing less would bring a man out on such a day, and at such an hour. But I take it that it is more likely to be some crony of the landlady's.'

Sherlock Holmes was wrong in his conjecture, however, for there came a step in the passage, and a tapping at the door. He stretched out his long arm to turn the lamp away from himself and towards the vacant chair upon which a newcomer must sit. 'Come in!' said he.

The man who entered was young, some two-and-twenty at the outside, well-groomed and trimly clad, with something of refinement and delicacy in his bearing. The streaming umbrella which he held in his hand, and his long shining waterproof told of the fierce weather through which he had come. He looked about him anxiously in the glare of the lamp, and I could see that his face was pale and his eyes heavy, like those of a man who is weighed down with some great anxiety.

'I owe you an apology,' he said, raising his golden pince-nez to his eyes. 'I trust that I am not intruding. I fear that I have brought some traces of the storm and rain into your snug chamber.'

'Give me your coat and umbrella,' said Holmes. 'They may rest

here on the hook, and will be dry presently. You have come up from the south-west, I see.'

'Yes, from Horsham.'

'That clay and chalk mixture which I see upon your toe-caps is quite distinctive.'

'I have come for advice.'

'That is easily got.'

'And help.'

'That is not always so easy.'

'I have heard of you, Mr Holmes. I heard from Major Prendergast how you saved him in the Tankerville Club Scandal.'

'Ah, of course. He was wrongfully accused of cheating at cards.'

'He said that you could solve anything.'

'He said too much.'

'That you are never beaten.'

'I have been beaten four times—three times by men and once by a woman.'

'But what is that compared with the number of your successes?'

'It is true that I have been generally successful.'

'Then you may be so with me.'

'I beg that you will draw your chair up to the fire, and favour me with some details as to your case.'

'It is no ordinary one.'

'None of those which come to me are. I am the last court of appeal.'

'And yet I question, sir, whether, in all your experience you have ever listened to a more mysterious and inexplicable chain of events than those which have happened in my own family.'

'You fill me with interest,' said Holmes. 'Pray give us the essential facts from the commencement, and I can afterwards question you as to those details which seem to me to be most important.'

The young man pulled his chair up and pushed his wet feet out towards the blaze.

'My name,' said he, 'is John Openshaw, but my own affairs have, so far as I can understand it, little to do with this awful business. It is a hereditary matter, so in order to give you an idea of the facts, I must go back to the commencement of the affair.

'You must know that my grandfather had two sons—my uncle Elias and my father Joseph. My father had a small factory at Coventry, which he enlarged at the time of the invention of bicycling. He was a patentee of the Openshaw unbreakable tyre, and his business met with such success that he was able to sell it, and to retire upon a handsome competence.

'My uncle Elias emigrated to America when he was a young man, and became a planter in Florida, where he was reported to have done very well. At the time of the war he fought in Jackson's army, and afterwards under Hood, where he rose to be a colonel. When Lee laid down his arms my uncle returned to his plantation, where he remained for three or four years. About 1869 or 1870 he came back to Europe, and took a small estate in Sussex, near Horsham. He had made a very considerable fortune in the States, and his reason for leaving them was his aversion to the negroes[13], and his dislike of the Republican policy in extending the franchise to them. He was a singular man, fierce and quick-tempered, very foul-mouthed when he was angry, and of a most retiring disposition. During all the years that he lived at Horsham I doubt if ever he set foot in the town. He had a garden and two or three fields round his house, and there he would take his exercise, though very often for weeks on end he would never leave his room. He drank a great deal of brandy, and smoked very heavily, but he would see no society, and did not want any friends, not even his own brother.

'He didn't mind me; in fact, he took a fancy to me, for at the time when he saw me first I was a youngster of twelve or so. This would be in the year 1878, after he had been eight or nine years in England. He begged my father to let me live with him, and he was very kind to me in his way. When he was sober he used to be fond of playing backgammon and draughts with me, and he would make me his representative both with the servants and with the tradespeople, so that by the time that I was sixteen I was quite master of the house. I kept all the keys, and could go where I liked and do what I liked, so long as I did not disturb him in his privacy. There was one singular exception, however, for he had a single room, a lumber-room up among the attics, which was invariably locked, and which he would never permit either me or anyone else to enter. With a boy's curiosity I have peeped through the keyhole, but I was never able to see more than such a collection of old trunks and bundles as would be expected in such a room.

'One day—it was in March, 1883—a letter with a foreign stamp lay upon the table in front of the Colonel's plate. It was not a common thing for him to receive letters, for his bills were all paid in ready money, and he had no friends of any sort. "From India!" said he, as he took it up. "Pondicherry postmark! What can this be?" Opening it hurriedly, out there jumped five little dried orange pips, which pattered down upon his plate. I began to laugh at this, but the laugh was struck from my lips at the sight of his face. His lip had fallen, his eyes were protruding, his skin the colour of putty, and he glared at the envelope which he still held in his trembling hand, "K. K. K.," he shrieked, and then, "My God, my God, my sins have overtaken me."

' "What is it, uncle!" I cried.

' "Death," said he, and rising from the table he retired to his room, leaving me palpitating with horror. I took up the envelope, and saw scrawled in red ink upon the inner flap, just above the gum, the letter K three times repeated. There was nothing else save the five dried pips. What could be the reason of his over-powering[14] terror? I left the breakfast-table[15], and as I ascended the stair I met him coming down with an old rusty key, which must have belonged to the attic, in one hand, and a small brass box, like a cash box, in the other.

' "They may do what they like, but I'll checkmate them still," said he, with an oath. "Tell Mary that I shall want a fire in my room today, and send down to Fordham, the Horsham lawyer."

'I did as he ordered, and when the lawyer arrived I was asked to step up to the room. The fire was burning brightly, and in the grate there was a mass of black, fluffy ashes, as of burned paper, while the brass box stood open and empty beside it. As I glanced at the box I noticed, with a start, that upon the lid was printed the treble K which I had read in the morning upon the envelope.

' "I wish you, John," said my uncle, "to witness my will. I leave my estate, with all its advantages and all its disadvantages to my brother, your father, whence it will, no doubt, descend to you. If you can enjoy it in peace, well and good! If you find you cannot, take my advice, my boy, and leave it to your deadliest enemy. I am sorry to give you such a two-edged thing, but I can't say what turn things are going to take. Kindly sign the paper where Mr Fordham shows you."

'I signed the paper as directed, and the lawyer took it away with him. The singular incident made, as you may think, the deepest impression upon me, and I pondered over it, and turned it every way in my mind without being able to make anything of it. Yet I could not shake off the vague feeling of dread which it left behind it, though the sensation grew less keen as the weeks passed, and nothing happened to disturb the usual routine of our lives. I could see a change in my uncle, however. He drank more than ever, and he was less inclined for any sort of society. Most of his time he would spend in his room, with the door locked upon the inside, but sometimes he would emerge in a sort of drunken frenzy and would burst out of the house and tear about the garden with a revolver in his hand, screaming out that he was afraid of no man, and that he was not to be cooped up, like a sheep in a pen, by man or devil. When these hot fits were over, however, he would rush tumultuously in at the door, and lock and bar it behind him, like a man who can brazen it out no longer against the terror which lies at the roots of his soul. At such times I have seen his face even on a cold day glisten with moisture as though it were new raised from a basin.

'Well, to come to an end of the matter, Mr Holmes, and not to abuse your patience, there came a night when he made one of those drunken sallies from which he never came back. We found him, when we went to search for him, face downwards in a little green-scummed pool, which lay at the foot of the garden. There was no sign of any violence, and the water was but two feet deep, so that the jury, having regard to his known eccentricity, brought in a verdict of suicide. But I, who knew how he winced from the very thought of death, had much ado to persuade myself

that he had gone out of his way to meet it. The matter passed, however, and my father entered into possession of the estate, and of some fourteen thousand pounds, which lay to his credit at the bank.'

'One moment,' Holmes interposed, 'Your statement is, I foresee, one of the most remarkable to which I have ever listened. Let me have the date of the reception by your uncle of the letter, and the date of his supposed suicide.'

'The letter arrived on March the 10th, 1883. His death was seven weeks later, upon the night of the 2nd of May.'

'Thank you. Pray proceed.'

'When my father took over the Horsham property, he, at my request, made a careful examination of the attic, which had been always locked up. We found the brass box there, although its contents had been destroyed. On the inside of the cover was a paper label, with the initials of K. K. K. repeated upon it, and "Letters, memoranda, receipts and a register" written beneath. These, we presume, indicated the nature of the papers which had been destroyed by Colonel Openshaw. For the rest, there was nothing of much importance in the attic, save a great many scattered papers and notebooks bearing upon my uncle's life in America. Some of them were of the war time, and showed that he had done his duty well, and had borne the repute of being a brave soldier. Others were of a date during the reconstruction of the Southern States, and were mostly concerned with politics, for he had evidently taken a strong part in opposing the carpet-bag politicians who had been sent down from the North.

'Well, it was the beginning of '84 when my father came to live at Horsham, and all went as well as possible with us until the January of '85. On the fourth day after the New Year I heard my father give a sharp cry of surprise as we sat together at the breakfast-table. There he was, sitting with a newly opened envelope in one hand and five dried orange pips in the outstretched palm of the other one. He had always laughed at what he called my cock-and-bull story about the Colonel, but he looked very puzzled and scared now that the same thing had come upon himself.

' "Why, what on earth does this mean, John?" he stammered.

'My heart had turned to lead. 'It is K. K. K.,' said I.

'He looked inside the envelope. 'So it is,' he cried. 'Here are the very letters. But what is this written above them?'

' "Put the papers on the sundial," I read, peeping over his shoulder.

' "What papers? What sundial?" he asked.

' "The sundial in the garden. There is no other," said I; "but the papers must be those that are destroyed."

' "Pooh!" said he, gripping hard at his courage. "We are in a civilized land here, and we can't have tomfoolery of this kind. Where does the thing come from?"

' "From Dundee," I answered, glancing at the postmark.

' "Some preposterous practical joke," said he. "What have I to do with sundials and papers? I shall take no notice of such nonsense."

' "I should certainly speak to the police," I said.

' "And be laughed at for my pains. Nothing of the sort."

' "Then let me do so."

' "No, I forbid you. I won't have a fuss made about such nonsense."

'It was in vain to argue with him, for he was a very obstinate man. I went about, however, with a heart which was full of forebodings.

'On the third day after the coming of the letter my father went from home to visit an old friend of his, Major Freebody, who is in command of one of the forts upon Portsdown Hill. I was glad that he should go, for it seemed to me that he was farther from danger when he was away from home. In that, however, I was in error. Upon the second day of his absence I received a telegram from the Major, imploring me to come at once. My father had fallen over one of the deep chalk-pits which abound in the neighbourhood, and was lying senseless, with a shattered skull. I hurried to him, but he passed away without having ever recovered his consciousness. He had, as it appears, been returning from Fareham in the twilight, and as the country was unknown to him, and the chalk-pit unfenced, the jury had no hesitation in bringing in a verdict of "Death from accidental causes". Carefully as I examined every fact connected with his death, I was unable to find anything which could suggest the idea of murder. There were no signs of violence, no footmarks, no robbery, no record of strangers having been seen upon the roads. And yet I need not tell you that my mind was far from at ease, and that I was well-nigh certain that some foul plot had been woven round him.

'In this sinister way I came into my inheritance. You will ask me why I did not dispose of it? I answer because I was well convinced that our troubles were in some way dependent upon an incident in my uncle's life, and that the danger would be as pressing in one house as in another.

'It was in January, '85, that my poor father met his end, and two years and eight months have elapsed since then. During that time I have lived happily at Horsham, and I had begun to hope that this curse had passed away from the family, and that it had ended with the last generation. I had begun to take comfort too soon, however; yesterday morning the blow fell in the very shape in which it had come upon my father.'

The young man took from his waistcoat a crumpled envelope, and, turning to the table, he shook out upon it five little dried orange pips.

'This is the envelope,' he continued. 'The postmark is London—eastern division. Within are the very words which were upon my father's last message. "K. K. K."; and then "Put the papers on the sundial".'

'What have you done?' asked Holmes.

'Nothing.'

'Nothing?'

'To tell the truth'—he sank his face into his thin, white

hands—'I have felt helpless. I have felt like one of those poor rabbits when the snake is writhing towards it. I seem to be in the grasp of some resistless, inexorable evil, which no foresight and no precautions can guard against.'

'Tut! Tut!' cried Sherlock Holmes. 'You must act, man, or you are lost. Nothing but energy can save you. This is no time for despair.'

'I have seen the police.'

'Ah?'

'But they listened to my story with a smile. I am convinced that the inspector has formed the opinion that the letters are all practical jokes, and that the deaths of my relations were really accidents, as the jury stated, and were not to be connected with the warnings.'

Holmes shook his clenched hands in the air. 'Incredible

imbecility!' he cried.

'They have, however, allowed me a policeman, who may remain in the house with me.'

'Has he come with you tonight?'

'No. His orders were to stay in the house.'

Again Holmes raved in the air.

'Why did you come to me?' he said; 'and, above all, why did you not come at once?'

'I did not know. It was only today that I spoke to Major Prendergast about my troubles, and was advised by him to come to you.'

'It is really two days since you had the letter. We should have acted before this. You have no further evidence, I suppose, than that which you have placed before us—no suggestive detail which might help us?'

'There is one thing,' said John Openshaw. He rummaged in his coat pocket, and drawing out a piece of discoloured, blue-tinted paper, he laid it out upon the table. 'I have some remembrance,' said he, 'that on the day when my uncle burned the papers I observed that the small, unburned margins which lay amid the ashes were of this particular colour. I found this single sheet upon the floor of his room, and I am inclined to think that it may be one of the papers which has, perhaps, fluttered out from among the others, and in that way has escaped destruction. Beyond the mention of pips, I do not see that it helps us much. I think myself that it is a page from some private diary. The writing is undoubtedly my uncle's.'

Holmes moved the lamp, and we both bent over the sheet of paper, which showed by its ragged edge that it had indeed been torn from a book. It was headed 'March, 1869,' and beneath were the following enigmatical notices:

> 4th. *Hudson came. Same old platform.*
>
> 7th. *Set the pips on McCauley, Paramore, and John Swain of St Augustine.*
>
> 9th. *McCauley cleared.*
>
> 10th. *John Swain cleared.*
>
> 12th. *Visited Paramore. All well.*

'Thank you!' said Holmes, folding up the paper and returning it to our visitor. 'And now you must on no account lose another instant. We cannot spare time even to discuss what you have told me. You must get home instantly and act.'

'What shall I do?'

'There is but one thing to do. It must be done at once. You must put this piece of paper which you have shown us into the brass box which you have described. You must also put in a note to say that all the other papers were burned by your uncle, and that this is the only one which remains. You must assert that in such words as will carry conviction with them. Having done this, you must at once put the box out upon the sundial, as directed. Do you understand?'

'Entirely.'

'Do not think of revenge, or anything of the sort, at present. I think that we may gain that by means of the law; but we have our web to weave, while theirs is already woven. The first consideration is to remove the pressing danger which threatens you. The second is to clear up the mystery, and to punish the guilty parties.'

'I thank you,' said the young man, rising, and pulling on his overcoat. 'You have given me fresh life and hope. I shall certainly do as you advise.'

'Do not lose an instant. And, above all, take care of yourself in the meanwhile, for I do not think that there can be a doubt that you are threatened by a very real and imminent danger. How do you go back?'

'By train from Waterloo.'

'It is not yet nine. The streets will be crowded, so I trust that you may be in safety. And yet you cannot guard yourself too closely.'

'I am armed.'

'That is well. Tomorrow I shall set to work upon your case.'

'I shall see you at Horsham, then?'

'No, your secret lies in London. It is there that I shall seek it.'

'Then I shall call upon you in a day, or in two days, with news as to the box and the papers. I shall take your advice in every particular.' He shook hands with us, and took his leave. Outside the wind still screamed, and the rain splashed and pattered against the windows. This strange, wild story seemed to have come to us from amid the mad elements—blown in upon us like a sheet of seaweed in a gale—and now to have been re-absorbed by them once more.

Sherlock Holmes sat for some time in silence with his head sunk forward, and his eyes bent upon the red glow of the fire. Then he lit his pipe, and leaning back in his chair he watched the blue smoke rings as they chased each other up to the ceiling.

'I think, Watson,' he remarked at last, 'that of all our cases we have had none more fantastic than this.'

'Save, perhaps, the Sign of Four.'

'Well, yes. Save, perhaps, that. And yet this John Openshaw seems to me to be walking amid even greater perils than did the Sholtos.'

'But have you,' I asked, 'formed any definite conception as to what these perils are?'

'There can be no question as to their nature,' he answered.

'Then what are they? Who is this K. K. K., and why does he pursue this unhappy family?'

Sherlock Holmes closed his eyes and placed his elbows upon the arms of his chair, with his fingertips together. 'The ideal reasoner,' he remarked, 'would, when he had once been shown a single fact in all its bearings, deduce from it not only all the chain of events which led up to it, but also all the results which would follow from it. As Cuvier could correctly describe a whole animal by the contemplation of a single bone, so the observer who has thoroughly understood one link in a series of incidents should be able to accurately state all the other ones, both before and after. We have not yet grasped the results which the reason alone can attain to. Problems may be solved in the study which have baffled all those who have sought a solution by the aid of their senses. To carry the art, however, to its highest pitch, it is necessary that the reasoner should be able to utilize all the facts which have come to his knowledge, and this in itself implies, as you will readily see, a possession of all knowledge, which, even in these days of free education and encyclopedias, is a somewhat rare accomplishment. It is not so impossible, however, that a man should possess all knowledge which is likely to be useful to him in his work, and this I have endeavoured in my case to do. If I remember rightly, you on one occasion, in the early days of our friendship, defined my limits in a very precise fashion.'

'Yes,' I answered, laughing. 'It was a singular document. Philosophy, astronomy, and politics were marked at zero, I remember. Botany variable, geology profound as regards the mud-stains[16] from any region within fifty miles of town, chemistry eccentric, anatomy unsystematic, sensational literature and crime records unique, violin player, boxer, swordsman, lawyer, and self-poisoner by cocaine and tobacco. Those, I think, were the main points of my analysis.'

Holmes grinned at the last item. 'Well,' he said, 'I say now, as I said then, that a man should keep his little brain attic stocked with all the furniture that he is likely to use, and the rest he can put away in the lumber-room of his library, where he can get it if he wants it. Now, for such a case as the one which has been submitted to us tonight, we need certainly to muster all our resources. Kindly hand me down the letter K of the American Encyclopedia which stands upon the shelf beside you. Thank you. Now let us consider the situation, and see what may be deduced from it. In the first place, we may start with a strong presumption that Colonel Openshaw had some very strong reason for leaving America. Men at his time of life do not change all their habits and exchange willingly the charming climate of Florida for the lonely life of an English provincial town. His extreme love of solitude in England suggests the idea that he was in fear of someone or something, so we may assume as a working hypothesis that it was fear of someone or something, which drove him from America. As to what it was he feared, we can only deduce that by considering the formidable letters which were received by himself and his successors. Did you remark the postmarks of those letters?'

'The first was from Pondicherry, the second from Dundee, and the third from London.'

'From East London. What do you deduce from that?'

'They are all seaports. That the writer was on board of a ship.'

'Excellent. We have already a clue. There can be no doubt that the probability—the strong probability—is that the writer was on board of a ship. And now let us consider another point. In the case of Pondicherry seven weeks elapsed between the threat and its fulfilment, in Dundee it was only some three or four days. Does that suggest anything?'

'A greater distance to travel.'

'But the letter had also a greater distance to come.'

'Then I do not see the point.'

'There is at least a presumption that the vessel in which the man or men are is a sailing ship. It looks as if they always send their singular warning or token before them when starting upon their mission. You see how quickly the deed followed the sign when it came from Dundee. If they had come from Pondicherry in a steamer they would have arrived almost as soon as their letter. But, as a matter of fact seven weeks elapsed. I think that those seven weeks represented the difference between the mail boat which brought the letter and the sailing vessel which brought the writer.'

'It is possible.'

'More than that. It is probable. And now you see the deadly urgency of this new case, and why I urged young Openshaw to caution. The blow has always fallen at the end of the time which it would take the senders to travel the distance. But this one comes from London, and therefore we cannot count upon delay.'

'Good God!' I cried. 'What can it mean, this relentless persecution?'

'The papers which Openshaw carried are obviously of vital importance to the person or persons in the sailing ship. I think that it is quite clear that there must be more than one of them. A single man could not have carried out two deaths in such a way as to deceive a coroner's jury. There must have been several in it, and they must have been men of resource and determination. Their papers they mean to have, be the holder of them who it may. In this way you see K. K. K. ceases to be the initials of an individual, and becomes the badge of a society.'

'But of what society?'

'Have you never—' said Sherlock Holmes, bending forward

and sinking his voice—'have you never heard of the Ku Klux Klan?'

'I never have.'

Holmes turned over the leaves of the book upon his knee. 'Here it is,' said he presently, "Ku Klux Klan. A name derived from the fanciful resemblance to the sound produced by cocking a rifle. This terrible secret society was formed by some ex-Confederate soldiers in the Southern states after the Civil War, and it rapidly formed local branches in different parts of the country, notably in Tennessee, Louisiana, the Carolinas, Georgia, and Florida. Its power was used for political purposes, principally for the terrorizing of the negro voters, and the murdering or driving from the country of those who were opposed to its views. Its outrages were usually preceded by a warning sent to the marked man in some fantastic but generally recognized shape—a sprig of oak leaves in some parts, melon seeds or orange pips in others. On receiving this the victim might either openly abjure his former ways, or might fly from the country. If he braved the matter out, death would unfailingly come upon him, and usually in some strange and unforeseen manner. So perfect was the organization of the society, and so systematic its methods, that there is hardly a case upon record where any man succeeded in braving it with impunity, or in which any of its outrages were traced home to the perpetrators. For some years the organization flourished, in spite of the efforts of the United States government, and of the better classes of the community in the South. Eventually, in the year 1869, the movement rather suddenly collapsed, although there have been sporadic outbreaks of the same sort since that date.'

'You will observe,' said Holmes, laying down the volume,

'that the sudden breaking up of the society was coincident with the disappearance of Openshaw from America with their papers. It may well have been cause and effect. It is no wonder that he and his family have some of the more implacable spirits upon their track. You can understand that this register and diary may implicate some of the first men in the South, and that there may be many who will not sleep easy at night until it is recovered.'

'Then the page we have seen—'

'Is such as we might expect. It ran, if I remember right, "sent the pips to A, B, and C"—that is, sent the society's warning to them. Then there are successive entries that A and B cleared, or left the country, and finally that C was visited, with, I fear, a sinister result for C. Well, I think, Doctor, that we may let some light into this dark place, and I believe that the only chance young Openshaw has in the meantime is to do what I have told him. There is nothing more to be said or to be done tonight, so hand me over my violin and let us try to forget for half an hour the miserable weather, and the still more miserable ways of our fellow-men.'

It had cleared in the morning, and the sun was shining with a subdued brightness through the dim veil which hangs over the great city. Sherlock Holmes was already at breakfast when I came down.

'You will excuse me for not waiting for you,' said he; 'I have, I foresee, a very busy day before me in looking into this case of young Openshaw's.'

'What steps will you take?' I asked.

'It will very much depend upon the results of my first inquiries. I may have to go down to Horsham after all.'

'You will not go there first?'

'No, I shall commence with the City. Just ring the bell, and the maid will bring up your coffee.'

As I waited, I lifted the unopened newspaper from the table and glanced my eye over it. It rested upon a heading which sent a chill to my heart.

'Holmes,' I cried, 'you are too late.'

'Ah!' said he, laying down his cup, 'I feared as much. How was it done?' He spoke calmly, but I could see that he was deeply moved.

'My eye caught the name of Openshaw, and the heading "Tragedy Near Waterloo Bridge". Here is the account: "Between nine and ten last night Police Constable Cook, of the H Division, on duty near Waterloo Bridge, heard a cry for help and a splash in the water. The night, however, was extremely dark and stormy, so that, in spite of the help of several passers-by, it was quite impossible to effect a rescue. The alarm, however, was given, and by the aid of the water police, the body was eventually recovered. It proved to be that of a young gentleman whose name, as it appears from an envelope which was found in his pocket, was John Openshaw, and whose residence is near Horsham. It is conjectured that he may have been hurrying down to catch the last train from Waterloo station, and that in his haste and the extreme darkness, he missed his path and walked over the edge of one of the small landing-places for river steamboats. The body exhibited no traces of violence, and there can be no doubt that the deceased had been the victim of an unfortunate accident, which should have the effect of calling the attention of the authorities to the condition of the riverside landing-stages." '

We sat in silence for some minutes, Holmes more depressed and shaken than I had ever seen him.

'That hurts my pride, Watson,' he said at last. 'It is a petty feeling, no doubt, but it hurts my pride. It becomes a personal matter with me now, and, if God sends me health, I shall set my hand upon this gang. That he should come to me for help, and that I should send him away to his death—!' He sprang from his chair, and paced about the room in uncontrollable agitation, with a flush upon his sallow cheeks, and a nervous clasping and unclasping of his long thin hands.

'They must be cunning devils,' he exclaimed at last. 'How could they have decoyed him down there? The Embankment is not on the direct line to the station. The bridge, no doubt, was too crowded, even on such a night, for their purpose. Well, Watson, we shall see who will win in the long run. I am going out now!'

'To the police?'

'No; I shall be my own police. When I have spun the web they may take the flies, but not before.'

All day I was engaged in my professional work, and it was late in the evening before I returned to Baker Street. Sherlock Holmes had not come back yet. It was nearly ten o'clock before he entered, looking pale and worn. He walked up to the sideboard, and, tearing a piece from the loaf, he devoured it voraciously, washing it down with a long draught of water.

'You are hungry,' I remarked.

'Starving. It had escaped my memory. I have had nothing since breakfast.'

'Nothing?'

'Not a bite. I had no time to think of it.'

'And how have you succeeded?'

'Well.'

'You have a clue?'

'I have them in the hollow of my hand. Young Openshaw shall not remain long unavenged. Why, Watson, let us put their own devilish trade-mark[17] upon them. It is well thought of!'

'What do you mean?'

He took an orange from the cupboard, and tearing it to pieces, he squeezed out the pips upon the table. Of these he took five, and thrust them into an envelope. On the inside of the flap he wrote, 'S. H. for J. O.' Then[18] he sealed it and addressed it to 'Captain James Calhoun, Barque Lone Star, Savannah, Georgia.'

'That will await him when he enters port,' said he, chuckling. 'It may give him a sleepless night. He will find it as sure a precursor of his fate as Openshaw did before him.'

'And who is this Captain Calhoun?'

'The leader of the gang. I shall have the others, but he first.'

'How did you trace it, then?'

He took a large sheet of paper from his pocket, all covered with dates and names.

'I have spent the whole day,' said he, 'over Lloyd's registers and files of the old papers, following the future career of every vessel which touched at Pondicherry in January and in February in '83. There were thirty-six ships of fair tonnage which were reported there during those months. Of these, one, the *Lone Star* instantly attracted my attention, since, although it was reported as having cleared from London, the name is that which is given to one of the states of the Union.'

'Texas, I think.'

'I was not and am not sure which; but I knew that the ship must have an American origin.'

'What then?'

'I searched the Dundee records, and when I found that the barque *Lone Star* was there in January, '85, my suspicion became a certainty. I then inquired as to the vessels which lay at present in the port of London.'

'Yes?'

'The *Lone Star* had arrived here last week. I went down to the Albert dock, and found that she had been taken down the river by the early tide this morning, homeward bound to Savannah. I wired to Gravesend, and learned that she had passed some time ago, and as the wind is easterly, I have no doubt that she is now past the Goodwins, and not very far from the Isle of Wight.'

'What will you do, then?'

'Oh, I have my hand upon him. He and the two mates are, as

I learn, the only native-born Americans in the ship. The others are Finns and Germans. I also know that they were all three away from the ship last night. I had it from the stevedore who has been loading their cargo. By the time that their sailing ship reaches Savannah the mail boat will have carried this letter, and the cable will have informed the police of Savannah that these three gentlemen are badly wanted here upon a charge of murder.'

There is ever a flaw, however, in the best laid of human plans, and the murderers of John Openshaw were never to receive the orange pips which would show them that another, as cunning and as resolute as themselves, was upon their track. Very long and very severe were the equinoctial gales of that year. We waited long for news of the *Lone Star* of Savannah, but none ever reached us. We did at last hear that somewhere far out in the Atlantic a shattered sternpost of a boat was seen swinging in the trough of a wave, with the letters 'L. S.' carved upon it, and that is all which we shall ever know of the fate of the *Lone Star*.

4.

The Man with the Twisted Lip

Isa Whitney, brother of the late Elias Whitney, D.D., Principal of the Theological College of St George's, was much addicted to opium. The habit grew upon him, as I understand, from some foolish freak when he was at college, for having read De Quincey's description of his dreams and sensations, he had drenched his tobacco with laudanum in an attempt to produce the same effects. He found, as so many more have done, that the practice is easier to attain than to get rid of, and for many years he continued to be a slave to the drug, an object of mingled horror and pity to his friends and relatives. I can see him now, with yellow, pasty face, drooping lids and pin-point[19] pupils, all huddled in a chair, the wreck and ruin of a noble man.

One night—it was in June, '89—there came a ring to my bell, about the hour when a man gives his first yawn and glances at the clock. I sat up in my chair, and my wife laid her needle-work down in her lap and made a little face of disappointment.

'A patient!' said she. 'You'll have to go out.'

I groaned, for I was newly come back from a weary day.

We heard the door open, a few hurried words, and then quick steps upon the linoleum. Our own door flew open, and a lady, clad in some dark-coloured stuff with a black veil, entered the room.

'You will excuse my calling so late,' she began, and then, suddenly losing her self-control, she ran forward, threw her arms about my wife's neck, and sobbed upon her shoulder. 'Oh! I'm in such trouble!' she cried; 'I do so want a little help.'

'Why,' said my wife, pulling up her veil, 'It is Kate Whitney. How you startled me, Kate! I had not an idea who you were when you came in.'

'I didn't know what to do, so I came straight to you.' That was always the way. Folk who were in grief came to my wife like birds to a lighthouse.

'It was very sweet of you to come. Now, you must have some wine and water, and sit here comfortably and tell us all about it. Or should you rather that I sent James off to bed?'

'Oh, no, no! I want the doctor's advice and help too. It's about Isa. He has not been home for two days. I am so frightened about him!'

It was not the first time that she had spoken to us of her husband's trouble, to me as a doctor, to my wife as an old friend and school companion. We soothed and comforted her by such words as we could find. Did she know where her husband was? Was it possible that we could bring him back to her?

It seems that it was. She had the surest information that of late he had, when the fit was on him, made use of an opium den in the farthest east of the City. Hitherto his orgies had always been confined to one day, and he had come back, twitching and shattered, in the evening. But now the spell had been upon him eight-and-forty hours, and he lay there, doubtless, among the dregs of the docks, breathing in the poison or sleeping off the effects. There he was to be found, she was sure of it, at the 'Bar of Gold', in Upper Swandam Lane. But what was she to do? How could she, a young and timid woman, make her way into such a place, and pluck her husband out from among the ruffians who surrounded him?

There was the case, and of course there was but one way out of it. Might I not escort her to this place? And then, as a second thought, why should she come at all? I was Isa Whitney's medical adviser, and as such I had influence over him. I could manage it better if I were alone. I promised her on my word that I would send him home in a cab within two hours if he were indeed at the address which she had given me. And so in ten minutes I had left my armchair and cheery sitting-room behind me, and was speeding eastward in a hansom on a strange errand, as it seemed to me at the time, though the future only could show how strange it was to be.

But there was no great difficulty in the first stage of my adventure. Upper Swandam Lane is a vile alley lurking behind the high wharves which line the north side of the river to the east of London Bridge. Between a slop shop and a gin shop, approached by a steep flight of steps leading down to a black gap like the mouth of a cave, I found the den of which I was in search. Ordering my cab to wait, I passed down the steps, worn hollow in the centre by the ceaseless tread of drunken feet, and by the light of a flickering oil lamp above the door I found the latch and made my way into a long, low room, thick and heavy with the brown opium smoke, and terraced with wooden berths, like the fore-castle of an emigrant ship.

Through the gloom one could dimly catch a glimpse of bodies lying in strange fantastic poses, bowed shoulders, bent knees, heads thrown back and chins pointing upward, with here and there a dark, lack-lustre eye turned upon the newcomer. Out of the black shadows there glimmered little red circles of light, now bright, now faint, as the burning poison waxed or waned in the bowls of the metal pipes. The most lay silent, but some muttered to themselves, and others talked together in a strange, low, monotonous voice, their conversation coming in gushes, and then suddenly tailing off into silence, each mumbling out his own thoughts and paying little heed to the words of his neighbour. At the farther end was a small brazier of burning charcoal, beside which on a three-legged wooden stool there sat a tall, thin old man, with his jaw resting upon his two fists, and his elbows upon his knees, staring into the fire.

As I entered, a sallow Malay attendant had hurried up with a pipe for me and a supply of the drug, beckoning me to an empty berth.

'Thank you, I have not come to stay,' said I. 'There is a friend of mine here, Mr Isa Whitney, and I wish to speak with him.'

There was a movement and an exclamation from my right, and peering through the gloom, I saw Whitney, pale, haggard, and unkempt, staring out at me.

'My God! It's Watson,' said he. He was in a pitiable state of reaction, with every nerve in a twitter. 'I say, Watson, what o'clock is it?'

'Nearly eleven.'

'Of what day?'

'Of Friday, June 19th.'

'Good heavens! I thought it was Wednesday. It is Wednesday. What d'you[20] want to frighten a chap for?' He sank his face onto his arms, and began to sob in a high treble key.

'I tell you that it is Friday, man. Your wife has been waiting this two days for you. You should be ashamed of yourself!'

'So I am. But you've got mixed, Watson, for I have only been here a few hours, three pipes, four pipes—I forget how many. But I'll go home with you. I wouldn't frighten Kate—poor little Kate. Give me your hand! Have you a cab?'

'Yes, I have one waiting.'

'Then I shall go in it. But I must owe something. Find what I owe, Watson. I am all off colour. I can do nothing for myself.'

I walked down the narrow passage between the double row of sleepers, holding my breath to keep out the vile, stupefying fumes of the drug, and looking about for the manager. As I passed the tall man who sat by the brazier I felt a sudden pluck at my skirt, and a low voice whispered, 'Walk past me, and then look back at me.' The words fell quite distinctly upon my ear. I glanced down. They could only have come from the old man at my side, and yet he sat now as absorbed as ever, very thin, very wrinkled, bent with age, an opium pipe dangling down from between his knees, as though it had dropped in sheer lassitude from his fingers. I took two steps forward and looked back. It took all my self-control to prevent me from breaking out into a cry of astonishment. He had turned his back so that none could see him but I. His form had filled out, his wrinkles were gone, the dull eyes had regained their fire, and there, sitting by the fire, and grinning at my surprise, was none other than Sherlock Holmes. He made a slight motion to me to approach him, and instantly, as he turned his face half round to the company once more, subsided into a doddering, loose-lipped senility.

'Holmes!' I whispered, 'what on earth are you doing in this den?'

'As low as you can,' he answered; 'I have excellent ears. If you would have the great kindness to get rid of that sottish friend of yours, I should be exceedingly glad to have a little talk with you.'

'I have a cab outside.'

'Then pray send him home in it. You may safely trust him, for he appears to be too limp to get into any mischief. I should recommend you also to send a note by the cabman to your wife to say that you have thrown in your lot with me. If you will wait outside, I shall be with you in five minutes.'

It was difficult to refuse any of Sherlock Holmes' requests, for they were always so exceedingly definite, and put forward with such a quiet air of mastery. I felt, however, that when Whitney was once confined in the cab, my mission was practically accomplished; and for the rest, I could not wish anything better than to be associated with my friend in one of those singular adventures which were the normal condition of his existence. In a few minutes I had written my note, paid Whitney's bill, led him out to the cab, and seen him driven through the darkness. In a very short time a decrepit figure had emerged from the opium den, and I was walking down the street with Sherlock Holmes. For two streets he shuffled along with a bent back and an uncertain foot. Then, glancing quickly round, he straightened himself out and burst into a hearty fit of laughter.

'I suppose, Watson,' said he, 'that you imagine that I have added opium-smoking to cocaine injections and all the other little weaknesses on which you have favoured me with your medical views.'

'I was certainly surprised to find you there.'

'But not more so than I to find you.'

'I came to find a friend.'

'And I to find an enemy.'

'An enemy?'

'Yes, one of my natural enemies, or, shall I say, my natural prey. Briefly, Watson, I am in the midst of a very remarkable inquiry, and I have hoped to find a clue in the incoherent ramblings of these sots, as I have done before now. Had I been recognized in that den my life would not have been worth an hour's purchase, for I have used it before now for my own purposes, and the rascally Lascar who runs it has sworn to have vengeance upon me. There is a trap-door[21] at the back of that building, near the corner of Paul's Wharf, which could tell some strange tales of what has passed through it upon the moonless nights.'

'What! You do not mean bodies?'

'Aye, bodies, Watson. We should be rich men if we had a thousand pounds for every poor devil who has been done to death in that den. It is the vilest murder-trap on the whole riverside, and I fear that Neville St Clair has entered it never to leave it more. But our trap should be here!' He put his two forefingers between his teeth and whistled shrilly, a signal which was answered by a similar whistle from the distance, followed shortly by the rattle of wheels and the clink of horses' hoofs. 'Now, Watson,' said Holmes, as a tall dog-cart dashed up through the gloom, throwing out two golden tunnels of yellow light from its side-lanterns, 'you'll come with me, won't you?'

'If I can be of use.'

'Oh, a trusty comrade is always of use. And a chronicler still more so. My room at the Cedars is a double-bedded one.'

'The Cedars?'

'Yes; that is Mr St Clair's house. I am staying there while I conduct the inquiry.'

'Where is it, then?'

'Near Lee, in Kent. We have a seven-mile drive before us.'

'But I am all in the dark.'

'Of course you are. You'll know all about it presently. Jump up here! All right, John, we shall not need you. Here's half-a-crown. Look out for me tomorrow about eleven. Give her her head! So long, then!'

He flicked the horse with his whip, and we dashed away through the endless succession of sombre and deserted streets, which widened gradually, until we were flying across a broad balustraded bridge, with the murky river flowing sluggishly beneath us. Beyond lay another dull wilderness of bricks and mortar, its silence broken only by the heavy, regular footfall of

the policeman, or the songs and shouts of some belated party of revellers. A dull wrack was drifting slowly across the sky, and a star or two twinkled dimly here and there through the rifts of the clouds. Holmes drove in silence, with his head sunk upon his breast, and the air of a man who is lost in thought, while I sat beside him curious to learn what this new quest might be which seemed to tax his powers so sorely, and yet afraid to break in upon the current of his thoughts. We had driven several miles, and were beginning to get to the fringe of the belt of suburban villas, when he shook himself, shrugged his shoulders, and lit up his pipe with the air of a man who has satisfied himself that he is acting for the best.

'You have a grand gift of silence, Watson,' said he. 'It makes you quite invaluable as a companion. 'Pon my word, it is a great thing for me to have someone to talk to, for my own thoughts are not over-pleasant. I was wondering what I should say to this dear little woman tonight when she meets me at the door.'

'You forget that I know nothing about it.'

'I shall just have time to tell you the facts of the case before we get to Lee. It seems absurdly simple, and yet, somehow, I can get nothing to go upon. There's plenty of thread, no doubt, but I can't get the end of it in my hand. Now, I'll state the case clearly and concisely to you, Watson, and maybe you can see a spark where all is dark to me.'

'Proceed, then.'

'Some years ago—to be definite, in May, 1884—there came to Lee a gentleman, Neville St Clair by name, who appeared to have plenty of money. He took a large villa, laid out the grounds very nicely, and lived generally in good style. By degrees he made friends in the neighbourhood, and in 1887 he married the daughter of a local brewer, by whom he has now had two children. He had no occupation, but was interested in several companies, and went into town as a rule in the morning, returning by the 5.14 from Cannon Street every night. Mr St Clair is now 37 of age, is a man of temperate habits, a good husband, a very affectionate father, and a man who is popular with all who know him. I may add that his whole debts at the present moment, as far as we have been able to ascertain, amount to £88 10s., while he has £220 standing to his credit in the Capital and Counties Bank. There is no reason, therefore, to think that money troubles have been weighing upon his mind.

'Last Monday Mr Neville St Clair went into town rather earlier than usual, remarking before he started that he had two important commissions to perform, and that he would bring his little boy home a box of bricks. Now, by the merest chance his wife received a telegram upon this same Monday, very shortly after his departure, to the effect that a small parcel of considerable value which she had been expecting was waiting for her at the offices of the Aberdeen Shipping Company. Now, if you are well up in your London, you will know that the office of the company is in Fresno Street, which branches out of Upper Swandam Lane, where you found me tonight. Mrs St Clair had her lunch, started for the City, did some shopping, proceeded to the Company's office, got her packet, and found herself at exactly 4.35 walking through Swandam Lane on her way back to the station. Have you followed me so far?'

'It is very clear.'

'If you remember, Monday was an exceedingly hot day, and Mrs St Clair walked slowly, glancing about in the hope of seeing a cab, as she did not like the neighbourhood in which she found herself. While she walked in this way down Swandam Lane she suddenly heard an ejaculation or cry, and was struck cold to see her husband looking down at her, and, as it seemed to her, beckoning to her from a second-floor window. The window was open, and she distinctly saw his face, which she describes as being terribly agitated. He waved his hands frantically to her, and then vanished from the window so suddenly that it seemed to her that he had been plucked back by some irresistible force from behind. One singular point which struck her quick feminine eye was that although he wore some dark coat, such as he had started to town in, he had on neither collar nor necktie.

'Convinced that something was amiss with him, she rushed down the steps—for the house was none other than the opium den in which you found me tonight—and, running through the front room, she attempted to ascend the stairs which led to the first floor. At the foot of the stairs, however, she met this Lascar scoundrel, of whom I have spoken, who thrust her back, and, aided by a Dane, who acts as assistant there, pushed her out into the street.

Filled with the most maddening doubts and fears, she rushed down the lane, and, by rare good fortune, met, in Fresno Street, a number of constables with an inspector, all on their way to their beat. The inspector and two men accompanied her back, and, in spite of the continued resistance of the proprietor, they made their way to the room in which Mr St Clair had last been seen. There was no sign of him there. In fact, in the whole of that floor there was no one to be found, save a crippled wretch of hideous aspect, who, it seems, made his home there. Both he and the Lascar stoutly swore that no one else had been in the front room during the afternoon. So determined was their denial that the inspector was staggered, and had almost come to believe that Mrs St Clair had been deluded when, with a cry, she sprang at a small deal box which lay upon the table, and tore the lid from it. Out there fell a cascade of children's bricks. It was the toy which he had promised to bring home.

'This discovery, and the evident confusion which the cripple showed, made the inspector realize that the matter was serious. The rooms were carefully examined, and results all pointed to an abominable crime. The front room was plainly furnished as a sitting-room, and led into a small bedroom, which looked out upon the back of one of the wharves. Between the wharf and the bedroom window is a narrow strip, which is dry at low tide, but is covered at high tide with at least four and a half feet of water. The bedroom window was a broad one, and opened from below. On examination traces of blood were to be seen upon the window-sill, and several scattered drops were visible upon the wooden floor of the bedroom. Thrust away behind a curtain in the front room were all the clothes of Mr Neville St Clair, with the exception of his coat. His boots, his socks, his hat, and his watch—all were there. There were no signs of violence upon any of these garments, and there were no other traces of Mr Neville St Clair. Out of the window he must apparently have gone, for no other exit could be discovered, and the ominous bloodstains upon the sill gave little promise that he could save himself by swimming, for the tide was at its very highest at the moment of the tragedy.

'And now as to the villains who seemed to be immediately implicated in the matter. The Lascar was known to be a man of the vilest antecedents, but as by Mrs St Clair's story he was known to have been at the foot of the stair within a very few seconds of her husband's appearance at the window, he could hardly have been more than an accessory to the crime. His defence was one of absolute ignorance, and he protested that he had no knowledge as to the doings of Hugh Boone, his lodger, and that he could not account in any way for the presence of the missing gentleman's clothes.

'So much for the Lascar manager. Now for the sinister cripple who lives upon the second floor of the opium den, and who was certainly the last human being whose eyes rested upon Neville St Clair. His name is Hugh Boone, and his hideous face is one which is familiar to every man who goes much to the City. He is a professional beggar, though in order to avoid the police regulations he pretends to a small trade in wax vestas. Some little distance down Threadneedle Street upon the left-hand side there is, as you may have remarked, a small angle in the wall. Here it is that this creature takes his daily seat, cross-legged, with his tiny stock of matches on his lap, and as he is a piteous spectacle a small rain of charity descends into the greasy leather cap which lies upon the pavement before him. I have watched the fellow more than once, before ever I thought of making his professional acquaintance, and I have been surprised at the harvest which he has reaped in so short a time. His appearance, you see, is so remarkable that no

one can pass him without observing him. A shock of orange hair, a pale face disfigured by a horrible scar, which, by its contraction, has turned up the outer edge of his upper lip, a bull-dog[22] chin, and a pair of very penetrating dark eyes, which present a singular contrast to the colour of his hair, all mark him out from amid the common crowd of mendicants, and so, too, does his wit, for he is ever ready with a reply to any piece of chaff which may be thrown at him by the passers-by. This is the man whom we now learn to have been the lodger at the opium den, and to have been the last man to see the gentleman of whom we are in quest.'

'But a cripple!' said I. 'What could he have done single-handed against a man in the prime of life?'

'He is a cripple in the sense that he walks with a limp; but, in other respects, he appears to be a powerful and well-nurtured man. Surely your medical experience would tell you, Watson, that weakness in one limb is often compensated for by exceptional strength in the others.'

'Pray continue your narrative.'

'Mrs St Clair had fainted at the sight of the blood upon the window, and she was escorted home in a cab by the police, as her presence could be of no help to them in their investigations. Inspector Barton, who had charge of the case, made a very careful examination of the premises, but without finding anything which threw any light upon the matter. One mistake had been made in not arresting Boone instantly, as he was allowed some few minutes during which he might have communicated with his friend the Lascar, but this fault was soon remedied, and he was seized and searched, without anything being found which could incriminate him. There were, it is true, some bloodstains upon his right shirt-sleeve, but he pointed to his ring finger, which had been cut near the nail, and explained that the bleeding came from there, adding that he had been to the window not long before, and that the stains which had been observed there came doubtless from the same source. He denied strenuously having ever seen Mr Neville St Clair, and swore that the presence of the clothes in his room was as much a mystery to him as to the police. As to Mrs St Clair's assertion, that she had actually seen her husband at the window, he declared that she must have been either mad or dreaming. He was removed, loudly protesting, to the police station, while the inspector remained upon the premises in the hope that the ebbing tide might afford some fresh clue.

'And it did, though they hardly found upon the mudbank what they had feared to find. It was Neville St Clair's coat, and not Neville St Clair, which lay uncovered as the tide receded. And what do you think they found in the pockets?'

'I cannot imagine.'

'No, I don't think you would guess. Every pocket stuffed with pennies and halfpennies—four hundred and twenty-one pennies, and two hundred and seventy halfpennies. It was no wonder that it had not been swept away by the tide. But a human body is a different matter. There is a fierce eddy between the wharf and the house. It seemed likely enough that the weighted coat had remained when the stripped body had been sucked away into the river.'

'But I understand that all the other clothes were found in the room. Would the body be dressed in a coat alone?'

'No, sir, but the facts might be met speciously enough. Suppose that this man Boone had thrust Neville St Clair through the window, there is no human eye which could have seen the deed. What would he do then? It would of course instantly strike him that he must get rid of the tell-tale garments. He would seize the coat then, and be in the act of throwing it out when it would occur to him that it would swim and not sink. He has little time, for he has heard the scuffle downstairs when the wife tried to force her way up, and perhaps he has already heard from his Lascar confederate that the police are hurrying up the street. There is not an instant to be lost. He rushes to some secret hoard, where he has accumulated the fruits of his beggary, and he stuffs all the coins upon which he can lay his hands into the pockets to make sure of the coat's sinking. He throws it out, and would have done the same with the other garments had not he heard the rush of steps below, and only just had time to close the window when the police appeared.'

'It certainly sounds feasible.'

'Well, we will take it as a working hypothesis for want of a better. Boone, as I have told you, was arrested and taken to the station, but it could not be shown that there had ever before been anything against him. He had for years been known as a professional beggar, but his life appeared to have been a very quiet and innocent one. There the matter stands at present, and the questions which have to be solved, what Neville St Clair was doing in the opium den, what happened to him when there, where is he now, and what Hugh Boone had to do with his disappearance, are all as far from a solution as ever. I confess that I cannot recall any case within my experience which looked at the first glance so simple, and yet which presented such difficulties.'

Whilst Sherlock Holmes had been detailing this singular series of events we had been whirling through the outskirts of the great town until the last straggling houses had been left behind, and we rattled along with a country hedge upon either side of us. Just as he finished, however, we drove through two scattered villages, where a few lights still glimmered in the windows.

'We are on the outskirts of Lee,' said my companion. 'We have touched on three English counties in our short drive, starting in Middlesex, passing over an angle of Surrey, and ending in Kent. See that light among the trees? That is the Cedars, and beside that lamp sits a woman whose anxious ears have already, I have little doubt, caught the clink of our horse's feet.'

'But why are you not conducting the case from Baker Street?' I asked.

'Because there are many inquiries which must be made out here. Mrs St Clair has most kindly put two rooms at my disposal, and you may rest assured that she will have nothing but a welcome for my friend and colleague. I hate to meet her, Watson, when I have no news of her husband. Here we are. Whoa, there, whoa!'

We had pulled up in front of a large villa which stood within its own grounds. A stable-boy had run out to the horse's head, and, springing down, I followed Holmes up the small, winding gravel drive which led to the house. As we approached, the door flew open, and a little blonde woman stood in the opening, clad in some sort of light *mousseline-de-soie*, with a touch of fluffy pink chiffon at her neck and wrists. She stood with her figure outlined against the flood of light, one hand upon the door, one half raised in her eagerness, her body slightly bent, her head and face protruded, with eager eyes and parted lips, a standing question.

'Well?' she cried, 'well[23]?' And then, seeing that there were two of us, she gave a cry of hope which sank into a groan as she saw that my companion shook his head and shrugged his shoulders.

'No good news?'

'None.'

'No bad?'

'No.'

'Thank God for that. But come in. You must be weary, for you have had a long day.'

'This is my friend, Dr Watson. He has been of most vital use to me in several of my cases, and a lucky chance has made it possible for me to bring him out and associate him with this investigation.'

'I am delighted to see you,' said she, pressing my hand warmly. 'You will, I am sure, forgive anything that may be wanting in our arrangements, when you consider the blow which has come so suddenly upon us.'

'My dear madam,' said I, 'I am an old campaigner, and if I were not, I can very well see that no apology is needed. If I can be of any assistance, either to you or to my friend here, I shall be indeed happy.'

'Now, Mr Sherlock Holmes,' said the lady as we entered a well-lit dining-room, upon the table of which a cold supper had been laid out, 'I should very much like to ask you one or two plain questions, to which I beg that you will give a plain answer.'

'Certainly, madam.'

'Do not trouble about my feelings. I am not hysterical, nor given to fainting. I simply wish to hear your real, real opinion.'

'Upon what point?'

'In your heart of hearts, do you think that Neville is alive?'

Sherlock Holmes seemed to be embarrassed by the question. 'Frankly now!' she repeated, standing upon the rug, and looking keenly down at him, as he leaned back in a basket chair.

'Frankly, then, madam, I do not.'

'You think that he is dead?'

'I do.'

'Murdered?'

'I don't say that. Perhaps.'

'And on what day did he meet his death?'

'On Monday.'

'Then perhaps, Mr Holmes, you will be good enough to explain how it is that I have received a letter from him today?'

Sherlock Holmes sprang out of his chair as if he had been galvanized.

'What!' he roared.

'Yes, today.' She stood smiling, holding up a little slip of paper in the air.

'May I see it?'

'Certainly.'

He snatched it from her in his eagerness, and smoothing it out upon the table, he drew over the lamp, and examined it intently. I had left my chair and was gazing at it over his shoulder. The envelope was a very coarse one, and was stamped with the Gravesend postmark, and with the date of that very day, or rather of the day before, for it was considerably after midnight.

'Coarse writing!' murmured Holmes. 'Surely this is not your husband's writing, madam.'

'No, but the enclosure is.'

'I perceive also that whoever addressed the envelope had to go and inquire as to the address.'

'How can you tell that?'

'The name, you see, is in perfectly black ink, which has dried itself. The rest is of the greyish colour which shows that blotting-paper has been used. If it had been written straight off, and then blotted, none would be of a deep black shade. This man has written the name, and there has then been a pause before he wrote the address, which can only mean that he was not familiar with it. It is, of course, a trifle, but there is nothing so important as trifles. Let us now see the letter! Ha! there has been an enclosure here!'

'Yes, there was a ring. His signet ring.'

'And you are sure that this is your husband's hand?'

'One of his hands.'

'One?'

'His hand when he wrote hurriedly. It is very unlike his usual writing, and yet I know it well.'

' "Dearest do not be frightened. All will come well. There is a huge error which it may take some little time to rectify. Wait in patience.—Neville." Written in pencil upon the flyleaf of a book, octavo size, no watermark. Posted today in Gravesend by a man with a dirty thumb. Ha! And the flap has been gummed, if I am not very much in error, by a person who has been chewing tobacco. And you have no doubt that it is your husband's hand, madam?'

'None. Neville wrote those words.'

'And they were posted today at Gravesend. Well, Mrs St Clair, the clouds lighten, though I should not venture to say that the danger is over.'

'But he must be alive, Mr Holmes.'

'Unless this is a clever forgery to put us on the wrong scent. The ring, after all, proves nothing. It may have been taken from him.'

'No, no; it is, it is his very own writing!'

'Very well. It may, however, have been written on Monday, and only posted today.'

'That is possible.'

'If so, much may have happened between.'

'Oh, you must not discourage me, Mr Holmes. I know that all is well with him. There is so keen a sympathy between us that I should know if evil came upon him. On the very day that I saw him last he cut himself in the bedroom, and yet I in the dining-room rushed upstairs instantly with the utmost certainty that something had happened. Do you think that I would respond to such a trifle, and yet be ignorant of his death?'

'I have seen too much not to know that the impression of a woman may be more valuable than the conclusion of an analytical reasoner. And in this letter you certainly have a very strong piece of evidence to corroborate your view. But if your husband is alive and able to write letters, why should he remain away from you?'

'I cannot imagine. It is unthinkable.'

'And on Monday he made no remarks before leaving you?'

'No.'

'And you were surprised to see him in Swandam Lane?'

'Very much so.'

'Was the window open?'

'Yes.'

'Then he might have called to you?'

'He might.'

'He only, as I understand, gave an inarticulate cry?'

'Yes.'

'A call for help, you thought?'

'Yes. He waved his hands.'

'But it might have been a cry of surprise. Astonishment at the unexpected sight of you might cause him to throw up his hands.'

'It is possible.'

'And you thought he was pulled back?'

'He disappeared so suddenly.'

'He might have leaped back. You did not see anyone else in the room?'

'No, but this horrible man confessed to having been there, and the Lascar was at the foot of the stairs.'

'Quite so. Your husband, as far as you could see, had his ordinary clothes on?'

'But without his collar or tie. I distinctly saw his bare throat.'

'Had he ever spoken of Swandam Lane?'

'Never.'

'Had he ever showed any signs of having taken opium?'

'Never.'

'Thank you, Mrs St Clair. Those are the principal points about which I wished to be absolutely clear. We shall now have a little supper and then retire, for we may have a very busy day tomorrow.'

A large and comfortable double-bedded room had been placed at our disposal, and I was quickly between the sheets, for I was weary after my night of adventure. Sherlock Holmes was a man, however, who when he had an unsolved problem upon his mind would go for days, and even for a week, without rest, turning it over, rearranging his facts, looking at it from every point of view, until he had either fathomed it, or convinced himself that his data were insufficient. It was soon evident to me that he was now preparing for an all-night sitting. He took off his coat and waistcoat, put on a large blue dressing-gown, and then wandered about the room collecting pillows from his bed, and cushions from the sofa and armchairs. With these he constructed a sort of Eastern divan, upon which he perched himself cross-legged, with an ounce of shag tobacco and a box of matches laid out in front of him. In the dim light of the lamp I saw him sitting there, an old briar pipe between his lips, his eyes fixed vacantly upon the corner of the ceiling, the blue smoke curling up from him, silent, motionless, with the light shining upon his strong-set aquiline features. So he sat as I dropped off to sleep, and so he sat when a sudden ejaculation caused me to wake up, and I found the summer sun shining into the apartment. The pipe was still between his lips, the smoke still curled upwards, and the room was full of a dense tobacco haze, but nothing remained of the heap of shag which I had seen upon the previous night.

'Awake, Watson?' he asked.

'Yes.'

'Game for a morning drive?'

'Certainly.'

'Then dress. No one is stirring yet, but I know where the stable-boy sleeps, and we shall soon have the trap out.' He chuckled to himself as he spoke, his eyes twinkled, and he seemed a different man to the sombre thinker of the previous night.

As I dressed I glanced at my watch. It was no wonder that no one was stirring. It was twenty-five minutes past four. I had hardly finished when Holmes returned with the news that the boy was putting in the horse.

'I want to test a little theory of mine,' said he, pulling on his boots. 'I think, Watson, that you are now standing in the presence of one of the most absolute fools in Europe. I deserve to be kicked from here to Charing Cross. But I think I have the key of the affair now.'

'And where is it?' I asked, smiling.

'In the bathroom,' he answered. 'Oh, yes, I am not joking,' he continued, seeing my look of incredulity. 'I have just been there, and I have taken it out, and I have got it in this Gladstone bag. Come on, my boy, and we shall see whether it will not fit the lock.'

We made our way downstairs as quietly as possible; and out into the bright morning sunshine. In the road stood our horse and trap, with the half-clad stable-boy waiting at the head. We both sprang in, and away we dashed down the London Road. A few country carts were stirring, bearing in vegetables to the metropolis, but the lines of villas on either side were as silent and lifeless as some city in a dream.

'It has been in some points a singular case,' said Holmes, flicking the horse on into a gallop. 'I confess that I have been as blind as a mole, but it is better to learn wisdom late than never to learn it at all.'

In town, the earliest risers were just beginning to look sleepily from their windows as we drove through the streets of the Surrey side. Passing down the Waterloo Bridge Road we crossed over the river, and dashing up Wellington Street wheeled sharply to the right, and found ourselves in Bow Street. Sherlock Holmes was well known to the force, and the two constables at the door saluted him. One of them held the horse's head while the other led us in.

'Who is on duty?' asked Holmes.

'Inspector Bradstreet, sir.'

'Ah, Bradstreet, how are you?' A tall, stout official had come down the stone-flagged passage, in a peaked cap and frogged jacket. 'I wish to have a quiet word with you, Bradstreet.'

'Certainly, Mr Holmes. Step into my room here.'

It was a small, office-like room, with a huge ledger upon the table, and a telephone projecting from the wall. The inspector sat down at his desk.

'What can I do for you, Mr Holmes?'

'I called about that beggar-man, Boone—the one who was charged with being concerned in the disappearance of Mr Neville St Clair, of Lee.'

'Yes. He was brought up and remanded for further inquiries.'

'So I heard. You have him here?'

'In the cells.'

'Is he quiet?'

'Oh, he gives no trouble. But he is a dirty scoundrel.'

'Dirty?'

'Yes, it is all we can do to make him wash his hands, and his face is as black as a tinker's. Well, when once his case has been settled he will have a regular prison bath; and I think, if you saw him you would agree with me that he needed it.'

'I should like to see him very much.'

'Would you? That is easily done. Come this way. You can leave your bag.'

'No, I think that I'll take it.'

'Very good. Come this way, if you please.' He led us down a passage, opened a barred door, passed down a winding stair, and brought us to a whitewashed corridor with a line of doors on each side.

'The third on the right is his,' said the inspector. 'Here it is!' He quietly shot back a panel in the upper part of the door, and glanced through.

'He is asleep,' said he. 'You can see him very well.'

We both put our eyes to the grating. The prisoner lay with his face towards us, in a very deep sleep, breathing slowly and heavily. He was a middle-sized man, coarsely clad as became his calling, with a coloured shirt protruding through the rent in his tattered coat. He was, as the inspector had said, extremely dirty, but the grime which covered his face could not conceal its repulsive ugliness. A broad weal from an old scar ran right across it from eye to chin, and by its contraction had turned up one side of the upper lip, so that three teeth were exposed in a perpetual snarl. A shock of very bright red hair grew low over his eyes and forehead.

'He's a beauty, isn't he?' said the inspector.

'He certainly needs a wash,' remarked Holmes. 'I had an idea that he might, and I took the liberty of bringing the tools with me.' He opened the Gladstone bag as he spoke, and took out, to my astonishment, a very large bath sponge.

'He! he[24]! You are a funny one,' chuckled the inspector.

'Now, if you will have the great goodness to open that door very quietly, we will soon make him cut a much more respectable figure.'

'Well, I don't know why not,' said the inspector. 'He doesn't look a credit to the Bow Street cells, does he?' He slipped his key into the lock, and we all very quietly entered the cell. The sleeper half turned, and then settled down once more into a deep slumber. Holmes stooped to the water jug, moistened his sponge, and then rubbed it twice vigorously across and down the prisoner's face.

'Let me introduce you,' he shouted, 'to Mr Neville St Clair, of Lee, in the county of Kent.'

Never in my life have I seen such a sight. The man's face peeled off under the sponge like the bark from a tree. Gone was the coarse brown tint! Gone, too, the horrid scar which had seamed it across, and the twisted lip which had given the repulsive sneer to the face! A twitch brought away the tangled red hair, and there, sitting up in his bed, was a pale, sad-faced, refined-looking man, black-haired and smooth-skinned, rubbing his eyes and staring about him with sleepy bewilderment. Then suddenly realizing the exposure, he broke into a scream, and threw himself down with his face to the pillow.

'Great heaven!' cried the inspector, 'it is, indeed, the missing man. I know him from the photograph.'

The prisoner turned with the reckless air of a man who abandons himself to his destiny. 'Be it so,' said he. 'And pray what am I charged with?'

'With making away with Mr Neville St—Oh, come, you can't be charged with that, unless they make a case of attempted suicide

of it,' said the inspector, with a grin. 'Well, I have been twenty-seven years in the Force, but this really takes the cake.'

'If I am Mr Neville St Clair, then it is obvious that no crime has been committed, and that, therefore, I am illegally detained.'

'No crime, but a very great error has been committed,' said Holmes. 'You would have done better to have trusted your wife.'

'It was not the wife, it was the children,' groaned the prisoner. 'God help me, I would not have them ashamed of their father. My God! What an exposure! What can I do?'

Sherlock Holmes sat down beside him on the couch, and patted him kindly on the shoulder.

'If you leave it to a court of law to clear the matter up,' said he, 'of course you can hardly avoid publicity. On the other hand, if you convince the police authorities that there is no possible case against you, I do not know that there is any reason that the details should find their way into the papers. Inspector Bradstreet would, I am sure, make notes upon anything which you might tell us, and submit it to the proper authorities. The case would then never go into court at all.'

'God bless you!' cried the prisoner passionately. 'I would have endured imprisonment, aye, even execution, rather than have left my miserable secret as a family blot to my children.

'You are the first who have ever heard my story. My father was a schoolmaster in Chesterfield, where I received an excellent education. I travelled in my youth, took to the stage, and finally became a reporter on an evening paper in London. One day my editor wished to have a series of articles upon begging in the metropolis, and I volunteered to supply them. There was the point from which all my adventures started. It was only by trying begging as an amateur that I could get the facts upon which to base my articles. When an actor I had, of course, learned all the secrets of making up, and had been famous in the green-room for my skill. I took advantage now of my attainments. I painted my face, and to make myself as pitiable as possible I made a good scar and fixed one side of my lip in a twist by the aid of a small slip of flesh-coloured plaster. Then with a red head of hair, and an appropriate dress, I took my station in the business part of the City, ostensibly as a match-seller, but really as a beggar. For seven hours I plied my trade, and when I returned home in the evening I found, to my surprise, that I had received no less than twenty-six shillings and fourpence.

'I wrote my articles, and thought little more of the matter until, some time later, I backed a bill for a friend, and had a writ served upon me for £25. I was at my wit's end where to get the money, but a sudden idea came to me. I begged a fortnight's grace from the creditor, asked for a holiday from my employers, and spent the time in begging in the City under my disguise. In ten days I had the money, and had paid the debt.

'Well, you can imagine how hard it was to settle down to arduous work at two pounds a week, when I knew that I could earn as much in a day by smearing my face with a little paint, laying my cap on the ground, and sitting still. It was a long fight between my pride and the money, but the dollars won at last, and I threw up reporting, and sat day after day in the corner which I had chosen, inspiring pity by my ghastly face and filling my pockets with coppers. Only one man knew my secret. He was the keeper of a low den in which I used to lodge in Swandam Lane, where I could every morning emerge as a squalid beggar and in the evenings transform myself into a well-dressed man about town. This fellow, a Lascar, was well paid by me for his rooms, so that I knew that my secret was safe in his possession.

'Well, very soon I found that I was saving considerable sums of money. I do not mean that any beggar in the streets of London could earn seven hundred pounds a year—which is less than my average takings—but I had exceptional advantages in my power of making up, and also in a facility in repartee, which improved by practice, and made me quite a recognized character in the City. All day a stream of pennies, varied by silver, poured in upon me, and it was a very bad day in which I failed to take two pounds.

'As I grew richer I grew more ambitious, took a house in the country, and eventually married, without anyone having a suspicion as to my real occupation. My dear wife knew that I had business in the City. She little knew what.

'Last Monday I had finished for the day, and was dressing in my room above the opium den, when I looked out of the window, and saw, to my horror and astonishment, that my wife was standing in the street, with her eyes fixed full upon me. I gave a cry of surprise, threw up my arms to cover my face, and rushing to my confidant, the Lascar, entreated him to prevent anyone from coming up to me. I heard her voice downstairs, but I knew that she could not ascend. Swiftly I threw off my clothes, pulled on those of a beggar, and put on my pigments and wig. Even a wife's eyes could not pierce so complete a disguise. But then it occurred to me that there might be a search in the room and that the clothes might betray me. I threw open the window, re-opening[25] by my violence a small cut which I had inflicted upon myself in the bedroom that morning. Then I seized my coat, which was weighted by the coppers which I had just transferred to it from the leather bag in which I carried my takings. I hurled it out of the window, and it disappeared into the Thames. The other clothes would have followed, but at that moment there was a rush of constables up the stairs, and a few minutes after I found, rather, I confess, to my relief, that instead of being identified as Mr Neville St Clair, I was arrested as his murderer.

'I do not know that there is anything else for me to explain. I was determined to preserve my disguise as long as possible, and hence my preference for a dirty face. Knowing that my wife would be terribly anxious, I slipped off my ring, and confided it to the Lascar at a moment when no constable was watching me, together with a hurried scrawl, telling her that she had no cause to fear.'

'That note only reached her yesterday,' said Holmes.

'Good God! What a week she must have spent.'

'The police have watched this Lascar,' said Inspector Bradstreet, 'and I can quite understand that he might find it difficult to post a letter unobserved. Probably he handed it to some sailor customer of his, who forgot all about it for some days.'

'That was it,' said Holmes, nodding approvingly, 'I have no doubt of it. But have you never been prosecuted for begging?'

'Many times; but what was a fine to me?'

'It must stop here, however,' said Bradstreet. 'If the police are to hush this thing up, there must be no more of Hugh Boone.'

'I have sworn it by the most solemn oaths which a man can take.'

'In that case I think that it is probable that no further steps may be taken. But if you are found again, then all must come out. I am sure, Mr Holmes, that we are very much indebted to you for having cleared the matter up. I wish I knew how you reach your results.'

'I reached this one,' said my friend, 'by sitting upon five pillows and consuming an ounce of shag. I think, Watson, that if we drive to Baker Street we shall just be in time for breakfast.'

5.

The Blue Carbuncle

I had called upon my friend Sherlock Holmes upon the second morning after Christmas, with the intention of wishing him the compliments of the season. He was lounging upon the sofa in a purple dressing gown, a pipe-rack within his reach upon the right, and a pile of crumpled morning papers, evidently newly studied, near at hand. Beside the couch was a wooden chair, and on the angle of the back hung a very seedy and disreputable hard felt hat, much the worse for wear, and cracked in several places. A lens and a forceps lying upon the seat of the chair suggested that the hat had been suspended in this manner for the purpose of examination.

'You are engaged,' said I; 'perhaps I interrupt you.'

'Not at all. I am glad to have a friend with whom I can discuss my results. The matter is a perfectly trivial one' (he jerked his thumb in the direction of the old hat), 'but there are points in connection with it which are not entirely devoid of interest, and even of instruction.'

I seated myself in his armchair, and warmed my hands before his crackling fire, for a sharp frost had set in, and the windows were thick with the ice crystals. 'I suppose,' I remarked, 'that, homely as it looks, this thing has some deadly story linked on to it—that it is the clue which will guide you in the solution of some mystery, and the punishment of some crime.'

'No, no. No crime,' said Sherlock Holmes, laughing. 'Only one of those whimsical little incidents which will happen when you have four million human beings all jostling each other within the space of a few square miles. Amid the action and reaction of so dense a swarm of humanity, every possible combination of events may be expected to take place, and many a little problem will be presented which may be striking and bizarre without being criminal. We have already had experience of such.'

'So much so,' I remarked, 'that, of the last six cases which I have added to my notes, three have been entirely free of any legal crime.'

'Precisely. You allude to my attempt to recover the Irene Adler papers, to the singular case of Miss Mary Sutherland, and to the adventure of the man with the twisted lip. Well, I have no doubt that this small matter will fall into the same innocent category. You know Peterson, the commissionaire?'

'Yes.'

'It is to him that this trophy belongs.'

'It is his hat.'

'No, no; he found it. Its owner is unknown. I beg that you will look upon it not, as a battered billycock, but as an intellectual problem. And, first as to how it came here. It arrived upon Christmas morning, in company with a good fat goose, which is, I have no doubt, roasting at this moment in front of Peterson's fire. The facts are these. About four o'clock on Christmas morning, Peterson, who, as you know, is a very honest fellow, was returning from some small jollification, and was making his way homewards down Tottenham Court Road. In front of him he saw, in the gaslight, a tallish man, walking with a slight stagger, and carrying a white goose slung over his shoulder. As he reached the corner of Goodge Street a row broke out between this stranger and a little knot of roughs. One of the latter knocked off the man's hat, on which he raised his stick to defend himself, and swinging it over his head, smashed the shop window behind him. Peterson had rushed forward to protect the stranger from his assailants, but the man, shocked at having broken the window and seeing an official-looking person in uniform rushing towards him, dropped his goose, took to his heels and vanished amid the labyrinth of small streets which lie at the back of Tottenham Court Road. The roughs had also fled at the appearance of Peterson, so that he was left in possession of the field of battle, and also of the spoils of victory in the shape of this battered hat and a most unimpeachable Christmas goose.'

'Which surely he restored to their owner?'

'My dear fellow, there lies the problem. It is true that "For Mrs Henry Baker" was printed upon a small card which was tied to the bird's left leg, and it is also true that the initials "H. B." are legible upon the lining of this hat; but, as there are some thousands of Bakers, and some hundreds of Henry Bakers in this city of ours, it is not easy to restore lost property to any one of them.'

'What, then, did Peterson do?'

'He brought round both hat and goose to me on Christmas morning, knowing that even the smallest problems are of interest to me. The goose we retained until this morning, when there were signs that, in spite of the slight frost, it would be well that it

should be eaten without unnecessary delay. Its finder has carried it off therefore to fulfil the ultimate destiny of a goose, while I continue to retain the hat of the unknown gentleman who lost his Christmas dinner.'

'Did he not advertise?'

'No.'

'Then, what clue could you have as to his identity?'

'Only as much as we can deduce.'

'From his hat?'

'Precisely.'

'But you are joking. What can you gather from this old battered felt?'

'Here is my lens. You know my methods. What can you gather yourself as to the individuality of the man who has worn this article?'

I took the tattered object in my hands, and turned it over rather ruefully. It was a very ordinary black hat of the usual round shape, hard and much the worse for wear. The lining had been of red silk, but was a good deal discoloured. There was no maker's name; but, as Holmes had remarked, the initials 'H. B.' were scrawled upon one side. It was pierced in the brim for a hat-securer, but the elastic was missing. For the rest, it was cracked, exceedingly dusty, and spotted in several places, although there seemed to have been some attempt to hide the discoloured patches by smearing them with ink.

'I can see nothing,' said I, handing it back to my friend.

'On the contrary, Watson, you can see everything. You fail, however, to reason from what you see. You are too timid in drawing your inferences.'

'Then, pray tell me what it is that you can infer from this hat?'

He picked it up, and gazed at it in the peculiar introspective fashion which was characteristic of him. 'It is perhaps less suggestive than it might have been,' he remarked, 'and yet there are a few inferences which are very distinct, and a few others which represent at least a strong balance of probability. That the man was highly intellectual is of course obvious upon the face of it, and also that he was fairly well-to-do within the last three years, although he has now fallen upon evil days. He had foresight, but has less now than formerly, pointing to a moral retrogression, which, when taken with the decline of his fortunes, seems to indicate some evil influence, probably drink, at work upon him. This may account also for the obvious fact that his wife has ceased to love him.'

'My dear Holmes!'

'He has, however, retained some degree of self-respect,' he continued, disregarding my remonstrance. 'He is a man who leads a sedentary life, goes out little, is out of training entirely, is middle-aged, has grizzled hair which he has had cut within the last few days, and which he anoints with lime-cream. These are the more patent facts which are to be deduced from his hat. Also, by the way, that it is extremely improbable that he has gas laid on his house.'

'You are certainly joking, Holmes.'

'Not in the least. Is it possible that even now when I give you these results you are unable to see how they are attained?'

'I have no doubt that I am very stupid; but I must confess that I am unable to follow you. For example, how did you deduce that this man was intellectual?'

For answer Holmes clapped the hat upon his head. It came

right over the forehead and settled upon the bridge of his nose. 'It is a question of cubic capacity,' said he; 'a man with so large a brain must have something in it.'

'The decline of his fortunes, then?'

'This hat is three years old. These flat brims curled at the edge came in then. It is a hat of the very best quality. Look at the band of ribbed silk, and the excellent lining. If this man could afford to buy so expensive a hat three years ago, and has had no hat since, then he has assuredly gone down in the world.'

'Well, that is clear enough, certainly. But how about the fore-sight, and the moral retrogression?'

Sherlock Holmes laughed. 'Here is the foresight,' said he, putting his finger upon the little disc and loop of the hat-securer. 'They are never sold upon hats. If this man ordered one, it is a sign of a certain amount of foresight, since he went out of his way to take this precaution against the wind. But since we see that he has broken the elastic and has not troubled to replace it, it is obvious that he has less foresight now than formerly, which is a distinct proof of a weakening nature. On the other hand, he has endeavoured to conceal some of these stains upon the felt by daubing them with ink, which is a sign that he has not entirely lost his self-respect.'

'Your reasoning is certainly plausible.'

'The further points, that he is middle-aged, that his hair is grizzled, that it has been recently cut, and that he uses lime-cream, are all to be gathered from a close examination of the lower part of the lining. The lens discloses a large number of hair-ends, clean cut by the scissors of the barber. They all appear to be adhesive, and there is a distinct odour of lime-cream. This dust, you will observe, is not the gritty, grey dust of the street, but the fluffy brown dust of the house, showing that it has been hung up indoors most of the time; while the marks of moisture upon the inside are proof positive that the wearer perspired very freely, and could, therefore, hardly be in the best of training.'

'But his wife—you said that she had ceased to love him.'

'This hat has not been brushed for weeks. When I see you, my dear Watson, with a week's accumulation of dust upon your hat, and when your wife allows you to go out in such a state, I shall fear that you also have been unfortunate enough to lose your wife's affection.'

'But he might be a bachelor.'

'Nay, he was bringing home the goose as a peace-offering to his wife. Remember the card upon the bird's leg.'

'You have an answer to everything. But how on earth do you deduce that the gas is not laid on in his house?'

'One tallow stain, or even two, might come by chance; but, when I see no less than five, I think that there can be little doubt that the individual must be brought into frequent contact with burning tallow—walks upstairs at night probably with his hat in one hand and a guttering candle in the other. Anyhow, he never got tallow-stains from a gas jet. Are you satisfied?'

'Well, it is very ingenious,' said I, laughing; 'but since, as you said just now, there has been no crime committed, and no harm done save the loss of a goose, all this seems to be rather a waste of energy.'

Sherlock Holmes had opened his mouth to reply, when the door flew open, and Peterson the commissionaire rushed into the apartment with flushed cheeks and the face of a man who is dazed with astonishment.

'The goose, Mr Holmes! The goose, sir!' he gasped.

'Eh! What of it, then? Has it returned to life, and flapped off through the kitchen window?' Holmes twisted himself round upon the sofa to get a fairer view of the man's excited face.

'See here, sir! See what my wife found in its crop!' He held out his hand, and displayed upon the centre of the palm a brilliantly scintillating blue stone, rather smaller than a bean in size, but of such purity and radiance that it twinkled like an electric point in the dark hollow of his hand.

Sherlock Holmes sat up with a whistle. 'By Jove, Peterson,' said he, 'this is treasure-trove indeed! I suppose you know what you have got?'

'A diamond, sir! A precious stone! It cuts into glass as though it were putty.'

'It's more than a precious stone. It is the precious stone.'

'Not the Countess of Morcar's blue carbuncle?' I ejaculated.

'Precisely so. I ought to know its size and shape, seeing that I have read the advertisement about it in The Times every day lately. It is absolutely unique, and its value can only be conjectured, but the reward offered of a thousand pounds is certainly not within a twentieth part of the market price.'

'A thousand pounds! Great Lord of mercy!' The commissionaire plumped down into a chair, and stared from one to the other of us.

'That is the reward, and I have reason to know that there are sentimental considerations in the background which would induce the Countess to part with half her fortune if she could but recover the gem.'

'It was lost, if I remember alright, at the Hotel Cosmopolitan,' I remarked.

'Precisely so, on the 22nd December, just five days ago. John Horner, a plumber, was accused of having abstracted it from the lady's jewel-case. The evidence against him was so strong that the case has been referred to the Assizes. I have some account of the matter here, I believe.' He rummaged amid his newspapers, glancing over the dates, until at last he smoothed one out, doubled it over, and read the following paragraph:

> 'Hotel Cosmopolitan Jewel Robbery. John Horner, 26, plumber, was brought up upon the charge of having upon the 22nd inst., abstracted from the jewel-case of the Countess of Morcar the valuable gem known as the blue carbuncle. James Ryder, upper-attendant at the hotel, gave his evidence to the effect that he had shown Horner up to the dressing-room of the Countess of Morcar upon the day of the robbery, in order that he might solder

the second bar of the grate, which was loose. He had remained with Horner some little time but had finally been called away. On returning he found that Horner had disappeared, that the bureau had been forced open, and that the small morocco casket in which, as it afterwards transpired, the Countess was accustomed to keep her jewel was lying empty upon the dressing-table. Ryder instantly gave the alarm, and Horner was arrested the same evening; but the stone could not be found either upon his person or in his rooms. Catherine Cusack, maid to the Countess, deposed to having heard Ryder's cry of dismay on discovering the robbery, and to having rushed into the room, where she found matters as described by the last witness. Inspector Bradstreet, B Division, gave evidence as to the arrest of Horner, who struggled frantically, and protested his innocence in the strongest terms. Evidence of a previous conviction for robbery having been given against the prisoner, the magistrate refused to deal summarily with the offence, but referred it to the Assizes. Horner, who had shown signs of intense emotion during the proceedings, fainted away at the conclusion and was carried out of court.'

'Hum! So much for the police-court,' said Holmes thoughtfully, tossing aside the paper. 'The question for us now to solve is the sequence of events leading from a rifled jewel-case at one end to the crop of a goose in Tottenham Court Road at the other. You see, Watson, our little deductions have suddenly assumed a much more important and less innocent aspect. Here is the stone; the stone came from the goose, and the goose came from Mr Henry Baker, the gentleman with the bad hat and all the other characteristics with which I have bored you. So now we must set ourselves very seriously to finding this gentleman, and ascertaining what part he has played in this little mystery. To do this, we must try the simplest means first, and these lie undoubtedly in an advertisement in all the evening papers. If this fail, I shall have recourse to other methods.'

'What will you say?'

'Give me a pencil, and that slip of paper. Now, then:

> *"Found at the corner of Goodge Street, a goose and a black felt hat. Mr Henry Baker can have the same by applying at 6.30 this evening at 221 B Baker Street."*

That is clear and concise.'

'Very. But will he see it?'

'Well, he is sure to keep an eye on the papers, since, to a poor man, the loss was a heavy one. He was clearly so scared by his mischance in breaking the window, and by the approach of Peterson, that he thought of nothing but flight; but since then he must have bitterly regretted the impulse which caused him to drop his bird. Then, again, the introduction of his name will cause him to see it, for everyone who knows him will direct his attention to it. Here you are, Peterson, run down to the advertising agency, and have this put in the evening papers.'

'In which, sir?'

'Oh, in the *Globe, Star, Pall Mall, St James's, Evening News, Standard, Echo,* and any others that occur to you.'

'Very well, sir, and this stone?'

'Ah, yes, I shall keep the stone. Thank you. And, I say, Peterson, just buy a goose on your way back, and leave it here with me, for we must have one to give to this gentleman in place of the one which your family is now devouring.'

When the commissionaire had gone, Holmes took up the stone and held it against the light. 'It's a bonny thing,' said he. 'Just see how it glints and sparkles. Of course it is a nucleus and focus of crime. Every good stone is. They are the devil's pet baits. In the larger and older jewels every facet may stand for a bloody deed. This stone is not yet twenty years old. It was found in the banks of the Amoy River in Southern China, and is remarkable in having every characteristic of the carbuncle, save that it is blue in shade, instead of ruby red. In spite of its youth, it has already a sinister history. There have been two murders, a vitriol-throwing, a suicide, and several robberies brought about for the sake of this forty-grain weight of crystallized charcoal. Who would think that so pretty a toy would be a purveyor to the gallows and the prison? I'll lock it up in my strong-box now, and drop a line to the Countess to say that we have it.'

'Do you think that this man Horner is innocent?'

'I cannot tell.'

'Well, then, do you imagine that this other one, Henry Baker, had anything to do with the matter?'

'It is, I think, much more likely that Henry Baker is an absolutely innocent man, who had no idea that the bird which he was carrying was of considerably more value than if it were made of solid gold. That, however, I shall determine by a very simple test, if . we have an answer to our advertisement.'

'And you can do nothing until then?'

'Nothing.'

'In that case I shall continue my professional round. But I shall come back in the evening at the hour you have mentioned, for I should like to see the solution of so tangled a business.'

'Very glad to see you. I dine at seven. There is a woodcock, I believe. By the way, in view of recent occurrences, perhaps I ought to ask Mrs Hudson to examine its crop.'

I had been delayed at a case, and it was a little after half-past six when I found myself in Baker Street once more. As I approached the house I saw a tall man in a Scotch bonnet, with a coat which was buttoned up to his chin, waiting outside in the bright semicircle which was thrown from the fanlight. Just as I arrived, the door was opened, and we were shown up together to Holmes' room.

'Mr Henry Baker, I believe,' said he, rising from his armchair, and greeting his visitor with the easy air of geniality which he could so readily assume. 'Pray take this chair by the fire, Mr Baker. It is a cold night, and I observe that your circulation is more adapted for summer than for winter. Ah, Watson, you have just come at the right time. Is that your hat, Mr Baker?'

'Yes, sir, that is undoubtedly my hat.'

He was a large man, with rounded shoulders, a massive head, and a broad, intelligent face, sloping down to a pointed beard of grizzled brown. A touch of red in nose and cheeks, with a slight tremor of his extended hand, recalled Holmes' surmise as to his habits. His rusty black frock-coat was buttoned right up in front, with the collar turned up, and his lank wrists protruded from his sleeves without a sign of cuff or shirt. He spoke in a slow staccato fashion, choosing his words with care, and gave the impression generally of a man of learning and letters who had had ill-usage at the hands of fortune.

'We have retained these things for some days,' said Holmes, 'because we expected to see an advertisement from you giving your address. I am at a loss to know now why you did not advertise.'

Our visitor gave a rather shamefaced laugh. 'Shillings have not been so plentiful with me as they once were,' he remarked. 'I had no doubt that the gang of roughs who assaulted me had carried off both my hat and the bird. I did not care to spend more money in a hopeless attempt at recovering them.'

'Very naturally. By the way, about the bird—we were compelled to eat it.'

'To eat it!' Our visitor half rose from his chair in his excitement.

'Yes, it would have been of no use to anyone had we not done so. But I presume that this other goose upon the sideboard, which is about the same weight and perfectly fresh, will answer your purpose equally well?'

'Oh, certainly, certainly!' answered Mr Baker, with a sigh of relief.

'Of course, we still have the feathers, legs, crop, and so on of your own bird, so if you wish—'

The man burst into a hearty laugh. 'They might be useful to me as relics of my adventure,' said he, 'but beyond that I can hardly see what use the *disjecta membra* of my late acquaintance are going to be to me. No, sir, I think that, with your permission, I will confine my attentions to the excellent bird which I perceive upon the sideboard.'

Sherlock Holmes glanced sharply across at me with a slight shrug of his shoulders.

'There is your hat, then, and there your bird,' said he. 'By the way, would it bore you to tell me where you got the other one from? I am somewhat of a fowl fancier, and I have seldom seen a better-grown goose.'

'Certainly, sir,' said Baker, who had risen and tucked his newly gained property under his arm. 'There are a few of us who frequent the Alpha Inn near the Museum—we are to be found in the Museum itself during the day, you understand. This year our good host, Windigate by name, instituted a goose-club, by which, on consideration of some few pence every week, we were each to receive a bird at Christmas. My pence were duly paid, and the rest is familiar to you. I am much indebted to you, sir, for a Scotch bonnet is fitted neither to my years nor my gravity.' With a comical pomposity of manner he bowed solemnly to both of us, and strode off upon his way.

'So much for Mr Henry Baker,' said Holmes, when he had closed the door behind him. 'It is quite certain that he knows

nothing whatever about the matter. Are you hungry, Watson?'

'Not particularly.'

'Then I suggest that we turn our dinner into a supper, and follow up this clue while it is still hot.'

'By all means.'

It was a bitter night, so we drew on our ulsters and wrapped cravats about our throats. Outside, the stars were shining coldly in a cloudless sky, and the breath of the passers-by blew out into smoke like so many pistol shots. Our footfalls rang out crisply and loudly as we swung through the doctors' quarter, Wimpole Street, Harley Street, and so through Wigmore Street into Oxford Street. In a quarter of an hour we were in Bloomsbury at the Alpha Inn, which is a small public-house at the corner of one of the streets which run down into Holborn. Holmes pushed open the door of the private bar, and ordered two glasses of beer from the ruddy-faced, white-aproned landlord.

'Your beer should be excellent if it is as good as your geese,' he said.

'My geese!' The man seemed surprised.

'Yes. I was speaking only half an hour ago to Mr Henry Baker, who was a member of your goose-club.'

'Ah! yes[26], I see. But you see, sir, them's[27] not our geese.'

'Indeed! Whose, then?'

'Well, I got the two dozen from a salesman in Covent Garden.'

'Indeed! I know some of them. Which was it?'

'Breckinridge is his name.'

'Ah! I don't know him. Well, here's your good health, landlord, and prosperity to your house. Good night!'

'Now for Mr Breckinridge,' he continued, buttoning up his

coat, as we came out into the frosty air. 'Remember, Watson, that though we have so homely a thing as a goose at one end of this chain, we have at the other a man who will certainly get seven years' penal servitude, unless we can establish his innocence. It is possible that our inquiry may but confirm his guilt; but, in any case, we have a line of investigation which has been missed by the police, and which a singular chance has placed in our hands. Let us follow it out to the bitter end. Faces to the south, then, and quick march!'

We passed across Holborn, down Endell Street, and so through a zigzag of slums to Covent Garden Market. One of the largest stalls bore the name of Breckinridge upon it and the proprietor, a horsey-looking man with a sharp face and trim side-whiskers, was helping a boy to put up the shutters.

'Good evening, it's a cold night,' said Holmes.

The salesman nodded, and shot a questioning glance at my companion.

'Sold out of geese, I see,' continued Holmes, pointing at the bare slabs of marble.

'Let you have five hundred tomorrow morning.'

'That's no good.'

'Well, there are some on the stall with the gas flare.'

'Ah, but I was recommended to you.'

'Who by?'

'The landlord of the "Alpha".'

'Ah, yes; I sent him a couple of dozen.'

'Fine birds they were, too. Now where did you get them from?'

To my surprise the question provoked a burst of anger from the salesman.

'Now, then, mister,' said he, with his head cocked and his arms akimbo, 'what are you driving at? Let's have it straight, now.'

'It is straight enough. I should like to know who sold you the geese which you supplied to the "Alpha".'

'Well, then, I shan't tell you. So now!'

'Oh, it is a matter of no importance; but I don't know why you should be so warm over such a trifle.'

'Warm! You'd be as warm, maybe, if you were as pestered as I am. When I pay good money for a good article there should be an end of the business; but it's "Where are the geese?" and "Who did you sell the geese to?" and "What will you take for the geese?" One would think they were the only geese in the world, to hear the fuss that is made over them.'

'Well, I have no connection with any other people who have been making inquiries,' said Holmes carelessly. 'If you won't tell us the bet is off, that is all. But I'm always ready to back my opinion on a matter of fowls, and I have a fiver on it that the bird I ate is country bred.'

'Well, then, you've lost your fiver, for it's town bred,' snapped the salesman.

'It's nothing of the kind.'

'I say it is.'

'I don't believe it.'

'D'you think you know more about fowls than I, who have handled them ever since I was a nipper? I tell you, all those birds that went to the "Alpha" were town bred.'

'You'll never persuade me to believe that.'

'Will you bet, then?'

'It's merely taking your money, for I know that I am right.

But I'll have a sovereign on with you, just to teach you not to be obstinate.'

The salesman chuckled grimly. 'Bring me the books. Bill,' said he.

The small boy brought round a small thin volume and a great greasy-backed one, laying them out together beneath the hanging lamp.

'Now then, Mr Cocksure,' said the salesman, 'I thought that I was out of geese, but before I finish you'll find that there is still one left in my shop. You see this little book?'

'Well?'

'That's the list of the folk from whom I buy. D'you see? Well, then, here on this page are the country folk, and the numbers after their names are where their accounts are in the big ledger. Now, then! You see this other page in red ink? Well, that is a list of my town suppliers. Now, look at that third name. Just read it out to me.'

'Mrs Oakshott, 117, Brixton Road—249,' read Holmes.

'Quite so. Now turn that up in the ledger.'

Holmes turned to the page indicated. 'Here you are, 'Mrs Oakshott, 117 Brixton Road, egg and poultry supplier.' '

'Now, then, what's the last entry?'

' "December 22. Twenty-four geese at 7s. 6d." '

'Quite so. There you are. And underneath?'

' "Sold to Mr Windigate of the 'Alpha' at 12s." '

'What have you to say now?'

Sherlock Holmes looked deeply chagrined. He drew a sovereign from his pocket and threw it down upon the slab, turning away with the air of a man whose disgust is too deep for words. A few yards off he stopped under a lamp-post, and laughed in the hearty, noiseless fashion which was peculiar to him.

'When you see a man with whiskers of that cut and the "Pink 'un" protruding out of his pocket, you can always draw him by a bet,' said he. 'I dare say that if I had put a hundred pounds down in front of him that man would not have given me such complete information as was drawn from him by the idea that he was doing me on a wager. Well, Watson, we are, I fancy, nearing the end of our quest, and the only point which remains to be determined is whether we should go on to this Mrs Oakshott tonight, or whether we should reserve it for tomorrow. It is clear from what that surly fellow said that there are others besides ourselves who are anxious about the matter, and I should—'

His remarks were suddenly cut short by a loud hubbub which broke out from the stall which we had just left. Turning round we saw a little rat-faced fellow, standing in the centre of the circle of yellow light which was thrown by the swinging lamp, while

Breckinridge, the salesman, framed in the door of his stall, was shaking his fists fiercely at the cringing figure.

'I've had enough of you and your geese,' he shouted. 'I wish you were all at the devil together. If you come pestering me any more with your silly talk I'll set the dog at you. You bring Mrs Oakshott here and I'll answer her, but what have you to do with it? Did I buy the geese off you?'

'No; but one of them was mine all the same,' whined the little man.

'Well, then, ask Mrs Oakshott for it.'

'She told me to ask you.'

'Well, you can ask the King of Proosia, for all I care. I've had enough of it. Get out of this!' He rushed fiercely forward, and the inquirer flitted away into the darkness.

'Ha, this may save us a visit to Brixton Road,' whispered Holmes. 'Come with me, and we will see what is to be made of this fellow.' Striding through the scattered knots of people who lounged round the flaring stalls, my companion speedily overtook the little man and touched him upon the shoulder. He sprang round, and I could see in the gaslight that every vestige of colour had been driven from his face.

'Who are you, then? What do you want?' he asked in a quavering voice.

'You will excuse me,' said Holmes blandly, 'but I could not help overhearing the questions which you put to the salesman just now. I think that I could be of assistance to you.'

'You? Who are you? How could you know anything of the matter?'

'My name is Sherlock Holmes. It is my business to know what

other people don't know.'

'But you can know nothing of this?'

'Excuse me, I know everything of it. You are endeavouring to trace some geese which were sold by Mrs Oakshott, of Brixton Road, to a salesman named Breckinridge, by him in turn to Mr Windigate, of the "Alpha", and by him to his club, of which Mr Henry Baker is a member.'

'Oh, sir, you are the very man whom I have longed to meet,' cried the little fellow, with outstretched hands and quivering fingers. 'I can hardly explain to you how interested I am in this matter.'

Sherlock Holmes hailed a four-wheeler which was passing. 'In that case we had better discuss it in a cosy room rather than in this wind-swept market-place,' said he. 'But pray tell me, before we go farther, who it is that I have the pleasure of assisting.'

The man hesitated for an instant. 'My name is John Robinson,' he answered, with a sidelong glance.

'No, no; the real name,' said Holmes sweetly. 'It is always awkward doing business with an alias.'

A flush sprang to the white cheeks of the stranger. 'Well, then,' said he, 'my real name is James Ryder.'

'Precisely so. Head attendant at the Hotel Cosmopolitan. Pray step into the cab, and I shall soon be able to tell you everything which you would wish to know.'

The little man stood glancing from one to the other of us with half-frightened, half-hopeful eyes, as one who is not sure whether he is on the verge of a windfall or of a catastrophe. Then he stepped into the cab, and in half an hour we were back in the sitting-room at Baker Street. Nothing had been said during our drive, but the high, thin breathing of our new companion, and the claspings and unclaspings of his hands, spoke of the nervous tension within him.

'Here we are!' said Holmes cheerily, as we filed into the room. 'The fire looks very seasonable in this weather. You look cold, Mr Ryder. Pray take the basket chair. I will just put on my slippers before we settle this little matter of yours. Now, then! You want to know what became of those geese?'

'Yes, sir.'

'Or rather, I fancy, of that goose. It was one bird, I imagine, in which you were interested—white, with a black bar across the tail.'

Ryder quivered with emotion. 'Oh, sir,' he cried, 'can you tell me where it went to?'

'It came here.'

'Here?'

'Yes, and a most remarkable bird it proved. I don't wonder that you should take an interest in it. It laid an egg after it was dead— the bonniest, brightest little blue egg that was ever seen. I have it here in my museum.'

Our visitor staggered to his feet, and clutched the mantelpiece with his right hand. Holmes unlocked his strong-box, and held up the blue carbuncle, which shone out like a star, with a cold, brilliant, many-pointed radiance. Ryder stood glaring with a drawn face, uncertain whether to claim or to disown it.

'The game's up, Ryder,' said Holmes quietly. 'Hold up, man, or you'll be into the fire. Give him an arm back into his chair, Watson. He's not got blood enough to go in for felony with impunity. Give him a dash of brandy. So! Now he looks a little more human. What a shrimp it is, to be sure!'

For a moment he had staggered and nearly fallen, but the brandy brought a tinge of colour into his cheeks, and he sat staring with frightened eyes at his accuser.

'I have almost every link in my hands, and all the proofs which I could possibly need, so there is little which you need tell[28] me. Still, that little may as well be cleared up to make the case complete. You had heard, Ryder, of this blue stone of the Countess of Morcar's?'

'It was Catherine Cusack who told me of it,' said he, in a crackling voice.

'I see. Her ladyship's waiting-maid. Well the temptation of sudden wealth so easily acquired was too much for you, as it has been for better men before you; but you were not very scrupulous in the means you used. It seems to me, Ryder, that there is the making of a very pretty villain in you. You knew that this man

Horner, the plumber, had been concerned in some such matter before, and that suspicion would rest the more readily upon him. What did you do, then? You made some small job in my lady's room—you and your confederate Cusack—and you managed that he should be the man sent for. Then, when he had left, you rifled the jewel-case, raised the alarm, and had this unfortunate man arrested. You then—'

Ryder threw himself down suddenly upon the rug, and clutched at my companion's knees. 'For God's sake, have mercy!' he shrieked. 'Think of my father! Of my mother! It would break their hearts. I never went wrong before! I never will again. I swear it. I'll swear it on a Bible. Oh, don't bring it into court! For Christ's sake, don't!'

'Get back into your chair!' said Holmes sternly. 'It is very well to cringe and crawl now, but you thought little enough of this poor Horner in the dock for a crime of which he knew nothing.'

'I will fly, Mr Holmes. I will leave the country, sir. Then the charge against him will break down.'

'Hum! We will talk about that. And now let us hear a true account of the next act. How came the stone into the goose, and how came the goose into the open market? Tell us the truth, for there lies your only hope of safety.'

Ryder passed his tongue over his parched lips. 'I will tell you it just as it happened, sir,' said he. 'When Horner had been arrested, it seemed to me that it would be best for me to get away with the stone at once, for I did not know at what moment the police might not take it into their heads to search me and my room. There was no place about the hotel where it would be safe. I went out, as if on some commission, and I made for my sister's house. She had married a man named Oakshott, and lived in Brixton Road, where she fattened fowls for the market. All the way there every man I met seemed to me to be a policeman or a detective, and for all that it was a cold night, the sweat was pouring down my face before I came to the Brixton Road. My sister asked me what was the matter, and why I was so pale; but I told her that I had been upset by the jewel robbery at the hotel. Then I went into the backyard, and smoked a pipe, and wondered what it would be best to do.

'I had a friend once called Maudsley, who went to the bad, and has just been serving his time in Pentonville. One day he had met me, and fell into talk about the ways of thieves and how they could get rid of what they stole. I knew that he would be true to me, for I knew one or two things about him, so I made up my mind to go right on to Kilburn, where he lived and take him into my confidence. He would show me how to turn the stone into money. But how to get to him in safety? I thought of the agonies

I had gone through in coming from the hotel. I might at any moment be seized and searched, and there would be the stone in my waistcoat pocket. I was leaning against the wall at the time, and looking at the geese which were waddling about round my feet, and suddenly an idea came into my head which showed me how I could beat the best detective that ever lived.

'My sister had told me some weeks before that I might have the pick of her geese for a Christmas present, and I knew that she was always as good as her word. I would take my goose now, and in it I would carry my stone to Kilburn. There was a little shed in the yard, and behind this I drove one of the birds, a fine big one, white, with a barred tail. I caught it and, prising its bill open, I thrust the stone down its throat as far as my finger could reach. The bird gave a gulp, and I felt the stone pass along its gullet and down into its crop. But the creature flapped and struggled, and out came my sister to know what was the matter. As I turned to speak to her the brute broke loose, and fluttered off among the others.

' "Whatever were you doing with that bird, Jem?" says she.

' "Well," said I, "you said you'd give me one for Christmas, and I was feeling which was the fattest."

' "Oh," says she, "we've set yours aside for you. Jem's bird, we call it. It's the big white one over yonder. There's twenty-six of them, which makes one for you, and one for us, and two dozen for the market."

' "Thank you, Maggie," says I; "but if it is all the same to you I'd rather have that one I was handling just now."

' "The other is a good three pound heavier," she said, "and we fattened it expressly for you."

' "Never mind. I'll have the other, and I'll take it now," said I.

' "Oh, just as you like," said she, a little huffed. "Which is it you want, then?"

' "That white one, with the barred tail, right in the middle of the flock."

' "Oh, very well. Kill it and take it with you."

'Well, I did what she said, Mr Holmes, and I carried the bird all the way to Kilburn. I told my pal what I had done, for he was a man that it was easy to tell a thing like that to. He laughed until he choked, and we got a knife and opened the goose. My heart turned to water, for there was no sign of the stone, and I knew that some terrible mistake had occurred. I left the bird, rushed back to my sister's, and hurried into the backyard. There was not a bird to be seen there.

' "Where are they all, Maggie?" I cried.

' "Gone to the dealer's."

' "Which dealer's?"

' "Breckinridge, of Covent Garden."

' "But was there another with a barred tail?" I asked, "the²⁹ same as the one I chose?"

' "Yes, Jem; there were two barred-tailed ones, and I could never tell them apart."

'Well, then, of course, I saw it all, and I ran off as hard as my feet would carry me to this man Breckinridge; but he had sold the lot at once, and not one word would he tell me as to where they had gone. You heard him yourselves tonight. Well, he has always answered me like that. My sister thinks that I am going mad. Sometimes I think that I am myself. And now—now I am myself a branded thief, without ever having touched the wealth for which I sold my character. God help me! God help me!' He burst into

convulsive sobbing, with his face buried in his hands.

There was a long silence, broken only by his heavy breathing, and by the measured tapping of Sherlock Holmes' fingertips upon the edge of the table. Then my friend rose, and threw open the door.

'Get out!' said he.

'What, sir! Oh, Heaven bless you!'

'No more words. Get out!'

And no more words were needed. There was a rush, a clatter upon the stairs, the bang of a door, and the crisp rattle of running footfalls from the street.

'After all, Watson,' said Holmes, reaching up his hand for his clay pipe, 'I am not retained by the police to supply their deficiencies. If Horner were in danger it would be another thing, but this fellow will not appear against him, and the case must collapse. I suppose that I am commuting a felony, but it is just possible that I am saving a soul. This fellow will not go wrong again. He is too terribly frightened. Send him to gaol now, and you make him a gaolbird for life. Besides, it is the season of forgiveness. Chance has put in our way a most singular and whimsical problem, and its solution is its own reward. If you will have the goodness to touch the bell, Doctor, we will begin another investigation, in which also a bird will be the chief feature.'

6.

The Speckled Band

In glancing over my notes of the seventy-odd cases in which I have during the last eight years studied the methods of my friend Sherlock Holmes, I find many tragic, some comic, a large number merely strange, but none commonplace; for, working as he did rather for the love of his art than for the acquirement of wealth, he refused to associate himself with any investigation which did not tend towards the unusual, and even the fantastic. Of all these varied cases, however, I cannot recall any which presented more singular features than that which was associated with the well-known Surrey family of the Roylotts of Stoke Moran. The events in question occurred in the early days of my association with Holmes, when we were sharing rooms as bachelors, in Baker Street. It is possible that I might have placed them upon record before, but a promise of secrecy was made at the time, from which I have only been freed during the last month by the untimely death of the lady to whom the pledge was given. It is perhaps as well that the facts should now come to light, for I have reasons to know that there are widespread rumours as to the death of Dr Grimesby Roylott which tend to make the matter even more terrible than the truth.

It was early in April, in the year '83, that I woke one morning to find Sherlock Holmes standing, fully dressed, by the side of my bed. He was a late riser as a rule, and, as the clock on the mantelpiece showed me that it was only a quarter past seven, I blinked up at him in some surprise, and perhaps just a little resentment, for I was myself regular in my habits.

'Very sorry to knock you up, Watson,' said he, 'but it's the common lot this morning. Mrs Hudson has been knocked up, she retorted upon me, and I on you.'

'What is it, then? A fire?'

'No, a client. It seems that a young lady has arrived in a considerable state of excitement, who insists upon seeing me. She is waiting now in the sitting-room. Now, when young ladies wander about the metropolis at this hour of the morning, and knock sleepy people up out of their beds, I presume that it is something very pressing which they have to communicate. Should it prove to be an interesting case, you would, I am sure, wish to follow it from the outset. I thought at any rate that I should call you, and give you the chance.'

'My dear fellow, I would not miss it for anything.'

I had no keener pleasure than in following Holmes in his professional investigations, and in admiring the rapid deductions, as swift as intuitions, and yet always founded on a logical basis, with which he unravelled the problems which were submitted to him. I rapidly threw on my clothes, and was ready in a few minutes to accompany my friend down to the sitting-room. A lady dressed in black and heavily veiled, who had been sitting in the window, rose as we entered.

'Good morning, madam,' said Holmes cheerily. 'My name is Sherlock Holmes. This is my intimate friend and associate, Dr Watson, before whom you can speak as freely as before myself. Ha, I am glad to see that Mrs Hudson has had the good sense to light the fire. Pray draw up to it, and I shall order you a cup of hot coffee, for I observe that you are shivering.'

'It is not cold which makes me shiver,' said the woman in a low voice, changing her seat as requested.

'What then?'

'It is fear, Mr Holmes. It is terror.' She raised her veil as she spoke, and we could see that she was indeed in a pitiable state of agitation, her face all drawn and grey, with restless, frightened eyes, like those of some hunted animal. Her features and figure were

those of a woman of thirty, but her hair was shot with premature grey, and her expression was weary and haggard. Sherlock Holmes ran her over with one of his quick, all-comprehensive glances.

'You must not fear,' said he soothingly, bending forward and patting her forearm. 'We shall soon set matters right, I have no doubt. You have come in by train this morning, I see.'

'You know me, then?'

'No, but I observe the second half of a return ticket in the palm of your left glove. You must have started early and yet you had a good drive in a dog-cart, along heavy roads, before you reached the station.'

The lady gave a violent start, and stared in bewilderment at my companion.

'There is no mystery, my dear madam,' said he, smiling. 'The left arm of your jacket is spattered with mud in no less than seven places. The marks are perfectly fresh. There is no vehicle save a dog-cart which throws up mud in that way, and then only when you sit on the left-hand side of the driver.'

'Whatever your reasons may be, you are perfectly correct,' said she. 'I started from home before six, reached Leatherhead at twenty past, and came in by the first train to Waterloo. Sir, I can stand this strain no longer, I shall go mad if it continues. I have no one to turn to—none, save only one, who cares for me, and he, poor fellow, can be of little aid. I have heard of you, Mr Holmes; I have heard of you from Mrs Farintosh, whom you helped in the hour of her sore need. It was from her that I had your address. Oh, sir, do you not think that you could help me too, and at least throw a little light through the dense darkness which surrounds me? At present it is out of my power to reward you for your services, but in a month or two I shall be married, with the control of my own income, and then at least you shall not find me ungrateful.'

Holmes turned to his desk, and unlocking it, drew out a small case-book[30] which he consulted.

'Farintosh,' said he. 'Ah, yes, I recall the case; it was concerned with an opal tiara. I think it was before your time, Watson. I can only say, madam, that I shall be happy to devote the same care to your case as I did to that of your friend. As to reward, my profession is its reward; but you are at liberty to defray whatever expenses I may be put to, at the time which suits you best. And now I beg that you will lay before us everything that may help us in forming an opinion upon the matter.'

'Alas!' replied our visitor. 'The very horror of my situation lies in the fact that my fears are so vague, and my suspicions depend so entirely upon small points, which might seem trivial to another, that even he to whom of all others I have a right to look for help and advice looks upon all that I tell him about it as the fancies of a nervous woman. He does not say so, but I can read it from his soothing answers and averted eyes. But I have heard, Mr Holmes, that you can see deeply into the manifold wickedness of the human heart. You may advise me how to walk amid the dangers which encompass me.'

'I am all attention, madam.'

'My name is Helen Stoner, and I am living with my stepfather, who is the last survivor of one of the oldest Saxon families in England, the Roylotts of Stoke Moran, on the western border of Surrey.'

Holmes nodded his head. 'The name is familiar to me,' said he.

'The family was at one time among the richest in England,

and the estates extended over the borders into Berkshire in the north, and Hampshire in the west. In the last century, however, four successive heirs were of a dissolute and wasteful disposition, and the family ruin was eventually completed by a gambler, in the days of the Regency. Nothing was left save a few acres of ground and the two-hundred-year-old house, which is itself crushed under a heavy mortgage. The last squire dragged out his existence there, living the horrible life of an aristocratic pauper; but his only son, my stepfather, seeing that he must adapt himself to the new conditions, obtained an advance from a relative, which enabled him to take a medical degree, and went out to Calcutta, where, by his professional skill and his force of character, he established a large practice. In a fit of anger, however, caused by some robberies which had been perpetrated in the house, he beat his native butler to death, and narrowly escaped a capital sentence. As it was, he suffered a long term of imprisonment, and afterwards returned to England a morose and disappointed man.

'When Dr Roylott was in India he married my mother, Mrs Stoner, the young widow of Major-General Stoner, of the Bengal Artillery. My sister Julia and I were twins, and we were only two years old at the time of my mother's remarriage. She had a considerable sum of money, not less than a thousand a year, and this she bequeathed to Dr Roylott entirely while we resided with him, with a provision that a certain annual sum should be allowed to each of us in the event of our marriage. Shortly after our return to England my mother died—she was killed eight years ago in a railway accident near Crewe. Dr Roylott then abandoned his attempts to establish himself in practice in London, and took us to live with him in the ancestral house at Stoke Moran. The money which my mother had left was enough for all our wants, and there seemed to be no obstacle to our happiness.

'But a terrible change came over our stepfather about this time. Instead of making friends and exchanging visits with our neighbours, who had at first been overjoyed to see a Roylott of Stoke Moran back in the old family seat, he shut himself up in his house, and seldom came out save to indulge in ferocious quarrels with whoever might cross his path. Violence of temper approaching to mania has been hereditary in the men of the family, and in my stepfather's case it had, I believe, been intensified by his long residence in the tropics. A series of disgraceful brawls took place, two of which ended in the police-court, until at last he became the terror of the village, and the folks would fly at his approach, for he is a man of immense strength, and absolutely uncontrollable in his anger.

'Last week he hurled the local blacksmith over a parapet into a stream and it was only by paying over all the money which I could gather together that I was able to avert another public exposure. He had no friends at all save the wandering gipsies, and he would give these vagabonds leave to encamp upon the few acres of bramble-covered land which represent the family estate, and would accept in return the hospitality of their tents, wandering away with them sometimes for weeks on end. He has a passion also for Indian animals, which are sent over to him by a correspondent, and he has at this moment a cheetah and a baboon, which wander freely over his grounds, and are feared by the villagers almost as much as their master.

'You can imagine from what I say that my poor sister Julia and I had no great pleasure in our lives. No servant would stay with us, and for a long time we did all the work of the house. She was but thirty at the time of her death, and yet her hair had already begun to whiten, even as mine has.'

'Your sister is dead, then?'

'She died just two years ago, and it is of her death that I wish to speak to you. You can understand that, living the life which I have described, we were little likely to see anyone of our own age and position. We had, however, an aunt, my mother's maiden sister, Miss Honoria Westphail, who lives near Harrow, and we were occasionally allowed to pay short visits at this lady's house. Julia went there at Christmas two years ago, and met there a half-pay Major of Marines, to whom she became engaged. My stepfather learned of the engagement when my sister returned, and offered no objection to the marriage; but within a fortnight of the day which had been fixed for the wedding, the terrible event occurred which has deprived me of my only companion.'

Sherlock Holmes had been leaning back in his chair with his eyes closed, and his head sunk in a cushion, but he half opened his lids now, and glanced across at his visitor.

'Pray be precise as to details,' said he.

'It is easy for me to be so, for every event of that dreadful time is seared into my memory. The manor house is, as I have already said, very old, and only one wing is now inhabited. The bedrooms in this wing are on the ground floor, the sitting-rooms being in the central block of the buildings. Of these bedrooms the first is Dr Roylott's, the second my sister's, and the third my own. There is no communication between them, but they all open out into the same corridor. Do I make myself plain?'

'Perfectly so.'

'The windows of the three rooms open out upon the lawn. That fatal night Dr Roylott had gone to his room early, though we knew that he had not retired to rest, for my sister was troubled by the smell of the strong Indian cigars which it was his custom to smoke. She left her room, therefore, and came into mine, where she sat for some time, chatting about her approaching wedding. At eleven o'clock she rose to leave me, but she paused at the door and looked back.

' "Tell me, Helen," said she, "have you ever heard anyone whistle in the dead of the night?"

' "Never," said I.

' "I suppose that you could not possibly whistle yourself in your sleep?"

' "Certainly not. But why?"

' "Because during the last few nights I have always, about three in the morning, heard a low clear whistle. I am a light sleeper, and it has awakened me. I cannot tell where it came from—perhaps from the next room, perhaps from the lawn. I thought that I would just ask you whether you had heard it."

' "No, I have not. It must be those wretched gipsies in the plantation."

' "Very likely. And yet if it were on the lawn I wonder that you did not hear it also."

' "Ah, but I sleep more heavily than you."

' "Well, it is of no great consequence, at any rate,' she smiled back at me, closed my door, and a few moments later I heard her key turn in the lock."

'Indeed,' said Holmes. 'Was it your custom always to lock yourselves in at night?'

'Always.'

'And why?'

'I think that I mentioned to you that the doctor kept a cheetah and a baboon. We had no feeling of security unless our doors were locked.'

'Quite so. Pray proceed with your statement.'

'I could not sleep that night. A vague feeling of impending misfortune impressed me. My sister and I, you will recollect, were twins, and you know how subtle are the links which bind two souls which are so closely allied. It was a wild night. The wind was howling outside, and the rain was beating and splashing against the windows. Suddenly, amid all the hubbub of the gale, there burst forth the wild scream of a terrified woman. I knew that it was my sister's voice. I sprang from my bed, wrapped a shawl round me, and rushed into the corridor. As I opened my door I seemed to hear a low whistle, such as my sister described, and a few moments later a clanging sound, as if a mass of metal had fallen. As I ran down the passage my sister's door was unlocked, and revolved slowly upon its hinges. I stared at it horror-stricken, not knowing what was about to issue from it. By the light of the corridor lamp I saw my sister appear at the opening, her face blanched with terror, her hands groping for help, her whole figure swaying to and fro like that of a drunkard. I ran to her and threw

my arms round her, but at that moment her knees seemed to give way and she fell to the ground. She writhed as one who is in terrible pain, and her limbs were dreadfully convulsed. At first I thought that she had not recognized me, but as I bent over her she suddenly shrieked out in a voice which I shall never forget, "Oh, my God! Helen! It was the band! The speckled band!" There was something else which she would fain have said, and she stabbed with her finger into the air in the direction of the Doctor's room, but a fresh convulsion seized her and choked her words. I rushed out, calling loudly for my stepfather, and I met him hastening from his room in his dressing-gown. When he reached my sister's side she was unconscious, and though he poured brandy down her throat, and sent for medical aid from the village, all efforts were in vain, for she slowly sank and died without having recovered her consciousness. Such was the dreadful end of my beloved sister.'

'One moment,' said Holmes, 'are you sure about this whistle and metallic sound? Could you swear to it?'

'That was what the county coroner asked me at the inquiry. It is my strong impression that I heard it, and yet among the crash of the gale, and the creaking of an old house, I may possibly have been deceived.'

'Was your sister dressed?'

'No, she was in her nightdress. In her right hand was found the charred stump of a match, and in her left a matchbox.'

'Showing that she had struck a light and looked about her when the alarm took place. That is important. And what conclusions did the coroner come to?'

'He investigated the case with great care, for Dr Roylott's conduct had long been notorious in the county, but he was unable to find any satisfactory cause of death. My evidence showed that the door had been fastened upon the inner side, and the windows were blocked by old-fashioned shutters with broad iron bars, which were secured every night. The walls were carefully sounded, and were shown to be quite solid all round, and the flooring was also thoroughly examined, with the same result. The chimney is wide, but is barred up by four large staples. It is certain, therefore, that my sister was quite alone when she met her end. Besides, there were no marks of any violence upon her.'

'How about poison?'

'The doctors examined her for it, but without success.'

'What do you think that this unfortunate lady died of, then?'

'It is my belief that she died of pure fear and nervous shock, though what it was which frightened her I cannot imagine.'

'Were there gipsies in the plantation at the time?'

'Yes, there are nearly always some there.'

'Ah, and what did you gather from this allusion to a band—a speckled band?'

'Sometimes I have thought that it was merely the wild talk of delirium, sometimes that it may have referred to some band of people, perhaps to these very gipsies in the plantation. I do not know whether the spotted handkerchiefs which so many of them wear over their heads might have suggested the strange adjective which she used.'

Holmes shook his head like a man who is far from being satisfied.

'These are very deep waters,' said he; 'pray go on with your narrative.'

'Two years have passed since then, and my life has been until lately lonelier than ever. A month ago, however, a dear friend, whom I have known for many years, has done me the honour to ask my hand in marriage. His name is Armitage—Percy Armitage—the second son of Mr Armitage, of Crane Water, near Reading. My stepfather has offered no opposition to the match, and we are to be married in the course of the spring. Two days ago some repairs were started in the west wing of the building, and my bedroom wall has been pierced, so that I have had to move into the chamber in which my sister died, and to sleep in the very bed in which she slept. Imagine, then, my thrill of terror when last night, as I lay awake, thinking over her terrible fate, I suddenly heard in the silence of the night the low whistle which had been the herald of her own death. I sprang up and lit the lamp, but nothing was to be seen in the room. I was too shaken to go to bed again, however, so I dressed, and as soon as it was daylight I slipped down, got a dog-cart at the Crown Inn, which is opposite, and drove to Leatherhead, from whence I have come on this morning, with the one object of seeing you and asking your advice.'

'You have done wisely,' said my friend. 'But have you told me all?'

'Yes, all.'

'Miss Stoner, you have not. You are screening your stepfather.'

'Why, what do you mean?'

For answer Holmes pushed back the frill of black lace which fringed the hand that lay upon our visitor's knee. Five little livid spots, the marks of four fingers and a thumb, were printed upon the white wrist.

'You have been cruelly used,' said Holmes.

The lady coloured deeply, and covered over her injured wrist. 'He is a hard man,' she said, 'and perhaps he hardly knows his own strength.'

There was a long silence, during which Holmes leaned his chin upon his hands and stared into the crackling fire.

'This is a very deep business,' he said at last. 'There are a thousand details which I should desire to know before I decide upon our course of action. Yet we have not a moment to lose. If we were to come to Stoke Moran today, would it be possible for us to see over these rooms without the knowledge of your stepfather?'

'As it happens, he spoke of coming into town today upon

some most important business. It is probable that he will be away all day, and that there would be nothing to disturb you. We have a housekeeper now, but she is old and foolish, and I could easily get her out of the way.'

'Excellent. You are not averse to this trip, Watson?'

'By no means.'

'Then we shall both come. What are you going to do yourself?'

'I have one or two things which I would wish to do now that I am in town. But I shall return by the twelve o'clock train, so as to be there in time for your coming.'

'And you may expect us early in the afternoon. I have myself some small business matters to attend to. Will you not wait and breakfast?'

'No, I must go. My heart is lightened already since I have confided my trouble to you. I shall look forward to seeing you again this afternoon.' She dropped her thick black veil over her face, and glided from the room.

'And what do you think of it all, Watson?' asked Sherlock Holmes, leaning back in his chair.

'It seems to me to be a most dark and sinister business.'

'Dark enough and sinister enough.'

'Yet if the lady is correct in saying that the flooring and walls are sound, and that the door, window, and chimney are impassable, then her sister must have been undoubtedly alone when she met her mysterious end.'

'What becomes, then, of these nocturnal whistles, and what of the very peculiar words of the dying woman?'

'I cannot think.'

'When you combine the ideas of whistles at night, the presence of a band of gipsies who are on intimate terms with this old doctor, the fact that we have every reason to believe that the doctor has an interest in preventing his stepdaughter's marriage, the dying allusion to a band, and finally, the fact that Miss Helen Stoner heard a metallic clang, which might have been caused by one of those metal bars that secured the shutters falling back into their place, I think that there is good ground to think that the mystery may be cleared along those lines.'

'But what, then, did the gipsies do?'

'I cannot imagine.'

'I see many objections to any such a theory.'

'And so do I. It is precisely for that reason that we are going to Stoke Moran this day. I want to see whether the objections are fatal, or if they may be explained away. But what, in the name of the devil!'

The ejaculation had been drawn from my companion by the fact that our door had been suddenly dashed open, and that a huge man had framed himself in the aperture. His costume was a peculiar mixture of the professional and of the agricultural, having a black top-hat, a long frock-coat, and a pair of high gaiters, with a hunting-crop swinging in his hand. So tall was he that his hat actually brushed the cross-bar of the doorway, and his breadth seemed to span it across from side to side. A large face, seared with a thousand wrinkles, burned yellow with the sun, and marked with every evil passion, was turned from one to the other of us, while his deep-set, bile-shot eyes, and his high thin fleshless nose, gave him somewhat the resemblance to a fierce old bird of prey.

'Which of you is Holmes?' asked this apparition.

'My name, sir, but you have the advantage of me,' said my

companion quietly.

'I am Dr Grimesby Roylott, of Stoke Moran.'

'Indeed, Doctor,' said Holmes blandly. 'Pray take a seat.'

'I will do nothing of the kind. My stepdaughter has been here. I have traced her. What has she been saying to you?'

'It is a little cold for the time of the year,' said Holmes.

'What has she been saying to you?' screamed the old man furiously.

'But I have heard that the crocuses promise well,' continued my companion imperturbably.

'Ha! You put me off, do you?' said our new visitor, taking a step forward, and shaking his hunting-crop. 'I know you, you scoundrel! I have heard of you before. You are Holmes the meddler.'

My friend smiled.

'Holmes, the busybody!'

His smile broadened.

'Holmes the Scotland Yard jack-in-office.'

Holmes chuckled heartily. 'Your conversation is most entertaining,' said he. 'When you go out close the door, for there is a decided draught.'

'I will go when I have said my say. Don't you dare to meddle with my affairs. I know that Miss Stoner has been here—I traced her! I am a dangerous man to fall foul of! See here.' He stepped swiftly forward, seized the poker, and bent it into a curve with his huge brown hands.

'See that you keep yourself out of my grip,' he snarled, and hurling the twisted poker into the fireplace, he strode out of the room.

'He seems a very amiable person,' said Holmes, laughing. 'I am not quite so bulky, but if he had remained I might have shown him that my grip was not much more feeble than his own.' As he spoke he picked up the steel poker, and with a sudden effort straightened it out again.

'Fancy his having the insolence to confound me with the official detective force! This incident gives zest to our investigation, however, and I only trust that our little friend will not suffer from her imprudence in allowing this brute to trace her. And now, Watson, we shall order breakfast, and afterwards I shall walk down to Doctors' Commons, where I hope to get some data which may help us in this matter.'

It was nearly one o'clock when Sherlock Holmes returned from his excursion. He held in his hand a sheet of blue paper, scrawled over with notes and figures.

'I have seen the will of the deceased wife,' said he. 'To determine its exact meaning I have been obliged to work out the present prices of the investments with which it is concerned. The total income, which at the time of the wife's death was little short of £1100, is now through the fall in agricultural prices not more than £750. Each daughter can claim an income of £250, in case of marriage. It is evident, therefore, that if both girls had married, this beauty would have had a mere pittance, while even one of them would cripple him to a very serious extent. My morning's work has not been wasted, since it has proved that he has the very strongest motives for standing in the way of anything of the sort. And now, Watson, this is too serious for dawdling, especially as the old man is aware that we are interesting ourselves in his affairs, so if you are ready we shall call a cab and drive to Waterloo. I should be very much obliged if you would slip your revolver into your pocket. An Eley's No. 2 is an excellent argument with gentlemen who can twist steel pokers into knots. That and a toothbrush are, I think, all that we need.'

At Waterloo we were fortunate in catching a train for Leatherhead, where we hired a trap at the station inn, and drove for four or five miles through the lovely Surrey lanes. It was a perfect day, with a bright sun and a few fleecy clouds in the heavens. The trees and wayside hedges were just throwing out their first green shoots, and the air was full of the pleasant smell of the moist earth. To me at least there was a strange contrast between the sweet promise of the spring and this sinister quest upon which we were engaged. My companion sat in the front of the trap, his arms folded, his hat pulled down over his eyes, and his chin sunk upon his breast, buried in the deepest thought. Suddenly, however, he started, tapped me on the shoulder, and pointed over the meadows.

'Look there!' said he.

A heavily timbered park stretched up in a gentle slope, thickening into a grove at the highest point. From amid the branches there jutted out the grey gables and high roof-tree of a very old mansion.

'Stoke Moran?' said he.

'Yes, sir, that be the house of Dr Grimesby Roylott,' remarked the driver.

'There is some building going on there,' said Holmes; 'that is where we are going.'

'There's the village,' said the driver, pointing to a cluster of roofs some distance to the left; 'but if you want to get to the house, you'll find it shorter to get over this stile, and so by the footpath over the fields. There it is, where the lady is walking.'

'And the lady, I fancy, is Miss Stoner,' observed Holmes, shading his eyes. 'Yes, I think we had better do as you suggest.'

We got off, paid our fare, and the trap rattled back on its way to Leatherhead.

'I thought it as well,' said Holmes, as we climbed the stile, 'that this fellow should think we had come here as architects, or on some definite business. It may stop his gossip. Good afternoon, Miss Stoner. You see that we have been as good as our word.'

Our client of the morning had hurried forward to meet us with a face which spoke her joy. 'I have been waiting so eagerly for you,' she cried, shaking hands with us warmly. 'All has turned out splendidly. Dr Roylott has gone to town, and it is unlikely that he will be back before evening.'

'We have had the pleasure of making the Doctor's acquaintance,' said Holmes, and in a few words he sketched out what had occurred. Miss Stoner turned white to the lips as she listened.

'Good heavens!' she cried, 'he has followed me, then.'

'So it appears.'

'He is so cunning that I never know when I am safe from him. What will he say when he returns?'

'He must guard himself, for he may find that there is someone more cunning than himself upon his track. You must lock yourself up from him tonight. If he is violent, we shall take you away to your aunt's at Harrow. Now, we must make the best use of our time, so kindly take us at once to the rooms which we are to examine.'

The building was of grey, lichen-blotched stone, with a high central portion, and two curving wings, like the claws of a crab, thrown out on each side. In one of these wings the windows were broken, and blocked with wooden boards, while the roof was partly caved in, a picture of ruin. The central portion was in little better repair, but the right-hand block was comparatively modern, and the blinds in the windows, with the blue smoke curling up from the chimneys, showed that this was where the family resided. Some scaffolding had been erected against the end wall, and the stone-work had been broken into, but there were no signs of any workmen at the moment of our visit. Holmes walked slowly up and down the ill-trimmed lawn, and examined with deep attention the outsides of the windows.

'This, I take it, belongs to the room in which you used to sleep, the centre one to your sister's, and the one next to the main building to Dr Roylott's chamber?'

'Exactly so. But I am now sleeping in the middle one.'

'Pending the alterations, as I understand. By the way, there does not seem to be any very pressing need for repairs at that end wall.'

'There were none. I believe that it was an excuse to move me from my room.'

'Ah! that[31] is suggestive. Now, on the other side of this narrow wing runs the corridor from which these three rooms open. There are windows in it, of course?'

'Yes, but very small ones. Too narrow for anyone to pass through.'

'As you both locked your doors at night, your rooms were unapproachable from that side. Now, would you have the kindness to go into your room, and to bar your shutters.'

Miss Stoner did so, and Holmes, after a careful examination through the open window, endeavoured in every way to force the shutter open, but without success. There was no slit through which a knife could be passed to raise the bar. Then with his lens he tested the hinges, but they were of solid iron, built firmly into the massive masonry. 'Hum!' said he, scratching his chin in some perplexity, 'my theory certainly presents some difficulties. No one could pass these shutters if they were bolted. Well, we shall see if the inside throws any light upon the matter.'

A small side-door led into the whitewashed corridor from which the three bedrooms opened. Holmes refused to examine the third chamber, so we passed at once to the second, that in which Miss Stoner was now sleeping, and in which her sister had met with her fate. It was a homely little room, with a low ceiling and a gaping fireplace, after the fashion of old country houses. A brown chest of drawers stood in one corner, a narrow white-counterpaned bed in another, and a dressing-table on the left-hand side of the window. These articles, with two small wicker-work chairs, made up all the furniture in the room save for a square of Wilton carpet in the centre. The boards round and the panelling of the walls were brown, worm-eaten oak, so old and discoloured that it may have dated from the original building of the house. Holmes drew one of the chairs into a corner and sat silent, while his eyes travelled round and round and up and down, taking in every detail of the apartment.

'Where does that bell communicate with?' he asked at last, pointing to a thick bell-rope which hung down beside the bed, the tassel actually lying upon the pillow.

'It goes to the housekeeper's room.'

'It looks newer than the other things?'

'Yes, it was only put there a couple of years ago.'

'Your sister asked for it, I suppose?'

'No, I never heard of her using it. We used always to get what we wanted for ourselves.'

'Indeed, it seemed unnecessary to put so nice a bell-pull there. You will excuse me for a few minutes while I satisfy myself as to this floor.' He threw himself down upon his face with his lens in his hand, and crawled swiftly backwards and forwards, examining minutely the cracks between the boards. Then he did the same with the woodwork with which the chamber was panelled. Finally he walked over to the bed and spent some time in staring at it, and in running his eye up and down the wall. Finally he took the bell-rope in his hand and gave it a brisk tug.

'Why, it's a dummy,' said he.

'Won't it ring?'

'No, it is not even attached to a wire. This is very interesting. You can see now that it is fastened to a hook just above where the little opening for the ventilator is.'

'How very absurd! I never noticed that before.'

'Very strange!' muttered Holmes, pulling at the rope. 'There are one or two very singular points about this room. For example, what a fool a builder must be to open a ventilator into another room, when, with the same trouble, he might have communicated with the outside air!'

'That is also quite modern,' said the lady.

'Done about the same time as the bell-rope?' remarked Holmes.

'Yes, there were several little changes carried out about that time.'

'They seem to have been of a most interesting character— dummy bell-ropes, and ventilators which do not ventilate. With your permission, Miss Stoner, we shall now carry our researches into the inner apartment.'

Dr Grimesby Roylott's chamber was larger than that of his stepdaughter, but was as plainly furnished. A camp bed, a small wooden shelf full of books, mostly of a technical character, an armchair beside the bed, a plain wooden chair against the wall, a round table, and a large iron safe were the principal things which met the eye. Holmes walked slowly round and examined each and all of them with the keenest interest.

'What's in here?' he asked, tapping the safe.

'My stepfather's business papers.'

'Oh! you[32] have seen inside, then?'

'Only once, some years ago. I remember that it was full of papers.'

'There isn't a cat in it, for example?'

'No. What a strange idea!'

'Well, look at this!' He took up a small saucer of milk which stood on the top of it.

'No; we don't keep a cat. But there is a cheetah and a baboon.'

'Ah, yes, of course! Well, a cheetah is just a big cat, and yet a saucer of milk does not go very far in satisfying its wants, I daresay.

There is one point which I should wish to determine.' He squatted down in front of the wooden chair, and examined the seat of it with the greatest attention.

'Thank you. That is quite settled,' said he, rising and putting his lens in his pocket. 'Hello! here[33] is something interesting!'

The object which had caught his eye was a small dog lash hung on one corner of the bed. The lash, however, was curled upon itself, and tied so as to make a loop of whipcord.

'What do you make of that, Watson?'

'It's a common enough lash. But I don't know why it should be tied.'

'That is not quite so common, is it? Ah, me! it's[34] a wicked world, and when a clever man turns his brains to crime it is the worst of all. I think that I have seen enough now, Miss Stoner, and, with your permission, we shall walk out upon the lawn.'

I had never seen my friend's face so grim, or his brow so dark, as it was when we turned from the scene of this investigation. We had walked several times up and down the lawn, neither Miss Stoner nor myself liking to break in upon his thoughts before he roused himself from his reverie.

'It is very essential, Miss Stoner,' said he, 'that you should absolutely follow my advice in every respect.'

'I shall most certainly do so.'

'The matter is too serious for any hesitation. Your life may depend upon your compliance.'

'I assure you that I am in your hands.'

'In the first place, both my friend and I must spend the night in your room.'

Both Miss Stoner and I gazed at him in astonishment.

'Yes, it must be so. Let me explain. I believe that that is the village inn over there?'

'Yes, that is the "Crown".'

'Very good. Your windows would be visible from there?'

'Certainly.'

'You must confine yourself to your room, on pretence of a headache, when your stepfather comes back. Then when you hear him retire for the night, you must open the shutters of your window, undo the hasp, put your lamp there as a signal to us, and then withdraw with everything which you are likely to want into the room which you used to occupy. I have no doubt that, in spite of the repairs, you could manage there for one night.'

'Oh, yes, easily.'

'The rest you will leave in our hands.'

'But what will you do?'

'We shall spend the night in your room, and we shall investigate the cause of this noise which has disturbed you.'

'I believe, Mr Holmes, that you have already made up your mind,' said Miss Stoner, laying her hand upon my companion's sleeve.

'Perhaps I have.'

'Then for pity's sake tell me what was the cause of my sister's death.'

'I should prefer to have clearer proofs before I speak.'

'You can at least tell me whether my own thought is correct, and if she died from some sudden fright.'

'No, I do not think so. I think that there was probably some more tangible cause. And now, Miss Stoner, we must leave you, for if Dr Roylott returned and saw us, our journey would be in vain.

Good-bye, and be brave, for if you will do what I have told you, you may rest assured that we shall soon drive away the dangers that threaten you.'

Sherlock Holmes and I had no difficulty in engaging a bed-room and sitting-room at the Crown Inn. They were on the upper floor, and from our window we could command a view of the avenue gate, and of the inhabited wing of Stoke Moran Manor House. At dusk we saw Dr Grimesby Roylott drive past, his huge form looming up beside the little figure of the lad who drove him. The boy had some slight difficulty in undoing the heavy iron gates, and we heard the hoarse roar of the Doctor's voice, and saw the fury with which he shook his clinched fists at him. The trap drove on, and a few minutes later we saw a sudden light spring up among the trees as the lamp was lit in one of the sitting-rooms.

'Do you know, Watson,' said Holmes, as we sat together in the gathering darkness, 'I have really some scruples as to taking you tonight. There is a distinct element of danger.'

'Can I be of assistance?'

'Your presence might be invaluable.'

'Then I shall certainly come.'

'It is very kind of you.'

'You speak of danger. You have evidently seen more in these rooms than was visible to me.'

'No, but I fancy that I may have deduced a little more. I imagine that you saw all that I did.'

'I saw nothing remarkable save the bell-rope, and what purpose that could answer I confess is more than I can imagine.'

'You saw the ventilator, too?'

'Yes, but I do not think that it is such a very unusual thing to have a small opening between two rooms. It was so small that a rat could hardly pass through.'

'I knew that we should find a ventilator before ever we came to Stoke Moran.'

'My dear Holmes!'

'Oh, yes, I did. You remember in her statement she said that her sister could smell Dr Roylott's cigar. Now, of course that suggested at once that there must be a communication between the two rooms. It could only be a small one, or it would have been remarked upon at the coroner's inquiry. I deduced a ventilator.'

'But what harm can there be in that?'

'Well, there is at least a curious coincidence of dates. A ventilator is made, a cord is hung, and a lady who sleeps in the bed dies. Does not that strike you?'

'I cannot as yet see any connection.'

'Did you observe anything very peculiar about that bed?'

'No.'

'It was clamped to the floor. Did you ever see a bed fastened like that before?'

'I cannot say that I have.'

'The lady could not move her bed. It must always be in the same relative position to the ventilator and to the rope—or so we may call it, since it was clearly never meant for a bell-pull.'

'Holmes,' I cried, 'I seem to see dimly what you are hitting at. We are only just in time to prevent some subtle and horrible crime.'

'Subtle enough and horrible enough. When a doctor does go wrong he is the first of criminals. He has nerve and he has knowledge. Palmer and Pritchard were among the heads of their profession. This man strikes even deeper, but, I think, Watson, that we shall be able to strike deeper still. But we shall have horrors enough before the night is over: for goodness' sake let us have a quiet pipe, and turn our minds for a few hours to something more cheerful.'

About nine o'clock the light among the trees was extinguished, and all was dark in the direction of the Manor House. Two hours passed slowly away, and then, suddenly, just at the stroke of eleven, a single bright light shone out right in front of us.

'That is our signal,' said Holmes, springing to his feet: 'it comes from the middle window.'

As we passed out he exchanged a few words with the landlord, explaining that we were going on a late visit to an acquaintance, and that it was possible that we might spend the night there. A moment later we were out on the dark road, a chill wind blowing in our faces, and one yellow light twinkling in front of us through the gloom to guide us on our sombre errand.

There was little difficulty in entering the grounds, for unrepaired breaches gaped in the old park wall. Making our way among the trees, we reached the lawn, crossed it, and were about to enter through the window, when out from a clump of laurel bushes there darted what seemed to be a hideous and distorted child, who threw itself upon the grass with writhing limbs, and then ran swiftly across the lawn into the darkness.

'My God!' I whispered; 'did you see it?'

Holmes was for the moment as startled as I. His hand closed like a vice upon my wrist in his agitation. Then he broke into a low laugh, and put his lips to my ear.

'It is a nice household,' he murmured. 'that is the baboon.'

I had forgotten the strange pets which the doctor affected. There was a cheetah, too; perhaps we might find it upon our shoulders at any moment. I confess that I felt easier in my mind when, after following Holmes' example and slipping off my shoes, I found myself inside the bedroom. My companion noiselessly closed the shutters, moved the lamp on to the table, and cast his eyes round the room. All was as we had seen it in the day-time. Then creeping up to me and making a trumpet of his hand, he whispered into my ear again so gently that it was all that I could do to distinguish the words:

'The least sound would be fatal to our plans.'

I nodded to show that I had heard.

'We must sit without light. He would see it through the ventilator.'

I nodded again.

'Do not go asleep; your very life may depend upon it. Have your pistol ready in case we should need it. I will sit on the side of the bed, and you in that chair.'

I took out my revolver and laid it on the corner of the table.

Holmes had brought up a long thin cane, and this he placed upon the bed beside him. By it he laid the box of matches and the stump of a candle. Then he turned down the lamp and we were left in darkness.

How shall I ever forget that dreadful vigil? I could not hear a sound, not even the drawing of a breath, and yet I knew that my companion sat open-eyed, within a few feet of me, in the same state of nervous tension in which I was myself. The shutters cut off the least ray of light, and we waited in absolute darkness. From outside came the occasional cry of a nightbird, and once at our very window a long drawn, cat-like whine, which told us that the cheetah was indeed at liberty. Far away we could hear the deep tones of the parish clock, which boomed out every quarter of an hour. How long they seemed, those quarters! Twelve o'clock, and one, and two, and three, and still we sat waiting silently for whatever might befall.

Suddenly there was the momentary gleam of a light up in the direction of the ventilator, which vanished immediately, but was succeeded by a strong smell of burning oil and heated metal. Someone in the next room had lit a dark lantern. I heard a gentle sound of movement, and then all was silent once more, though the smell grew stronger. For half an hour I sat with straining ears. Then suddenly another sound became audible—a very gentle, soothing sound, like that of a small jet of steam escaping continually from a

kettle. The instant that we heard it, Holmes sprang from the bed, struck a match, and lashed furiously with his cane at the bell-pull.

'You see it. Watson?' he yelled. 'You see it?'

But I saw nothing. At the moment when Holmes struck the light I heard a low, clear whistle, but the sudden glare flashing into my weary eyes made it impossible for me to tell what it was at which my friend lashed so savagely. I could, however, see that his face was deadly pale, and filled with horror and loathing.

He had ceased to strike, and was gazing up at the ventilator, when suddenly there broke from the silence of the night the most horrible cry to which I have ever listened. It swelled up louder and louder, a hoarse yell of pain and fear and anger all mingled in the one dreadful shriek. They say that away down in the village, and even in the distant parsonage, that cry raised the sleepers from their beds. It struck cold to our hearts, and I stood gazing at Holmes, and he at me, until the last echoes of it had died away into the silence from which it rose.

'What can it mean?' I gasped.

'It means that it is all over,' Holmes answered. 'And perhaps, after all, it is for the best. Take your pistol, and we shall enter Dr Roylott's room.'

With a grave face he lit the lamp, and led the way down the corridor. Twice he struck at the chamber door without any reply from within. Then he turned the handle and entered, I at his heels, with the cocked pistol in my hand.

It was a singular sight which met our eyes. On the table stood a dark lantern with the shutter half open, throwing a brilliant beam of light upon the iron safe, the door of which was ajar. Beside this table, on the wooden chair, sat Dr Grimesby Roylott, clad in a long grey dressing-gown, his bare ankles protruding beneath, and his feet thrust into red heelless Turkish slippers. Across his lap lay the short stock with the long lash which we had noticed during the day. His chin was cocked upwards, and his eyes were fixed in a dreadful rigid stare at the corner of the ceiling. Round his brow he had a peculiar yellow band, with brownish speckles, which seemed to be bound tightly round his head. As we entered he made neither sound nor motion.

'The band! the speckled band!' whispered Holmes.

I took a step forward: in an instant his strange headgear began to move, and there reared itself from among his hair the squat diamond-shaped head and puffed neck of a loathsome serpent.

'It is a swamp adder!' cried Holmes—'the deadliest snake in India. He has died within ten seconds of being bitten. Violence does, in truth, recoil upon the violent, and the schemer falls into the pit which he digs for another. Let us thrust this creature back into its den, and we can then remove Miss Stoner to some place of shelter, and let the county police know what has happened.'

As he spoke he drew the dog whip swiftly from the dead man's lap, and throwing the noose round the reptile's neck, he drew it from its horrid perch, and carrying it at arm's length, threw it into the iron safe, which he closed upon it.

Such are the true facts of the death of Dr Grimesby Roylott, of Stoke Moran. It is not necessary that I should prolong a narrative which has already run to too great a length, by telling how we broke the sad news to the terrified girl, how we conveyed her by the morning train to the care of her good aunt at Harrow, of how the slow process of official inquiry came to the conclusion that the Doctor met his fate while indiscreetly playing with a dangerous pet. The little which I had yet to learn of the case was told me by Sherlock Holmes as we travelled back next day.

'I had,' said he, 'come to an entirely erroneous conclusion, which shows, my dear Watson, how dangerous it always is to reason from insufficient data. The presence of the gipsies, and the use of the word "band", which was used by the poor girl, no doubt, to explain the appearance which she had caught a hurried glimpse of by the light of her match, were sufficient to put me upon an entirely wrong scent. I can only claim the merit that I instantly reconsidered my position when, however, it became clear to me that whatever danger threatened an occupant of the room could not come either from the window or the door. My attention was speedily drawn, as I have already remarked to you, to this ventilator, and to the bell-rope which hung down to the bed. The discovery that this was a dummy, and that the bed was clamped to the floor, instantly gave rise to the suspicion that the rope was there as a bridge for something passing through the hole, and coming to the bed. The idea of a snake instantly occurred to me, and when I coupled it with my knowledge that the Doctor was furnished with a supply of creatures from India, I felt that I was probably on the right track. The idea of using a form of poison which could not possibly be discovered by any chemical test was just such a one as would occur to a clever and ruthless man who had an Eastern training. The rapidity with which such a poison would take effect would also, from his point of view, be an advantage. It would be a sharp-eyed coroner indeed who could distinguish the two little dark punctures which would show where the poison fangs had done their work. Then I thought of the whistle. Of course, he must recall the snake before the morning light revealed it to the victim. He had trained it, probably by the use of the milk which we saw, to return to him when summoned. He would put it through this ventilator at the hour that he thought best, with the certainty that it would crawl down the rope, and land on the bed. It might or might not bite the occupant, perhaps she might escape every night for a week, but sooner or later she must fall a victim.

'I had come to these conclusions before ever I had entered his room. An inspection of his chair showed me that he had been in the habit of standing on it, which, of course, would be necessary in order that he should reach the ventilator. The sight of the safe, the saucer of milk, and the loop of whipcord were enough to finally dispel any doubts which may have remained. The metallic clang heard by Miss Stoner was obviously caused by her stepfather hastily closing the door of his safe upon its terrible occupant. Having once made up my mind, you know the steps which I took in order to put the matter to the proof. I heard the creature hiss, as I have no doubt that you did also, and I instantly lit the light and attacked it.'

'With the result of driving it through the ventilator.'

'And also with the result of causing it to turn upon its master at the other side. Some of the blows of my cane came home, and roused its snakish temper, so that it flew upon the first person it saw. In this way I am no doubt indirectly responsible for Dr Grimesby Roylott's death, and I cannot say that it is likely to weigh very heavily upon my conscience.'

7.

The Copper Beeches

'To the man who loves art for its own sake,' remarked Sherlock Holmes, tossing aside the advertisement sheet of the *Daily Telegraph*, 'it is frequently in its least important and lowliest manifestations that the keenest pleasure is to be derived. It is pleasant to me to observe, Watson, that you have so far grasped this truth that in these little records of our cases which you have been good enough to draw up, and, I am bound to say, occasionally to embellish, you have given prominence not so much to the many *causes célèbres* and sensational trials in which I have figured, but rather to those incidents which may have been trivial in themselves, but which have given room for those faculties of deduction and of logical synthesis which I have made my special province.'

'And yet,' said I, smiling, 'I cannot quite hold myself absolved from the charge of sensationalism which has been urged against my records.'

'You have erred, perhaps,' he observed, taking up a glowing cinder with the tongs, and lighting with it the long cherrywood pipe which was wont to replace his clay when he was in a disputatious rather than a meditative mood—'you have erred, perhaps, in attempting to put colour and life into each of your statements, instead of confining yourself to the task of placing upon record that severe reasoning from cause to effect which is really the only notable feature about the thing.'

'It seems to me that I have done you full justice in the matter,' I remarked with some coldness, for I was repelled by the egotism which I had more than once observed to be a strong factor in my friend's singular character.

'No, it is not selfishness or conceit,' said he, answering, as was his wont, my thoughts rather than my words. 'If I claim full justice for my art, it is because it is an impersonal thing—a thing beyond myself. Crime is common. Logic is rare. Therefore it is upon the logic rather than upon the crime that you should dwell. You have degraded what should have been a course of lectures into a series of tales.'

It was a cold morning of the early spring, and we sat after breakfast on either side of a cheery fire in the old room at Baker Street. A thick fog rolled down between the lines of dun-coloured houses, and the opposing windows loomed like dark, shapeless blurs, through the heavy yellow wreaths. Our gas was lit and shone on the white cloth, and glimmer of china and metal, for the table had not been cleared yet. Sherlock Holmes had been silent all the morning, dipping continuously into the advertisement columns of a succession of papers, until at last, having apparently given up his search, he had emerged in no very sweet temper to lecture me upon my literary shortcomings.

'At the same time,' he remarked, after a pause, during which he had sat puffing at his long pipe and gazing down into the fire, 'you can hardly be open to a charge of sensationalism, for out of these cases which you have been so kind as to interest yourself in, a fair proportion do not treat of crime, in its legal sense, at all. The small matter in which I endeavoured to help the King of Bohemia, the singular experience of Miss Mary Sutherland, the problem connected with the man with the twisted lip, and the incident of the noble bachelor, were all matters which are outside the pale of the law. But in avoiding the sensational, I fear that you may have bordered on the trivial.'

'The end may have been so,' I answered, 'but the methods I hold to have been novel and of interest.'

'Pshaw, my dear fellow, what do the public, the great unobservant public, who could hardly tell a weaver by his tooth or a compositor by his left thumb, care about the finer shades of analysis and deduction! But, indeed, if you are trivial, I cannot blame you, for the days of the great cases are past. Man, or at least criminal man, has lost all enterprise and originality. As to my own little practice, it seems to be degenerating into an agency for recovering lost lead pencils and giving advice to young ladies from boarding-schools[35]. I think that I have touched bottom at last, however. This note I had this morning marks my zero point, I fancy. Read it!' He tossed a crumpled letter across to me.

It was dated from Montague Place upon the preceding evening, and ran thus:

> *Dear Mr Holmes,*
>
> *I am very anxious to consult you as to whether I should or should not accept a situation which has been offered to me as governess. I shall call at half-past ten tomorrow if I do not inconvenience you.*
>
> *Yours faithfully,*
> *VIOLET HUNTER*

'Do you know the young lady?' I asked.

'Not I.'

'It is half past ten now.'

'Yes, and I have no doubt that is her ring.'

'It may turn out to be of more interest than you think. You remember that the affair of the blue carbuncle, which appeared to be a mere whim at first, developed into a serious investigation. It may be so in this case, also.'

'Well, let us hope so! But our doubts will very soon be solved, for here, unless I am much mistaken, is the person in question.'

As he spoke the door opened, and a young lady entered the room. She was plainly but neatly dressed, with a bright, quick face, freckled like a plover's egg, and with the brisk manner of a woman who has had her own way to make in the world.

'You will excuse my troubling you, I am sure,' said she, as my companion rose to greet her; 'but I have had a very strange experience, and as I have no parents or relations of any sort from whom I could ask advice, I thought that perhaps you would be kind enough to tell me what I should do.'

'Pray take a seat, Miss Hunter. I shall be happy to do anything that I can to serve you.'

I could see that Holmes was favourably impressed by the manner and speech of his new client. He looked her over in his searching fashion, and then composed himself, with his lids drooping and his fingertips together to listen to her story.

'I have been a governess for five years,' said she, 'in the family of Colonel Spence Munro, but two months ago the Colonel received an appointment at Halifax, in Nova Scotia, and took his children over to America with him, so that I found myself without a situation. I advertised and I answered advertisements, but without success. At last the little money which I had saved began to run short, and I was at my wits' end as to what I should do.

'There is a well-known agency for governesses in the West End called Westaway's, and there I used to call about once a week in order to see whether anything had turned up which might suit me. Westaway was the name of the founder of the business, but it is really managed by Miss Stoper. She sits in her own little office, and the ladies who are seeking employment wait in an anteroom, and are then shown in one by one, when she consults her ledgers, and sees whether she has anything which would suit them.

'Well, when I called last week I was shown into the little office as usual, but I found that Miss Stoper was not alone. A prodigiously stout man with a very smiling face, and a great heavy chin which rolled down in fold upon fold over his throat, sat at her elbow with a pair of glasses on his nose, looking very earnestly at the ladies who entered. As I came in he gave quite a jump in his chair, and turned quickly to Miss Stoper:

' "That will do,' said he; "I could not ask for anything better. Capital! Capital!" He seemed quite enthusiastic and rubbed his hands together in the most genial fashion. He was such a comfortable-looking man that it was quite a pleasure to look at him.

' "You are looking for a situation, miss?" he asked.

' "Yes, sir."

' "As governess?"

' "Yes, sir."

' "And what salary do you ask?"

' "I had four pounds a month in my last place with Colonel Spence Munro."

' "Oh, tut, tut! sweating[36]—rank sweating!" he cried, throwing his fat hands out into the air like a man who is in a boiling passion. "How could anyone offer so pitiful a sum to a lady with such attractions and accomplishments?"

' "My accomplishments, sir, may be less than you imagine," said I. "A little French, a little German, music, and drawing—"

' "Tut, tut!" he cried. "This is all quite beside the question. The point is, have you or have you not the bearing and deportment of a lady? There it is in a nutshell. If you have not, you are not fitted for the rearing of a child who may some day play a considerable part in the history of the country. But if you have, why, then how could any gentleman ask you to condescend to accept anything under the three figures? Your salary with me, madam, would commence at a hundred pounds a year."

'You may imagine, Mr Holmes, that to me, destitute as I was, such an offer seemed almost too good to be true. The gentleman, however, seeing perhaps the look of incredulity upon my face, opened a pocket-book[37] and took out a note.

' "It is also my custom," said he, smiling in the most pleasant fashion until his eyes were just two little shining slits, amidst the white creases of his face, "to advance to my young ladies half their salary beforehand, so that they may meet any little expenses of their journey and their wardrobe."

'It seemed to me that I had never met so fascinating and so

thoughtful a man. As I was already in debt to my tradesmen, the advance was a great convenience, and yet there was something unnatural about the whole transaction which made me wish to know a little more before I quite committed myself.

' "May I ask where you live, sir?" said I.

' "Hampshire. Charming rural place. The Copper Beeches, five miles on the far side of Winchester. It is the most lovely country, my dear young lady, and the dearest old country house."

' "And my duties, sir? I should be glad to know what they would be."

' "One child—one dear little romper just six years old. Oh, if you could see him killing cockroaches with a slipper! Smack! smack[38]! smack! Three gone before you could wink!" He leaned back in his chair and laughed his eyes into his head again.

'I was a little startled at the nature of the child's amusement, but the father's laughter made me think that perhaps he was joking.

' "My sole duties, then," I asked, "are to take charge of a single child?"

' "No, no, not the sole, not the sole, my dear young lady," he cried. "Your duty would be as I am sure your good sense would suggest, to obey any little commands my wife might give, provided always that they were such commands as a lady might with propriety obey. You see no difficulty, heh?"

' "I should be happy to make myself useful."

' "Quite so. In dress now, for example! We are faddy people, you know—faddy, but kind-hearted. If you were asked to wear any dress which we might give you, you would not object to our little whim. Heh?"

' "No," said I, considerably astonished at his words.

' "Or to sit here, or sit there, that would not be offensive to you?"

' "Oh, no."

' "Or to cut your hair quite short before you come to us?"

'I could hardly believe my ears. As you may observe, Mr Holmes, my hair is somewhat luxuriant, and of a rather peculiar tint of chestnut. It has been considered artistic. I could not dream of sacrificing it in this off-hand fashion.

' "I am afraid that that is quite impossible," said I. He had been watching me eagerly out of his small eyes and I could see a shadow pass over his face as I spoke.

' "I am afraid that it is quite essential," said he. "It is a little fancy of my wife's, and ladies' fancies, you know, madam, ladies' fancies must be consulted. And so you won't cut your hair?"

' "No, sir, I really could not," I answered firmly.

' "Ah, very well; then that quite settles the matter. It is a pity, because in other respects you would really have done very nicely. In that case, Miss Stoper, I had best inspect a few more of your young ladies."

'The manageress had sat all this while busy with her papers without a word to either of us, but she glanced at me now with so much annoyance upon her face that I could not help suspecting that she had lost a handsome commission through my refusal.

' "Do you desire your name to be kept upon the books?" she asked.

' "If you please, Miss Stoper."

' "Well, really, it seems rather useless, since you refuse the most excellent offers in this fashion," said she sharply. "You can hardly expect us to exert ourselves to find another such opening for you. Good day to you, Miss Hunter." She struck a gong upon the table, and I was shown out by the page.

'Well, Mr Holmes, when I got back to my lodgings and found little enough in the cupboard, and two or three bills upon the table, I began to ask myself whether I had not done a very foolish thing. After all, if these people had strange fads, and expected obedience on the most extraordinary matters, they were at least ready to pay for their eccentricity. Very few governesses in England are getting a hundred a year. Besides, what use was my hair to me? Many people are improved by wearing it short, and perhaps I should be among the number. Next day I was inclined to think that I had made a mistake, and by the day after I was sure of it. I had almost overcome my pride, so far as to go back to the agency and inquire whether the place was still open, when I received this letter from the gentleman himself. I have it here and I will read it to you:

The Copper Beeches, near Winchester

Dear Miss Hunter,

Miss Stoper has very kindly given me your address, and I write from here to ask you whether you have reconsidered your decision. My wife is very anxious that you should come, for she has been much attracted by my description of you. We are willing to give thirty pounds a quarter, or £120 a year, so as to recompense you for any little inconvenience which our fads may cause you. They are not very exacting after all. My wife is fond of a particular shade of electric blue, and would like you to wear such a dress indoors in the morning. You need not, however, go to the expense of purchasing new, as we have one belonging to my dear daughter Alice (now in Philadelphia) which would, I should think, fit you very well. Then, as to sitting here or there, or amusing yourself in any manner indicated, that need cause you no inconvenience. As regards your hair, it is no doubt a pity, especially as I could not help remarking its beauty during our short interview, but I am afraid that I must remain firm upon this point, and I only hope that the increased salary may recompense you for the loss. Your duties, as far as the child is concerned, are very light. Now do try to come, and I shall meet you with the dog-cart at Winchester. Let me know your train.

Yours faithfully,
JEPHRO RUCASTLE

'That is the letter which I have just received, Mr Holmes, and my mind is made up that I will accept it. I thought, however, that before taking the final step, I should like to submit the whole matter to your consideration.'

'Well, Miss Hunter, if your mind is made up, that settles the question,' said Holmes, smiling.

'But you would not advise me to refuse?'

'I confess that it is not the situation which I should like to see a sister of mine apply for.'

'What is the meaning of it all, Mr Holmes?'

'Ah, I have no data. I cannot tell. Perhaps you have yourself formed some opinion?'

'Well, there seems to me to be only one possible solution.

Mr Rucastle seemed to be a very kind, good-natured man. Is it not possible that his wife is a lunatic, that he desires to keep the matter quiet for fear she should be taken to an asylum, and that he humours her fancies in every way in order to prevent an outbreak?'

'That is a possible solution—in fact, as matters stand, it is the most probable one. But in any case it does not seem to be a nice household for a young lady.'

'But the money, Mr Holmes, the money!'

'Well, yes, of course, the pay is good—too good. That is what makes me uneasy. Why should they give you £120 a year, when they could have their pick for £40? There must be some strong reason behind.'

'I thought that if I told you the circumstances you would understand afterwards if I wanted your help. I should feel so much stronger if I felt that you were at the back of me.'

'Oh, you may carry that feeling away with you. I assure you that your little problem promises to be the most interesting which has come my way for some months. There is something distinctly novel about some of the features. If you should find yourself in doubt or in danger—'

'Danger! What danger do you foresee?'

Holmes shook his head gravely. 'It would cease to be a danger if we could define it,' said he. 'But at any time, day or night, a telegram would bring me down to your help.'

'That is enough.' She rose briskly from her chair with the anxiety all swept from her face. 'I shall go down to Hampshire quite easy in my mind now. I shall write to Mr Rucastle at once, sacrifice my poor hair tonight, and start for Winchester tomorrow.' With a few grateful words to Holmes she bade us both goodnight,

and bustled off upon her way.

'At least,' said I, as we heard her quick, firm steps descending the stairs, 'she seems to be a young lady who is very well able to take care of herself.'

'And she would need to be,' said Holmes gravely. 'I am much mistaken if we do not hear from her before many days are past.'

It was not very long before my friend's prediction was fulfilled. A fortnight went by, during which I frequently found my thoughts turning in her direction, and wondering what strange side-alley of human experience this lonely woman had strayed into. The unusual salary, the curious conditions, the light duties, all pointed to something abnormal, though whether a fad or a plot, or whether the man were a philanthropist or a villain, it was quite beyond my powers to determine. As to Holmes, I observed that he sat frequently for half an hour on end, with knitted brows and an abstracted air, but he swept the matter away with a wave of his hand when I mentioned it. 'Data! data[39]! data!' he cried impatiently. 'I can't make bricks without clay.' And yet he would always wind up by muttering that no sister of his should ever have accepted such a situation.

The telegram which we eventually received came late one night, just as I was thinking of turning in, and Holmes was settling down to one of those all-night chemical researches which he frequently indulged in, when I would leave him stooping over a retort and a test-tube at night and find him in the same position when I came down to breakfast in the morning. He opened the yellow envelope, and then, glancing at the message, threw it across to me.

'Just look up the trains in Bradshaw,' said he, and turned back to his chemical studies.

The summons was a brief and urgent one.

> *Please be at the Black Swan Hotel at Winchester at midday tomorrow (it said). Do come! I am at my wits' end.*
>
> *HUNTER*

'Will you come with me?' asked Holmes, glancing up.

'I should wish to.'

'Just look it up, then.'

'There is a train at half past nine,' said I, glancing over my Bradshaw. 'It is due at Winchester at 11:30.'

'That will do very nicely. Then perhaps I had better postpone my analysis of the acetones, as we may need to be at our best in the morning.'

By eleven o'clock the next day we were well upon our way to the old English capital. Holmes had been buried in the morning papers all the way down, but after we had passed the Hampshire border he threw them down, and began to admire the scenery. It was an ideal spring day, a light blue sky, flecked with little fleecy white clouds drifting across from west to east. The sun was shining very brightly, and yet there was an exhilarating nip in the air, which set an edge to a man's energy. All over the countryside, away to the rolling hills around Aldershot, the little red and grey roofs of the farm-steadings peeped out from amidst the light green of the new foliage.

'Are they not fresh and beautiful?' I cried, with all the enthusiasm of a man fresh from the fogs of Baker Street.

But Holmes shook his head gravely.

'Do you know, Watson,' said he, 'that it is one of the curses of a mind with a turn like mine that I must look at everything with reference to my own special subject. You look at these scattered houses, and you are impressed by their beauty. I look at them, and the only thought which comes to me is a feeling of their isolation, and of the impunity with which crime may be committed there.'

'Good heavens!' I cried. 'Who would associate crime with these dear old homesteads?'

'They always fill me with a certain horror. It is my belief, Watson, founded upon my experience, that the lowest and vilest alleys in London do not present a more dreadful record of sin than does the smiling and beautiful countryside.'

'You horrify me!'

'But the reason is very obvious. The pressure of public opinion can do in the town what the law cannot accomplish. There is no lane so vile that the scream of a tortured child, or the thud of a drunkard's blow, does not beget sympathy and indignation among the neighbours, and then the whole machinery of justice is ever so close that a word of complaint can set it going, and there is but a step between the crime and the dock. But look at these lonely houses, each in its own fields, filled for the most part with poor ignorant folk who know little of the law. Think of the deeds of hellish cruelty, the hidden wickedness which may go on, year in, year out, in such places, and none the wiser. Had this lady who appeals to us for help gone to live in Winchester, I should never have had a fear for her. It is the five miles of country which makes the danger. Still, it is clear that she is not personally threatened.'

'No. If she can come to Winchester to meet us she can get away.'

'Quite so. She has her freedom.'

'What *can* be the matter, then? Can you suggest no explanation?'

'I have devised seven separate explanations, each of which would cover the facts as far as we know them. But which of these is correct can only be determined by the fresh information which we shall no doubt find waiting for us. Well, there is the tower of the Cathedral, and we shall soon learn all that Miss Hunter has to tell.'

The 'Black Swan' is an inn of repute in the High Street, at no distance from the station, and there we found the young lady waiting for us. She had engaged a sitting-room, and our lunch awaited us upon the table.

'I am so delighted that you have come,' she said earnestly, 'it is so kind of you both; but indeed I do not know what I should do. Your advice will be altogether invaluable to me.'

'Pray tell us what has happened to you.'

'I will do so, and I must be quick, for I have promised Mr Rucastle to be back before three. I got his leave to come into town this morning, though he little knew for what purpose.'

'Let us have everything in its due order.' Holmes thrust his long thin legs out towards the fire, and composed himself to listen.

'In the first place, I may say that I have met, on the whole, with no actual ill-treatment from Mr and Mrs Rucastle. It is only fair to them to say that. But I cannot understand them, and I am not easy in my mind about them.'

'What can you not understand?'

'Their reasons for their conduct. But you shall have it all just as it occurred. When I came down Mr Rucastle met me here, and drove me in his dog-cart to the Copper Beeches. It is, as he said, beautifully situated, but it is not beautiful in itself, for it is a large square block of a house, whitewashed, but all stained and streaked with damp and bad weather. There are grounds round it, woods on three sides, and on the fourth a field which slopes down to the Southampton high-road, which curves past about a hundred yards from the front door. This ground in front belongs to the house, but the woods all round are part of Lord Southerton's preserves. A clump of copper beeches immediately in front of the hall door has given its name to the place.

'I was driven over by my employer, who was as amiable as ever, and was introduced by him that evening to his wife and the child. There was no truth, Mr Holmes, in the conjecture which seemed to us to be probable in your rooms at Baker Street. Mrs Rucastle is not mad. I found her to be a silent, pale-faced woman, much younger than her husband, not more than thirty, I should think, while he can hardly be less than forty-five. From their conversation I have gathered that they have been married about seven years, that he was a widower, and that his only child by the first wife was the daughter who has gone to Philadelphia. Mr Rucastle told me in private that the reason why she had left them was that she had an unreasoning aversion to her stepmother. As the daughter could not have been less than twenty, I can quite imagine that her position must have been uncomfortable with her father's young wife.

'Mrs Rucastle seemed to me to be colourless in mind as well as in feature. She impressed me neither favourably nor the reverse. She was a nonentity. It was easy to see that she was passionately devoted both to her husband and to her little son. Her light grey eyes wandered continually from one to the other, noting every little want and forestalling it if possible. He was kind to her also in his bluff boisterous fashion, and on the whole they seemed to be a happy couple. And yet she had some secret sorrow, this woman. She would often be lost in deep thought, with the saddest look upon her face. More than once I have surprised her in tears. I have thought sometimes that it was the disposition of her child which weighed upon her mind, for I have never met so utterly spoiled and so ill-natured a little creature. He is small for his age, with a head which is quite disproportionately large. His whole life appears to be spent in an alternation between savage fits of passion and gloomy intervals of sulking. Giving pain to any creature weaker than himself seems to be his one idea of amusement, and he shows quite remarkable talent in planning the capture of mice, little birds, and insects. But I would rather not talk about the creature, Mr Holmes, and, indeed, he has little to do with my story.'

'I am glad of all details,' remarked my friend, 'whether they seem to you to be relevant or not.'

'I shall try not to miss anything of importance. The one un-pleasant thing about the house, which struck me at once, was the appearance and conduct of the servants. There are only two, a man and his wife. Toller, for that is his name, is a rough, uncouth man, with grizzled hair and whiskers, and a perpetual smell of drink. Twice since I have been with them he has been quite drunk, and yet Mr Rucastle seemed to take no notice of it. His wife is a very tall and strong woman with a sour face, as silent as Mrs Rucastle, and much less amiable. They are a most unpleasant couple, but fortunately I spend most of my time in the nursery and my own room, which are next to each other in one corner of the building.

'For two days after my arrival at the Copper Beeches my life was very quiet; on the third, Mrs Rucastle came down just after breakfast and whispered something to her husband.

' "Oh yes," said he, turning to me, "we are very much obliged to you, Miss Hunter, for falling in with our whims so far as to cut your hair. I assure you that it has not detracted in the tiniest iota from your appearance. We shall now see how the electric-blue dress will become you. You will find it laid out upon the bed in your room, and if you would be so good as to put it on we should both be extremely obliged."

'The dress which I found waiting for me was of a peculiar shade of blue. It was of excellent material, a sort of beige, but it bore unmistakable signs of having been worn before. It could not have been a better fit if I had been measured for it. Both Mr and Mrs Rucastle expressed a delight at the look of it which seemed quite exaggerated in its vehemence. They were waiting for me in the drawing-room, which is a very large room, stretching along the entire front of the house, with three long windows reaching down to the floor. A chair had been placed close to the central window, with its back turned towards it. In this I was asked to sit, and then Mr Rucastle, walking up and down on the other side of the room, began to tell me a series of the funniest stories that I have ever listened to. You cannot imagine how comical he was, and I laughed until I was quite weary. Mrs Rucastle, however, who has evidently no sense of humour, never so much as smiled, but sat with her hands in her lap, and a sad, anxious look upon her face. After an hour or so Mr Rucastle suddenly remarked that it was time to commence the duties of the day, and that I might change my dress, and go to little Edward in the nursery.

'Two days later this same performance was gone through under exactly similar circumstances. Again I changed my dress, again I sat in the window, and again I laughed very heartily at the funny stories of which my employer had an immense repertoire, and which he told inimitably. Then he handed me a yellow-backed novel, and, moving my chair a little sideways, that my own shadow might not fall upon the page, he begged me to read aloud to him. I read for about ten minutes, beginning in the heart of a chapter,

and then suddenly, in the middle of a sentence, he ordered me to cease and to change my dress.

'You can easily imagine, Mr Holmes, how curious I became as to what the meaning of this extraordinary performance could possibly be. They were always very careful, I observed, to turn my face away from the window, so that I became consumed with the desire to see what was going on behind my back. At first it seemed to be impossible, but I soon devised a means. My hand mirror had been broken, so a happy thought seized me, and I concealed a piece of the glass in my handkerchief. On the next occasion, in the midst of my laughter, I put my handkerchief up to my eyes, and was able with a little management to see all that there was behind me. I confess that I was disappointed. There was nothing.

At least, that was my first impression. At the second glance, however, I perceived that there was a man standing in the Southampton Road, a small bearded man in a grey suit, who seemed to be looking in my direction. The road is an important highway, and there are usually people there. This man, however, was leaning against the railings which bordered our field, and was looking earnestly. I lowered my handkerchief, and glanced at Mrs Rucastle to find her eyes fixed upon me with a most searching gaze. She said nothing, but I am convinced that she had divined that I had a mirror in my hand, and had seen what was behind me. She rose at once.

' "Jephro," said she, "there is an impertinent fellow upon the road there who stares up at Miss Hunter."

' "No friend of yours, Miss Hunter?" he asked.

' "No; I know no one in these parts."

' "Dear me! How very impertinent! Kindly turn round, and motion to him to go away."

' "Surely it would be better to take no notice?"

' "No, no, we should have him loitering here always. Kindly turn round, and wave him away like that."

'I did as I was told, and at the same instant Mrs Rucastle drew down the blind. That was a week ago, and from that time I have not sat again in the window, nor have I worn the blue dress, nor seen the man in the road.'

'Pray continue,' said Holmes. 'Your narrative promises to be a most interesting one.'

'You will find it rather disconnected, I fear, and there may prove to be little relation between the different incidents of which I speak. On the very first day that I was at the Copper Beeches, Mr Rucastle took me to a small outhouse which stands near the kitchen door, as we approached it I heard the sharp rattling of a chain, and the sound as of a large animal moving about.

' "Look in here!" said Mr Rucastle, showing me a slit between two planks. "Is he not a beauty?"

'I looked through, and was conscious of two glowing eyes, and of a vague figure huddled up in the darkness.

' "Don't be frightened," said my employer, laughing at the start which I had given. "It's only Carlo, my mastiff. I call him mine, but really old Toller, my groom, is the only man who can do anything with him. We feed him once a day, and not too much then, so that he is always as keen as mustard. Toller lets him loose every night, and God help the trespasser whom he lays his fangs upon. For goodness' sake don't you ever on any pretext set your foot over the threshold at night, for it's as much as your life is worth."

'The warning was no idle one, for two nights later I happened to look out of my bedroom window about two o'clock in the morning. It was a beautiful moonlight night, and the lawn in front of the house was silvered over and almost as bright as day. I was standing wrapped in the peaceful beauty of the scene, when I was aware that something was moving under the shadow of the copper beeches. As it emerged into the moonshine I saw what it was. It was a giant dog, as large as a calf, tawny-tinted, with hanging jowl, black muzzle, and huge projecting bones. It walked slowly across the lawn and vanished into the shadow upon the other side. That dreadful silent sentinel sent a chill to my heart which I do not think that any burglar could have done.

'And now I have a very strange experience to tell you. I had, as you know, cut off my hair in London, and I had placed it in a great coil at the bottom of my trunk. One evening, after the child was in bed, I began to amuse myself by examining the furniture of my room and by rearranging my own little things. There was an old chest of drawers in the room, the two upper ones empty and open, the lower one locked. I had filled the first two with my linen and as I had still much to pack away I was naturally annoyed at not having the use of the third drawer. It struck me that it might have been fastened by a mere oversight, so I took out my bunch of keys and tried to open it. The very first key fitted to perfection, and I drew the drawer open. There was only one thing in it, but I am sure that you would never guess what it was. It was my coil of hair.

'I took it up and examined it. It was of the same peculiar tint, and the same thickness. But then the impossibility of the thing obtruded itself upon me. How *could* my hair have been locked in the drawer? With trembling hands I undid my trunk, turned out the contents and drew from the bottom my own hair. I laid the two tresses together, and I assure you that they were identical. Was it not extraordinary? Puzzle as I would, I could make nothing at all of what it meant. I returned the strange hair to the drawer, and I said nothing of the matter to the Rucastles as I felt that I had put myself in the wrong by opening a drawer which they had locked.

'I am naturally observant, as you may have remarked, Mr Holmes, and I soon had a pretty good plan of the whole house

in my head. There was one wing, however, which appeared not to be inhabited at all. A door which faced that which led into the quarters of the Tollers opened into this suite, but it was invariably locked. One day, however, as I ascended the stair, I met Mr Rucastle coming out through this door, his keys in his hand, and a look on his face which made him a very different person to the round jovial man to whom I was accustomed. His cheeks were red, his brow was all crinkled with anger, and the veins stood out at his temples with passion. He locked the door, and hurried past me without a word or a look.

'This aroused my curiosity; so when I went out for a walk in the grounds with my charge, I strolled round to the side from which I could see the windows of this part of the house. There were four of them in a row, three of which were simply dirty, while the fourth was shuttered up. They were evidently all deserted. As I strolled up and down, glancing at them occasionally, Mr Rucastle came out to me, looking as merry and jovial as ever.

' "Ah!" said he, "you must not think me rude if I passed you without a word, my dear young lady. I was preoccupied with business matters."

'I assured him that I was not offended. "By the way," said I, "you seem to have quite a suite of spare rooms up there, and one of them has the shutters up."

' "He looked surprised and, as it seemed to me, a little startled at my remark.

' "Photography is one of my hobbies," said he. "I have made my dark-room[40] up there. But, dear me! what[41] an observant young lady we have come upon. Who would have believed it? Who would have ever believed it?" He spoke in a jesting tone, but there was no jest in his eyes as he looked at me. I read suspicion there, and annoyance, but no jest.

'Well, Mr Holmes, from the moment that I understood that there was something about that suite of rooms which I was not to know, I was all on fire to go over them. It was not mere curiosity, though I have my share of that. It was more a feeling of duty— a feeling that some good might come from my penetrating to this place. They talk of woman's instinct; perhaps it was woman's instinct which gave me that feeling. At any rate, it was there; and I was keenly on the look-out for any chance to pass the forbidden door.

'It was only yesterday that the chance came. I may tell you that, besides Mr Rucastle, both Toller and his wife find something to do in these deserted rooms, and I once saw him carrying a large black linen bag with him through the door. Recently he has been drinking hard, and yesterday evening he was very drunk; and, when I came upstairs, there was a key in the door. I have no doubt at all that he had left it there. Mr and Mrs Rucastle were both downstairs, and the child was with them, so that I had an admirable opportunity. I turned the key gently in the lock, opened the door, and slipped through.

'There was a little passage in front of me, unpapered and uncarpeted, which turned at a right angle at the farther end. Round this corner were three doors in a line, the first and third of which were open. They each led into an empty room, dusty and cheerless, with two windows in the one, and one in the other, so thick with dirt that the evening light glimmered dimly through them. The centre door was closed, and across the outside of it had been fastened one of the broad bars of an iron bed, padlocked at one end to a ring in the wall, and fastened at the other with stout cord. The door itself was locked as well, and the key was not there. This barricaded door corresponded clearly with the shuttered window outside, and yet I could see by the glimmer from beneath it that the room was not in darkness. Evidently there was a skylight which let in light from above. As I stood in the passage gazing at the sinister door and wondering what secret it might veil, I suddenly heard the sound of steps within the room, and saw a shadow pass backwards and forwards against the little slit of dim light which shone out from under the door. A mad, unreasoning terror rose up in me at the sight, Mr Holmes. My overstrung nerves failed me suddenly, and I turned and ran—ran as though some dreadful hand were behind me, clutching at the skirt of my dress. I rushed down the passage, through the door, and straight into the arms of Mr Rucastle, who was waiting outside.

' "So," said he, smiling, "it was you, then. I thought that it must be when I saw the door open."

' "Oh, I am so frightened!" I panted.

' "My dear young lady! my[42] dear young lady!"—you cannot think how caressing and soothing his manner was—"and what has frightened you, my dear young lady?"

'But his voice was just a little too coaxing. He overdid it. I was keenly on my guard against him.

' "I was foolish enough to go into the empty wing," I answered. "But it is so lonely and eerie in this dim light that I was frightened and ran out again. Oh, it is so dreadfully still in there!"

' "Only that?" said he, looking at me keenly.

' "Why, what did you think?" I asked.

' "Why do you think that I lock this door?"

' "I am sure that I do not know."

' "It is to keep people out who have no business there. Do you see?" He was still smiling in the most amiable manner.

' "I am sure if I had known—"

' "Well, then, you know now. And if you ever put your foot over that threshold again—" here in an instant the smile hardened into a grin of rage, and he glared down at me with the face of a demon—"I'll throw you to the mastiff."

'I was so terrified that I do not know what I did. I suppose that I must have rushed past him into my room. I remember nothing until I found myself lying on my bed trembling all over. Then I thought of you, Mr Holmes. I could not live there longer without some advice. I was frightened of the house, of the man, of the woman, of the servants, even of the child. They were all horrible to me. If I could only bring you down all would be well. Of course I might have fled from the house, but my curiosity was almost as strong as my fears. My mind was soon made up. I would send you a wire. I put on my hat and cloak, went down to the office, which is about half a mile from the house, and then returned, feeling very much easier. A horrible doubt came into my mind as I approached the door lest the dog might be loose, but I remembered that Toller had drunk himself into a state of insensibility that evening, and I knew that he was the only one in the household who had any influence with the savage creature, or who would venture to set him free. I slipped in in safety, and lay awake half the night in my joy at the thought of seeing you. I had no difficulty in getting leave to come into Winchester this morning, but I must be back before three o'clock, for Mr and Mrs Rucastle are going on a visit, and will be away all the evening, so that I must look after the child. Now I have told you all my adventures, Mr Holmes, and I should be very glad if you could tell me what it all means, and, above all, what I should do.'

Holmes and I had listened spellbound to this extraordinary story. My friend rose now, and paced up and down the room, his hands in his pockets, and an expression of the most profound gravity upon his face.

'Is Toller still drunk?' he asked.

'Yes. I heard his wife tell Mrs Rucastle that she could do nothing with him.'

'That is well. And the Rucastles go out tonight?'

'Yes.'

'Is there a cellar with a good strong lock?'

'Yes, the wine cellar.'

'You seem to me to have acted all through this matter like a very brave and sensible girl, Miss Hunter. Do you think that you could perform one more feat? I should not ask it of you if I did not think you a quite exceptional woman.'

'I will try. What is it?'

'We shall be at the Copper Beeches by seven o'clock, my friend and I. The Rucastles will be gone by that time, and Toller will, we hope, be incapable. There only remains Mrs Toller, who might give the alarm. If you could send her into the cellar, on some errand, and then turn the key upon her, you would facilitate matters immensely.'

'I will do it.'

'Excellent! We shall then look thoroughly into the affair. Of course there is only one feasible explanation. You have been brought there to personate someone, and the real person is imprisoned in this chamber. That is obvious. As to who this prisoner is, I have no doubt that it is the daughter, Miss Alice Rucastle, if I remember right, who was said to have gone to America. You were chosen, doubtless, as resembling her in height, figure, and the colour of your hair. Hers had been cut off very possibly in some illness through which she has passed, and so, of course, yours had to be sacrificed also. By a curious chance you came upon her tresses. The man in the road was, undoubtedly, some friend of hers—possibly her fiancé—and no doubt as you wore the girl's dress, and were so like her, he was convinced from your laughter, whenever he saw you, and afterwards from your gesture, that Miss Rucastle was perfectly happy, and that she no longer desired his attentions. The dog is let loose at night to prevent him from endeavouring to communicate with her. So much is fairly clear. The most serious point in the case is the disposition of the child.'

'What on earth has that to do with it?' I ejaculated.

'My dear Watson, you as a medical man are continually gaining light as to the tendencies of a child by the study of the parents. Don't you see that the converse is equally valid. I have frequently gained my first real insight into the character of parents by studying their children. This child's disposition is abnormally cruel, merely for cruelty's sake, and whether he derives this from his smiling father, as I should suspect, or from his mother, it bodes evil for the poor girl who is in their power.'

'I am sure that you are right, Mr Holmes,' cried our client. 'A thousand things come back to me which make me certain that you have hit it. Oh, let us lose not an instant in bringing help to this poor creature.'

'We must be circumspect, for we are dealing with a very cunning man. We can do nothing until seven o'clock. At that hour we shall be with you, and it will not be long before we solve the mystery.'

We were as good as our word, for it was just seven when we reached the Copper Beeches, having put up our trap at a wayside public house. The group of trees, with their dark leaves shining like burnished metal in the light of the setting sun, were sufficient to mark the house even had Miss Hunter not been standing smiling on the doorstep.

'Have you managed it?' asked Holmes.

A loud thudding noise came from somewhere downstairs. 'That is Mrs Toller in the cellar,' said she. 'Her husband lies snoring on the kitchen rug. Here are his keys, which are the duplicates of Mr Rucastle's.'

'You have done well indeed!' cried Holmes, with enthusiasm. 'Now lead the way, and we shall soon see the end of this black business.'

We passed up the stair, unlocked the door, followed on down a passage, and found ourselves in front of the barricade which Miss Hunter had described. Holmes cut the cord and removed the transverse bar. Then he tried the various keys in the lock, but without success. No sound came from within, and at the silence Holmes' face clouded over.

'I trust that we are not too late,' said he. 'I think, Miss Hunter, that we had better go in without you. Now, Watson, put your shoulder to it, and we shall see whether we cannot make our way in.'

It was an old rickety door and gave at once before our united strength. Together we rushed into the room. It was empty. There was no furniture save a little pallet bed, a small table, and a basketful of linen. The skylight above was open, and the prisoner gone.

'There has been some villainy here,' said Holmes; 'this beauty has guessed Miss Hunter's intentions, and has carried his victim off.'

'But how?'

'Through the skylight. We shall soon see how he managed it.' He swung himself up onto the roof. 'Ah, yes,' he cried, 'here's the end of a long light ladder against the eaves. That is how he did it.'

'But it is impossible,' said Miss Hunter; 'the ladder was not there when the Rucastles went away.'

'He has come back and done it. I tell you that he is a clever and dangerous man. I should not be very much surprised if this were he whose step I hear now upon the stair. I think, Watson, that it would be as well for you to have your pistol ready.'

The words were hardly out of his mouth before a man appeared at the door of the room, a very fat and burly man, with a heavy stick in his hand. Miss Hunter screamed and shrunk against the wall at the sight of him, but Sherlock Holmes sprang forward and confronted him.

'You villain!' said he, 'where's[43] your daughter?'

The fat man cast his eyes round, and then up at the open skylight.

'It is for me to ask you that,' he shrieked, 'you thieves! Spies and thieves! I have caught you, have I? You are in my power. I'll serve you!' He turned and clattered down the stairs as hard as he could go.

'He's gone for the dog!' cried Miss Hunter.

'I have my revolver,' said I.

'Better close the front door,' cried Holmes, and we all rushed down the stairs together. We had hardly reached the hall when we heard the baying of a hound and then a scream of agony, with a horrible worrying sound which it was dreadful to listen to. An elderly man with a red face and shaking limbs came staggering out at a side door.

'My God!' he cried. 'Someone has loosed the dog. It's not been fed for two days. Quick, quick, or it'll be too late!'

Holmes and I rushed out, and round the angle of the house, with Toller hurrying behind us. There was the huge famished brute, its black muzzle buried in Rucastle's throat, while he writhed and screamed upon the ground. Running up, I blew its brains out, and it fell over with its keen white teeth still meeting in the great creases of his neck. With much labour we separated them, and carried him, living but horribly mangled, into the house. We laid him upon the drawing-room sofa, and having dispatched the sobered Toller to bear the news to his wife, I did what I could to relieve his pain. We were all assembled round him when the door opened, and a tall, gaunt woman entered the room.

'Mrs Toller!' cried Miss Hunter.

'Yes, miss. Mr Rucastle let me out when he came back before he went up to you. Ah, miss, it is a pity you didn't let me know what you were planning, for I would have told you that your pains were wasted.'

'Ha!' said Holmes, looking keenly at her. 'It is clear that Mrs Toller knows more about this matter than anyone else.'

'Yes, sir, I do, and I am ready enough to tell what I know.'

'Then pray sit down, and let us hear it, for there are several points on which I must confess that I am still in the dark.'

'I will soon make it clear to you,' said she; 'and I'd have done so before now if I could ha' got out from the cellar. If there's police-court business over this, you'll remember that I was the one that stood your friend, and that I was Miss Alice's friend too.

'She was never happy at home, Miss Alice wasn't, from the time that her father married again. She was slighted like, and had no say in anything; but it never really became bad for her until after she met Mr Fowler at a friend's house. As well as I could learn, Miss Alice had rights of her own by will, but she was so quiet and patient, she was, that she never said a word about them, but just left everything in Mr Rucastle's hands. He knew he was safe with her; but when there was a chance of a husband coming forward, who would ask for all that the law would give him, then her father thought it time to put a stop on it. He wanted her to sign a paper, so that whether she married or not, he could use her money. When she wouldn't do it, he kept on worrying her until she got brain fever, and for six weeks was at death's door. Then she got better at last, all worn to a shadow, and with her beautiful hair cut off; but that didn't make no change in her young man, and he stuck to her as true as man could be.'

'Ah,' said Holmes, 'I think that what you have been good enough to tell us makes the matter fairly clear, and that I can deduce all that remains. Mr Rucastle, then, I presume, took to this system of imprisonment?'

'Yes, sir.'

'And brought Miss Hunter down from London in order to get rid of the disagreeable persistence of Mr Fowler.'

'That was it, sir.'

'But Mr Fowler being a persevering man, as a good seaman should be, blockaded the house, and having met you, succeeded by certain arguments, metallic or otherwise, in convincing you that your interests were the same as his.'

'Mr Fowler was a very kind-spoken, free-handed gentleman,' said Mrs Toller serenely.

'And in this way he managed that your good man should have no want of drink, and that a ladder should be ready at the moment when your master had gone out.'

'You have it, sir, just as it happened.'

'I am sure we owe you an apology, Mrs Toller,' said Holmes, 'for you have certainly cleared up everything which puzzled us. And here comes the country surgeon and Mrs Rucastle, so I think, Watson, that we had best escort Miss Hunter back to Winchester, as it seems to me that our locus standi now is rather a questionable one.'

And thus was solved the mystery of the sinister house with the copper beeches in front of the door. Mr Rucastle survived, but was always a broken man, kept alive solely through the care of his devoted wife. They still live with their old servants, who probably know so much of Rucastle's past life that he finds it difficult to part from them. Mr Fowler and Miss Rucastle were married, by special license, in Southampton the day after their flight, and he is now the holder of a Government appointment in the Island of Mauritius. As to Miss Violet Hunter, my friend Holmes, rather to my disappointment, manifested no further interest in her when once she had ceased to be the centre of one of his problems, and she is now the head of a private school at Walsall, where I believe that she has met with considerable success.

THE END

Notes

1	notepaper	16	mud stains	31	That
2	cheekbones	17	trademark	32	You
3	where	18	then	33	Here
4	madam	19	pinpoint	34	It's
5	drawing room	20	do you	35	boarding schools
6	top hat	21	trapdoor	36	Sweating
7	simpler	22	bulldog	37	pocketbook
8	earrings	23	Well	38	Smack
9	There	24	He	39	Data
10	...not denser	25	reopening	40	darkroom
11	quarter past	26	Yes	41	What
12	quieter	27	these are	42	My
13	Negroes	28	...need to tell	43	Where's
14	overpowering	29	The		
15	breakfast table	30	casebook		

福爾摩斯七大奇案

Preface to the Chinese Translation
中文譯本序

福爾摩斯探案故事自 19 世紀 90 年代出版以來，一直暢銷不衰而擁有廣大讀者，迄今幾乎已有世界上各種文字譯本。阿瑟・柯南・道爾塑造的福爾摩斯神探的形象，可以說在世界各國家傳戶曉。

他曾說，"我在一所醫學院接受極為嚴謹的教育，尤其受到了愛丁堡大學那位具有非凡觀察力的貝爾教授的深刻影響。貝爾教授在觀察病人時，不僅能指出他患的病症，而且還能道出他的職業和居住地。我閱讀當今一些偵探故事後，發覺幾乎每宗案件都是由於偶然機遇而予以破案的。我覺得我會試寫些偵探故事，那位偵探會像貝爾醫生觀察治療病人那樣偵破罪案，以科學方式取代偶然機遇的方式。"

確實，柯南・道爾寫的案件，最終都是以縝密的調查研究和邏輯推理破案的，他首創了偵探小說中着重推理的流派，對後來流行的這一流派產生了重要影響。福爾摩斯探案故事的情節一般都離奇曲折，撲朔迷離，十分引人入勝，同時也揭示了當時英國社會上的陰暗面，並對形形色色的犯罪和不道德行為進行了譴責，在一定程度上具有勸人萬勿作惡的警世涵義，讀後會給人留下這樣的印象：罪犯不管多麼狡猾地作案，最後都會被睿智的福爾摩斯偵破，由警方緝拿歸案，繩之以法，真可說是"天網恢恢，疏而不漏"。

阿瑟‧柯南‧道爾 1859 年出生於蘇格蘭愛丁堡市一個篤信天主教的中產階級家庭，父親是政府建工部門的公務員，母親靠丈夫微薄的工資撫養十個子女，阿瑟排行老二。青少年時代，他在耶穌會創辦的學校讀書，後來放棄天主教信仰。1876 年進愛丁堡大學攻讀醫學，並先後在赴格陵蘭的捕鯨船和赴西非洲的貨輪上任隨船醫師，以掙取工資接濟家庭。大學畢業後，他在樸茨茅斯市郊區索思西開業行醫，因對文學懷有濃厚興趣，不時業餘寫作投稿。1885 年，他獲愛丁堡大學醫學博士學位；1887 年，首篇福爾摩斯探案小說《血字的研究》在《畢頓聖誕年刊》發表，引起美國《利平科特》月刊總編約翰‧斯托達德的興趣，他赴倫敦為刊物安排英國版時，宴請柯南‧道爾和王爾德並向他們兩個約稿。1890 年，柯南‧道爾的另一篇偵探小說《四簽名》和王爾德的《道林‧格雷的肖像》相繼在該刊發表。同年，柯南‧道爾赴維也納鑽研眼科醫學。

1891 年，他在倫敦開辦眼科治療業務，因生意清淡遂決定棄醫從文，開始為《河濱雜誌》撰寫福爾摩斯探案短篇故事，第一組以《波希米亞醜聞》為首的六篇引起讀者極大興趣，雜誌社要求他續寫六篇，但柯南・道爾並不積極，索要每篇 50 鎊稿酬，雜誌社一口同意，於是他又寫了第二組故事，1892 年這 12 篇彙編成《福爾摩斯探奇歷險記》出版。隨後他厭倦續寫偵探小說，而願仿效沃爾特・司各特從事嚴肅的歷史小說創作，後經母親勸說才擱置這一打算，但他向《河濱雜誌》社提出 12 篇故事需付一千英鎊的優厚稿酬，未料雜誌社慨然允諾，他遂再次續寫《銀額駒》等 12 篇探案故事，不過在最後一篇《最後的問題》中他還是讓福爾摩斯和他的宿敵莫里亞蒂在瑞士頓興巴赫瀑布懸崖上搏鬥，雙雙墮入深淵而亡。這 12 篇短篇於 1893 年匯集成《回憶錄》一書出版。

後經近十年的間隔，柯南・道爾聽到朋友講述一個鬼怪似的獵犬奇聞，乃決定把它作為福爾摩斯早期探案的情節，於 1902 年發表《巴斯克維爾的獵犬》，作品大受讀者歡迎。1903 年，他不再固執己見，在《空屋》那個短篇中使福爾摩斯死而復生，從而為刊物續寫另一組故事，後匯集為《歸來記》於 1905 年出版。嗣後，他又寫了《恐怖谷》(1915)、《最後的致意》(1917) 和《新探案》(1927) 三組偵探故事。《福爾摩斯探案全集》於 1928 至 1929 年出版，共收集四部中長篇和 56 部短篇。

柯南・道爾另寫過多部歷史小說、科幻小說和劇本，但最終他在英國文學史上主要是以偵探小說聞名於世。他因對英國在南非戰爭的政策的辯護而於 1902 年被封為爵士。晚年他由於其子在第一次世界大戰中負傷不治身亡而沉迷於通靈，宣稱能與亡靈對話，並著有《唯靈論歷史》等書。1930 年 7 月 7 日，柯南・道爾心臟病發作，病逝於薩塞克斯郡家中，享年 71 歲。

柯南‧道爾繼承西方文學傳統，在探案中還塑造了福爾摩斯的一個陪襯人物——記述他的探奇歷險事跡的華生醫師淳厚忠誠的形象。福爾摩斯和華生，就像唐吉訶德和桑丘、約翰遜和鮑斯韋爾、匹克威克先生和薩姆‧韋勒那樣，是一對令人難忘的美好搭檔。時至今日，西方仍有不少讀者視福爾摩斯為真人，投郵至倫敦百加街向他諮詢各種問題，請他協助破案。福爾摩斯探案故事自 1901 年被拍攝成默片以來，至今屢經改編成電影和電視片，越拍越精彩。

在重譯過程中，我們改正了坊間舊譯本中的一些誤譯。這裏僅舉數例，諸如《波希米亞醜聞》裏有一句原文是 "He is Mr. Godfrey Norton, of the Inner Temple"，被誤譯成"他是住在坦普爾的戈弗里‧諾頓先生。"其實 the Inner Temple 是指英國倫敦四個培養律師的組織之一的內殿律師學院。《紅髮會》中"On account of the bequest of the late Ezekiah Hopkins, of Lebannon, Penn., USA"一句譯成了"賓夕法尼亞州已故黎巴嫩人伊喬基亞‧霍普金斯之遺贈。"這裏的 Lebannon 實為賓夕法尼亞州的黎巴嫩市。

最後，我們這個新譯本當也有不足之處，尚祈讀者不吝批評指正。

梅紹武　屠珍

波希米亞醜聞

夏洛克‧福爾摩斯一向稱呼她做「那個女人」。我很少聽到他用別的稱呼提過她。在他的心目中，她在所有女性中當屬才貌超群，別的女人都為之黯然失色。這倒並非說他對艾蓮‧艾德勒有甚麼近乎愛情的感情，因為對他那種嚴謹精確而令人欽佩的沉着冷靜的頭腦來說，一切情感，尤其是愛情那種感情，都是格格不入的。我認為他簡直就是人世間一架用於推理和觀察的最完美無缺的機器，但是作為情人，他勢必會把自己置身於錯誤地位。他從不談及溫柔的感情，只會對之加以嘲諷。樂於觀察的人讚賞那種感情——那種極好地揭示人們的動機和行為的感情。然而，對訓練有素、善於推理的人來說，容許這種感情侵擾自己那種調整得挺好的靈敏性情，無異於引進一種使人分心的因素，從而可能會使他對自己的智力成果都產生懷疑。一粒沙落入精密儀器裏也好，一條裂紋出現在他那副高倍數鏡片中的一片上也好，都比不上一種強烈感情混入他那種性情更起擾亂作用。然而，對他來說，唯獨一個女人，就是那已故的艾蓮‧艾德勒，卻令他疑惑不解地耿耿於懷，難以忘卻。

近來我很少跟福爾摩斯見面。我因為結了婚，彼此就較疏遠了。我自己的美滿幸福啦，那種首次感到自己成為一家之主而對家務事的關心啦，都足以使我專心一致、無暇旁顧；福爾摩斯則懷着他那種豪放不羈的氣質，厭惡社交界的繁縟禮儀，依舊住在我們先前合租的百加街住所裏，整天埋頭於他的舊書堆裏，一週週地交替於這樣的狀態之間：時而用可卡因提提神，時而因毒品而引起瞌睡，時而又因自身天生的好體質而精力旺盛。他仍然一如既往，專心研究犯罪活動，並用他那卓越的才能和超凡的觀察力追查線索，偵破謎案，那些案件都是警方無能為力而放棄的。我時不時聽到一些有關他的活動的含糊報導，例如他給召喚到敖德薩去調查特雷波夫謀殺案啦，偵破亭可馬里那宗阿特金森兄弟的古怪慘案啦，最近又為荷蘭王室成功完成那麼一項微妙的使命啦，等等。這些情況，我跟各位讀者一樣，都是從日報上讀到的；除此之外，我對這位老朋友和夥伴的情況就知之甚少了。

一天晚上——1888 年 3 月 20 日那天夜晚——我在出診回家的途中（我現在又已開業行醫），經過百加街。那扇我熟悉的大門，在我頭腦裏，總跟《血字的研究》一案中那些陰森事件以及後來我的求婚聯繫在一起，我突然極想見見福爾摩斯，了解一下目前他正在怎樣發揮他那非凡的本領。他那數間房間裏點着明亮的燈，我抬頭仰視，看到窗簾上兩次掠過他那瘦高的黑側影。他垂着頭，反背着手，正在室內急切而快速地來回踱步。我一向對他的種種情緒、生活習慣、態度舉止都很熟悉，他又在工作了。他無疑已從毒品產生的夢幻中清醒過來，正在苦苦思考某個新問題的線索。我拉一下門鈴，接着就給引進那間先前我也有份的房間。

他的態度並不很熱情，這種情況倒是少見的，可我心想他還是很高興見到我吧。他幾乎沒吭聲，目光卻挺親切，用手指着一張扶手椅讓我坐下，然後把他那個雪茄煙盒扔過來，又指一下角落裏那個放酒和飲料的架以及蘇打水罐。接着，他便站在壁爐前，帶着他那種獨特的內心反思的神態望着我。

"你倒挺適合結婚，"他說。"華生，自從我們上次見面以來，你的體重恐怕增加了七磅半。"

"七磅，"我答道。

"真的，我認為該是七磅多。華生，七磅多一點。我注意到你又開業行醫了，可你並沒跟我說過要出診啊。"

"這你是怎麼知道的？"

"我是看出來的，推斷出來的，否則我怎麼會知道你近來經常淋雨，而且家裏有個粗心大意、笨拙的女僕呢？"

"親愛的福爾摩斯，"我說，"你可真有兩下子。你要是活在數個世紀前，準會遭受宗教火刑給活活燒死。星期四我確實步行到鄉下去了一趟，回家時讓雨淋得變了落湯雞。可我已經換了衣服，真猜不透你是怎樣推斷出來的。至於女僕瑪麗·簡，她簡直無可救藥，我太太已經把她辭退了；可我還是不明白你這是怎樣推斷出來的。"

他格格笑了起來，搓着他那雙細長而神經質的手。

"這事簡單得很呢，"他說，"我的一雙眼告訴我，你左腳那隻鞋左側，也就是爐火剛好照到的地方，皮面上有六道幾乎是平行的裂痕，這些裂痕明明是有人要除掉鞋底沾上的泥，便順着鞋跟笨手笨腳地刮掉時弄出來的。因此，你看，我就得出兩項推斷：一是你曾經在惡劣的天氣中出過門，二是你僱用了一個刷靴子刷出不少裂紋的特別笨的倫敦女僕。至於行醫的事，那是因為一位先生走進我的房間，身上帶有一股碘酒氣味道，右手食指上有硝酸銀的黑斑點，大禮帽一邊突出一塊，表明他在那裏面放進去過聽診器。我要是不說他是醫學界的一位積極份子，那可真夠愚蠢的了。"

他解釋完這一推理過程，我不由得笑出聲來。"聽你說這些推理，"我說道，"事情彷彿總是顯得簡單到了荒唐可笑的程度，連我自已也很容易辦得到；不過我對你這一系列推理的每一步還是感到困惑不解，直到你解釋完了整個過程才明白。可我還是相信在眼力上我跟你不相上下。"

"沒錯，"他點燃一支煙，坐進一張扶手椅，答道，"但是你只是在看，沒有觀察。這兩種情況的區別十分明顯，比如說，你常看到那段從樓下過道到這間屋外面的樓梯台階吧？"

"經常看到。"

"多久會見一次？"

"嗯，至少數百次了吧。"

"那麼，說說看，一共有多少級台階？"

"多少級台階？我不知道。"

"這就對了！因為你沒觀察，光是看見。這就是我要指出來的。我卻知道，總共有 17 級台階，因為我既看見也觀察了。順便說說，你既然對這類小問題挺感興趣，又樂意記錄下我的一兩個小經驗，那你可能對這個也會感興趣。"他把桌上放着的一張粉紅色厚信紙扔過來，說道，"這是最近一班郵差送來的。大聲唸唸吧！"

信上沒寫日期，也沒有署名和地址。

"今晚七時三刻有位先生前去拜訪，有件要事相商。"信上寫道，"你最近致力為歐洲一王室效勞，表明委託你承辦一件絕非誇張的大事是足可信賴的。有關你的事蹟報導我們已從四面八方得到。屆時望勿外出。來訪者若戴面具，請勿介意為幸。"

"這確實是件神秘的事，"我說。"你想像得出這是甚麼意思嗎？"

"我現在還沒有甚麼論據，在沒有論據之前就任意加以推測，那是大錯特錯的。有人不知不覺地歪曲事實以解釋理論，而不是拿理論來解釋事實。不過，這封信在這兒，你能從中推斷出甚麼嗎？"

我仔細檢查那張信紙，辨認筆跡。

"寫這封信的人大概相當闊氣，"我說，盡力模仿我的夥伴那種推理方法。"這種信紙少說要花半個克朗才能買到一疊，質量特別硬、特別強韌。"

"特別，這個詞用得對，"福爾摩斯說。"它根本不是英國造的紙。你舉起它來，朝亮處照照看。"

我照辦了，看到紙的紋理中有個大"E"字母和一個小"g"字母，有個"P"，另有個"G"和一個小"t"兩個字母連在一起。

"你理解這是甚麼意思嗎？"福爾摩斯問道。

"當然是製造者的名字，要麼毋寧說是他的姓名縮寫標記。"

"完全錯了，'G'和't'代表的是'Gesellschaft'，也就是德文裏'公司'這個單詞，跟我們常用的'Co.'這個縮寫一樣。'P'當然代表的是'Papier'——'紙'。現在該説説'Eg'。我們查一下《歐洲大陸地名詞典》。"他從書架上取下一部棕色書皮的厚書。"Eglow, Eglonitz——有了，Egria。那是在一個説德語的國家裏——也就是在波希米亞，離卡爾斯巴德不遠。'該地以華倫斯坦猝於此處以及眾多玻璃工廠和造紙廠而聞名於世。'哈哈，老弟，你理解這是甚麼意思嗎？"他兩眼閃閃發光，洋洋得意地噴出一大口煙的藍色煙霧。

"這種紙是在波希米亞製造的。"

"完全正確。寫這封信的人是個德國人。你有沒有注意到'有關你的事蹟報導我們已從四面八方得到'這個句子的特殊結構？法國人或俄國人是不會這樣寫的。只有德國人才這樣沒有禮貌地運用動詞。因此，現在要查明這個用波希米亞紙寫信、寧願戴面具而不露真面目的德國人想做甚麼。嗯，要是我沒弄錯的話，他來了，很快就會解除我們的疑問。"

就在他説話那時候，外面響起一陣清脆的馬蹄聲和車輪磨蹭路邊石的嘎嘎聲，接着就有人猛拉一陣門鈴。福爾摩斯吹聲口哨。

"聽聲響是兩匹馬的蹄聲，"他説。"沒錯，"他朝窗外瞥一眼，接着説，"一輛精緻的小馬車和兩匹駿馬，每匹值150畿尼呢。別説別的，華生，這件案有的是錢可賺呢。"

"我最好還是離開吧，福爾摩斯。"

"別介意，醫生，就坐在那兒。我若沒有我的鮑斯韋爾[1]，就會不知所措。這事看來一定會挺有趣，錯過它未免太可惜了。"

"可是你這位委託人會不會……"

"不用管他，我也許需要你的協助，他也可能同樣需要。他來了。醫生，就坐在那張扶手椅裏，請多留心吧。"

我們聽到一陣緩慢而沉重的腳步聲，先在樓梯上，後在過道裏，到了門口驟然停止。隨即是一記響亮而帶權威命令式的敲門聲。

"請進！"福爾摩斯說。

一個男人走進來，身高不低於六尺六寸[2]，長着海格力斯那樣的寬胸脯和壯實的四肢。他衣着闊綽華麗，華麗得在英國會讓人覺得有點俗氣。那件雙排扣的上衣前襟和袖口都鑲着阿斯特拉罕黑羊皮。他肩上披一件用猩紅色絲綢作襯裏的深藍色披風，領口扣着一枚鑲嵌綠寶石的火焰形飾針，腳踏一雙到他小腿腰的皮靴，靴口上鑲着棕色毛皮，整個外表給人留下一種粗野奢華的深刻印象。他手裏拿着一頂寬邊帽，臉的上半部戴着一個蓋過顴骨的黑色假面具。顯然他剛剛調整過那副面具，因為他在進屋時，手還舉在面具上。從他那張臉的下半部來看，嘴唇厚而下垂，下巴長而直，顯出他是個性格堅強、近乎頑固而果斷的男人。

"收到我的短信了嗎？"他問道，嗓音深沉沙啞，帶着濃重的德國人口音。"我告訴過你我要前來拜訪。"他朝我們看來看去，像是拿不準該跟誰說話才好。

"請坐，"福爾摩斯說，"這位是我的朋友兼同事——華生醫生，他偶爾好心幫我調查案件。請問，該怎麼稱呼您？"

"可以稱呼我馮·克拉姆伯爵，我是波希米亞貴族。我理解你這位朋友是個值得尊敬和謹慎的人，我也可以把一件特別重要的事信任地託付給他吧。要不然，我寧願跟你單獨談談。"

我於是站起來準備離開，福爾摩斯卻一把拉住我的手腕，又把我推進扶手椅。"要麼跟我們一起談，要麼就甚麼也不談，"他說。"要對我說的話，您都可以在這位先生面前說。"

伯爵聳聳他那寬肩膀，說道："那我首先要求兩位要為我要說的事保守兩年秘密。兩年後，這事就無關重要了。目前說這事重要得可能會影響到整個歐洲歷史都不為過！"

"我保證遵守，"福爾摩斯答道。

"我也保證！"

"請原諒我戴着面具，"我們這位古怪的來客接着說，"那位僱用我的貴人不願意讓你們知道他派來的代理人是誰，因此我可以承認我剛才報的姓名也並非是我的真實姓名。"

"這我早已料到，"福爾摩斯乾巴巴地說。

"情況非常微妙，必須採取一切預防措施，才能防止事態不會發展成為一大醜聞，以免使一個歐洲王室遭受嚴重傷害。簡單說吧，這事會使偉大的奧姆斯坦家族——波希米亞世襲王室受到牽連！"

"這我也已料到，"福爾摩斯喃喃道，隨即坐進扶手椅，閉上兩眼。

這時候，我們的來客不由得用顯然十分驚訝的目光，往這個體態懶洋洋而倦怠的人掃一眼，在他心目中，這人曾被描述為歐洲分析問題最透徹的推理專家和精力最充沛的大偵探啊！福爾摩斯又慢慢睜開兩眼，不耐煩地望着那個體魄魁偉的委託人。

"陛下若肯屈尊闡明案情，"他說，"我就可以更好地為您效勞了。"

那個人立刻站起來，激動得無法控制地在室內來回踱步。接着，他打個絕望的手勢，一把扯下臉上的面具，把它扔在地上。"你説得對，"他喊道，"我就是國王，為何要隱瞞呢？"

"就是呢！"福爾摩斯喃喃道，"陛下還沒開口，我就知道我是在跟卡賽爾費爾斯坦大公爵、波希米亞世襲國王威廉·戈特萊希·西格斯蒙德·馮·奧姆斯坦交談呢。"

"不過，你能理解，"我們這位怪客又坐下來，撫摸一下他那又高又白的額頭，説道，"你能理解我不習慣親自出馬處理這種事。這事卻又那麼敏感，叫我簡直沒法委託別人代辦而又不受那個人的擺佈。我是為了向你徵詢意見才微服私訪，從布拉格來到這裏。"

"那就請説説吧，"福爾摩斯又閉上雙眼。

"簡單説吧，事情是這樣的：大約五年前，我有一次去華沙，逗留了很久，結識了那位大名鼎鼎的交際花艾蓮·艾德勒。你一定熟悉這個名字吧。"

"醫生，請在我的資料索引裏查一查艾蓮·艾德勒這個女人，"福爾摩斯連眼睛也沒睜一睜，對我喃喃道。他多年來養成一個習慣，就是把許多人事材料摘編入卡片備查。因此，要想讓他沒法立刻提供某人某事的情況，那是很不容易辦到的。在這件事上，我找到了她的個人簡歷，給夾在一位猶太法學博士和一名寫過一篇深海魚類專題論文的指揮官兩份材料之間。

"讓我看看，"福爾摩斯説。"唔！1858 年出生在新澤西州。女低音——唔！意大利歌劇院——唔！華沙帝國歌劇院首席女歌手。從歌劇舞台退休——哈！住在倫敦——是這麼一回事！據我理解，陛下跟這位年輕女人有過瓜葛，給她寫過數封有失體面的信，現在急想把那些信收回來吧。"

"就是這麼一回事，可怎樣才能……？"

"你們有沒有秘密結過婚？"

"沒有。"

"沒有甚麼法律文件或證明嗎？"

"沒有。"

"那我就不明白了，陛下。這個年輕女人如果想拿那些信來敲詐或者為了甚麼別的目的，她又怎麼能夠證明那些信是真的呢？"

"我親筆寫的字啊！"

"哼！偽造的。"

"我私人的信箋。"

"偷的。"

"我自己的印鑒。"

"仿造的。"

"我的照片。"

"買的。"

"我們合照的啊！"

"噢，老天！那就太糟糕了。陛下確實犯了太不謹慎的錯誤。"

"我當時真是昏了頭——神經錯亂。"

"您已經嚴重地傷害了自己。"

"當時我只是王儲，年紀很輕，現在也不過 30 歲。"

"那就要把那張照片收回來。"

"我們已經試過，卻失敗了。"

"陛下要出錢，把照片買回來。"

"她不肯賣。"

"那就偷吧。"

"這我們也試過五次。兩次我花錢僱了小偷搜遍了她的屋；一次她在旅行時，我們調換了她的行李；另有兩次對她進行攔路搶劫。可是都一無所獲。"

"沒有那張照片的蹤影？"

"一點也沒有。"

福爾摩斯笑着說："這還真是件不小的麻煩事呢。"

"可這對我來說卻挺嚴重，"國王用責備的口氣頂他一句。

"倒也確實挺嚴重。她打算拿那張照片做甚麼呢？"

"毀掉我！"

"怎麼毀？"

"我快要結婚了。"

"這我倒也聽說了。"

"是跟斯堪的納維亞國王的二公主克洛蒂爾德‧洛特曼‧馮‧薩克斯曼寧根結婚。你也許知道這個家族嚴厲的家規吧。她本人就是個很敏感的女人，只要對我的行為有一絲懷疑，就會終止這個婚約。"

"艾蓮‧艾德勒打算怎麼樣呢？"

"威脅要把那張照片送交他們。她會那樣做的。我知道她會的。你不了解她，她有鋼鐵般的意志。她既有女人最美貌的容顏，也有男人最倔強的個性。只要我跟另外一個女人結婚，她甚麼事都做得出來——絕對會的。"

"您肯定她還沒把那張照片寄出去嗎？"

"這我敢肯定。"

"為甚麼？"

"因為她說過她會在公開宣佈婚禮那天把它寄出，那就是下星期一。"

"噢，那我們還有三天時間呢，"福爾摩斯打個呵欠，說道。"目前我還有一兩件重要的事要處理。陛下當然還要留在倫敦吧？"

"當然。你可以在蘭厄姆酒店找到我，用的是馮·克拉姆伯爵這個姓名。"

"那我們會寫信把進展情況告訴您。"

"請一定要這樣做。我會焦急地等待。"

"那麼，費用怎麼算呢？"

"全由你自行決定。"

"沒有任何條件嗎？"

"不瞞你說，我寧願付出我領土上的一個省份換回那張照片。"

"那麼眼前的費用呢？"

國王從他的披風裏面拿出一個很沉的羚羊皮錢袋，放在桌上。

"這裏有三百鎊金幣和七百鎊鈔票，"他說。

福爾摩斯在筆記本中一頁上潦草地寫了收條，撕下來遞給國王。

"那位小姐的地址呢？"他問道。

"聖約翰・伍德區塞潘廷大街布里奧尼邸宅。"

福爾摩斯記下來。"還有個問題，"他說，"照片是六寸的嗎？"

"是的。"

"那麼，再見，陛下。我們相信不久就會給您帶來好消息。"國王的馬車走遠後，福爾摩斯對我說，"華生，我們也再見吧。明天下午三時你再來，我跟你好好聊聊這件小事。"

三時正，我來到百加街，福爾摩斯出門還沒回來。房東太太告訴我他早上八時一過就出去了。可我還是在壁爐旁坐下，不管他何時才能回來，我都準備等他，因為我已經對他的調查工作深感興趣，儘管這件案並沒有我記錄過的那兩宗犯罪案件所具有的那種殘忍而奇特的特徵，可是此案的性質和委託人的顯貴身份，仍然使它具有非同尋常的特色。確實，除了我的朋友着手調查此案的性質以外，還有他掌握情況的那種高明手法啦，那種敏銳而透徹的推理啦，那種破解最難解決的謎案的快速而精細的方式啦，都叫我樂意研究和學習。我已經那麼習慣他一貫會取勝，從沒想到他會有失敗的可能。

接近四時那時候，房門開了，進來一個醉醺醺的馬夫，蓄着絡腮鬍子，面紅耳赤，衣衫襤褸，一副邋遢樣子。我雖然很熟悉我朋友那種驚人的喬裝技巧，可還是要再三審視一番才敢肯定那個人的確是他。他朝我點下頭就走進臥室。沒過五分鐘，他便像往常那樣身穿一套花呢服裝，體面地出現在我面前。他把手插在褲袋裏，在壁爐前舒展開雙腿，開心地笑了好幾分鐘。

「哈哈哈，真是的！」他笑道，接着嗆住了，隨後又大笑起來，笑得渾身無力，不得不癱在椅上。

「這是怎麼一回事？」

「簡直太好笑了。我敢肯定你絕對猜不出整個上午我在忙些甚麼，忙出甚麼結果。」

「我猜不出來。你大概一直在偵察艾蓮‧艾德勒小姐的生活習慣，也許還有她的住處吧。」

「就是就是，結果卻很不尋常。可我還是要告訴你，今天早晨一過八時我就離開了這裏，打扮成一名失業的馬夫。那些馬夫有股互相同情、互助友愛的深厚感情。你若成為他們當中的一員，就能了解到你想知道的一切。我很快便找到了布里奧尼邸宅，那是一幢小巧雅致的兩層樓房，後面有個花園，正對着馬路。大門上裝有朱伯保險鎖。寬敞的客廳在右側，佈置得很華麗，長窗戶幾乎挨到地面，那些荒唐的英國窗栓連小孩都打得開。屋後身沒有甚麼值得注意的，只有過道那扇窗戶倒可以從馬廄房頂觸得到。我圍着那幢屋轉了一圈，從各個角度仔細觀察一番，沒再發現甚麼令人感興趣的了。

「隨後我便在街上閒逛，果然不出我所料，我在花園一面牆外找到一條小巷，那裏有一排馬廄。我便幫助那些馬夫刷洗馬匹。他們給我兩便士酬勞，一杯淡啤酒混黑啤酒的混合酒，兩斗滿滿的板煙，還說了許多我想知道的有關艾德勒小姐的情況給我知，更不用提還有我並不感興趣的附近住家六七個人的底細，我只好耐心地聽。」

「都說艾德勒小姐甚麼了？」我問道。

"哦，她把那一帶的男人都迷得暈頭轉向。她是這個行星上最秀麗誘人的美人。塞潘廷馬廄的馬夫無一例外地都這麼說。她過着寧靜的生活，在音樂會上演唱，每天下午五時乘馬車出門，準時七時回家吃晚飯。她除了去演唱外，其他時間均深居簡出。她只跟一個男人交往，而且過往甚密。那個人一頭深髮，相貌英俊，一身帥氣，每天至少來看她一次，經常是兩次。他是內殿律師學院的戈弗雷・諾頓先生。看出把馬車夫作為心腹朋友的好處了吧。他們趕車從塞潘廷馬廄那兒送他回家多次，對他的底細一清二楚。我聽完他們所説的一切，再次在布里奧尼邸宅附近來回走走，思考我的下一步行動計劃。

"戈弗雷・諾頓這個人顯然是這事當中的一位關鍵性人物。他是一名律師。聽起來可不太妙。他們兩人之間究竟是甚麼關係？他一再來看她，目的何在呢？艾蓮・艾德勒小姐是他的委託人，他的朋友，還是他的情人？如果是委託人，那她大概已經把那張照片交給他保管了。如果是他的情人，那她就不大會那樣做了。要弄清楚這個問題，我就要決定該繼續對布里奧尼邸宅進行調查呢，還是把注意力轉移到那位先生在內殿律師學院裏的住所。這是個挺微妙的問題，而且也擴展了我調查的範圍。華生，這些瑣碎的細節恐怕惹你厭煩了吧。可是你如果想了解情況，我就不得不讓你知道我的一些小小困難。"

"我在洗耳恭聽呢，"我答道。

"我正在斟酌這個問題，忽然有輛雙輪馬車在布里奧尼邸宅門前停下，從車上跳下一位先生。他是個相貌很英俊的男子，深膚色，高鼻樑，留着鬍——顯然就是我剛才聽説的那個男人。看起來他像是有急事，叫車夫等着他。他從開門的女僕身旁擦身而過，透着一副在那個邸宅裏無拘無束的態度。

"他在屋裏逗留了約半個小時，我通過客廳窗戶隱約看見他在室內踱來踱去，揮動雙臂，激動地談着甚麼。至於女主人，我甚麼也沒看見。隨後，他便走出來，顯得比剛才還要急的樣子。他登上馬車，從褲袋裏掏出一隻金錶，鄭重地看看，隨即喊道：'給我拼命趕，先去攝政街格羅斯‧漢基旅館，然後去埃格韋爾路聖莫尼卡教堂。你要是能在 20 分鐘之內趕到，我就賞你半個畿尼！'

"他們便一溜煙走了，我正在尋思要不要跟去，這時忽然從小巷那邊來了一輛小巧潔淨的四輪馬車，車夫那件外衣的鈕扣只扣上了一半，領帶歪在耳朵下面，馬匹馬具上的金屬箍環都還沒扣好。車還沒停穩，艾德勒小姐便從大門裏飛奔出來。我在那一瞬間只瞥見了她一眼，卻已看出她真是個可愛的人兒，容貌艷美得足以叫男人傾倒。

"'約翰，去聖莫尼卡教堂！'她喊道，'你要是能在 20 分鐘之內趕到那裏，我就賞你半鎊金幣！'

"華生，這可是千載難逢的好機會，不能錯過。我正在琢磨該跟在馬車後面跑呢，還是偷偷攀登在馬車後面的踏板上，這時候又過來一輛馬車。車夫對我手舉的微薄車費瞟了兩眼，我沒等他拒絕就跳上馬車。'去聖莫尼卡教堂。20 分鐘能趕到，我就付你半鎊！'當時是差 25 分鐘到 12 時；甚麼重要的事即將發生，是夠清楚的了。

"馬車夫趕得飛快，我平生恐怕還從來沒乘坐過比這更快的車了，但是那兩輛馬車卻已先行到達。我抵達時，那輛出租馬車和那輛四輪馬車以及兩匹冒汗喘氣的馬，都已停在教堂門前。我連忙付了車錢，走進教堂。那裏只有我跟蹤的那兩個人和一位身穿白色法袍的牧師，別無他人。牧師像是在規勸他們兩人。他們三個圍在一起，站在聖壇前。我就像個偶然來教堂閒逛的人，順着旁邊的通道朝前走。令我吃驚的是，聖壇前那三個人忽然間都把臉轉向我。戈弗雷‧諾頓飛快地朝我跑來。

"'謝天謝地！'他喊道。'有了你就行了。來！來！'

"'甚麼事？'我問道。

"'來，老兄，來，只消三分鐘，否則就不合法了。'

"我給半拉半拖地弄到聖壇前。還沒弄清做甚麼，我就發覺自己在對耳邊低聲的話語作出喃喃的答覆，為我一無所知的事在作證，總的來說，就是相助未婚女子艾蓮‧艾德勒小姐和單身漢戈弗雷‧諾頓先生結為連理。這一切是在很短的時間內完成的。緊跟着就是男方在我這一邊道謝，女方在我那一邊表示感謝，牧師則站在我對面對我微笑。這可是我有生以來從來沒遇到過的最荒謬的場面。剛才我就是一想起這事便不由得大笑起來。看來是他們的結婚證書不夠合法，牧師在沒有證人的情況下斷然拒絕給他們兩人證婚。幸虧我的出現才使新郎不必跑到大街上去找一位伴郎。新娘賞我一鎊金幣，我打算把它串在錶鏈上戴着，作為這次奇遇的紀念。"

"這真是出乎意料的轉折，"我說。"後來呢？"

"唉，我發現我的計劃受到了嚴重干擾。看來這對新婚夫婦可能會立刻離開這裏，因此我要採取迅速而有效的措施。他們兩人在教堂門口分別後，他乘車回內殿律師學院，她則回自己的住處。'我還像往常那樣，五時乘車到公園去，'她辭別時對他說。我只聽到這句。他們兩人自乘車駛向不同方向。我也離開那裏，為自己做些安排。"

"甚麼安排呢？"

"來杯啤酒和一點滷牛肉！"他搖搖鈴，答道，"我一直忙得都忘了吃東西。今天晚上看來還會更忙。順便說一句，醫生，今晚我需要你的合作。"

"我很樂意幫助你。"

"你不怕犯法嗎？"

"一點也不怕。"

"也不怕萬一給逮捕嗎？"

"要是為了一件好事，那就不怕。"

"哦，這事是再好不過了。"

"那我聽從你的吩咐。"

"我早就確信能夠指望你的幫助。"

"可你究竟想做甚麼？"

"等特納太太端進來食物，我就跟你說明。"房東太太送進來簡單食物，他便一邊狼吞虎嚥地吃着，一邊說道，"目前我不得不邊吃邊談這件事，因為時間很緊迫，目前已經快到五時。我們要在兩小時之內趕到行動地點。艾蓮小姐，要麼該稱夫人了，七時會乘車回家。我們要在布里奧尼邸宅跟她會面。"

"然後呢？"

"以後的事由我來辦。將會發生甚麼事我都做好了安排。只有一點我要堅持，那就是不管發生甚麼事，你都別插手干預。明白嗎？"

"完全不介入嗎？"

"對，甚麼事都別管。可能會發生一點不大愉快的事，你別介入。我一給帶進屋，事情就馬上會結束。四五分鐘過後，那扇窗會打開，你要守候在窗那兒。"

"嗯。"

"你一定要盯着我，我會讓你看見。"

"嗯。"

"等我一舉手——就是這樣——你就把我叫你扔的東西扔進房間裏，同時扯起嗓門高喊'起火了！'聽明白了嗎？"

"明白了。"

"沒甚麼可怕的，"福爾摩斯從衣袋裏掏出一個像雪茄煙那樣的長卷筒，說道："這是水管工的噴煙器，兩頭都有火藥帽使它自行點火。你的任務就是專管這玩意。你一大喊起火了，肯定招來不少人救火。那時候你就可以走到街的盡頭那邊去，不出十分鐘我便去跟你會合。我說的你都聽明白了吧？"

"我要一直保持不介入的態度；挨近那扇窗盯視着你；一看到信號就把這玩意扔進去；接着高喊起火了；然後到街頭轉角那邊去等你。"

"完全正確。"

"那你就放心等着看我的吧。"

"太好了。現在大概到了我該去扮演新角色的時候了。"

他進入臥室，過了數分鐘再出來時，已經喬裝改扮成一名純樸而和藹可親的新教牧師。那頂寬大的黑帽啦，那條鼓鼓囊囊的褲啦，那條白領帶啦，那種同情的微笑啦，那種仁慈而好奇的凝視神態啦，只有約翰・黑爾先生[3]能與之相比。福爾摩斯不只是換了裝束，就連他的表情、舉止和靈魂似乎都隨着他扮的新角色而起了變化。他成為一名研究犯罪的專家時，舞台上便少了一名優秀演員，連科學界都少了一名敏銳的理論家。

我們六時一刻離開百加街，提前十分鐘到達了塞潘廷大街。天色已暗，我們兩人在布里奧尼邸宅外面來回踱步，等待女主人回來，這時街燈剛剛點亮。那幢屋正如我根據夏洛克・福爾摩斯的簡單描述所想像的那樣，只是地點並不像我所預料的那樣僻靜。恰恰相反，附近地區雖然挺安靜，這條小街卻挺熱鬧。街頭轉角那邊有一群穿着破衣爛衫、抽着煙卷、說說笑笑的人，一個帶着砂輪的磨剪的人，兩個正在跟一個女僕調情的警衛，還有兩三個衣着體面、叼着雪茄煙周圍走動的男孩。

"你看，"我們在那幢屋前面踱來踱去時，福爾摩斯說，"這件婚事倒把事情簡單化了。那張照片現在已成為一把雙刃劍。情況可能是她不願意讓戈弗雷・諾頓看到那張照片，就像我們那位委託人害怕照片出現在公主眼前一樣。因此，目前的問題是我們到哪兒去找到那張照片？"

"真的，到哪兒去找呢？"

"她不大可能隨身帶着它，因為那是一張六寸的照片，大得很難藏在一個女人的衣服裏。她也明白國王會攔劫她或者搜查她，這種辦法已經試過兩次。因此，我們可以肯定她不會隨身攜帶着它。"

"那又能在哪兒呢？"

"在為她管理錢財的銀行家或她的律師手裏。有這兩種可能性，可我又覺得這兩種可能性都不現實。女人天生愛保密，喜歡自己想辦法藏東西。她為何要把東西交到別人手中呢？她信得過自己的保管能力，可這就可能會給一個受託辦事的人帶來何等程度的間接或政治壓力，她就不知道了。除此之外，別忘了她決定數天之內要利用那張照片，因此那張照片肯定在她隨手拿得到的地方。一定在她自己家裏。"

"可她家已經兩次在夜間被盜過了。"

"哼，那些小偷不知道怎樣尋找呢。"

"你又怎樣尋找呢？"

"我不必去尋找。"

"那怎麼辦呢？"

"我要讓她親自給我看。"

"可她會拒絕的。"

"她不會拒絕。我聽見車輪聲了，那是她乘坐的馬車。現在要嚴格按照我的命令行事。"

他正說着，街道轉角那邊出現了一輛馬車的側燈閃爍的亮光。那是一輛漂亮的四輪馬車轆轆地駛到布里奧尼邸宅門前。馬車剛一停下，街道轉角那兒一個流浪漢立刻衝上前去開車門，希望能賺一個銅子的賞錢，卻被另一個有同樣想法而衝過去的流浪漢用手肘頂開。於是兩人激烈地爭吵起來，兩名警衛介入，站在一名流浪漢一邊，而那個磨剪人則同樣站在另一名流浪漢一邊，爭吵便由此而加劇。有人動手揮了一拳，這時候那位夫人正好下車，立刻就被圍困在那些糾纏在一起的人群當中。那夥人面紅耳赤，拳打棒擊，扭在一起野蠻地毆鬥。福爾摩斯連忙衝進人群去保護那位夫人，可他剛到她身邊，就大叫一聲，倒臥在地，鮮血順着臉淌下來。眾人見他倒下，那兩名警衛拔腿就朝一個方向逃走，兩名流浪漢則朝另一方向逃之夭夭，數個衣着體面、沒參加毆鬥而站在一旁看熱鬧的人便擠進去為夫人解圍並照顧那位受傷的先生。艾蓮·艾德勒——我還是願意這麼稱呼她——急忙跑上台階。她在最高一級台階那兒站住了，在門廳裏的燈光背景襯托下顯現出她那極其優美的身材輪廓。她回頭望着街道。

"那位可憐的先生傷得厲害嗎？"

"他死了，"數個人異口同聲地喊道。

"沒有，沒有，他還活着，"另一個人嚷道，"可您要是不趕緊把他送醫院，那他可就沒命了！"

"他真是個勇敢的好漢，"一個女人說。"要不是他，夫人的錢包和手錶早就讓那群流浪漢搶走了。他們是一幫的，都是些粗暴的人。啊，他喘氣了！"

"不能讓他這樣躺在街上，我們能不能把他抬進屋去，夫人？"

"當然，把他抬進客廳去吧，那兒有張舒服的沙發。請走這邊！"

於是，大夥兒慢慢而嚴肅地把福爾摩斯抬進布里奧尼邸宅，把他安頓在那個主要的房間裏，而這時我依然站在窗戶旁邊我那個位置上沒動，一直觀察着這事的整個過程。燈都給點亮了，窗簾卻沒給拉上，所以我看見福爾摩斯躺在沙發上。我弄不清他當時是否對自己所扮演的角色感到有點內疚，可我卻覺得自己平生從來沒有比目前更感到羞愧了，因為我看到自己協力反對的那個美人兒正在溫柔親切地服侍傷者。然而，現在我如果拂袖不做福爾摩斯委託我的事，那可是一種最卑鄙的背叛。我於是硬起心腸，從我寬大的長外套裏取出那個噴煙器，心想反正我們並非要傷害她，只是想讓她別傷害別人罷了。

福爾摩斯靠在那張沙發上。我看到他好像呼吸挺困難似的，一名女僕趕緊跑過去打開窗戶。這時我見到他舉起手來，一見這個信號，我就立刻把那個玩意扔進房間，高聲喊道："起火了！"我的喊聲剛一落音，那夥看熱鬧的人，衣着整齊的和破衣爛衫的——紳士啦，馬夫啦，男僕啦，女僕啦——全都異口同聲地尖叫："起火了！"滾滾濃煙繚繞全室，從那扇敞開的窗戶冒出來。我瞥見一群慌張奔跑的身影。片刻後，我聽到從屋裏傳出福爾摩斯的喊聲，叫大家不要驚慌，這只是一場虛驚。我急忙穿過大聲喊叫的人群，跑到街道轉角那兒。不出十分鐘，我欣喜地發現我的朋友挎着我的手逃離了那亂哄哄的現場。他一言不發地快步走了好幾分鐘，等我們走進一條通往愛吉韋爾街的安靜小巷，他才開口。

"醫生，你剛才做得很好，"他說。"簡直不能再好了。一切順利。"

"莫非你拿到了那張照片？"

"我弄清楚它給放在哪兒了。"

"這你是怎樣發現的？"

"就像我跟你說過的那樣，她給我看了。"

"我還是不明白。"

"我並不想把這事弄得神秘兮兮，"他笑着說。"這事挺簡單呢。你當然看得出來街上那些人都是我們的同黨。他們今天晚上都是花錢僱用的。"

"這我倒也猜到了。"

"那陣騷亂一開始，我便手握一塊濕漉漉的紅顏料，急忙衝過去，跌倒在地，把手捂在臉上就成了一副可憐相。這是老招了。"

"這我也揣摩出來了。"

"然後他們就把我抬進屋去。她沒法不把我弄進去。在那種情況下，她不那麼做，又能怎麼辦？我就進了她的客廳，正是我猜疑過的那間房。那張照片不是藏在那間房裏，就是在她的臥室裏。我倒要看看究竟藏在哪間房裏。他們把我安頓在沙發上，我便裝出喘不過氣的樣子，他們只好打開窗，你就有了機會。"

"這樣做對你又有甚麼幫助呢？"

"太重要了。女人一看到自己的屋起火，首先就會本能地搶救自己最珍貴的東西。這種不可抗拒的強烈衝動我已經不止一次利用過。在達林頓調包醜聞一案中，我用過一次；在那宗阿恩斯沃斯城堡案中也用過。結了婚的女人會趕緊去抱起她的嬰孩，未婚女子則會首先去抓起她的首飾盒。我早已明白，對今天這位夫人來說，家裏沒有甚麼再比我們在尋找的那樣東西更寶貴的了。她會衝向前去把它搶救出來。起火的警報真不賴，煙霧和喊叫聲足以震驚鋼鐵般的神經。她的反應妙極了。那張照片就藏在室內拉鈴繩索上方那塊能挪動的嵌板後面的壁龕裏。她立刻奔到那裏，我瞥見她把那張照片抽出了一半。我一喊這只是一場虛驚，她又把它放回去了。她瞟一眼那個噴煙器就匆匆走出那間屋，此後我就沒再看到她了。我站起來，找個藉口便偷偷離開那幢屋。當時我曾猶豫是不是該立刻把那張照片弄到手，但是馬車夫那時候進來了；他死盯住我。為了保險起見，看來還是另等良機吧。過份急躁，反倒會破壞事情。"

"現在該怎麼辦呢？"我問道。

"我們的調查差不多結束了。明天我要跟國王一起去拜訪她。你如果願意去，也可以一起去。僕人會把我們引進那間大廳等候夫人，可是等她一出來，恐怕既見不到我們，也見不到那張照片了。陛下如果親手拿回那張照片，一定會感到非常滿意的。"

"那你們準備甚麼時候去拜訪呢？"

"早上八時。趁她還沒起來，我們可以不受干擾地做。再者，我們不能耽誤，因為這件婚事可能會改變她的生活習慣。我要馬上打個電報給國王。"

我們已經走到百加街，在門口停下來。他在衣袋裏掏摸鑰匙的時候，忽然有人路過，向他打個招呼：

"晚安，福爾摩斯先生！"

當時人行道上有好幾個人，那句問候像是出自一個身穿寬大的長外套、匆匆走過的瘦小子之口。

"這聲音我以前聽過，"福爾摩斯注視着昏暗的街道，説道，"可是目前一時弄不清剛才打招呼的那個人究竟是誰了。"

那天晚上，我就在百加街過夜。清晨起牀後，我們正在吃烤麵包片，喝咖啡，波希米亞國王匆匆忙忙進來了。

"你真拿到那張照片了嗎？"他用雙手緊緊抓住夏洛克·福爾摩斯的兩個肩膀，焦急地望着他，大聲問道。

"還沒有呢。"

"可是有沒有希望?"

"有希望。"

"那就趕快去吧,我都等不及了。"

"我們要租輛馬車。"

"不必了,我那輛四輪馬車在外面等着呢。"

"那可就省事多了。"我們便走下台階,再次動身去布里奧尼邸宅。

"艾蓮‧艾德勒結婚了,"福爾摩斯説。

"結婚了!甚麼時候?"

"昨天。"

"跟誰?"

"跟一位姓諾頓的英國律師。"

"可她不會愛他。"

"我倒巴不得她愛他。"

"為甚麼這樣想呢?"

"因為這樣就可以使陛下今後不必擔心一切麻煩了。那位女士如果愛她的丈夫,就不愛陛下了。她要是不愛陛下,就沒有理由要阻止陛下的計劃了。"

"這倒是實在的,可是⋯⋯!唉,我真希望她跟我的身份一樣就好了!她會是一位多麼了不起的王后啊!"在我們的馬車抵達塞潘廷大街之前,國王一直陷入悶悶不樂的沉思。

布里奧尼邸宅的大門敞着呢,台階上站着一位上了年紀的女僕。她用蔑視的目光望着我們從馬車上下來。

"我想您是夏洛克·福爾摩斯先生吧？"

"是啊，"我的夥伴有點吃驚而詫異地注視着她，答道。

"真是的！我的女主人告訴我您多半會來。今天清晨她跟她丈夫一起走了，從查林十字街乘 5 時 15 分那班火車去歐洲大陸了。"

"甚麼！"夏洛克·福爾摩斯往後跌，驚訝懊惱得臉色煞白。

"你是說她已經離開英國了嗎？"

"再也不回來了。"

"那些信件呢？"國王粗暴地問道。"完了，完了，徹底完了！"

"我們進去看個究竟吧，"福爾摩斯推開那個女僕，匆匆進入客廳，我和國王緊跟在後。室內傢具到處亂放着，壁櫥擱板給卸了下來，抽屜都給拉開了，好像夫人臨走之前翻箱倒櫃地匆匆忙忙翻查了一遍似的。福爾摩斯衝到鈴索那兒，打開一扇小拉門，伸手掏出一張照片和一封信。照片是艾蓮·艾德勒本人穿着晚禮服照的單人照。信封上寫着："致夏洛克·福爾摩斯先生。留交本人親收。"我的朋友撕開信封，我們三個一起看信。寫信日期是今天凌晨，內容如下：

敬愛的夏洛克·福爾摩斯先生：

您做得的確挺精彩。您把我完全蒙騙了。在發生火警之前，我一點也沒起疑。可我後來發現自己洩露了機密，便開始思索。數個月前就有人忠告過我要提防您。他們告訴我國王要是僱用偵探的話，那準是閣下。他們把您的地址告訴我了。儘管如此，您還是讓我洩露了您想知道的事。我甚至在開始懷疑時，都難以把那麼一位上了歲數、和藹可親的牧師想得那麼壞！但是，您該知道，我本人是個訓練有素的演員。男人的服裝對我來說並不生疏。我常常女扮男裝，利用作為男性的方便。我當時派馬車夫約翰去客廳監視您，自己跑上樓去換上我稱之為散步的便服。我下樓時，您剛剛離開。

隨後，我便尾隨您，走到您家門口。於是我肯定了自己真是大名鼎鼎的夏洛克·福爾摩斯先生感興趣的一名對象。我便相當冒失地向您道個晚安，然後就去內殿律師學院找我的丈夫。

我們都認為受到這樣一位可怕的對手追逐，最好的辦法就是逃走吧，所以您今天前來寒舍時會發現這裏已經是一個空巢。至於那張照片，請您那位委託人儘管放心。我愛上了一個比他強得多的男人，那個人也深深愛着我。國王愛做甚麼就做甚麼吧，不必顧慮他錯待過的人會出面阻礙。那張照片我是要保留的，只是為了保護自己，保留一件永遠防備他將來可能會採取任何手段來對付我的武器。我現在留給他一張他可能樂意收下的照片。

謹向敬愛的夏洛克·福爾摩斯先生致意。

艾蓮·艾德勒敬啟

"噢，這個女人可了不得！——哎呀呀，一個多麼了不起的女人啊！"我們三個看完那封信，波希米亞國王高聲嚷道。"我不是跟你們說過她多麼機靈，多麼果斷嗎？她要是當上了王后，真會是一位令人讚美的王后啊！怪可惜的是她跟我門不當、戶不對，不是同一個階層，是不是？”

“我倒從這位女士身上看出，論水平，她似乎確實跟陛下大不一樣，”福爾摩斯冷淡地答道，“很遺憾我沒能使陛下的事得到一個更圓滿的結局。”

“親愛的先生，恰恰相反，”國王大聲說。“沒有甚麼比這個結局更圓滿的了。我知道她說話算數。那張照片現在就跟給燒掉了一樣叫我放心了。”

“聽陛下這麼說，我也很高興。”

“真是十分感謝你。請告訴我該怎樣酬謝你。這隻戒指……”國王從手指上脫下一枚蛇形的綠寶石戒指，托在手掌上遞給他。

“陛下有件我認為比這枚戒指更有價值的東西。”

“那你就明說吧。”

“這張照片！”

國王驚訝地望着福爾摩斯。

“艾蓮的照片！”他大聲說，“當然當然，你要是想要，就拿去吧。”

“謝謝陛下。這事就到此結束了吧。祝您早安！”他鞠個躬，轉身沒再答理國王向他伸出的手，就跟我一起返回他的住處。

這就是波希米亞國王怎樣受到一宗特大醜聞的威脅，夏洛克·福爾摩斯的傑出計劃又怎樣讓一個女人的才智給挫敗的經過。他以往總是對女人的聰明機智加以嘲諷，可近來我沒再聽到他這種譏笑了。如今每逢一提到艾蓮·艾德勒或者她那張照片，他總是用那個女人這一尊稱來稱呼她。

2.
紅髮會

去年秋季，有一天我去拜訪我的朋友夏洛克·福爾摩斯先生，他正在跟一位滿頭紅髮、面色紅潤、上了年紀的胖紳士深談呢。我為自己的打擾道歉，就打算離開，我的朋友卻突然把我拉進室內，關上房門。

"你來得真是再巧不過了，親愛的華生，"他熱情地說。

"我看你正忙着呢。"

"對，正忙着呢，而且忙得可以。"

"那我暫到隔壁房間裏去等你吧。"

"不用。威爾遜先生，在我過去許多成功的偵破案例中，這位先生是我的好拍檔好助手。我敢肯定在我調查你這件案時，他也會是我極好的幫手。"

那位胖紳士從座位上微微欠身向我行個屈膝禮，那雙厚眼皮下的小眼睛即閃現一絲懷疑的目光。

"坐在那張靠背椅上吧，"福爾摩斯說，自己又坐回他的扶手椅，把雙手的指尖抵在一起，這是他審慎思考時的習慣。"親愛的華生，我知道你跟我一樣喜歡稀奇古怪的事物，而不是日常生活當中平凡單調的常規慣例。你那股熱情促使你把那些怪事都記錄了下來，足見你對它們挺感興趣，恕我這樣說，同時也給我那些小小的奇遇多多少少增添了點光彩。"

"我對你處理的案件確實都挺感興趣，"我答道。

"你還記得那天我們在談論瑪麗·薩瑟蘭[4]小姐提出的那個挺簡單的問題前我說的一番話吧，為了取得新奇的效果和驚人的配合，我們兩個要深入到生活當中去，任何奇思遐想都一向遠不及生活當中某些事物那樣大膽。"

"記得，我當時還曾冒昧地對你這種看法產生過懷疑呢。"

"是啊，醫生，可你還是要同意我的看法，要不然我就會不斷地給你列舉事實，非攻破你的道理，叫你承認我說得對才罷休。現在，這位傑貝斯·威爾遜先生今天上午來訪，說了我近些日子聽到的一件最離奇的事。你聽我說過最離奇最獨特的事，往往並非跟較大罪行而是跟較小罪行有關聯，有時確實還可以懷疑是否確實犯了罪。這件事，就我聽來，我還不能斷定它是否真是個犯罪行為。不過，事情經過也確實是我平生所聽到最離奇的了。威爾遜先生，我想請你把這事再從頭說一遍，不僅是因為我的朋友華生醫生沒聽到開頭那部份，也因為這事離奇得讓我更想再聽你把細節說一遍。一般來說，我一聽到一點說明事情經過的情節，就能讓我聯想到其他上千件類似的案件來作為我的指南。可是這一次我不得不承認，在我看來這些事實真是怪獨特的。"

那位矮胖的委託人挺起胸膛，帶着頗為自負的樣子，從大衣袋裏掏出一張又髒又皺的報紙，把它攤平在膝頭。他探頭掃視廣告欄目，我這時趁機仔細打量一下這個人，力圖模仿我夥伴的方法，從他的衣着或外表上看出點底細來。

　　可我審視的收穫並不大。我們這位來客具有一名普通英國商人的種種特點：肥胖、浮誇自負、動作遲緩。他穿一條鬆垮垮的灰格褲子和一件不大乾淨的黑燕尾服，燕尾服前面沒扣上鈕扣，露出裏面那件土灰色馬甲，那小袋上掛着一條粗銅錶鏈，上面墜着一個有個方孔的圓金屬飾品。他身旁那張椅上，放着一頂磨損了的禮帽和一件絲絨領皺巴巴、褪了色的棕色大衣。依我看，這人除了長着一頭火紅的頭髮，臉上現出極端懊惱和不滿的表情之外，沒甚麼特別的地方。

　　夏洛克・福爾摩斯敏銳的目光看出我在做甚麼。他發現我那種疑問的眼神，便微微一笑，搖搖頭。"他做過一段時期的體力工作，吸鼻煙，是一名共濟會會員，到過中國，最近還寫過不少字，除了這些顯而易見的事實外，別的我就推斷不出甚麼來了。"

　　傑貝斯・威爾遜先生在座位上吃驚得挺直身體，食指還點着那張報紙，兩眼卻望着我的夥伴。

　　"福爾摩斯先生，我真驚訝你究竟怎麼知道得這麼多？"他問道，"比如，你怎麼知道我做過體力工作？這跟福音一樣千真萬確，當初我就是在船上當木匠的。"

　　"親愛的先生，你的右手比左手大得多。你用右手工作，所以右手的肌肉就比較發達。"

　　"唔，那麼吸鼻煙和共濟會會員又是怎麼一回事呢？"

"我不願告訴你我是怎麼看出來的，以此來低估你的智慧，何況你還違背了你那個團體的嚴格會規，佩戴了一枚指南針模樣、彎弓的胸針呢。"

"哦，當然，我忘了這一點。可是寫字呢？"

"你右手的袖上足有五寸長的地方磨得光溜溜的，左袖手臂肘那兒由於經常靠在桌面上而縫了一個整潔的補釘啊。"

"那麼，中國呢？"

"靠近你手腕那兒紋的一條魚，只能是在中國紋的。我對紋身花紋作過一點研究，甚至還寫過這方面的文章呢。把魚鱗染成淡淡的粉紅色是中國才有的絕技。此外，我還看到你那條錶鏈墜着一枚中國錢幣，這不就更加一目了然、十分簡單了嗎？"

傑貝斯・威爾遜先生大笑起來，說道："唔，這我怎樣也沒料到！起初我還當你簡直是神機妙算，可說穿了，這也畢竟沒甚麼了不起。"

福爾摩斯說："華生，我開始覺得這樣詳盡解釋是做錯了。要知道，人要'Omne ignotum pro magnifico[5]'才對。如果太直接，我這可憐的小小名氣就會一敗塗地了。威爾遜先生，你找到那個廣告了嗎？"

"找到了，就在這兒，"他答道，那又粗又紅的手指正指在那欄廣告中間。"就在這兒，這就是這事的起因。兩位，你們自己看看吧。"

我接過報紙，唸出如下內容：

謹致紅髮會會員

由於原住美國賓夕法尼亞州黎巴嫩市已故伊喬基亞·霍普金斯的遺贈，現有一空缺名額，薪金每週四鎊，純屬掛名職務。凡紅髮會男性會員，年滿 21 歲，身體健康，智力健全，皆有資格申請。有意者請於星期一上午 11 時親至弗利特街教皇院 7 號紅髮會辦公室鄧肯·羅斯處提出申請為荷。

我讀了兩遍這條極不尋常的廣告，不由得大聲說：“這到底是甚麼意思？”

福爾摩斯在座椅上扭動兩下，格格笑出聲來，他興致高的時候素來這樣。“這個廣告有點離奇古怪，是不是？”他說。“好了，威爾遜先生，你就從頭說說你自己，你家裏的人，還有這個廣告給你帶來的好運吧。華生，請先把這份報紙名稱和日期記下來。”

“這是 1890 年 4 月 27 日，正好是兩個月前的晨紀事報。”

“很好，現在，威爾遜先生，請說吧。”

“唔，夏洛克·福爾摩斯先生，就像我剛才跟你說的，”傑貝斯擦擦前額，說道，“我在市區附近的科伯格廣場開了一家小當鋪。買賣不大，近數年來只能勉強靠它維持生計。過去我還僱用得起兩個員工，可現在只能聘請一個了；就連這一個不大負擔得起，這個員工為了要學會這行買賣，自願只拿一半工資。”

夏洛克·福爾摩斯問道：“這個如此慷慨的男孩叫甚麼名字？”

“他叫文森·斯波爾丁，算不上是個男孩了。我也說不清他究竟多大。福爾摩斯先生，我再也找不到比這個員工更精明能幹的了，我心裏也挺明白他本來可以把生活改善得好些，能比我付給他的工錢多賺一倍。可他自己如果挺滿意，我又何必讓他有這個想法呢？"

"可不是呢，看來你能出比市價低得多的工錢僱用到一個員工，運氣真不錯。這年頭，老闆僱人真不容易啊。我不知道你那個員工是不是跟那個廣告一樣非同一般。"

"哦，他也有他的毛病，"威爾遜先生說。"再也沒有誰比他更愛照相了。他不在工作上多用點腦，而是整天拿着照相機四處去拍照，然後就像兔子鑽洞那樣，飛快地進入地下室去沖印。這就是他的主要毛病。不過，總的來說，他是個好員工，沒有甚麼壞心腸。"

"他大概還在你那兒工作吧？"

"對，先生。除他之外，還有一個 14 歲的小女孩負責做飯、打掃房間——我那間屋裏就是這樣，因為我是個單身漢，從來沒成過家。先生，我們三個住在一起過着很安靜的日子。我們住在同一個屋簷下，欠了債一起還，沒有更多的事做。

"頭一件打擾我們的事就是這個廣告。正好在八個星期前那天，斯波爾丁走進辦公室，手裏拿着這張報紙，說道：

"'威爾遜先生，上帝啊，但願我是個紅頭髮的人！'

"'為甚麼呢？'我問他。

"'為甚麼？'他說，'紅髮會現在又有個空缺職位。誰要是得到這份美差，簡直就等於發筆小財呢。據我了解，空缺多得很，那些負責管理那筆資金的理事真不知該怎麼辦才好。我的頭髮要

是能變顏色就好了，這個美好的安樂窩就等着我進去了。'

"'甚麼事？'我問道。要知道，福爾摩斯先生，我是個深居簡出的人，因為我的買賣都是別人送上門來的，不用我到外面去招攬生意，我經常一連數個星期足不出戶。因此，我對外界的事孤陋寡聞，總樂意聽到點甚麼消息。

"'您完全沒聽説過紅髮會嗎？'他瞪大兩眼，問道。

"'完全沒聽説過。'

"'怎麼，我還真有點不明白，因為您本人就有資格申請那個空缺啊。'

"'那職位能賺多少錢？'我問道。

"'哦，一年只給二百鎊，不過工作很輕鬆，也不會過多阻礙您別的業務。'

"你們不難想見這事叫我多麼動心，因為這些年來我的生意並不太好，一筆額外的二百鎊收入，想必會很有用的。

"'那就給我説説全部情況吧，'我説。

"他便把那個廣告指給我看，説道：'您自己看看吧，這個紅髮會有個空缺職位，上面有地址，您可以去辦理申請手續。據我所知，紅髮會的發起人是一位叫伊喬基亞·霍普金斯的美國百萬富翁。這人作風十分古怪。他本人長了一頭紅髮，並對所有紅頭髮的人都懷有深厚感情；他死後，大家才發現他把巨額財產移交給數位受託人管理，留下遺言要用他的遺產利息給紅頭髮的人提供一份舒適的工作。據我所知，待遇十分豐厚，要做的工作卻很少。'

"'可是，'我説，'那會有成上千萬的紅髮人去申請啊。'

"'不會像您想的那麼多,'他答道。'您看,這只限於倫敦人和成年男子。這個美國人年輕時是在倫敦發蹟的,他想回報一下這座古老的城市。我還聽說,如果你的頭髮是淺紅色或深紅色,而不是真正發亮的火紅色,你去申請也沒用。威爾遜先生,您如果現在願意去申請,走進去一定成功;不過,為了這區區二百鎊,您也許不值得走一趟。'

"兩位,你們現在可以看到這一事實:我的頭髮真是火紅的,所以我覺得若去爭取一下的話,我比誰都更有希望。文森·斯波爾丁似乎對這事挺了解,因此我想他可能對我有幫助,我就叫他關好百葉窗歇業,馬上跟我走一趟。他很樂意放一天假,我們就動身前往那個廣告上刊登的地址。

"福爾摩斯先生,我永遠不希望再見到那種情景了。紅髮深淺不等的男人從東南西北、四面八方,湧到這座城市來應徵廣告上那個空缺職位。弗利特街上擠滿了紅髮人群,教皇院看起來就像叫賣水果的小販放滿柑橙的一輛手推車。我沒料到那樣一個廣告竟召集到了全國那麼多人。他們的頭髮甚麼顏色都有——草黃色、檸檬色、柑橙色、磚紅色、愛爾蘭長毛獵狗那種紅棕色、肝色、土黃色等等;但是,正如斯波爾丁所說的那樣,真正鮮豔的火紅色倒不多。我一見那麼多等待的人,頓時心涼了,真想放棄算了;斯波爾丁卻說甚麼也不同意。我真想像不到他哪兒來的那股力量,連推帶撞地帶我從人群中硬擠過去,一直擠到那個辦公室的台階前。台階上有兩股人流,一些人滿懷希望地往上走,另一些人垂頭喪氣地往下走;我們拼命往裏面擠,很快就進入了辦公室。"

"你這段經歷真夠有趣的，"那位委託人停頓一下，猛吸一口鼻煙以喚醒自己的記憶時，福爾摩斯插嘴道。"請接着往下講述你這件挺有趣的事吧。"

"辦公室裏除了兩三張木椅和一張松木板寫字枱外，甚麼也沒有。寫字枱後面坐着一個頭髮顏色比我的還要紅的矮小男人；他對每一個走上前去的候選人都說上數句話，接着總是想法挑他們一點毛病，說不合格。想得到這樣一個空缺職位原來並非那麼容易。然而，輪到我時，那個矮小男人對我卻比對別人都客氣得多；我們兩人進去後，他就把門關上，好跟我們單獨談談。"

"'這位是傑貝斯·威爾遜先生，'我那個員工說，'他願意填補紅髮會這個空缺職位。'

"那個人答道：'他倒挺適合這個職務，完全符合我們的一切條件。我不記得見過還有誰的頭髮顏色比他的更火紅的了，'他往後退一步，歪着頭，凝視我的頭髮，看得我都不好意思了。隨即他突然撲過來，拉住我的手，熱烈祝賀我求職成功。

"他說：'我要是再猶豫不決，就太不對勁了。不過，我不得不採取明顯的謹慎措施，相信你不會介意吧，'他一邊說，一邊就用雙手狠狠揪住我的頭髮，用力往上拔，痛得我喊叫起來，他才停手。'你眼淚都流出來了！'他鬆手後，對我說，'我看出全都符合條件，可是我們不得不小心謹慎，因為我有兩次讓戴假髮的男人、一次讓染髮的小子騙過。我還可以告訴你一些鞋線蠟的事，會叫你聽了感到噁心。'他走到窗前，往外面聲嘶力竭地高聲宣佈那個空缺職位已經有人填補。窗下傳來一陣大失所望的嘆息聲。人群便朝四面八方散開，只剩下了我本人和那位幹事，再也見不到其他紅髮人。

"'我叫鄧肯‧羅斯，'他說，'我就是那位高貴施主遺留下的基金的一名養老金領取人。威爾遜先生，你有沒有結婚？成家了嗎？'

"我回答說沒有。

"他的臉色頓時一沉。

"他一本正經地說：'哎呀！這事可的確挺嚴重！很遺憾聽你這麼說。設立這項基金的目的當然既是為了維持也是為了繁殖生育更多的紅髮人。你居然是個單身漢，真是太糟糕了。'

"福爾摩斯先生，我一聽這話，頭頓時垂下來了，因為我認為自己最終還是沒能得到那個空缺職位；可他考慮一會，又聲稱這也沒有多大關係。

"'要是換了另一個人，'他說，'這缺點就不可解決了，可你的頭髮長得這麼好，我們對你要特別照顧。你甚麼時候能來上班？'

"'嗯，這事真有點尷尬，因為我已有盤生意了，'我說。

"'那不礙事，我能替您管理好您的店鋪，'文森‧斯波爾丁插嘴道。

"'上班時間是甚麼時間？'我問道。

"'上午十時到下午二時。'

"福爾摩斯先生，開當鋪的人多半在晚上做買賣，尤其是在發薪前的星期四和星期五晚上，所以我在上午額外賺點錢倒也挺合適。再說，我知道我那個員工是個好人，要是有甚麼買賣，他會替我照料好的。

"我於是就説：'這對我來説挺合適。但不知薪金多少？'

"'每週四鎊。'

"'做甚麼工作呢？'

"'那純屬掛名而已。'

"'純屬掛名是甚麼意思呢？'

"'嗯，那就是説在那段工作時間你要留在辦公室裏，或者説至少也要在這棟樓裏。你如果離開一會，就永遠失去這個職位。那份遺囑上對這一點説得明明白白，清清楚楚。你要是在那段時間裏離開辦公室一步，就沒照章辦事。'

"我説，'一天只工作四小時，我該不會想離開的。'

"'那就好，記住不得以任何藉口離開，'鄧肯·羅斯先生又説，'無論是生病，還是有事等等原因都不行。你要留在這裏，否則你就會失去這個職位。'

"'做甚麼工作呢？'

"'你的工作就是抄寫《大英百科全書》，這兒有這個版本的第一卷。你自備墨水、筆和吸墨紙，我們只提供這張桌和椅。明天能來上班嗎？'

"'當然可以，'我答道。

"'那麼，傑貝斯·威爾遜先生，再見！讓我再一次祝賀你這麼幸運地得到這個重要職位。'他鞠一躬，把我送出房間；我便跟我的員工回家，為自己的好運氣真是高興得不知所措。

"可是我整天都在思量這件事，到了晚上情緒又低沉下來，因為整件事讓我不禁覺得必定是一場大騙局或大詭計，儘管我猜不出其目的是甚麼。有人竟會立下這樣一個遺囑，付那麼多錢讓人只抄寫《大英百科全書》這樣簡單的工作，簡直不可思議。文森·斯波爾丁盡力鼓勵我；後來去睡覺時，我自己對整件事作出了結論。不管怎麼說，我決定第二天早晨去看看究竟是怎麼一回事，我於是買一瓶一個便士的墨水、一支羽毛筆和七大張書寫紙，就前往教皇院。

"嗯，叫我又驚又喜的是，那裏安排得很讓人滿意，桌子已經給我擺放好，鄧肯·羅斯先生已經在那裏，好讓我順利開始工作。他讓我從字母 A 開始抄寫，隨後就走了；不過他不時進來一下看我做得是否妥當。下午二時他向我道聲再見，還讚揚我抄得真不少。我一走出辦公室，他就把門鎖上。

"福爾摩斯先生，事情便這樣一天天延續下去，星期六那位幹事進來，付給我四鎊作為一週的工資。第二個星期依然這樣，第三個星期也如此。我每天早晨十時準時開始工作，每天下午二時離開。鄧肯·羅斯先生逐漸每天上午只來一次了，又過了些日子，他根本就不來了。我當然依舊一刻也不敢離開辦公室，因為我不敢肯定他會甚麼時候進來，再說這份工作那麼輕鬆對我也挺合適，我真不敢冒失去這個職位的風險。

"就這樣過了八個星期，我已經抄寫了 'Abbots'（修道士）、'Archery'（箭術）、'Armour'（盔甲）、'Architecture'（建築學）、'Attica'（阿提卡）等等條目，希望由於我的勤奮，不久就可以開始抄寫以 B 字母為首的詞條了。我花了不少錢買了大頁書寫紙，抄寫的東西幾乎堆滿一個書架了。隨後，這事就突然一下子結束了。"

"結束了？"

"是啊，先生。就是今天上午結束的。我照常十時去上班，門卻關着還上了鎖，房門的嵌板上用圖釘釘着一張方形卡片。就是這張卡片，兩位可以自己看看。"

他舉着一張便條紙大小的白卡片，上面寫着：

紅髮會現已解散。
此啟。
1890 年 10 月 9 日

夏洛克·福爾摩斯和我仔細看了看這張簡短通告和後面那個人懊惱的臉容。這事滑稽可笑的一面超過了其他各方面，我們兩人禁不住哈哈大笑起來。

"我看不出這有甚麼可笑的地方，"我們那位委託人氣得滿面通紅，生氣地嚷，"你們如果只會取笑我，甚麼也做不了，那我可以到別處請教。"

"不，不，"福爾摩斯連忙一邊大聲説，一邊把欠起身的威爾遜先生推回那張椅子裏。"我真的決不會放棄你這件案。這事太不尋常，太新鮮了。不過，恕我直説，這事實在有點滑稽可笑。請告訴我，你一發現門上這張卡片，當時做了甚麼？"

"先生，我真是大吃一驚，不知該怎麼辦才好。我向周圍的辦公室打聽，可他們看來也弄不清這是怎麼一回事。最後，我去找房東。他是一位會計師，就住在地下；我問他可否告訴我紅髮會發生了甚麼事。他説他從來沒聽説過有這樣一個團體。我又問鄧肯·羅斯先生是做甚麼的。他説他從來也沒聽説過這個姓名。

"我就説：'就是住在四號的那位先生。'

"'甚麼，那個紅頭髮的男人嗎？'

"'是啊。'

"'哦，'他答道，'那個人叫威廉·莫里斯。他是一名律師，暫時租住我的一間房間，因為他的辦公室還沒佈置好。他昨天搬走了。'

"'那我能在哪兒找到他呢？'

"'噢，在他的新辦公室。他確實把他的地址告訴我了。嗯，愛德華國王街 17 號，就在聖保羅教堂附近。'

"我立刻就趕到那兒去了，福爾摩斯先生。可我一找到那個地方，卻發現是個護膝製造廠，那個廠裏誰也沒聽説過有個叫威廉·莫里斯或鄧肯·羅斯的人。"

"那你怎麼辦呢？"福爾摩斯問道。

"我只好返回我在薩克斯科伯格廣場的家。我接受了我那個員工的勸告。可是他甚麼忙也幫不上，只是勸我等待，或許會收到來信，得知消息。可是，福爾摩斯先生，這樣做可不大妙。我不甘心連爭都不爭一下就失去這樣一個美差，於是我聽説你肯給那些需要幫助的可憐人出主意，我就徑直找你來了。"

"你這樣做很明智，"福爾摩斯説。"你這件案非同一般，我樂意管一管。從你講述的情況來看，它牽連的問題可能比乍看起來要嚴重得多。"

"夠嚴重的！"傑貝斯·威爾遜先生説。"想想看，我每週損失四鎊呢！"

"對你個人來説，"福爾摩斯説，"我看不出你該抱怨這個極不尋常的紅髮會。正相反，據我所知，你賺了 30 多鎊，更不提還抄寫了那麼多 A 字母為首的詞條，大長了知識。你做這事並不吃虧呢！"

"是不吃虧，先生。可我想弄明白這到底是怎麼一回事，他們是些甚麼人，他們開我這個玩笑——如果真是玩笑——是為了甚麼目的。開這個玩笑可真花了不少錢，足足花了 32 鎊呢！"

"這些問題我們會盡力替你弄清楚。威爾遜先生，首先我想先問你一兩個問題。那位叫你注意看那個廣告的員工在你那兒工作多久了？"

"這事發生之前，他大概做了一個月左右吧。"

"他是怎麼來的？"

"看廣告應徵來的。"

"他是唯一的應徵人嗎？"

"不是，有十多個人申請。"

"你為甚麼選中了他呢？"

"因為他精明能幹，要的工錢也低。"

"其實只要一半工錢。"

"對。"

"這個文森・斯波爾丁是甚麼模樣的？"

"矮小，身型健壯，動作很敏捷；他雖然 30 出頭了，面皮倒是光溜溜的，額頭上有塊硫酸燒傷的白傷疤。"

福爾摩斯挺興奮地在座位上挺直身體。"這些我都想到了，"他說。"你有沒有注意到他兩耳有耳孔？"

"注意到了，先生。他跟我說是他少年時一個吉卜賽人給他的耳朵穿了孔。"

"嗯，"福爾摩斯陷入沉思，接着問道，"他還在你那裏嗎？"

"在，先生，我剛離開他一會而已。"

"你不在的時候，他一直管理你的生意嗎？"

"先生，我對他的工作沒甚麼可抱怨的。每天上午本來就沒有多少買賣。"

"就這樣吧，威爾遜先生。一兩天之內，我就會告訴你我對這事的看法。今天是星期六，我希望星期一我們就可以得出結論。"

客人走後，福爾摩斯問我："華生，依你看，這是怎麼一回事呢？"

"我甚麼也沒看出來，"我坦率地答道。"這事太神秘了。"

福爾摩斯説："一般來説，越是離奇的事，一旦真相大白，就越不神秘。反倒是那些普普通通、毫不起眼的罪行才真讓人困惑不解，就跟一張平淡無奇的面孔叫人最難辨認一樣。可我要馬上處理這件事。"

"那你打算怎麼辦呢？"我問道。

他答道："抽煙，這是個要抽三斗煙才能解決的問題；50 分鐘之內，請你別跟我説話。"他便坐在椅上，蜷起兩腿，瘦膝蓋對着他那鷹鉤鼻，閉着兩眼，嘴裏叼着的那個陶製黑煙斗很像某種珍禽長長的尖嘴。我原以為他睡着了，自己也就打起盹來。就在那時候，他忽然像個拿定了主意的人從座位上一躍而起，把煙斗放在壁爐台上。

"今天下午薩拉薩特在聖詹姆斯會堂演出，"他説，"怎麼樣，華生？你的病人能給你兩三個小時的假嗎？"

"我今天沒事做。業務也從來不是那麼離不開的。"

"那就戴上帽子，我們走吧。我要先經過市區，我們順路還可以吃頓午飯。我注意到節目單上有不少德國音樂，比起意大利或法國音樂我更喜歡德國音樂，它能令人深思反省，我正想做點反思呢，走吧！"

我們乘地鐵一直到阿爾德斯門，再走一小段路便到了薩克斯科伯格廣場。這裏就是我們上午聽到的那件怪事發生的地點。這是一條狹窄破舊的窮街陋巷，四排灰暗的兩層磚房座落在周圍有鐵欄杆的圍牆裏。院子裏有一片雜草叢生的草坪，上面有數簇枯萎的月桂樹叢在一片煙霧瀰漫、很不相宜的環境裏頑強地生長着。街道轉角一幢屋上有三個鍍金圓球[6]和一塊棕色木板，木板上標有"傑貝斯·威爾遜"白字招牌，說明這裏就是我們那位紅髮委託人做生意的地點。夏洛克·福爾摩斯在那間屋面前站住，歪着頭仔細觀察，兩眼在起皺的眼瞼下炯炯有神。接着，他在街上慢慢踱步片刻，又返回那個轉角，注視着那些房屋。最後，他回到那家當鋪前，用他的手杖用力戳敲兩三下那裏的人行道，然後走到當鋪門前敲門。一個看樣子挺精神、鬍子刮得乾淨的男孩立即打開門，請他入內。

"謝謝，"福爾摩斯說，"我只想打聽一下從這兒到河濱大街怎麼去。"

"從第三個路口往右轉，到第四個路口再往左轉，"那個員工立刻答道，隨即關上門。

我們從那裏走開時，福爾摩斯說："真是個精明能幹的男孩。依我判斷，他稱得上是倫敦城裏第四個最精明能幹的人；至於膽量方面，我不敢説他是不是數第三。我以前對他有些了解。"

"威爾遜先生的員工，"我説，"在這個紅髮會謎案中顯然起了很大的作用。我肯定你去問路只是想看看他罷了。"

"不是看他。"

"那又是為了甚麼呢？"

"是看看他褲腿膝蓋那個地方。"

"看見了甚麼？"

"看到了我想要看的東西。"

"剛才你為何又戳又敲人行道啊？"

"親愛的醫生，目前是注意觀察而不是閒聊的時候。我們現在是在敵人領域裏偵查呢。我們知道了薩克斯科伯格廣場的一些情況。現在再去偵察一下廣場後面那些地方。"

我們從那偏僻的薩克斯科伯格廣場轉角一轉彎，發現前面那條路上，是一種截然不同的景象，就跟一幅畫正反兩面迥然不同一樣。那是市區通往西北的一條交通大動脈。街道上車水馬龍，熙來攘往，堵塞不暢；行人道上黑壓壓一片匆匆趕路的行人。我們看到一排華麗商店和富麗堂皇的商業樓宇，簡直叫人難以相信它們竟跟我們剛離開的荒涼蕭條的廣場毗鄰。

福爾摩斯站在轉角那裏，順着那排屋望過去，説道："讓我想想，我要記住這些屋的順序。準確了解倫敦是我的一大癖好。這裏有一家莫蒂麥煙草店，一家售報小店，一家城市和郊區銀行的科伯格分行，一家素菜餐廳和麥克法蘭馬車製造廠。這裏把我們兩人一直帶到另一街區。現在，醫生，我們已經完成該做的工作，該去消遣一下了。來一客三文治和一杯咖啡，然後就到小提琴演奏廳去享受一番悦耳、優雅而和諧的氣氛，那裏沒有紅髮委託人拿猜不透的難題來打擾我們。"

我朋友是個熱情奔放的音樂家，不但是位技藝精湛的演奏家，而且還是個才藝超群的作曲家。整個下午，他坐在觀眾席裏，沉浸於最完美的歡悅境界，隨着音樂節拍輕輕揮動自己瘦長的手指；他面帶微笑，眼神倦怠恍惚，那種神情跟那個鐵面無私、多謀善斷、果敢敏捷的刑事大偵探福爾摩斯的神態迴異，儼然判若兩人。在他那獨特性格中，這種雙重性交替展現，我常常認為他那種極嚴謹的作風，跟他那種有時在他身上佔主導地位、富詩意的沉思神態，形成明顯反差。他的性格就是這樣，使他從一個極端轉換到另一個極端，時而疲憊倦怠，時而精神亢奮。正如我很熟悉那樣，他最令人敬畏的時候，莫過於接連數天，一直靠在他那張四周圍着他的即興作品和已印成白紙黑字的著作的扶手椅上，沉思冥想那一階段。接着，一股強烈的追捕慾望突然湧上心頭，這時刻他的推理本領便會提升到直覺程度，使那些不熟悉他工作方法的人，會以疑惑目光把他看成是個料事如神的人。那天下午，我看到他在聖詹姆斯會堂徹底沉醉在音樂當中，就知道他決意要追捕的那些人該倒霉了。

我們走出會堂時，他說："醫生，你一定想回家了吧。"

"對，該回去了。"

"我還要花數小時辦件事。科伯格廣場這件事很嚴重。"

"為甚麼嚴重呢？"

"有人正在密謀一宗重大的犯罪案件。我有充份理由相信我們能及時制止他們。可是今天是星期六，事情變得有點複雜了。

今天晚上我需要你的協助。”

“甚麼時間？”

“十時來就行了。”

“那我十時準時到達百加街。”

“很好。不過，醫生，這事可能有點危險，請把你在部隊裏使用過的那把手槍放在衣袋裏。”他揚一下手，轉過身去，立即消失在人群中。

我敢說我這個人並不比世人愚鈍，可我和夏洛克·福爾摩斯交往，總是沉重地覺得自己太笨。就拿這件事來說吧，他聽到的我也都聽到了，他見到的我也都見到了，可是從他的言談話語中，明顯聽出他不但看清了已發生的事，而且還能預見到將會發生的事；而在我看來，整件事仍然雜亂無章而荒誕離奇。我乘車回到肯辛頓我家時，又把這事從頭到尾思索一遍，從抄寫《大英百科全書》的那個紅髮人離奇古怪的事，直到去訪問薩克斯科伯格廣場，再到福爾摩斯跟我分別時說的不祥之詞。今夜探險是怎麼一回事呢？為何要帶上武器？我們要去哪兒？去做甚麼？我從福爾摩斯口中得到暗示，當鋪老闆那個顏面光溜溜的員工是個可怕的人——一個可能玩弄狡猾花招的人。我試圖破解這個謎，最後卻在失望中作罷，只好把它擱在一邊，等到晚上讓它真相大白吧。

九時一刻我從家裏出來，穿過公園，路經牛津街到達百加街。門口停着兩輛馬車。我一走進過道，就聽到樓上傳來說話聲。走進福爾摩斯的房間，我看見他正跟兩個人談得很熱烈，一人是警局的彼得·瓊斯偵探，另一人面帶愁容、瘦瘦高高，頭戴一頂亮晃晃的大禮帽，身穿一件很講究的厚禮服大衣。

「好！我們人都到齊了，」福爾摩斯一邊說，一邊扣上粗呢上衣的鈕扣，又從架上取下他那根沉重的打獵鞭子。「華生，你大概認識倫敦警局的瓊斯先生吧。讓我介紹你認識一下麥里韋瑟先生，他也是我們今夜冒險行動的夥伴。」

「醫生，你看，我們又一起拍檔追捕了，」瓊斯趾高氣揚地說，「我們這位朋友是位追捕能手。他需要的只是一隻老狗幫他把獵物抓獲。」

麥里韋瑟憂鬱地說：「我倒期望這次追捕不要成為一場徒勞無功的行動。」

那位警探高傲地說：「先生，您可以對福爾摩斯先生充滿信心。他有自己的一些小辦法。這套辦法，恕我直言，就是有點太理論化和異想天開。他倒具有一名偵探所必備的質素。有那麼一兩次，比如舒爾托兇殺案和阿格拉寶物盜竊案[7]，他都比官方偵探判斷得更接近正確，我這樣說並非誇大其詞。」

那個陌生人順從地說：「瓊斯先生，你要這樣說，我也沒意見！可我還是要聲明，我錯過了玩橋牌的時間，這是我 27 年來頭一次星期六晚上不玩橋牌。」

福爾摩斯說：「我想您會發現您今晚下的賭注比您以往下過的都大。這場牌局會更加激動人心。麥里韋瑟先生，您的賭注約三萬鎊呢；而對你來說，瓊斯，那個人會是你一直想逮捕的人。」

「約翰·克萊這個殺人犯、盜竊犯、搶劫犯、詐騙犯是個年輕人，麥里韋瑟先生，但他是那個犯罪集團的頭目。我銬住他比銬住其他任何倫敦罪犯都要緊。約翰·克萊這個男孩是個非凡人物，他爺爺是位公爵，他本人在伊頓公學和牛津大學讀過書，頭腦跟雙手都一樣靈活，我們雖然經常聽說他出沒的蹤跡，卻始終不清楚能在哪裏找到他。他這個星期在蘇格蘭闖入民居偷盜，下個星期卻又在康沃爾郡籌款興建一個孤兒院。我已經跟蹤他多年，至今還沒見過他一面。"

"我希望今晚能榮幸地把你介紹給他。我也跟約翰・克萊先生交過一兩次手，我同意你剛才說的，他是一個盜竊集團的頭目。目前已經過了十時，該是我們出發的時刻了。如果你們兩人乘坐頭一輛馬車，我和華生就坐第二輛跟着。"

挺長的一段路途中，夏洛克・福爾摩斯很少說話；他靠在車座上，哼着下午聽過的樂曲。馬車在沒有盡頭、迷宮般的點着煤氣燈的馬路上轔轔行駛，一直駛入法林頓街。

"我們快到了，"我的朋友說。"麥里韋瑟這人是位銀行董事，他本人對這件案挺感興趣。我想讓瓊斯跟我們一起來也好。這人不壞，只是在他那個行業裏他純粹是個笨蛋。不過他也有個優點。那就是他一旦遇到了罪犯，就勇猛得像隻鬥牛犬，頑強得像隻大龍蝦。好，我們到了，他們在等着呢。"

我們到達上午去過的那條人群熙來攘往的大街。馬車給打發掉之後，我們便在麥里韋瑟先生的帶領下，經過一條窄巷，走進他打開的一扇門。那裏面有條小過道，盡頭是一扇結實的大鐵門。這扇門也給打開，進門後是盤旋式石板台階通向另一扇令人望而生畏的大門。麥里韋瑟先生停下來把提燈點着，接着就帶領我們進入一條泥土味的過道，隨後打開第三道門，走進一個龐大的拱頂地下室，那裏面四周堆滿着板條箱和沉重的大箱。

福爾摩斯把提燈舉起來四周察看，說道：“你們這個地下室要從上面突破倒不容易。”

　　“從下面也一樣不容易，”麥里韋瑟先生一邊說，一邊用手杖敲打着地上的石板。接着他忽然驚訝地抬起頭來說，“哎呀，老天，這兒聽起來怎麼是空洞的！”

　　“我真的要請求您安靜一些，”福爾摩斯嚴厲地說，“您已經危及我們這次探險的全面勝利。我請您找個箱坐下，別再打擾，好不好？”

　　這位儀表堂堂的麥里韋瑟先生只好坐在一個板條箱上，滿臉帶着受了委屈的表情。這時候，福爾摩斯跪在石板地上，拿着提燈和一個放大鏡，開始仔細檢查石板之間的隙縫。短短兩三秒鐘的檢查就使他滿足了，他站起來，把放大鏡放回衣袋裏。

　　“我們至少還要等待一個小時，”他說，“因為他們只能等那位好心腸的當鋪老闆睡着才會採取行動。他們會分秒必爭地抓緊時間動手，因為他們越早下手，逃跑的時間就越充裕。醫生，你肯定已經猜到我們現在是在倫敦一家大銀行的市內分行的地下室裏吧。麥里韋瑟先生是這家大銀行的董事長，他會向你們解釋倫敦那些膽大包天的罪犯現在為甚麼對這個地下室那麼感興趣。”

　　那位董事長低聲說：“這裏儲存着我們的法國黃金。我們已經多次接到警告，提醒我們有人可能在這上面打主意呢。”

　　“你們的法國黃金？”

　　“對，數個月前我們恰好有個機會增加我們的資金來源，為此我們就向法國銀行借了三萬法國拿破崙頭像金幣。世人都已知道我們一直沒時間開箱取出這筆錢，因此錢仍舊放在我們的地下室裏。我坐着的這個板條箱裏就有二千枚法國金幣，用錫箔一層一層的包着呢。我們現在的黃金儲備比一家分行平時儲存的數量要多得多。董事們一直對這事挺擔心。”

“他們擔心是有道理的，”福爾摩斯説。“現在是我們安排一下小小的計劃的時候了。我估計過不了一小時，情況就會達到重要關頭。現在，麥里韋瑟先生，我們要把這盞燈遮隱一下。”

“坐在黑暗裏等着嗎？”

“恐怕要這樣。我衣袋裏倒是帶來了一副撲克牌，我們恰好湊成 partie carrée[8]，本來您可以照樣玩玩橋牌。可我覺得敵人已經準備就緒，我們不能冒露出亮光的風險。首先，我們要選好自己的位置。那些人都是膽大妄為的亡命徒，我們雖然可以打他們個措手不及，可是除非我們小心謹慎，他們還是可能會令我們受些傷害的。我站在這個板條箱後面，你們都藏在那些箱後面。等我一用燈光照亮他們，你們就迅速撲過去。他們如果開槍，華生，你就毫不含糊地擊倒他們。”

我把上好子彈的手槍放在我蹲在後面的木箱上。福爾摩斯立刻拉下提燈滑板遮住亮光，我們便陷入一片漆黑之中——我還從來沒體驗過這樣黑漆漆的環境呢。烤熱了的鐵皮氣味叫我確信燈還亮着呢，一到時機就會亮出燈光。我呢，在那陰濕冰涼的地下室裏神經緊張地靜候着，那突如其來的黑暗真給人一種壓抑而沮喪的感覺。

福爾摩斯悄聲説：“他們只有一條退路，就是奔回那間屋，逃出去，退到薩克斯科伯格廣場。瓊斯，我想你已經照我的囑咐安排好了吧。”

"我已經派好一名督察和兩名警員守候在前門那兒。"

"那我們就把所有的洞口都堵上了,目前我們要靜靜地在這兒等待。"

時間過得真慢!事後我們核對了一下筆記,其實只等了一小時十五分鐘,可我當時卻以為熬了一整夜,曙光差不多就將來臨似的。我不敢變換位置,手腳又累又麻,神經緊張到了極點,可是我的聽覺卻十分敏銳,不但能聽到數位夥伴輕微的呼吸聲,還能分辨出體型健碩的瓊斯發出的粗聲粗氣和那位銀行董事長悄悄的嘆息聲。從我的位置,我可以從箱上方望到石板地那個方向。我驀地發現那兒隱約閃現一絲亮光。

起初只是石板地上顯露一星半點灰黃色亮光,接着連成亮晃晃的一條黃線。隨後沒有任何預兆或聲響,地面似乎忽然出現一條裂縫,從裏面伸出一隻手,一隻幾乎像女人那樣白嫩的手,在那一小塊亮的地方摸索。約一分鐘後,那隻蠕動手指頭的手伸出地面,隨即又像伸出來那樣突然縮回去,周圍又是一片漆黑,只有那一星半點的灰黃亮光標示出那條裂縫。

然而,那隻手只隱沒了一會。緊接着便是一陣刺耳的撕裂聲響,一塊寬大的白石板翻了起來倒向一邊,露出一個四方洞口,從洞口裏透出一盞提燈的亮光。洞邊出現一張清秀的男孩似的臉,他向四周敏捷地觀察一下,然後便用兩手按住缺口兩邊把身體撐上來,先是肩膀,接着是腰部升到缺口上面,隨後一個膝蓋跪在洞口邊緣。轉眼間,他就站在洞口一邊,彎腰拉上來另一個跟他同樣輕巧靈活的、面色蒼白、頭髮火紅的矮小男人。

他悄聲說:"一切順利,把鑿和袋遞給我。老天爺,大事不妙！阿爾奇，快跳進去！我來對付！"

夏洛克‧福爾摩斯已經一躍而起，竄過去一把揪住那個闖入者的衣領。另外那個人聳身跳進洞去；我聽見瓊斯抓住他的襯衫，喳地一聲撕扯下來的聲響。一把左輪手槍的槍管倏地在亮光下一閃，福爾摩斯那根獵鞭嗖地一聲抽在那個人的手腕上，手槍應聲落地。

"約翰‧克萊，那沒有用，"福爾摩斯平穩地説。"這次你逃不掉了！"

"算我倒霉，"對方極其冷靜地答道，"可我的夥伴會平安無事，儘管我看見你們揪下了他的上衣後襬。"

福爾摩斯説："三個人正在門口那邊等着他呢。"

"噢，真是的，你們這事辦得倒挺周到，我該稱讚你們！"

"我也該誇獎你，"福爾摩斯答道。"你出的紅頭髮那個主意挺新穎別致，也挺有效呢！"

"你很快就會見到你那位同黨，"瓊斯説。"他鑽洞的本事真比我快一手。伸出手來，讓我銬上！"

"請你別用你那髒手碰我。你們也許不知道我是王室後裔。我還要請你們跟我説話，任何時候都要用'先生'和'請'字。"我們銬住那名罪犯的手腕時，他抗議道。

瓊斯瞪他一眼，譏諷道："好吧，那就請先生上台階吧，到了上面，我們再叫輛馬車把閣下送往警局。"

"這還像話，"約翰‧克萊安詳地説。他向我們三個很快地鞠一躬，由那名警探押着，默默無言地走出去。

我們跟在他們身後走出地下室，麥里韋瑟先生説："我真不知銀行該怎麼感謝和酬勞你們才好。你們無疑用了最嚴謹周密的方式，偵察並破獲了這宗我平生從沒見過的最精心策劃的銀行盜竊案。"

"我自己也有一兩筆賬要跟約翰·克萊算清，"福爾摩斯說。"為了破這件案，我花了點錢，我想銀行會付給我的。除此之外，我還要到了其他方面的優厚報酬。這次破案的經驗在許多方面都是獨一無二的，光是聽到紅髮會這件不尋常的事就收穫不小。"

凌晨，我們兩人在百加街喝混蘇打水的威士忌時，福爾摩斯解釋道："華生，你看，一開始就很明顯，紅髮會那個奇特的廣告，加上抄寫《大英百科全書》那種事，唯一可能的目的，就是要叫那個頭腦糊塗的當鋪老闆每天離開他的店鋪數小時。這個做法挺新奇，卻很難再想出比這更絕妙的辦法了。這個辦法無疑是克萊那個同黨的頭髮顏色引起他精明頭腦想出來的。每週四鎊是引當鋪老闆上鉤的誘餌，而這對他們想把成千上萬鎊弄到手的人來說又算得了甚麼，對不對？他們登出那條廣告之後，一個流氓租一間臨時辦公室，另一個流氓就慫恿那個人去申請那份美差。他們兩個確保那個人每週一到週五上午都會離開他的店。我一聽到那名員工只要一半工錢，就看出他去當鋪當員工明明有某種重要的特殊動機。"

"但你是怎樣猜出了他的動機？"

"如果那家店鋪裏有女人，我想必就該懷疑無非是做些庸俗的風流韻事。然而根本不是那麼一回事。那個老闆經營的是小買賣，店裏沒有甚麼值錢的玩意，根本用不着他們那麼精心策劃，花那麼多錢。因此，他們的目標肯定在當鋪那間屋之外。那又可能是甚麼呢？我想到了那個員工喜歡照相，還經常消失在地下室那個花招。地下室！這就找到了這宗錯綜複雜的案子線索。隨後我便調查了這個神秘員工的底細，發現我是在跟倫敦一個頭腦最酷、膽最大的罪犯打交道。他正在地下室裏弄甚麼，每天要做數小時，一連做數個月才行。那可能是甚麼呢？我想除了是挖一條通往其他屋的地道之外，不會有別的。

"我一去察看作案地點，心裏就明白了。我用手杖戳敲行人道，曾經使你感到驚訝。當時我是想弄清楚那條地道是往前還是往後延伸。它不是往前。隨後我就敲當鋪的門，正如我們期望的那樣，是那個員工開門。我跟他過去有過數次較量，但彼此從未見過面。我幾乎沒看他的臉，只想看看他的膝蓋。你也一定注意到了他那條褲子的膝部磨得那麼破舊，又皺又髒。這說明他花了不少時間在挖地道。唯一沒解決的問題是他們挖地道想做甚麼？於是，我在那個拐角周圍巡視一番，發現原來那家城市和郊區銀行的分行，跟我們朋友那間屋緊靠着，便覺得問題解決了。我們聽完音樂會，你乘車回家了，我就先後走訪了倫敦警局和那家銀行的董事長，結果你已經見到了。"

"那你怎麼斷定他們會在今晚動手呢？"我問道。

"哦，那個紅髮會關門大吉就是個徵兆。他們已經不在乎傑貝斯·威爾遜先生是不是留在當鋪裏了，換句話說，他們的地道已經挖通。但是，最重要的是因為地道可能會被人發現，黃金也可能會給搬走，因此他們要盡快利用地道。對他們來說，星期六比其他日子更合適，這樣就會有兩天時間可以供他們逃跑。根據這些理由，我斷定他們會在今天晚上下手。"

我毫不掩飾自己的欽佩心情，讚嘆道："你的推理真是太妙了。這一連串推理，每個環節連連相扣，都是實在的正確！"

"這就讓我不感到無聊了，"他打個呵欠，答道，"唉！我近些日子已經深感無聊。我就是力求不要庸庸碌碌地虛度一輩子。這些小案真幫 - 了我的忙。"

"你真是個造福人類的英才！"我說。

他聳聳肩說："唔，這畢竟也許有點用處吧，正如居斯塔夫·福樓拜給喬治·桑的信中所說的 'L'homme c'est rien—l'ouvre c'est tout![9]'。

3.

五顆橙核

我翻閱自己記載的 1882 年至 1890 年間有關福爾摩斯探案的筆記和記錄，發現竟有那麼多具有特色的離奇而有趣的案子，想寫篇東西，真不知該怎樣取捨才好。有些案已經通過報章廣為流傳，可是有些案卻沒有使我這位朋友盡情發揮他的傑出才能，而那種本領正是報章想報導的題材。另有些案又使他的分析本事受到了挫折，正跟某些記事那樣有了頭，卻無尾；還有一些案子只弄清了案情一部份，而那種解釋是出於推測或臆斷，也不是基於我朋友所珍視的那種準確無誤的邏輯論證。但是，在上述最後一類的案子當中有一件案，情節那麼離奇，結局又那麼驚人，使我不由得想在這裏說一說，儘管該案當中有數個細節完全不能弄明白，而且恐怕永遠也沒法完全弄明白了。

1887 年，我們經手了一系列趣味或大或小的案件，這些案件的記錄我都保存着呢。在這一年 12 個月裏的記錄標題下，有以下各案的記載:《帕拉多爾密室案》啦 ，一個團體在一家傢具店庫房地下室，設有一個窮奢極侈的俱樂部的《業餘乞丐團案》啦，與之關連的《英國帆船'索菲‧安德遜'號失事真相案》啦，《格賴斯‧彼德遜在烏法島上的奇遇案》啦，最後還有《坎伯韋爾放毒案》。在最後那宗案件調查中，大家也許還記得夏洛克‧福爾摩斯在給死者的懷錶上發條時，居然發現那隻錶兩小時前就已經上緊發條，從而證明死者在那段時間裏已上牀睡覺，這一推論對弄清案情來説至關重要。這些案子我以後也許會略述其詳。不過，其中沒有哪件案，在情節上像我現在要提筆敘述的這件案那樣撲朔迷離，那樣怪誕不經。

那是在 9 月下旬，秋分時節的暴風雨猛烈異常。全天狂風呼嘯，大雨擊窗，以至於連這座靠人類雙手辛勤興建起來、了不起的倫敦市中心，我們也不得不承認自然界無比威力的存在，而使我們一時失去從事日常工作的心情。那就像沒給馴服的籠中獸，通過人類文明那道鐵柵欄在向人類怒吼呢。隨着夜幕降臨，暴風雨更加猛烈，風時而大聲呼嘯，時而低聲咽泣，頗像從壁爐煙囱裏傳出的嬰兒哭泣聲。福爾摩斯心情憂鬱地坐在壁爐一旁，編製他破獲的罪案記錄互見索引；我則坐在另一端，埋頭閲讀一本克拉克‧拉塞爾著的精彩的海洋小説，這時候，屋外的狂風咆哮，瓢潑大雨漸漸猶如海浪衝擊，彷彿在跟小説題材相呼應，融為一體似的。我的妻子近日正回娘家探親，因此我又成為百加街舊居的一名房客。

"咦，"我抬頭瞥一眼我的夥伴，"肯定有人在拉門鈴。今天晚上有誰還會來呢？要麼是你的哪位朋友？"

"除了老兄外，我沒有甚麼別的朋友，"他答道，"我向來不鼓勵人們來訪。"

"那一定是位委託人吧？"

"如果是的話，案情肯定很嚴重。否則在這種天氣，這個時間，若不是很嚴重的事，決不會有人來的。可我覺得來人大概是房東太太的親友吧。"

然而，福爾摩斯卻猜錯了，因為過道裏有腳步聲，接着便有人敲門。福爾摩斯立即伸出長手臂把那盞照着自己的燈，轉向那把來客必定會坐的空椅那邊，然後便說聲"請進！"。

進來的是個年輕人，從外貌上看約 22 歲左右，衣着講究，服飾整潔，舉止文雅。他手裏那把水流如注的雨傘和身上那件水珠閃亮的雨衣，都說明他一路上飽嘗風吹雨打。他在燈光下焦急地四處張望。我看得出他臉色蒼白，眼神憂鬱，一個讓沉重憂慮壓得喘不過氣的人往往現出那種神情。

"我該向您道歉，"他一邊說，一邊戴上一副金絲框夾鼻眼鏡。"但願我沒打擾您！我擔心我已經把外面暴風雨的污水帶進來弄髒了您這間整潔的屋。"

"把你的雨傘和雨衣交給我吧，"福爾摩斯說。"把它們掛在掛鉤上，一會就會乾。我看出你是從西南那邊來的。"

"對，是從霍舍姆來的。"

"從你鞋尖上沾着的那種混着黏土和白灰的污跡就可以看出這一點。"

"我是專程來向您求教的。"

"這不困難。"

"還需要您的幫助。"

"那可就不總是那麼容易了。"

"我久聞閣下大名,福爾摩斯先生。我聽普倫德加斯特少校説過,您是怎樣把他從坦克維爾俱樂部醜聞一案中拯救出來的。"

"哦,當然。有人誣告他玩牌時作弊。"

"他説您甚麼問題都能解決。"

"這太過獎了。"

"他説您從來沒失敗過。"

"不,我失敗過四次——三次栽在數個男人手下,一次敗給一個女人。"

"可這跟您取勝的數量沒法相比。"

"我一般都能成功,這倒是事實。"

"那您對我這件事想必也會成功。"

"請把椅子挪近壁爐這邊來一點,告訴我你這件案的一些細節。"

"這是一件極不尋常的案。"

"到我這兒來談的都説極不尋常,我這裏成了最高上訴法院了。"

"不過,先生,我懷疑您有沒有在您的經歷中,聽説過比我家族中發生的一連串事故更神秘更難解釋的了。"

"這話説得倒叫我挺感興趣,"福爾摩斯説。"那就把這件事的主要事實從頭跟我們説説,隨後我認為其中最重要的細節會提出來問問。"

那個年輕人把椅子挪近一點,兩隻濕腳伸向爐邊。

他說："我叫約翰·奧彭肖，就我個人的理解，我本人跟這件可怕的事沒多大關係。這是長輩遺留下來的問題。為了讓您對這事有個大致的概念，我要從頭說起。

　　"您該知道我爺爺有兩個兒子——我伯父伊萊西斯和我爸約瑟夫。我爸在科芬特里開了一家小工廠，在發明自行車時代他擴展了業務，享有奧彭肖防裂車胎的專利權，生意由此興隆得使他後來能賣掉工廠，過着富裕的退休生活。

　　"我伯父年輕時移居美國，成了佛羅里達州一名種植園主，據說他也經營得不錯。南北戰爭期間，他參加傑克遜部隊作戰，後來又隸屬胡德部下，升任上校。南軍統帥投降後，我伯父便解甲歸田，重返他的種植園，在那裏又住了三四年。大約在 1869 年或 1870 年，他返回歐洲，在薩塞克斯郡霍舍姆附近購置了一小塊地。他在美國賺了不少錢，離美返英是因為他厭惡黑人，也不喜歡共和黨給予黑人選舉權的政策。他是個怪人，兇狠急躁，發怒時出言不遜，性情極為孤僻。他在霍舍姆居住那些年月裏深居簡出，我都懷疑他是否去過城鎮。他有座花園，屋周圍有兩三塊田地，他可以在那裏活動身體，可他卻經常一連數個星期都足不出戶。他喝大量白蘭地，煙癮也很大。他不喜歡社交，也不交甚麼朋友，連跟自己的親弟弟也不來往。

　　"他不討厭我，其實還挺喜歡我，因為他初次見我時，我才 12 歲左右。那是 1878 年，他已經回國八九年了。他要求我爸讓我住到他家裏去，他按照自己的方式疼愛我。他清醒不醉時，喜歡跟我玩雙陸棋，下象棋。有時他還讓我代他跟僕人和商販打交道，所以我到了 16 歲，已經在家裏像個小當家了。我掌管所有鑰匙，我想去哪兒就去哪兒，想做甚麼就做甚麼，只要我不打擾他的隱居生活就行。但是，有個例外，那就是閣樓上有一個儲物室，長年上着鎖，無論是我還是別人他都不許進去。我曾經懷着小男孩的好奇心，從鑰匙孔向裏面窺視，看到除了預料中那樣一間房裏會存放的一堆破舊箱子和包裹外，別無他物。

"有一天——那是在 1883 年 3 月，一封貼有外國郵票的信在餐桌上，放在上校的餐盤前。對他來說，一封來信是件極不尋常的事，因為他的賬單都用現款支付，再說，他甚麼樣的朋友也沒有啊。'從印度來的！'他拿起信封，說道，'彭地治里的郵戳！這是怎麼一回事？'他急忙拆開信封，只見五顆乾癟的橙核從中掉落他的盤裏。我正想發笑，可是一見他的臉色，頓時從嘴邊收斂了笑容。他的嘴唇向下垂，兩眼鼓出，面色發灰，他瞪視着自己發顫的手還拿着的信封。'K.K.K.'他尖叫一聲，接着喊道，'我的上帝！我的上帝！我的罪孽真是難逃啊！'

"'甚麼事，伯父？'我問道。

"'死亡。'他答道，隨即從餐桌前站起來，回自己的房間，剩下我獨自一人在那裏嚇得直發抖。我拿起那個信封，看到信封口裏面塗膠水處的上端，有用紅墨水潦草寫下的三個 K 字。除了那五顆乾癟的橙核外，別無他物。甚麼原因把他嚇得那樣魂飛魄散呢？我離開餐桌上樓時，碰見他手裏拿着一把生了銹的鑰匙走下樓來，那準是閣樓上那間屋的房門鑰匙，另一隻手托着一個像錢箱那樣的小銅盒。

"'他們愛做甚麼就做甚麼吧，可我還是會戰勝他們，'他賭咒道。'去告訴瑪麗，今天把我房間裏的壁爐生起火來，再派人

去把霍舍姆的福德姆律師請來！'

"我照他的吩咐辦了；律師來後，我也給喚進室內。爐火生得挺旺，壁爐欄裏有一堆焚燒了的蓬鬆的黑紙灰。爐邊放着那個銅盒，盒蓋開着，裏面空空如也。我瞥一眼那個盒，吃驚地發現盒蓋上印着跟早上那個信封上一樣的三個 K 字。

"'我要你，約翰，'伯父說，'做我的遺囑見證人。我把我的財產，連帶它的有利和不利的影響，都留給我的弟弟——也就是你爸。到時候，肯定都會轉給你。但願你能平安而順利地享用！如果你認為辦不到，我的孩子，那就聽從我的勸告，把它留給你那不共戴天的敵人吧。我很遺憾給你這樣一個有利也有弊的遺產。可我又沒法說準事情會向哪個方向發展。現在請照福德姆律師指給你的地方，在這份遺囑上簽個名吧。'

"我在指定的地方簽了名，律師就帶走了遺囑。您可以想像這件怪事給我留下多麼深刻的印象，我翻來覆去地琢磨，也沒弄清楚其中的奧秘。可我卻沒法擺脫這給我留下的隱約的恐怖感，儘管隨着時光的流逝，這種感覺漸趨緩和，何況也沒發生甚麼干擾我們日常生活的事。然而，我卻看出伯父舉止上的一些變化。他喝酒喝得比以前更多了，更不願意參加任何社交活動。大部份時間他都倒鎖上門獨自留在自己的房裏，可有時他又會像發酒瘋那樣衝出房，手裏握着一把手槍，在花園裏狂奔亂跑，嘴裏大聲喊着他誰也不怕，還說不管是人是鬼，誰也別想把他像頭綿羊那樣圈禁起來。等這陣激烈的酒瘋發作之後，他又急急忙忙奔回屋裏，鎖上門，還插上門栓，好像再也沒法掩飾自己內心深處的恐懼。在這種時刻，我看見他那張臉，即使在寒冷的天，也淨是冷汗，就跟剛從洗臉盆裏抬起頭來那樣濕漉漉的。

「嗯，福爾摩斯先生，現在説説這事的結局吧，不再辜負您的一片耐心。有一天晚上，他又發一回酒瘋，奔跑出去，再也沒有回來。我們四處尋找，結果在花園一端發現他臉朝下跌進一個泛起綠泡沫的小池塘裏。沒有發現任何受到暴力襲擊的跡象，池塘的水也不過兩英尺深。因此，陪審團鑒於眾所周知他平日那種古怪行徑，判定為‘自殺’事件。可是我深知伯父多麼懼怕死亡，怎麼也説服不了自己相信他竟會跑出去自尋短見。然而，這事也就這麼過去了，我爸繼承了物業以及約一萬四千鎊的銀行存款。」

「等一下，」福爾摩斯插嘴道，「我預料你説的這件事會是我聽到過的一宗最離奇的案。請告訴我，尊伯父收到那封信的日期以及他被人推測是‘自殺’的那個日期。」

「信是 1883 年 3 月 10 日收到的。他是在七個星期後的 5 月 2 日那天晚上死的。」

「謝謝。請接着往下説吧。」

「我爸接管了霍舍姆房物業後，在我的請求下，仔細檢查了閣樓上那間一向鎖着的房間，我們在室內找到了那個銅盒，儘管裏面的東西都已銷毀。盒蓋內層貼着一張紙標籤，上面寫着 K.K.K. 三個大寫字母，下面寫着‘信件、記事、收據和一份登記冊’的字樣。我們斷定這就説明了奧彭肖上校銷毀的東西的本質。此外，還有不少散亂的文件和一些記錄伯父在美國生活的筆記本，除此之外，閣樓那間房間裏就沒有甚麼別的重要東西了。那些散亂文件中，有些是關於戰爭時期的情況和他恪盡職守而榮獲英勇戰士稱號的記載，有些是關於南方各州重建時期的記述，大都跟政治相關，因為伯父曾經明顯積極參加過反對那些由北方派來、隨身只帶一個毯製手提包前來南方投機的政客。

"嗯，自從我爸 1884 年遷到霍舍姆來住，直到 1885 年前，我們一直生活得稱心如意。新年過後的第四天，我們坐在一起吃早餐，我忽然聽到我爸尖叫一聲，只見他一手拿着一個剛拆開的信封，另一隻五指伸開的手掌上有五顆乾癟的橙核。他平時總譏笑我所説的伯父的遭遇純屬無稽之談，但是目前同樣的事也發生在他身上時，他卻大驚失色，困惑不解了。

"'怎麼，這究竟是怎麼一回事，約翰？'他結結巴巴地問道。

"我心頭十分沉重，便説：'這是 K.K.K.。'

"他又看看信封裏面，大聲説道：'不錯，就是這三個字母，可那上面寫的是甚麼？'

"我從他肩膀上方望過去，唸道：'把那些文件放在日晷上。'

"'甚麼文件，甚麼日晷？'他問道。

"'花園裏那個日晷，別處沒有，'我答道。'文件一定指的是那些已經銷毀了的東西。'

"'呸！'他壯着膽說，'我們這裏是文明國土，不容許存在這類蠢事。這封信是從哪兒寄來的？'

"我看一下郵戳，答道：'是從鄧迪寄來的。'

"'一個荒唐的惡作劇，'他説。'我跟文件和日晷有甚麼關係？我才不理會這種無聊的事呢。'

"'該去報警，'我説。

"'讓別人取笑我的痛苦。我不做。'

"'那由我去報警吧？'

"'不行，我不准你去。我不願為這種事庸人自擾。'

"跟他爭辯也沒用，因為他生性固執。可是我離開後，心中充滿不祥預感。

"收到來信後的第三天，我爸出門去拜訪一位老友弗里博迪少校，少校現在是波茲當山要塞的指揮官。他出門我很樂意，因為我覺得他不在家倒離危險遠些。他出門的第二天，我收到少校打來電報，囑我立刻去他家。我爸跌進了附近一個很深的石灰坑，頭骨摔碎，躺在那裏不省人事。我急忙趕去，可他老人家沒再恢復知覺就去世了。看來他是在黃昏時份從費勒姆回家，由於對鄉間道路不熟悉，那個石灰坑又沒有柵欄遮擋，就掉進去了。陪審團毫不猶豫地作出'由意外事故致死'的裁決。我仔細檢查了一切跟他死亡有關的事，也找不出甚麼跟謀殺有所關聯。現場沒有任何暴力跡象，沒有腳印，沒有發生搶劫，也沒有甚麼陌生人出現在路上被人發現的記錄。可是，不瞞您說，我的內心非常不安，我敢肯定有人對我爸策劃了某種卑鄙的陰謀。

"我便在這種不祥的情況下繼承了遺產，您會問我為何不處理掉那些物業呢？我的回答是，因為我深信我們家這些災難在一定程度上跟我伯父生前某件事有關聯，因此不管是在這間屋裏還是在另一間屋裏都同樣會受到威脅。

"可憐的老爸是 1885 年 1 月慘遭不幸身亡的，至今已有兩年八個月；在這段期間，我在霍舍姆生活得還算幸福，我開始奢望這種詛咒已遠離我而去，已跟我的長輩了結。可我沾沾自喜得太早了。昨天早上，災禍再次臨門，就跟當年降臨到我爸頭上的過程完全一樣。"

那個年輕人從馬甲衣袋取出一個皺巴巴的信封，轉身走到桌前，從信封裏倒出五顆乾癟的橙核。

"這就是那個信封，"他接着説。"郵戳蓋的是倫敦東區。裏面寫的話跟上次給我爸那封信一樣，'K.K.K.'，然後是'把那些文件放在日晷上！'"

"那你怎麼辦呢？"福爾摩斯問道。

"甚麼也沒做。"

"甚麼也沒做？"

"説實話，"——他低下頭，兩隻又瘦又白的手捂住臉——"我不知道該怎麼辦。我覺得自己就像一隻可憐的小白兔面對一條蜿蜒前來的毒蛇。我好像陷入一雙沒法對抗的殘酷無情的魔爪中，任何遠見和預防措施都防範不了。"

"嘖！嘖！"福爾摩斯大聲説。"你必須採取行動，男子漢，否則你可就完了。只有振作起精神來才能得救。目前可不是失望洩氣的時候。"

"我報過警了。"

"是嗎？"

"可他們聽我訴説後，只付之一笑。我相信那個警員已有固定看法，認為那些信純屬惡作劇，我兩位長輩的死亡，正如陪審團所説的，確實出於意外，因此不必跟那些前兆聯繫在一起。"

福爾摩斯揮動着他緊握的雙拳，大聲説道："真是一群白癡！"

"他們倒是派來一名警察留住在我家中。"

"今天晚上他跟你一起來了嗎？"

"沒有，他奉命留在我的住宅裏。"

福爾摩斯又氣得揮舞起拳頭。

"那你為何又來找我？"他問道。"再說，你為何不一開始就來找我呢？"

"我先前不知道，直到今天我跟普倫德加斯特少校談起我的情況，他才建議我來找您。"

"你收到那封信已經整整兩天了。我們本應該早就行動起來。除了你放在我們面前這五顆橙核外，大概沒有甚麼別的憑證──沒有甚麼可能會有助我們的啟發性細節了吧？"

"還有一件，"約翰‧奧彭肖一邊說，一邊在上衣袋裏摸索一下，掏出一張褪色的藍紙，把它攤開放在桌上。"我記得伯父焚燒文件那天，我發現灰堆裏有些沒燒着的紙邊就是這種特殊顏色。後來我在伯父屋裏的地板上發現了這張紙，料想這可能是從那疊文件裏掉下的一頁沒被燒掉。這張紙上除了提到橙核之外，我看不出它對我們有甚麼幫助。我個人認為這可能是私人日記裏的一頁，字跡無疑是我伯父的手筆。"

福爾摩斯移動一下枱燈，我們兩人便俯身察看那張紙，紙邊參差不齊，的確是從一本簿上撕下來的。上端寫着"1869 年 3 月"的字樣，下面是莫名其妙的記載：

4 日：赫德森來，抱着同樣的舊政見。
7 日：把橙核交給聖‧奧古斯丁的麥考利、帕拉莫爾和約翰‧斯溫。
9 日：麥考利已給清除。
10 日：約翰‧斯溫已給清除。

12 日：走訪帕拉莫爾。一切順利。

福爾摩斯把那張紙摺好交還給來訪人，説道：「謝謝！你現在連一分鐘也不能再耽擱了。我們甚至沒時間討論你剛才告訴我的一切了。你要立刻回家行動。」

「該做甚麼呢？」

「只做一件事，而且馬上就要做。你要把這張給我們看過的紙，放在你説的那個銅盒裏。還要寫封短信説明其他文件都已經讓你伯父焚毀了，這張紙是唯一留下的一頁。信上的措詞必須誠懇得讓他們相信。然後，立刻把那個盒放在日晷上。明白了嗎？」

「明白了。」

「目前先別想復仇甚麼的。我認為我們可以靠法律來解決。他們已經佈下羅網，我們也要安排好我們的法網。首先要考慮的是消除那種正在臨近威脅你的危機。其次才是破解這個謎，嚴懲那個犯罪集團。」

「謝謝您，」年輕人起身，穿上大衣，説道，「您真是給了我新的生命和希望。我一定按照您的指點去做。」

「一定要分秒必爭。目前最重要的是你該注意自身的安全，因為我認為你現在無疑正面臨一種真正而緊迫的危險威脅。你怎樣回去呢？」

「從滑鐵盧車站乘車回去。」

「現在還不到九時，街上的人還不少，所以我相信你會平安無事。你一定要嚴加保護自己。」

「我帶着武器呢！」

"那就好。明天我就開始辦理你這件案。"

"那明天我們在霍舍姆見，行嗎？"

"不，你這件案的奧秘在倫敦。我要在這裏搜尋線索。"

"那我過一兩天再來，把有關銅盒和文件的結果告訴您。我會按照您指點的每個細節去做。"他和我們握手告別。門外狂風依舊在呼嘯，大雨滂沱，雨點嗒嗒地打在玻璃窗上。這件離奇凶險的事似乎是隨着狂風暴雨來到我們這兒的——宛如一根由狂風吹到我們身上的海草——現在又讓暴風雨席捲走了。

福爾摩斯默默地坐了片刻，頭向前探着，兩眼凝視着壁爐裏的紅火苗。隨後，他點燃煙斗，背靠在椅上，望着嘴裏噴出來的藍色煙圈一個接一個地升向天花板。

"華生，"他終於開口道，"在我們辦理的所有案件中，此案大概是最離奇的了。"

"除了《四簽名》那個案子外，也許是的。"

"嗯，對，除了那個案子，也許是這樣的。可我卻覺得這位約翰·奧彭肖比舒爾托那家人[10]面臨更大的危險。"

"這是怎樣的危險你是否已有明確看法？"我問道。

"性質是沒有甚麼疑問的了，"他答道。

"是甚麼呢？K.K.K. 是誰？他們為何一直糾纏這個不幸的家庭呢？"

夏洛克·福爾摩斯閉上兩眼，把兩肘放在椅子扶手上，雙手的指尖抵在一起，說道："對一個理想的推理家來說，一旦有人向他指出一個事實的一個方面，他就能從這方面不僅推斷出導致這個事實的各個方面，而且還能推測出由此而產生的一切後果。

正像居維葉經過深思熟慮，就能根據一塊骨頭準確地描繪出一頭完整的動物那樣，一個觀察家，既然已經徹底了解一系列事件中的一環，就該能正確說明前前後後所有的其他環節。我們現在還沒掌握那只有靠推理才能得出的結論。有些問題難倒了所有那些曾經企圖憑感性知覺來解決的人，倒可能在書房裏得到解決。然而，要使這種本領達到登峰造極的地步，推理家就該能夠利用他已掌握的全部事實，這是必須的；而這本身就意味着要掌握一切知識，這一點你很快就會理解，但是要做到這一點，即使當今已有免費教育和百科全書，這種成就也還是有點稀罕的。不過，一個人要掌握可能對自己工作有用的全部知識，倒也未必絕對辦不到，我本人就一直在朝那個方向努力呢。我如果沒記錯的話，我們兩人初交時，你曾經在一次場合挺精確地指出了我在知識上的局限性。"

"對，"我笑着說。"那是一份獨特文獻。我記得：哲學、天文學、政治學，我打了零分給你；植物學，說不準；地質學，就辨認倫敦 50 里以內，任何地區的泥土污跡來說，算得上造詣極深；化學，異乎尋常；解剖學，全無系統；驚險文學和罪行記錄方面，那是獨一無二的；同時又是小提琴演奏家、拳擊手、劍手、律師以及可卡因和煙草的自我毒害者。我認為這些全是我分析的要點。"

福爾摩斯一聽我說的最後一項，咧嘴笑了。"嗯，我現在一如既往，還是要說一個人該給自己那個小小的頭腦閣樓裏，裝滿他可能需要使用的一切知識，其餘的可以暫放到他的藏書室裏，需要時隨取隨用。目前，為了今晚我們接辦的這件案，我們肯定需要集中所有資料。麻煩把你身邊書架上的《美國百科全書》K字部首那一卷遞給我。謝謝！讓我們考慮一下情況，看看從中可能作出甚麼推斷。首先，我們完全可以推斷奧彭肖少校離開美國是有很重要的原因。一般來說，他那個年齡的人不大容易改變生活習慣，可他卻甘願放棄佛羅里達州那種宜人氣候，而跑回英國住在一個小鄉鎮裏過寂寞生活。他在英國那麼罕見地熱愛孤獨生活，這就暗示他是在懼怕某人或某事，因此作為工作前提，我們可以假定他就是由於對某人或某事的恐懼而被迫離開了美國。至於他懼怕甚麼，我們只能憑他本人和他繼承人接到的那三封可怕的信來推斷。你注意到那數封信的郵戳沒有？"

"第一封是從彭地治里，第二封是從鄧迪，第三封是從倫敦。"

"是從倫敦東區，你從這上面又能推斷出甚麼呢？"

"那數處都是港口。寄信人是在船上寫信。"

"太厲害了。我們現在已經有了一個線索。毫無疑問，很可能——極其可能——寫信的人是在一艘船上。現在再考慮另一點。就那封由彭地治里寄的信來說，從收到這封恐嚇信到出事那天，其間經過了七個星期。而從鄧迪寄的那封信，只經過了三四天。這說明了甚麼問題呢？"

"前者路程較遠。"

"可是那封信也要經過一段較遠路程？"

"這我就不明白了。"

"這至少叫我們又有個設想：那個人或那夥人乘的是一艘帆船。看來他們那些怪誕的警告或信號，好像總是在他們啟程執行任務之前發出的。你看，從鄧迪發出信號後，事情發生得多快。他們如果是乘輪船從彭地治里來的，那他們便可以跟信同時抵達。然而，事實上，隔了七個星期才出事。我認為這七個星期就說明那封信是郵船載來的，而寫信人則是乘帆船來的，由此而構成這一時差。"

"這倒是可能的。"

"不僅可能，而且恐怕就是如此。現在你可以看出這件新案致命的緊迫性，也可以看出我為甚麼告誡奧彭肖要多加小心。災禍總是在發信人旅程終結時來臨的。而這封信是從倫敦發出的，因此我們一分一秒也不能耽誤了。"

"老天爺！"我喊道。"這種無情的迫害究竟為的是甚麼呢？"

"奧彭肖帶回來的那些文件，明明對帆船上那個人或一夥人有着生死攸關的重要性。我認為這分明不止一個人，單獨一個人不可能接連殺害兩個人，而所用的手法又居然騙過了驗屍陪審團。這想必是一夥又有智謀又有決心的人做的。別管那些文件藏在何人手中，他們非把它們弄到手不可。從這個角度可以看出 K.K.K. 不是某人的姓名縮寫，而是一個團體的標誌。"

"但那是個怎樣的團體呢？"

福爾摩斯探身向前，壓低嗓音說："你從來沒聽說過三 K 黨嗎？"

"從來沒聽說過。"

福爾摩斯一頁一頁地翻着膝蓋上那卷書。"看這兒！"隨後他唸道，"克・克魯克斯・克蘭英文為 Kn Klux Klan，即三 K 黨。這個名字來源於想像中那種酷似扳起槍支的擊鐵聲。這個可怕的秘密組織是南方各州前聯邦士兵在南北戰爭後組成的，並迅速在全國各地成立了分會，其中在田納西、路易斯安那、卡羅來納、佐治亞和佛羅里達各州的尤為引人注目。它的勢力在於實現其政治目的，主要是對黑人選民使用恐怖手段，謀殺或驅逐反對他們觀點的人出國。他們施行殘酷手段之前，通常是先寄給受到敵視的人一種形狀奇怪而尚可辨認的東西——有些地方是一小根帶葉的橡樹枝，有些地方是兩三顆西瓜種子或橙核，作為警告。受到威脅的人接到警告後，可以放棄原有觀點或逃亡國外。如果置之不理，則必將遭到殺害，而且通常是用一種奇怪或意想不到的方式執行的。那個團體組織得那麼嚴密，使用方法又那麼有系統，竟使那些有案可稽的案件中，幾乎從未見有哪個敢與之對抗的人能夠免遭殺害，也從未能追查出執行暴行的犯案者。儘管美國政府和南方上層社會竭力阻止，這個團體在數年內還是到處蔓延滋長。最後到了 1869 年，這個三 K 黨活動突然瓦解，儘管此後還偶爾發生這類暴行。"

福爾摩斯放下手中那卷百科全書，說道："你一定注意到那個組織突然瓦解，是跟奧彭肖帶着文件逃出美國同時發生的。這兩件事很可能互為因果。怪不得奧彭肖和他的家人總有一些死對頭在追蹤他們。你可以理解那本記事本和日記可能牽涉到美國南方的某些頭面人物，另外還可能有不少人不重新找到那些東西是連覺都睡不踏實的。"

"那我們見過的那一頁……"

"正如我們所料想的。我如果沒有記錯的話，那上面寫着'送橙核給甲、乙和丙'——就是說把團體的警告通知他們。接着又寫道：甲和乙已給清除或者已出國；最後還說走訪過丙；我擔心這會給丙帶來不祥後果。對，醫生，我想我們可以讓那個黑暗地方獲得一線光明。我相信奧彭肖目前唯一的機會，就是按照我的指點去做。今天晚上沒有甚麼更多可説、更多可做的了，那就請把小提琴遞給我，讓我們把這種煩人天氣和我們夥伴更不幸的遭遇忘掉半個小時吧！"

翌日清晨，天已放晴，太陽透過籠罩在這座了不起的城市上空的朦朧雲霧，閃爍着柔和的光芒。我下樓時，福爾摩斯已經在吃早餐。

"原諒我沒等你，"他説，"我預感要為小奧彭肖的案忙碌一整天。"

"你打算採取甚麼行動呢？"我問道。

"這要看我初步調查的結果。我畢竟還是要去一趟霍舍姆。"

"你不首先去那裏嗎？"

"不，我要從城裏開始。你拉一下鈴，女僕就會給你端來咖啡。"

我在等待咖啡時，拿起桌上一份還沒打開的報紙，瀏覽一下內容。我的目光停留在一個叫我打了個冷顫的標題上。

"福爾摩斯，"我喊道，"你晚了一步！"

"啊！"他放下杯，説道。"我也一直在為這事擔心。甚麼事？"他很冷靜地問道，但我還是看得出他內心很不平靜。

"我看到了奧彭肖的名字和'滑鐵盧橋畔的悲劇'這個標題，內容是這樣的：'昨晚九時至十時之間，H 分局巡警庫克在滑鐵盧橋附近值勤，忽然聽到有人呼救和落水聲。是夜伸手不見五指，再加狂風暴雨肆虐，雖然有過路數人協助，也根本無法營救。但是當即發出了警報，經水上警察的協同努力，終於撈獲那具屍體。經驗明該屍體為一年輕紳士，從其衣袋取出一個信封，得知該人姓名為約翰·奧彭肖，生前住在霍舍姆附近。據推測，可能是急於趕搭滑鐵盧車站開出的末班火車，匆忙間在一片漆黑中迷途，誤踩一輪渡小碼頭的邊緣而失足落水。屍體未見有任何暴力痕跡。死者無疑是因意外不幸遇難，此事應引起市政當局對河濱碼頭登岸設施予以關注。'"

我們默默地坐了數分鐘，我從沒見過福爾摩斯的情緒如此低沉沮喪。

"這事傷害了我的自尊心，華生，"他終於開口道。"這無疑是微不足道的情感，卻傷害了我的自尊心。現在這事成為我個人的事了，上帝若賜我健康，我就要親手抓住那幫匪徒。小奧彭肖跑來向我求救，而我竟然送他去死……！"他從椅上一躍而起，灰黃的面頰漲得通紅，情緒激動，難以克制地在室內踱來踱去，兩隻瘦長的手一會神經質地緊握在一起，一會又鬆開。

"那些人一定是狡猾的魔鬼，"他終於說道。"他們怎麼竟會把他騙到那兒去的呢？那個堤岸並不在直達車站那條路線上啊！即使在這樣一個黑夜裏，那座橋上來來往往的人肯定還是不少，對他們下手並不是很有利啊。唉，華生，我們倒要看看誰贏得最後勝利！目前我要出去一趟！"

"去警局嗎？"

"不，我自己當警察。等我把網撒好，警方就可以捉拿那班敗類了，而不是在這之前。"

我一整天都在忙着醫務工作，晚上很遲才回到百加街。夏洛克·福爾摩斯還沒回來。快到十時，他才面色蒼白、筋疲力盡地進來。他走到櫥櫃前，撕下一塊麵包，狼吞虎嚥地吃着，喝一大杯水把它沖下去。

　　"你餓了，"我説。

　　"餓極了。我一直忘記吃東西了，從早餐後到現在甚麼也沒吃。"

　　"沒吃東西？"

　　"一點也沒吃。哪有時間想到吃。"

　　"那有了甚麼進展嗎？"

　　"不錯。"

　　"有了線索？"

　　"他們已經在我的手掌中了。小奧彭肖的仇不會報不了的。嘿，華生，讓我們以其人之道還治其人之身。這是經過深思熟慮想到的！"

　　"你這是甚麼意思？"

　　他從碗櫃裏拿出一個橙，分成數塊，把橙核擠出來，放在桌上，從中選出五顆，裝進一個信封。在信封封口裏面他寫上"S.H. 代 J.O."夏洛克·福爾摩斯（Sherlock Holmes）代約翰·奧彭肖（John Openshaw）之意。他把信封好，又添上"美國佐治亞州薩瓦納，'孤星'號三桅船，詹姆斯·卡爾霍恩船長收"等字樣。

　　"等他進港時，這封信已經在等着他了，"他格格笑着説。"這會讓他夜不成眠。他還會發現這封信是他死亡的預兆，正如奧彭肖在他之前所遭遇的命運一樣。"

"這個卡爾霍恩是甚麼人？"

"那個集團的頭目，別的人我也要處理，不過首先解決他。"

"你是怎樣追查出來的呢？"

福爾摩斯從衣袋裏掏出一張紙，上面都是日期和姓名。

"我花了一整天，"他說，"查閱了勞埃德船級社船名錄和文件案卷，追查 1883 年一月和二月，在彭地治里港停靠過的每艘船離港以後的航程。從報導上看，在那兩個月裏，抵達那裏噸位較大的船隻共有 36 艘，其中一艘叫作'孤星'號，它立刻引起了我的注意，因為這艘船雖然據報是在倫敦離港的，船名卻用了美國一個州的別稱孤星州（Lone Star State），因該州州旗和州印的圖飾中都只有一顆星而得名。"

"我想是德薩斯州吧。"

"是哪個州我當時和現在都說不準，可是我明白那艘船一定是艘美國船。"

"又怎樣了呢？"

"我又查閱鄧迪的記錄，一找到那艘'孤星'號船到過那裏，原來的猜疑就變成確信無疑了。我接着又查查目前停泊在倫敦港內的船隻。"

"結果呢？"

"那艘'孤星'號船上星期抵達了這裏。我便到艾伯特船塢，查到那艘船今天早晨已趁早潮順流而下，返航到薩瓦納港去了。我打電報到格雷夫森德，得知那艘船已在不久前駛過該港口，由於風向是朝東的，我敢肯定那艘船目前已駛過古德溫斯，離懷特島不遠了。"

“那你怎麼辦呢？”

“我要逮住他。據我了解，卡爾霍恩船長和大副二副是那艘船上僅有的美國人，其餘的都是芬蘭人和德國人。我還了解到他們三人昨天晚上離船上過岸，這是當時正在給他們裝貨的碼頭工人告訴我的。等他們那艘船一到達薩瓦納，郵船已把我那封信載到那裏了，同時我也發了電報通知薩瓦納警方，說明這三位先生是倫敦正在通緝的犯有謀殺罪的要犯。”

然而，人佈置下的天羅地網，有時也會出現漏洞。那三位謀殺約翰·奧彭肖的兇手，竟然沒收到那五顆橙核，而那數顆橙核原本可以讓他們知道世上另有一個跟他們一樣狡猾而堅決的人，正在追捕他們呢。那年秋分時節暴風颳得很久，而且十分猛烈。我們等了很長時間想得到薩瓦納“孤星”號船的消息，卻一直落空。後來我們才終於聽說：在遙遠的大西洋某處，有人看到在一次海浪的退潮中，漂泊着一塊破碎的船尾柱，上面刻着“L.S.”兩個字母（“L.S.”是“孤星”“Lone Star”的縮寫）；有關“孤星”號船的命運我們只是知道這些了。

歪唇男人

艾薩·惠特尼是聖·喬治文學神學院已故院長、科學博士伊萊亞斯·惠特尼的弟弟,他很沉迷鴉片煙這個嗜好。據我了解,他是由於在大學讀書時,閱讀了德·昆西描述吸毒後的夢幻和快感而染上了這個壞習慣的,他把煙葉浸在鴉片酊裏之後再抽,企圖獲得同樣效果。艾薩·惠特尼跟許多人一樣,後來才發現這種做法上癮易,戒掉難,多年來便一直成了毒品的奴隸,一個叫親友既厭惡又憐憫的對象。他那個樣子我至今記憶猶新,面色蠟黃,憔悴不堪,眼皮下垂,瞳孔縮小,全身蜷縮在一張椅裏,活像一副衰敗貴族的落魄相。

一天晚上——那是在 1889 年 6 月裏——有人拉響我的門鈴。那時候已是人們打呵欠,瞥一眼時鐘的時間。我當即在椅上坐起身來,我太太把手中的針線放在膝上,臉上略顯不大高興的樣子。

"病人!"她說,"你又要出診了!"

我哼一聲，因為我今天忙了一整天，已經疲憊不堪，剛回到家。

我們聽到開門聲和數句急促的聲音，隨即是一陣快步走過氈毯的聲響。我們的房門給打開了，一個身穿深色衣服、蒙着黑面紗的女人走了進來。

"請原諒我這麼晚來打擾你們，"她說道，接着就失控地奔向前摟住我太太的頸項，伏在她肩上哭起來。"唉，我真倒霉極了！"她哭着說，"太需要有人幫幫我了。"

我太太把她的面紗掀起來 ，說道："哦，原來是凱蒂·惠特尼。你可真嚇了我一大跳，凱蒂！你方才進來，我一點也沒想到是你。"

"我真不知道該怎麼辦了，就直接找你來了。"事情總是這樣的，人們有時遇到了麻煩，都會來找我的賢妻，就跟鳥在黑夜撲向燈塔似的。

"你來找我，我很高興。那就先喝點酒和水，舒舒服服地坐一會，再慢慢告訴我發生了甚麼事，要麼我讓華生先去睡，我們兩人私下談談，好不好？"

"哦，不，不，我也需要聽聽醫生的指點和幫助。是關於艾薩，他有兩天沒回家了。我真為他擔心。"

我作為一名醫生，我太太作為她的一個老朋友和老同學，聽她說她先生的麻煩事，已經不止一次了。我們盡量用諸如此類的話來安慰她，例如，她知道她先生去哪兒了嗎？我們有可能把他找回來嗎？

看來這倒是可以辦到的。她掌握了確切的信息：她丈夫近來上了鴉片煙癮，就去老城區最東邊一家鴉片煙館廝混。迄今為止，他一向只在外一天，晚上渾身抽搐，散了架那樣返回家來。可是，這次，他竟鬼迷心竅，出去了 48 小時都沒回來，他現在準是跟碼頭上那些社會渣滓一起躺在煙館裏吞雲吐霧，要麼就是過足了癮，倒頭酣睡，等慢慢恢復過來。她敢肯定能在北天鵝壩巷那家"黃金窟"裏找到他。可是她又能怎麼辦呢？她這樣一個年輕弱女子，怎能進入那樣的地方，從那幫無賴當中帶走她的丈夫呢？

情況就是如此，當然也只有一個辦法可想，那就是我能否陪她一起去呢？可我後來轉念一想，她又何必去呢？我本人是艾薩·惠特尼的健康顧問，對他也有些影響力。我如果獨自前去，也許會處理得更好。我便答應她，艾薩要是真在她說的那個地方，我就會在兩小時之內租一輛馬車送他回家。於是，四分鐘後，我便離開我的安樂椅和溫馨的客廳，乘一輛出租馬車急速趕往東區，去完成一項怪使命。當時我是這麼想的，可是後來竟會是那麼離奇古怪，真叫我沒有料到。

不過，我這次探奇歷險活動頭一階段倒沒遇到多大麻煩。北天鵝壩巷隱藏在倫敦橋東沿河北岸的高大碼頭建築場後邊，是一條最髒的小巷，夾在一家出售廉價現成服裝的商店和一個小酒吧之間，有條陡峭的台階直通下面一個洞口般的黑門，我在那兒找到了我要尋訪的那家煙館。我吩咐馬車夫停下車等着，便順着台階走下去，這段石台階中間已讓那些川流不息、搖搖晃晃的腳步踩得凹陷不平；我借助那扇門上方一盞閃爍不定的油燈亮光，找到了門閂，便走進一個矮矮的長房間，裏面瀰漫着濃重的棕褐色鴉片煙霧，靠牆排列着一長串木榻，就跟移民船隻甲板下面的統艙一樣。

透過昏暗的燈光，你可以隱約瞥見一些躺在木榻上面東倒西歪的人影，有的縮頭聳肩，有的屈膝蜷臥，有的頭向後仰，下巴朝天，這兒那兒都有倦怠無神的目光望着新來的客人。那些陰影裏閃爍着紅紅的小光圈，隨着點燃的毒品融化進金屬的煙槍鍋而忽明忽暗。大多數煙鬼都靜悄悄地躺在那裏，也有個別人在自言自語，還有兩三個用一種單調古怪的腔調在交頭接耳，竊竊私語，滔滔不絕，接着話音又突然越來越低而沉寂，各人低聲自言自語，說起自己的心事，對旁邊人的話充耳不聞。遠處那頭有個小火盆，炭火熊熊，盆旁邊有個瘦高的老頭坐在一張三條腿的矮木凳上，雙拳托腮，兩肘支在膝蓋上，雙目盯視着炭火。

我一進去，就有一個膚色灰黃的馬來員工急忙走過來，遞給我一支煙槍和一份鴉片煙，招呼我到一張空榻那邊去。

"謝謝，我不是來抽煙的，"我說。"我有個朋友艾薩·惠特尼先生在這兒，我想找他說說話。"

有人在我右邊蠕動，喊了一聲；我透過昏暗燈光看見面色蒼白、憔悴不堪、邋遢的惠特尼，瞪着大眼在望着我呢。

"老天爺！原來是華生，"他說道，反應出一副可憐兮兮的樣子，激動得每根神經都在發顫。"我說呀，華生，現在甚麼時間了？"

"快 11 時了。"

"是哪天呢？"

"6 月 19 號，星期五。"

"我的天！我還以為是星期三呢。今天明明是星期三，你為何要嚇人？"他低下頭，把臉埋在雙臂之間，尖聲刺耳地嗚咽起來。

"我跟你説，今天就是星期五。尊夫人在家裏整整等你兩天了。你該感到羞恥。"

"對，我是該感到羞恥，可是你弄錯了，華生，我到這裏才數小時，只抽了三鍋煙，四鍋煙——我都記不清多少鍋了。不過，我會跟你回家。我不該讓凱蒂擔心害怕，可憐的小凱蒂，扶我一把！你租馬車了嗎？"

"早就租了一輛，在外面等着呢。"

"那我就乘坐它吧，可我還要付賬呢，華生，去算一下我欠了多少錢。我真是一點精神也沒有了，沒法自己辦事了。"

我從那條窄過道穿過去，兩邊的木榻上都躺着人，我屏住呼吸，免得吸進那令人麻木噁心的鴉片臭氣，到處尋找店老闆。我走過那個坐在炭火盆旁邊的瘦高男人身旁，覺得有人猛揪一下我的襯衫，還有人在悄聲説："往前走數步，再回頭看看我！"這兩句話清清楚楚地傳入我的耳中。我低頭一看，這話只能是出自我身旁那個老伯伯，可是他坐在那裏跟剛才一樣沉思呢，他骨瘦如柴，滿臉皺紋，衰老佝僂，一支煙槍搖搖晃晃地垂在他的雙膝間，好像是因為他手指無力握着才滑落下去的。我朝前走兩步，回頭一看，真是大吃一驚，幸好我竭力克制才沒喊出聲來。他轉過身來，除我之外，不讓別人看到他的臉。他舒展身體，臉上的皺紋消失了，呆滯的兩眼又炯炯有神。那個坐在炭盆旁邊咧嘴笑我吃驚的神情的人不是別人，正是夏洛克·福爾摩斯。他微微暗示叫我走近，隨即轉身側面朝向眾人，又顯出一副老態龍鍾、哆哆嗦嗦的癡呆樣子。

"福爾摩斯！"我喃喃問道，"你在這煙館裏做甚麼？"

"嗓音盡量放低些，我耳朵靈得很，"他答道。"你如果能打發掉你那個癮君子朋友，我倒很想跟你談談話。"

"外面有輛小馬車在等着呢。"

"那就叫車送他回家吧。你可以完全放心，他分明已經沒精神再惹是生非了。我還建議你寫個便條讓車夫給尊夫人，就說我們兩人又搭上夥了。你先到外邊等一會，我過五分鐘就來找你。"

要拒絕夏洛克‧福爾摩斯的任何請求，那是很困難的，因為他的請求一向極其明確，總是以挺高超的溫和氣度提出來，因此我也認為一旦把惠特尼關進馬車裏，我的任務也就實際上完成了；剩下的事呢，能跟我的朋友一道去進行一次探奇歷險活動，那可是再好不過的事了，而那對福爾摩斯來説，則是他正常的生活境況。我花了數分鐘寫好短信，付清惠特尼欠的賬，領他出去上了車，目送他在黑夜中乘車而去。沒多久，就從鴉片館裏走出來一個衰頹老頭，我便跟夏洛克‧福爾摩斯順着街道走下去。在兩條街的路程上，他都駝着背，晃晃悠悠地蹣跚而行。接着，他向四周迅速望一下，便挺直身體，放聲哈哈大笑起來。

"華生，"他説，"我猜想你大概認為我除了可卡因注射以及你從醫學觀點加給我的其他小毛病之外，現在又增添了抽鴉片煙這個癖好了吧。"

"在這裏碰到你，當然叫我感到驚訝。"

"可是決不會比我在這裏見到你更驚訝吧。"

"我是來這兒找一個朋友。"

"我卻是找一個敵人！"

"一個敵人？"

"對，我的一個天然敵人，要麼可以說我的一個天然獵物。簡單說吧，華生，我在進行一次極不平凡的偵察呢。我想按照從前做過的那樣，從那些煙鬼的胡言亂語中找出一條線索。我如果在那個煙館裏讓人認出來，過不了一小時性命就會不保，因為以前我為了破案在那裏偵察過。那個開煙館的流氓拉斯卡發過誓要找我報仇。那間屋後面有個活暗門，就在保羅碼頭轉角附近，黑漆漆的深夜裏那扇門裏面發生過不少怪事。"

"甚麼？你不是指屍體吧？"

"對，華生，正是屍體。我們如果為每一個在那煙館裏給弄死的倒霉人伸冤而賺到一千鎊，我們就該會成為富人了。那裏是整個沿河一帶最險惡的殺人陷阱。我擔心奈維爾·聖克萊爾先生走了進去，就再也出不來了。哦，我們的輕便馬車應該就在這裏等着呢！"他把兩手的食指塞進上下牙之間，吹出一聲尖哨，遠處回應了一聲同樣的哨聲，沒多會就傳來一陣轆轆的車輪聲和噠噠的馬蹄聲。一輛單匹馬拉的雙輪馬車從黑暗的地方駛過來，兩旁的吊燈射出黃光。福爾摩斯說："華生，你現在願意跟我一起去嗎？"

"我如果能派上用場，當然樂意去。"

"嗯，一個信得過的夥伴總是有用的，更不用提還是一個記錄我事蹟的人呢。我在杉園那間房裏有兩張牀。"

"杉園？"

"對，那是聖克萊爾先生的屋。我調查這件案時就住在那裏。”

“那在哪兒？”

“在肯特郡，離李鎮不遠。馬車要走七里路。”

“但我真是一無所知啊。”

“你當然馬上就會知道。上車吧！好了，約翰，不麻煩你了，這兒是半克朗。明天 11 時左右等我。把韁繩交給我吧，再見！”

他輕抽那匹馬一鞭子，馬車就行駛起來，經過一條條寂靜無人的漆黑街道，隨後路面漸漸展寬，我們飛快駛過一座兩側有欄杆的大橋，橋下緩緩流着黑沉沉的河水。前方出現一片淨是磚頭灰泥的荒地，只有巡警沉重的腳步聲，或一些狂歡尋樂的人在晚歸中唱歌喊叫聲，打破了那裏的寂靜。一堆散亂的烏雲從天空緩慢飄過，這兒那兒一兩顆星星在雲縫中微微閃亮。福爾摩斯默默地駕駛着馬車，頭垂在胸前，像是陷入了沉思；我坐在他身旁，好奇地想知道這到底是一件甚麼案件，竟會使他耗費如此大的精力，可是我又不敢打斷他的思路。我們行駛了數英里，漸漸來到郊外別墅區的邊緣，這時他忽然振作起來，聳聳肩，點燃他的煙斗，現出洋洋自得的神氣。

“華生，你可真有保持沉默的天賦，”他說，“這使你成為一個非常難得的好夥伴。哎，說真話，有個可以推心置腹地說說話的人，對我來說，倒也至關重要，因為我的想法不一定討人喜歡。我正躊躇今天晚上，那位可親的年輕夫人在門口迎接我時，我該對她說甚麼。”

“你忘了我對這事一無所知啊。”

“我們到達李鎮之前，我正好有時間把案情說給你聽。這事看起來簡單得出奇，可是我不知怎的，卻摸不清頭腦。線索倒是很多，卻讓我抓不到頭緒。我現在簡明扼要把案情說給你聽，華生，也許你能替我看出點眉目來。"

"那就說吧。"

"數年前——更確切地說是 1884 年 5 月——有位紳士叫奈維爾·聖克萊爾，來到了李鎮，看樣子他挺有錢，購置了一棟大屋，周邊也修飾得挺漂亮，過着挺體面的日子。他跟鄰居逐漸交了朋友，1887 年娶了當地一位釀酒商的女兒，現在他已經有了兩個孩子。他沒有固定職業，卻對數家公司挺感興趣，作一些投資，他平常每天早晨進城，傍晚 5 時 15 分從坎農街乘車回家。聖克萊爾先生現在 37 歲，沒有甚麼不良嗜好，是個好丈夫，有愛心的父親，受相識者歡迎的人。我還可以補充說，他目前就我們已經可以查明的全部債務是 88 鎊 10 先令，而他在那家首都與郡府銀行裏存有 220 鎊呢。因此沒有理由認為他有財務上的壓力。

"上星期一聖克萊爾先生比往常要早些進城。臨走前，他提到有兩件重要的事要辦，還說會給小兒子帶回一盒積木。說來也巧，就在同一天早晨，他走後不久，他太太收到一封電報，說有個相當貴重的小包裹——一個她一直在等待的包裹——已經寄到亞伯丁運輸公司辦事處，請她去取。喏，你如果熟悉倫敦街道，就會知道那家公司辦事處在弗雷斯諾街，那是天鵝壩巷上的一條岔道，也就是你今夜見到我的那個地方。聖克萊爾太太吃過午飯就進城了，在商店買了些東西便到公司辦事處去取了她那個包裹，正好在午後 4 時 35 分穿過天鵝壩巷前去車站。你聽明白了嗎？"

"聽得清清楚楚。"

"你還記得星期一那天特別熱吧，聖克萊爾太太慢慢走着，朝四下張望，期望租到一輛馬車，因為她不喜歡那四周的環境。她沿着天鵝壩巷朝前走，驀地聽到一聲驚叫或喊聲，抬頭一看，只見她老公在一棟樓房的三層樓窗口那兒朝下望着她，像是在朝她招手呢，這真叫她驚嚇得渾身冰涼。那扇窗戶是敞着的，她清楚看到他的臉，據她形容，那樣子十分焦慮不安。他向她拼命揮手，卻又突然一下子從窗口消失，像是讓後面一種沒法抗拒的力量揪了回去。她那雙女性敏感的眼睛發現了一個異常現象，那就是她丈夫雖然還穿着進城時穿的那件深色上衣，頸項那兒卻沒有硬領，也沒有領帶。

"她確信她丈夫一定發生了甚麼事，便急忙奔下台階——因為那幢屋正是今晚你發現我在那兒逗留過的煙館——她穿過前屋，打算登上通往二樓的樓梯，卻在樓梯口遇到了我剛才提到過的那個流氓拉斯卡，他把她推開，並在一名丹麥籍員工的幫助下，把她推到街頭。她滿懷焦慮和恐懼心情，極其惱火地順着小巷跑出去，難得幸運地在弗雷斯諾大街，遇到了正在巡邏的一名警官和數名警員，他們便跟她返回。儘管煙館老闆再三阻攔，他們還是進入了聖克萊爾先生剛才讓人發現的那個房間，可是房裏卻沒有他逗留過的任何跡象。整個那層樓裏其實除了有個面目醜陋的癮子住在那裏之外，別無他人。癮子和拉斯卡都賭咒發誓說，那天下午沒有人來過這間前房。他們兩人說得那麼肯定，連警官也動搖了，正想認為聖克萊爾太太準是看錯了人，這時她忽然大叫一聲，撲到桌上放着的一個松木盒前，打開盒蓋，嘩啦啦地倒出一大堆兒童積木玩具。這正是聖克萊爾曾經答應要帶回家的玩具。

"這一發現和那個瘸子明顯驚惶失措的神情，讓那位警官意識到了事態的嚴重性。於是，那數間房都給仔細搜查了一通，結果表明一切都跟一宗可憎的罪行相關。前屋陳設簡樸，是一間客廳，通向一間小臥室，從臥室窗戶可以望見一個碼頭的後方。碼頭和臥室窗戶之間有條窄溝，落潮時是乾涸地面，漲潮時至少讓四尺半的深水淹沒。臥室那扇窗戶挺寬敞，由底下朝上開啟。大家在檢查時，發現窗台上有斑斑血跡，臥室地板上也有兩三滴血。拉開前房裏一道布簾，後面竟放着聖克萊爾先生的全套衣服，只缺那件上衣。他的靴呀，襪呀，帽呀，手錶呀，全都在那裏。從那些衣物上倒看不出發生過甚麼暴力的痕跡，卻也不見聖克萊爾先生的蹤影。他想必是從窗口跳出去的，因為沒發現房裏還另有別的出口；從窗台上不祥的血跡來看，他想游泳逃生是不大可能的，原因是這場悲劇發生時，潮水正漲得高極了。

"再說說那些看來跟此案有直接牽連的歹徒吧。那個拉斯卡是個臭名昭彰的地痞流氓。可是按聖克萊爾太太的說法，她丈夫在窗口出現後僅僅數秒，拉斯卡便已經站在樓梯口那兒，這個人至多是這宗犯罪案件的一個幫兇而已。拉斯卡分辯說自己對這事一無所知，對樓上的房客修・波恩的所作所為也完全不清楚，對那位失蹤先生的衣服出現在現場，更說不出個所以然來。

"拉斯卡老闆的情況就是這樣。現在再說說那個住在鴉片煙館三樓，樣子陰險的瘸子吧。他當然是最後一個親眼見到聖克萊爾先生的人。他叫修・波恩，凡是常去市中心的人都熟悉他那張醜陋的臉。他是個職業乞丐，由於要避免警方管制，他裝作賣蠟火柴的小販。在離針線街不遠的地方，靠左那邊，你可能也注意到過，有個小牆角，那個可憐人每天就坐在那裏，盤着雙腿，把少得可憐的數盒火柴放在膝上；由於他那副可憐相，人們施捨給他的硬幣就像雨點那樣，落進他放在身邊行人道上一頂油膩的皮革便帽裏。我曾經不止一次注意過這個人，後來我了解了一下他的乞討情況，才對他瞬間工夫就有那麼豐盛的收入深感吃驚。要知道，他的形象那麼異常，誰在他面前走過，都會看他一眼的。一頭蓬鬆的紅頭髮；一張蒼白的臉讓一塊可怕的傷疤毀了容，那塊傷疤一收縮就把上唇外部邊緣翻捲上去；一副哈巴狗似的下巴；一雙目光挺銳利的深色眼睛，那兩隻眼跟他的頭髮在顏色上形成奇特的鮮明對比；這一切都顯出他跟其他一般乞丐迥然不同；此外，他的智力也非一般，別管過路人投給他甚麼破爛東西，他都能脫口道出一句相應回答。我們現在知道他就是那個煙館樓上的房客，也是最後一個親眼見到我們正在尋找的那位紳士的人。"

"可是一個瘸子！"我說。"他獨自一人又能把一個正當壯年的人怎樣了呢？"

"就走路一瘸一拐這點來說，他是個殘疾人，可是在其他方面，他看樣子卻是個挺有力氣、有充足營養的人。華生，你的醫學知識肯定會告訴你，人一肢不靈活的弱點，常常可以由其他肢體格外強壯有力而得到補償呢。"

"請接着往下說吧。"

"聖克萊爾太太一見到窗台上的血跡就暈倒，隨即便由一名警察租一輛馬車護送她回家了，因為她在場，對他們的調查毫無幫助。巴頓警長負責此案，非常仔細地檢查了現場，卻沒找到甚麼弄清此案的線索。當時犯了一個錯誤，沒有立即逮捕修·波恩，因此想必使他有了數分鐘時間可以跟他的朋友拉斯卡串口供。不過，這個錯誤很快就給糾正了；他被拘捕，並受到搜查，可是並沒發現甚麼可以定他罪的證據。他襯衫右袖上確實有些血跡，可是他指着自己左手第四指的指甲邊緣被刀割破的地方，解釋說血是從那兒流出來的，還補充說他剛才曾到窗口那邊，那裏發現的血跡無疑也是這麼來的。他堅決否認曾經見過奈維爾·聖克萊爾先生，並且賭咒發誓說那些衣服出現在他的房間裏，他也跟警方一樣覺得是個謎。至於聖克萊爾太太確認她確實看見了她丈夫出現在窗口，他聲稱她想必不是瘋了，就是在做夢。他在大聲抗議下給押往警察局，而警長仍留在案發現場，希望等退潮後能發現些新線索。

"他們雖然沒在泥灘上找到他們擔心會找到的屍體，可還是找到了一樣東西，那不是聖克萊爾先生本人，而是他的上衣。那件上衣在退潮後暴露在泥灘上。你猜他們在那件上衣衣袋裏發現了甚麼？"

"不知道。"

"嗯，我料你也猜不出。每個衣袋裏都裝滿了一便士和半便士的硬幣——總共有 421 枚一便士硬幣和 275 枚半便士硬幣。怪不得這件上衣沒讓潮水沖走。可是人的軀體就是另外一回事了。那座碼頭和那棟樓房之間有一股水勢洶湧的退潮。看來很可能是那件挺沉的上衣給留了下來，而那赤裸的身軀卻給捲進河裏去了。"

"可我理解警員發現別的衣服都在那間房裏啊。難道他只穿了一件上衣嗎？"

"不，華生，這事也許能自圓其説。假定波恩這東西把奈維爾·聖克萊爾推出了窗外，卻沒人親眼目睹這件事。隨後，他會再做些甚麼呢？他當然馬上會想到要那些會趕快處理掉洩露天機的衣服。他就拿起那件上衣，正要往外扔的時候，一轉念想到那件衣服會飄浮在水面上而沉不下去。這時候，他已經聽見那位太太非要上樓不可的吵鬧聲，也許還聽見他的同黨拉斯卡説，街上已有數名警察正朝這裏跑過來。他剩下的時間不多了，刻不容緩。他就衝到那個藏着自己靠乞討而積下來的錢的密櫃，能抓出多少硬幣就抓出多少，塞進那件上衣的衣袋，確保它能沉入水底。他扔出上衣後，想必還打算依樣處理另外數件衣服，卻聽到了樓下急促的腳步聲，因此警察出現在那間房裏時，他只來得及關上那扇窗。"

"聽起來確實像是這麼一回事。"

"好，我們在沒有更好的推測前，就暫且把這當作有用的假設吧。我剛才跟你説了，波恩給逮捕帶到警局裏去了，可是警方又拿不出甚麼證據，證明他犯過甚麼前科而可以控告他。他多年來一直是眾人皆知的乞丐，過着似乎挺安靜而於人無害的生活。目前情況就是這樣擺在我們面前。該弄清的問題不少，諸如奈維爾·聖克萊爾到煙館去做甚麼？他在那裏究竟發生了甚麼事？目前他身在何處？修·波恩跟他的失蹤有甚麼關係？這些問題都還遠遠沒有得到解答。我不記得我經辦過的案件當中，曾經有這樣一件乍看似乎挺簡單卻出現這麼多難題的案件。"

福爾摩斯在詳述這一連串怪事時，我們乘坐的馬車正飛快駛過這座大城市的郊區，後來把那些零零落落的屋也甩在後面了。馬車隨即順着兩旁有籬笆的鄉間小道行走。他剛説完，馬車便駛過兩旁有疏疏落落農舍的村莊，有數家窗戶微閃着燈光呢。

"我們現在到了李鎮邊緣，"我的夥伴説。"在這短短的旅途中，我們竟路過了英格蘭的三個郡，從米德爾賽克斯郡出發，經過薩里郡一角，最後抵達肯特郡。你看到樹叢中的燈光嗎？那裏就是杉園，那盞燈旁邊坐着一位婦女，她憂心如焚，豎起耳朵傾聽着呢，無疑已經聽到我們的馬車奔馳的噠噠聲。"

"可是你為何不在百加街辦這件案呢？"

"因為有不少事要在這裏詢問。聖克萊爾太太已經盛情安排了兩個房間供我使用。你儘管放心，她一定會對我的朋友兼同事表示熱烈歡迎。華生，我沒有得到她丈夫的消息之前，真不想見到她。我們到了。吁，吁！"

我們在一座大別墅前停下車，這座別墅座落在庭園中。一個馬童跑過來，拉住馬頭。我跳下車，跟福爾摩斯踏上一條通往樓房的彎曲小碎石道。我們走近時，屋的前門開了，一位金髮小婦人站在門口，身穿一套淺色真絲薄綢衣服，領口和袖口鑲着蓬鬆的粉紅薄紗花邊；她在燈光襯映下，輪廓鮮明，一手扶門，一手急切地半舉着，腰微微彎傾，探首向前，雙唇微張，目光充滿着渴望，一副詢問的神情。

"怎樣了？"她喊道，"怎樣了？"隨後她看到我們是兩個人，又見我的夥伴搖頭聳肩，起初還充滿着希望地喊着，便轉而陷入嘆息。

"沒有好消息嗎？"

"還沒有。"

"沒有壞消息嗎？"

"也沒有。"

"那我謝天謝地！請進來吧。兩位足足辛苦了一整天，一定很累了吧。"

"這是我的好友華生醫生。他在我以往辦的一些案裏幫了我很大忙。我很幸運能請他來跟我一起調查這宗案。"

"很高興見到您，"她說，跟我熱情地握手，"您要是能考慮到我們遭受的打擊，就會原諒我們任何接待不周的地方。"

"尊敬的夫人，"我說，"我可是個久經沙場的老戰士，即使不是，也看得出您根本沒必要道甚麼歉。我要是能對您或者對我的朋友有所幫助，那就真是太高興了。"

"福爾摩斯先生，"那位夫人說，這時我們走進一間燈光明亮的餐室，桌上放好了已放涼的飯菜，"我很想問您一兩個直截了當的問題，請您給我一個坦率的答案。"

"當然可以，夫人。"

"請不必擔心我的情緒。我不會歇斯底里，也不會輕易暈倒。我只想聽聽您實實在在的意見。"

"哪方面呢？"

"請您說真心實話，您認為奈維爾還活着嗎？"

夏洛克・福爾摩斯好像被這個問題窘住了。"請說真心實話！"她又說了一遍，站在地毯那兒俯視着正坐在一張藤椅的福爾摩斯。

"那麼，説實話，夫人，我不認為。"

"您認為他已經死了嗎？"

"對。"

"讓人謀殺了？"

"我沒那麼説，也許吧。"

"那他是哪天被害的？"

"星期一。"

"福爾摩斯先生，那就請您解釋一下我怎會在今天收到了他寄給我的這封信呢？"

夏洛克・福爾摩斯像觸了電似的，從椅上跳起來。

"甚麼？"他喊道。

"沒錯，就在今天。"她面帶微笑站在那裏，高高舉起一張紙。

"我可以看看嗎？"

"當然可以。"

他從她手中抓過來那封信，把它撫平在桌上，挪過燈來，仔細審視。我也離開座椅，從他背後注視那封信。信封挺粗糙，蓋着格雷夫森德的郵戳，發信日期是當天，要麼可以説是昨天，因為現在已經過了半夜。

"字跡潦草，"福爾摩斯喃喃道。"這肯定不是您先生的字跡吧，夫人。"

"不是，不過信中附來的一樣東西卻是他的。"

"我還看出，信封不管是誰寫的，那個人都要先打聽一下地址。"

"您怎能這樣説呢？"

"您看，人名是用深黑墨水寫的，自動乾的，其餘部份則是淡灰色，說明用吸墨紙吸過。要是一口氣寫下來的，再用吸墨紙吸過，便不會有深黑色字了。這人寫下姓名，停頓了一下，才寫地址，這只能表明他不熟悉這個地址。這當然是件區區小事，然而再也沒有甚麼比小事更重要的了。現在我們看看這封信！嘿！隨信還附來一樣東西呢！"

"對，一枚戒指，他的圖章戒指。"

"您能肯定這是您先生的筆跡嗎？"

"是他的其中一種筆跡。"

"其中一種？"

"一種他在匆忙中寫字的筆跡，跟他平時的筆跡不大一樣，可我還是認得出來。"

"'親愛的，不用害怕。一切都會好轉的。事已鑄成大錯，也許需要些時間來糾正。請耐心等待。奈維爾。'這封信是用鉛筆寫在一張八開本書的扉頁上的，紙上沒有水紋。嗯，這封信是由一個大拇指挺髒的人今天從格雷夫森德寄出的。嘿！信封蓋是用膠水黏的，我如果沒弄錯的話，封信的人是一個一直在嚼煙草的人。您敢肯定這是您先生的筆跡嗎，夫人？"

"這我敢肯定，是奈維爾寫的字。"

"而且信和戒指都是今天從格雷夫森德寄來的。那就好，聖克萊爾太太，烏雲已散，可我還不敢說危險已過。"

"這麼說，他一定還活着呢，福爾摩斯先生。"

"除非這封信是巧妙偽造的，想誤導我們。這枚戒指也畢竟證明不了甚麼，那可以從他手上拿下來呢！"

“不，不，這是——這是他親筆寫的！”

“那好，可是這封信也可能是星期一寫的，今天才寄出。”

“這倒也可能。”

“如果是這樣的話，這段時間裏也可能發生不少事。”

“哦，福爾摩斯先生，請您別叫我喪失信心。我知道他一定沒事。我跟他之間有一種敏銳的心靈感應，他要是遭到不幸，我就會感覺得到。我最後見到他那天，他在臥室裏劃破了手指，而我在樓下飯廳裏心裏一驚，就知道他準是發生了甚麼事，馬上奔上樓去。您想我對這麼一件小事都有反應，難道對他的死亡會一點反應都沒有嗎？”

“我遇過的事太多了，哪能不知道一位婦女的直覺也許會比一位分析推理家做出的論斷更有價值呢。何況您從這封信得到一個強有力的證據來支持您的看法。不過，您的先生如果還活在世上，又能寫信，卻為甚麼不回家來呢？”

“我想不出為甚麼。這真叫人不可思議。”

“他星期一出門時沒對您說甚麼嗎？”

“沒有。”

“您在天鵝壩巷望見他時吃驚了嗎？”

“真是大吃一驚。”

“窗戶敞着嗎？”

“敞着呢。”

“那他可能是在喊您？”

“可能是的。”

“按我理解，他只模糊地喊了一聲。”

"對。"

"您認為那是呼救聲嗎？"

"是的。他還擺動雙手呢。"

"但那也可能是一聲驚呼。出乎意料地見到了您，使他可能驚訝得舉起了雙手。"

"這倒也可能。"

"可是您認為他是讓人從後面給拉開的嗎？"

"他一下子就消失了。"

"那也可能是他朝後跳開了。您沒見到房裏還有別人嗎？"

"沒有，可是那個面目醜陋的人承認自己一直在那裏，還有那個拉斯卡在樓梯口那兒。"

"這倒也是。就您所見到的情況來說，您先生身上穿的是他平時穿的那身衣服嗎？"

"是的，只是沒了硬領和領帶。我清清楚楚看到他光着頸項呢。"

"他以前提起過天鵝壩巷沒有？"

"從來沒有。"

"他以往顯露過抽鴉片煙的跡象嗎？"

"從來沒有。"

"謝謝您，聖克萊爾太太。這正是我絕對要弄清楚的數個重點。我們現在先吃點晚飯，然後就休息，因為我們明天可能要忙碌一整天呢。"

一間寬敞舒適的房間裏放着兩張牀供我們使用。經過一夜探奇歷險的奔波，我已經累得筋疲力盡，很快便鑽進被窩了。夏洛克·福爾摩斯卻是這樣一個人,他每逢心中有個尚未解決的問題就會連續數天,甚至一個星期,廢寢忘食地反覆思考,重新梳理自己掌握的各種情況,從各個角度審查那個問題,一直要麼弄個水落石出,要麼深信自己搜集的材料還不夠充份時才肯罷休。我很快就明白他又準備坐個通宵了。他脫掉外衣和馬甲,穿上一件大的藍睡袍,然後在房間裏四處踱步,把牀上的枕頭以及沙發和扶手椅上的靠墊收攏在一起,擺成一個東方式沙發。他盤腿坐在上面,面前放好一益司劣質板煙絲和一盒火柴。在那昏暗的燈光下,我看見他端坐在那裏,嘴裏叼着一個歐石楠根雕成的老煙斗,兩眼茫然地凝視着天花板,藍色煙霧從他嘴邊盤旋繚繞冉冉升起。他默默不語,紋絲不動,燈光照在他那山鷹般堅定的容貌上。他就那樣坐在那裏,我則漸漸墮入夢鄉。突然聽到他大喊一聲,我從夢中驚醒,他還那樣坐着呢。最後,我睜開兩眼,夏日朝暉已經照進屋裏。那個煙斗依然叼在他嘴裏,青煙在他頭上繚繞。濃重的煙霧瀰漫全房,昨夜我見到的那堆板煙絲已經吸光了。

"睡醒了,華生?"他問道。

"嗯。"

"早上駕車出去遛一趟如何?"

"好吧。"

"那就趕快穿上衣服。目前誰都還沒起牀呢。我知道小馬童睡在哪兒,我們可以立刻把馬車套好出去。"他一邊說,一邊格格發笑,兩眼閃爍着光芒,似乎跟昨夜冥思苦想的他判若兩人。

我穿上衣服,看一下錶,這時才清晨 4 時 25 分,怪不得還沒有人起牀。我剛穿好衣服,福爾摩斯就走進來說小馬童正在套車呢。

"我要去檢驗一下我這個小小的推理，"他穿上靴，說道。"華生，你現在大概正站在全歐洲一個最笨的蠢人面前。我該讓人一腳從這裏踢到倫敦查林十字街去！可是我目前已找到開啟這個謎案的那把鎖匙了。"

"在哪兒呢？"我微笑着問道。

"在洗手間裏呢，"他答道。"哦，是的，我沒在開玩笑。"他發現我不大相信的樣子，又接着說。"我剛去過那兒，已把它拿出來了，放在這個格萊德斯通手提包裏了。走吧，朋友，讓我們看看我這把鑰匙對不對得上鎖。"

我們盡量不吭聲，悄悄下樓，走出大門，迎向明媚的晨曦。那輛套好的馬車在路邊，那個還沒穿好衣服的小馬童站在車前拉住馬。我們兩人躍上馬車，順着倫敦大道飛奔而去。路上有數輛往城市運輸蔬菜的農村大車在走動，可是路旁兩邊一排排別墅還寂然無聲，了無生氣，宛如夢境中的城鎮。

"有些疑點顯示這是件奇案，"福爾摩斯一邊說，一邊揚鞭驅馬疾駛。"我承認先前我的兩眼瞎得像鼴鼠，不過，聰明才智學得雖晚，總比不學強。"

我們的馬車經過薩里郡邊緣一帶街道時，城鎮裏起牀最早的人，剛剛睡眼惺忪地朝窗外眺望呢。馬車駛過滑鐵盧大橋，越過泰晤士河，飛快奔駛在威靈頓大街上，然後向右急轉彎，來到博街。警方人員都認識福爾摩斯，看守所門旁兩名警察向他致敬，其中一名接過韁繩，拉住馬，另一名便引我們進去。

"今天誰值班？"福爾摩斯問道。

"布萊德斯特里特警長，先生。"

"布萊德斯特里特警長，你好！"一位身材魁梧的警員從石板鋪的通道走出來，頭戴一頂鴨舌帽，身穿帶有盤花鈕扣的上衣。"我想跟你悄悄商量一些事，布萊德斯特里特。"

"當然可以，福爾摩斯先生，請進房來吧。"

那是一間像辦公室的小房間，桌上放着一本厚實的分類登記簿，牆上掛着一個電話。警員臨桌坐下。

"大駕光臨，不知有何吩咐，福爾摩斯先生？"

"我是來看看那個乞丐波恩——那個人被控跟李鎮奈維爾·聖克萊爾先生失蹤一案有關。"

"對，他是給押到這裏來候審的。"

"這我聽說了。他在這兒嗎？"

"在牢房裏。"

"他有沒有鬧事？"

"哦，一點也沒有搗亂，但他是個髒透了的壞蛋。"

"髒得很？"

"沒錯，我們只能做到叫他洗了洗手。他那張臉黑得跟補鍋匠的一樣。哼，等他的案判完後，他要按監獄的規定洗個澡；我想，您見到了他，也會同意他真該好好洗澡了。"

"我倒真想見見他。"

"您想見他嗎？那好辦。請跟我來。您可以把手提包留在這裏。"

"不，不，我還是隨身拿着吧。"

"那也好，請跟我來，"他領着我們走過通道，打開一道上了門的門，從盤旋式樓梯下去，把我們帶到一條兩邊牆刷得粉白的通道，兩旁各有一排牢房。

"右邊第三間就是他的牢房，"警員說。"就是這間！"他輕輕打開牢門上的一扇小窗，朝裏面望一眼。

"這人睡着了，"他說，"您可以從這兒很清楚地看到他。"

我們兩人通過小窗的格柵往裏面窺視。那名囚犯臉朝着我們躺在那裏正在酣睡，氣喘得又重又慢。他中等身形，穿着一套跟他那個行業相稱的粗料衣服，貼身一件黑襯衫從那件破爛的上衣數處裂縫中顯露出來。他確實像警員所說的那樣骯髒，臉上的污垢還是掩蓋不住他那叫人噁心的醜容，從眼角到下巴有一道寬寬的舊傷疤，這道傷疤一收縮便把上唇一邊翻捲起來，那張歪嘴就露出三顆牙齒，像是一直在吼叫的樣子。一頭亂蓬蓬的亮紅髮低低覆蓋着額頭和兩眼。

"是個俊男，對不對？"警員說。

"他的確要好好洗澡，"福爾摩斯說，"我倒想了一個可以給他洗澡的好主意，還擅自帶來了些工具。"他一邊說，一邊打開他那個手提包，從裏面取出一塊挺大的洗澡海綿，這真叫我大吃一驚。

"嘻，嘻！您可真會逗樂人，"警長格格笑着說。

"現在，麻煩您輕輕打開門，我們馬上就會讓他變成一個挺體面的人物！"

"行，這有何不可，"警長說。"他這副醜樣子一點也沒給我們博街這個看守所增光，對不對？"他把鑰匙插入門鎖，我們便悄悄走進牢房。那個睡着的人翻一下身，又睡着了。福爾摩斯彎腰着水罐蘸濕了那塊海綿，便在囚犯那張臉上上下下用力擦了數下。

"讓我給各位介紹一下，"他大聲說，"這位是肯特郡李鎮的奈維爾・聖克萊爾先生！"

我一輩子也沒見過這種場面。那個人的臉就像剝去樹皮那樣讓海綿剝下一層皮。粗糙的棕色不見了！臉上縫着的那道可怕的傷疤和那顯出一副可憎的、冷笑的歪嘴唇也不見了。那一頭亂蓬蓬的紅頭髮也一下子給揪掉了。這時候，牀上坐起來的是個面色蒼白、愁眉不展、相貌英俊的男子，一頭黑髮，皮膚平滑，揉着惺忪的雙眼，困惑地四下裏張望。接着，他忽然領悟到事已敗露，不由得尖叫一聲，撲倒在牀上，把臉埋在枕頭裏。

"老天！"警長驚呼道，"他的確是那個失蹤的人，我從相片認出他來了！"

那名囚犯轉過身來，擺出一副聽天由命、滿不在乎的架勢，說："就算是，你又能控告我犯了甚麼罪？"

"犯了藏匿奈維爾・聖——先生的罪。哦，好了，除非他們把這件案當做自殺未遂案，否則不會控告你這個罪名，"警長咧嘴一笑，說道。"我已經做了 27 年警察，這次可真中了大獎。"

"如果我本人就是奈維爾・聖克萊爾先生，那我就分明沒犯甚麼罪，因此我現在是被非法拘留。"

"沒犯罪，可是犯了一個很大的錯誤，"福爾摩斯說。"你要是信得過尊夫人，想必就會更好地跟我們配合。"

"倒不是因為我的太太，而是為了我的孩子們，"那名囚犯嘟噥道，"願上帝保佑，我不願意他們因為他們的爸爸做的事而感到羞恥。天哪！這事暴露出去多丟人！我該怎麼辦？」

福爾摩斯坐在那張牀上他的身邊，和藹地拍拍他的肩膀。

「這事你若讓法庭來查清就難免會宣揚出去，」他說，「但你只要讓警察當局相信，這不是一件甚麼可以控告你的案，我想也就沒理由把案情細節由媒體公諸於世。我相信布萊德斯特里特警長會把你告訴我們的話記錄下來，上報有關當局。這樣一來，這事就根本不會上法庭了。」

「上帝保佑您！」那名囚犯激動地大聲說。「我寧願忍受拘禁關押，唉，甚至處決，也不願把我這悲慘的秘密作為家庭的一個污點留給孩子。

「您是第一個聽到我的身世的人。我爸是切斯特菲爾德的小學校長，我在那裏受過優良的教育。年輕時，我愛旅遊，愛演戲，後來在倫敦一家晚報社當了記者。有一天，總編想登一組反映大城市裏乞丐生涯的報導文章。我自告奮勇承擔這個任務。這就成了我平生探奇歷險的開端。「我只能喬裝成乞丐，才收集得到寫這組文章所需的一些基本材料。我當過演員，當然就學會了喬裝秘訣。我的喬裝技巧在劇場後台是很有名氣的。我便利用這個本事，先用油彩抹臉，然後為了盡量將自己打扮成最叫人憐憫的模樣，便用一小塊肉色橡皮膏做出一個唯肖唯妙的傷疤，把嘴唇一邊向上捲起來，戴上一個紅色假髮套，配上相應的服裝，就在城裏最熱鬧的地區選定一個地方，表面上是個賣火柴的小販，實際上是個乞丐。我這樣乞討了七個小時，晚上回到家，驚訝地發現竟得到了 26 先令 4 便士。

「我寫完那組報導文章，就不再想到那事了；後來過了一段時間，我在一位朋友的一張票據背面簽了名做了擔保，沒想到後來接到一張傳票要我賠償 25 鎊。這真叫我不知所措，我不知從哪兒能弄來這麼多錢，可我靈機一動，想出一個主意。我請求債主容我半個月時間籌款，又向報社請了半個月假，便喬裝成乞丐到市裏去乞討。只用了十天光景，我就有了錢，償還了那筆債務。

"嗯，您想像得到在報社一週賺兩鎊薪金，多麼辛苦！何況我知道只消在臉上塗抹點油彩，把帽放在地上，靜靜地坐着，一天就能賺那麼多錢。是要自尊心呢，還是要錢，我思想鬥爭了很久，最後還是金錢佔了上風，我便放棄了記者工作，天天坐在我第一次選定的那條街的拐角，借着我那副可怕的面容引起人們的惻隱之心，銅幣就裝滿了我的袋。只有一個人知道我這個秘密，那個人就是我在天鵝壩巷寄宿的那個下等煙館的老闆；我在那裏可以每天清早以一個邋遢的乞丐模樣出現，晚上又變成一個衣着體面的男人走出來。這個拉斯卡，我付給他高額的房租，這樣我就感到踏實，深信他不會洩露我的秘密。

"嗯，我很快就發現自己已經積存了一大筆錢財。我並非說倫敦街頭的任何一個乞丐都能每年賺到七百鎊——這數還比不上我的平均收入——我本人有喬裝特技，又有機智的應付本領，這兩方面真是越練越精，就使我成了城裏大眾熟悉的人物。全天都有大批各式各樣的銀幣流水般進入我的私囊，如果哪天收入不到兩鎊，那就算運氣不濟了。

"我越有錢越有野心，就在郊區買了一棟屋，還結了婚，也從沒引起誰對我的職業產生過懷疑。我那愛妻只知道我在城裏做生意，卻不曉得我究竟做甚麼。

"上星期一，我完成了一天的工作，正在煙館樓上的房間裏換衣服，朝窗外看了一眼。叫我大為驚恐的是，見到了我太太站在街中央，正兩眼看着我呢。我不由得驚呼一聲，趕緊用兩隻胳臂遮住臉，隨即立刻跑去找我那位知己朋友拉斯卡，請求他別讓任何人上樓來找我。我聽到她在樓下說話的聲音，心裏明白她一時半會還不會上樓來，便連忙脫掉身上的衣服，換上乞丐那身裝束，又戴上假髮，臉上塗好油彩，連我太太都沒法看出我這種偽裝。隨後我又想到他們也許會搜查我那個房間，我的秘密就可能讓那些衣服敗露，我便連忙打開窗戶，由於用力過猛，竟又碰破我清晨在臥室裏割破的那個小傷口；平時我把討來的錢都放在一個皮革袋裏，我就把裏面的硬幣掏出來塞進我那件上衣衣袋裏，好讓它增添分量，然後就把它扔出窗外，它就沉入泰晤士河沒影了。別的衣服我本想也都扔下去，可是那時候，樓梯上傳來了警察衝上來的腳步聲；片刻後，我發現自己沒被認出是奈維爾·聖克萊爾先生，反倒給當成殺害他的兇手，並遭到了拘捕，但我承認這倒讓我鬆了口氣。

"我不知道還有甚麼別的情況需要解釋。我當時下定決心盡可能長期保持我的喬裝樣子，這就是我寧願保留着一張髒兮兮的面孔的原因。我知道我太太會焦急萬分，便在警察沒注意時除掉手指上的戒指，匆匆寫封短信塞進拉斯卡手裏，託他轉告我太太不必着急。"

"但她昨天才收到你那封短信，"福爾摩斯說。

"老天！這一週她該是怎麼熬過來的！"

"警方監視住拉斯卡，"布萊德斯特里特警長說，"這我完全可以理解，他要想把信發出去而又不讓人注意，是很困難的。也許他把信又託給了他的某位海員顧客寄，那個人又把這事忘了好幾天。”

　　“就是這麼一回事，”福爾摩斯同意地點點頭，“這我一點也不懷疑。可你從來也沒因為乞討而捱過處罰嗎？”

　　“捱過多次，可罰點錢在我又算得了甚麼。”

　　“事情就到此為止吧，”布萊德斯特里特警長説。“如果警方聲張出去，那麼修‧波恩就該不再存在了。”

　　“我已經鄭重發過誓，保證説話算話。”

　　“要是這樣，我想這事也就大可不必再深究下去了。可你如果再讓我們發現在街頭行乞，那我們便會把這事和盤托出。我要説，福爾摩斯先生，我們非常感謝您幫助我們澄清了這件案！我很想知道您是怎樣得出了這個答案的呢？”

　　“這個答案呢，”福爾摩斯説，“是全靠坐在五個枕頭上，抽完一盎司板煙絲得出來的。我想，華生，我們兩人如果現在乘車回百加街，正好趕上吃早餐呢。”

5

藍寶石案

聖誕節的翌日早晨，我為了向好友夏洛克・福爾摩斯祝賀佳節，便去探望他。他身穿一件紫紅色晨袍，懶洋洋地斜靠在躺椅上，右手所及之處有個放煙斗的架，身邊還有一堆揉皺了的晨報，顯然都剛剛翻閱過了。躺椅旁邊是一張木椅，椅背一角上掛着一頂骯髒、破爛不堪的硬禮帽，那頂帽簡直糟得都沒法再戴了，上面有好幾處長了裂縫。椅座上放着一個放大鏡和一個鉗，這說明那頂帽給那樣掛在那裏，是為了便於查看。

"你正忙着呢，"我說，"我大概打擾你了。"

"一點也沒打擾，我倒樂意有個朋友能跟我一起討論一下我得出的結論。這純粹是件瑣碎小事，"（他用大拇指指一下那頂破舊的帽）"不過有數點跟這頂帽有關的事，卻並非索然無味，甚至還會大有教益呢。"

我在一張扶手椅上坐下，就着劈啪作響的爐火暖暖雙手，因為嚴寒已至，玻璃窗上都結了晶瑩冰花。"我料想，"我說，"這頂帽儘管看起來並不雅觀，卻跟某宗人命案有牽連——你從它可以找到破解一宗奇案的線索，懲治那麼一項犯罪行為吧。"

"不，不。沒有甚麼犯罪行為。"夏洛克・福爾摩斯笑着說。"這只是那些離奇小事當中的一件罷了。想想看，四百萬人擁擠不堪地居住在一塊僅有兩三平方英里的彈丸之地上，這類小事少不了。在這樣稠密的人群互相角逐中，各種各樣錯綜複雜的事件都可能發生，而且不少問題也許會出現得古怪而驚人，卻並非是犯罪行為。這類事我們早就體驗過。"

"是啊，"我說，"我最近增添記載的六個案例，其中就有三宗就跟法律上的犯罪完全無關。"

"正是這樣。你指的是我想方設法找回艾蓮・艾德勒的相片那一回事、瑪麗・薩瑟蘭小姐奇案和那個歪嘴男人的案件吧。嗯，我敢肯定這件小事也會屬於這類無罪範疇。那個看門人彼得森你認識嗎？"

"認識。"

"這個戰利品是他的。"

"是他的帽。"

"不是，不是，是他撿來的，帽的主人是誰目前還沒弄清楚。請你不要把它簡簡單單看成是頂破帽，而該把它當做一個靠智力來破解的問題。首先，它是怎樣來到了我這兒的。這是在聖誕節早晨跟一隻大肥鵝一起給送到我這兒來的，我敢肯定那隻鵝目前正在彼德森的爐火上烘烤着呢。情況是這樣的：聖誕節凌晨四時左右，彼德森你也知道是個挺誠實的人，參加一個小型聯歡慶祝會之後，沿着托特納姆法院路往家走的時候，在煤氣燈下看見一個高大的男人在他前面有點蹣跚地走着，肩上搭着一隻白鵝。彼德森正路過古治街拐角時，那個高大男人忽然跟一小群流氓爭吵起來。一個流氓把他的帽打落在地，他便舉起手杖在自己頭上方揮舞自衛，一不留神把身後一家店鋪的玻璃窗打得粉碎。彼德森見此情景，便奔過去保護那個陌生人別再受到襲擊，但那個人由於打碎了玻璃窗而驚恐不已，又見一個穿制服的警察模樣的人朝他跑來，就丟下那隻鵝，拔腿逃之夭夭，很快便消失在托特納姆法院路後面彎彎曲曲的小巷裏。那夥流氓看到彼德森趕過來，也四散而逃，結果只剩下他獨自一人留在那個打鬥的戰場上，而且掠奪了兩樣戰利品：這頂破帽和一隻完美的聖誕節大肥鵝。"

"他一定把東西歸還原主了吧？"

"親愛的夥伴，問題就出在這裏。那隻鵝的左腿上確實繫着一張寫着‘獻給亨利·貝克夫人’的小卡片，這頂帽的襯裏上也標着字跡清楚的姓名縮寫‘H·B’字樣；可是在我們這座城市裏，姓貝克的人數以千計，而叫亨利·貝克的人又何止數百。因此，要在這麼多人當中找到失主，把東西還給他，決非一件容易辦得到的事。"

"那彼德森後來怎麼辦呢？"

"他知道我連最細小的問題都會感興趣，便在聖誕節那天清晨，把帽和鵝送到我這裏來了。我們把那隻鵝留到今天早上，雖然天氣較冷，可還是有跡象表明沒必要再保存下去，還是趁早吃掉牠算了。因此，彼德森就把牠拿走，去了結那隻鵝，我則保留了那位失去了聖誕佳餚的陌生先生的帽。"

"他沒登報尋找失物嗎？"

"沒有。"

"那你有甚麼線索能找到那個人的身份嗎？"

"只能盡量推測了。"

"從這頂帽？"

"沒錯。"

"你是在開玩笑吧。你又能從這頂破帽找到甚麼呢？"

"我的放大鏡在這兒呢。你素來知道我的工作方法。你自己能否推測出那戴過這頂帽的人有甚麼特徵嗎？"

我把那頂破帽拿在手中，無奈地把它翻過來看看，這是一頂極其普通的圓形黑帽，硬邦邦的，破舊得真沒法再戴了。紅色絲綢襯裏已大大褪色，製帽商的商標也沒有了，但是正像福爾摩斯所說的那樣，一側卻有潦草寫下的姓名縮寫"H·B"兩個字母。帽邊上有箍帶的穿孔，可是那鬆緊帶已經沒有了。其他方面呢，那頂帽儘管看來有數處褪了色的地方都用墨水塗黑了，卻還是有數處裂開了，灰塵僕僕，污點斑斑。

"我甚麼也看不出來，"我說，把帽交還給我的朋友。

"恰恰相反，你甚麼都看得出來，但你沒有作出推理。你啊，太膽怯，不敢推論。"

"那就請你說說你能從這頂帽作出甚麼推論嗎？"

他拿起帽，用他那種獨特的內心思考方式琢磨，目光凝視着它，說道："這頂帽可能提供的引人聯想的事物或許並不多，但還是有數點明明可以推論出來，另有一些至少也很有可能給推測出來。從表面上看，這人當然明顯是個學識淵博的人，而且在過去三年裏，生活相當富裕，儘管目前他處境窘迫。他以往頗有遠見，目前卻今非昔比了，再加上經濟狀況每況愈下，家道中落，導致他精神萎靡不振，某種不良嗜好，也許是酗酒吧，看來便乘虛而入。這也分明可以看出他的夫人不再愛他了。"

"哪裏會呢，親愛的福爾摩斯！"

"不過他還保持着某種程度的自尊心，"他沒理會我的反駁，接着說。"他這個人一向深居簡出，根本不鍛煉身體，是個中年人，頭髮灰白了，最近數天剛理過髮，塗過檸檬髮膏，這些都是從他那頂帽推斷出來的明顯事實。順便說一下，他家中絕對不大可能安裝有煤氣燈。"

"你準是在開玩笑吧，福爾摩斯！"

"一點也不是。即使我現在跟你說了這些結論，你可能還是沒看出這都是怎麼得出來的吧？"

"我不否認自己太笨，但我要承認沒法領會你說的話。譬如，你怎麼推斷出這人是個學識淵博的人呢？"

福爾摩斯把那頂帽啪的一下扣在自己的頭上作為答覆。帽蓋住了他的額頭，搭在鼻樑上。"這無非是個容量問題，"他說，"一個人有這麼大的頭，腦裏想必存有不少玩意吧！"

"那麼，家道中落又是怎麼推斷出來的呢？"

"這頂帽已經買了三年，當時這種帽邊向上捲的平檐帽很時興，是質量最優良的帽。看看這條羅紋絲綢箍帶，還有這講究的襯裏！這人三年前如果買得起這麼昂貴的一頂帽，但後來再也沒買過別的帽，那他肯定是走下坡路了。"

"嗯，這一點倒也說得通，可是說這人頗有遠見，又說他精神萎靡不振，這是怎麼一回事呢？"

　　福爾摩斯笑了。"看這兒，說明他有遠見，"他一邊說，一邊把手指放在那個釘鬆緊帶的小圓環和搭扣上。"這種帽出售時並不帶這些小東西。這人如果訂造了這些，正好說明他頗有遠見，因為他特地用這個辦法來預防帽被風颳走。但我們又看到他把鬆緊帶弄壞了，而又不願意費點功夫重新釘上一條，這顯然說明他已不如以前那樣有遠見了，也是他意志日漸消沉的明證。另一方面，他設法用墨水塗抹來遮蓋帽上污跡，又表明他還沒完全喪失自尊心。"

　　"你的推論似乎言之有理。"

　　"再者，他是個中年人，頭髮灰白了，最近剛理過髮，頭上抹過檸檬髮膏，這些都是從帽襯裏底部仔細檢查後得出來的。通過放大鏡，看到了不少新頭髮碎，是理髮師用剪刀剪下來的，那些髮碎都黏在一起，還有股檸檬膏味。你也會注意到帽上的塵土不是街上那種顆粒灰砂，而是屋裏揚起的絨毛灰塵，說明這頂帽大部份時間都給掛在室內，裏面的濕印又明顯證明戴帽的人愛出汗，因此不可能是個身體鍛煉得很好的人。"

　　"可是他的夫人——你說她不再愛他了。"

　　"這頂帽已經有好幾個星期沒給刷過了。親愛的華生，我要是見到你的帽上落了一個星期的塵土，而且尊夫人就讓你那副髒樣子出門，我便會擔心閣下也不幸失去了尊夫人的愛情。"

　　"但他也可能是個單身漢啊！"

　　"不可能，那天晚上他要把那隻鵝帶回家去，作為一件向夫人提出和解的禮物啊。別忘了鵝腿上繫着那張小卡片呢。"

"你對每個問題都作了解答，可你究竟怎麼推斷出他家裏沒安裝煤氣燈呢？"

"要是一滴蠟燭油，甚至兩滴，那可能是偶然滴上去的，但我一看到至少有五滴燭油，就肯定這人經常接觸到點燃的蠟燭了——也許是每天夜晚上樓時，一手托着淌油的蠟燭，一手拿着帽。反正，他絕不可能從煤氣燈沾上燭油污跡。你滿意了嗎？"

"嗯，你真是個機靈鬼！"我笑着說，"但你既然剛才說這裏面沒有甚麼犯罪行為，除了遺失一隻鵝之外，沒造成甚麼危害，那你這樣仔細察看來真是白浪費了精力。"

夏洛克·福爾摩斯正要張嘴答話，這時房門突然打開，看門人彼德森跑了進來，兩頰通紅，面帶茫然吃驚的神情。

"那隻鵝，福爾摩斯先生！那隻鵝，先生！"他氣喘吁吁地說。

"呃？怎麼了？莫非鵝又活了，拍打着翅膀從廚房窗口飛出去了嗎？"福爾摩斯為了把那個人激動的表情看得更清楚，從躺椅上轉過身來。

"您看看，先生！您看我老婆在鵝的嗉囊裏發現了甚麼！"他伸出手，手心上展現一顆光芒四射的藍寶石。那顆藍寶石比一粒蠶豆稍微小一些，卻那麼晶瑩潔淨，光輝奪目，就像一道電光在他那黝黑的手掌裏閃爍。

夏洛克·福爾摩斯吹聲口哨，坐起來。"老天，彼德森！"他說，"這確實是一件珍藏的寶貝啊！你大概知道你得到的是甚麼吧？"

"一顆鑽石，先生！一顆寶石！用它切割就像切油灰一樣。"

"這顆寶石可非同一般，而是那顆名貴寶石。"

"莫非就是莫卡伯爵夫人那顆寶石嗎？"我驀地喊道。

"正是！我最近每天都看《泰晤士報》有關這顆寶石的報導，因此知道它的形狀大小。這顆寶石絕對是獨一無二的珍寶，它的價值只能猜測，那筆懸賞報酬一千鎊肯定還不到這顆寶石市價的二十分之一。"

"一千鎊！我的天！"那個看門人撲通一下跌坐在椅上，瞪着大眼來回望着我和福爾摩斯。

"那只是尋找失物的懸賞金額而已，我確實知道伯爵夫人還出於某種感情上的考慮，只要能夠找回這顆寶石，她寧可把財產分一半給人也心甘情願。"

"我如果沒記錯的話，這顆寶石是在大世界酒店遺失的，"我說道。

"完全正確，12 月 22 日，也就是五天前，一名水管工人約翰·霍納被指控從伯爵夫人的首飾盒裏偷走了這顆寶石。由於他犯罪的證據確鑿，這件案現已提交巡迴審判庭處理，我相信我這裏還有些關於這事的報導呢。"他翻弄那堆報紙，掃視每份上面的日期，最後撫平一張，再對摺一下，唸出下面的段落：

> "大世界酒店寶石失竊案。約翰·霍納，26 歲，水管工人，因本月 22 日從莫卡伯爵夫人首飾盒中竊取一顆名貴的、著名的'藍寶石'而被送交法院起訴。酒店服務員領班詹姆士·賴德，對此案作證如下：盜竊發生那天，他曾帶約翰·霍納到樓上莫卡夫人的化粧室內，焊接壁爐前第二根已鬆動的欄杆。他陪同霍納逗留一會，就給召喚離去。他回來時，發現霍納已不見蹤

影，而梳粧台抽屜則已被撬開，一個空空的摩洛哥皮革小首飾匣給丟棄在梳粧台上，後來聽說伯爵夫人習慣把首飾存放在那個盒裏。賴德當即報了警。於是霍納當晚即被捕，可是從他身上和他的住所裏都沒找到那顆寶石。伯爵夫人的女僕凱瑟琳・古錫宣誓作證，說她聽到賴德發現寶石被竊後的驚叫聲，就衝進房間，看到室內的情況跟上述證人所述相符。B區分局布萊德斯特里特警長證明霍納被逮捕時拼命抗拒，並用最強烈的措詞申辯自己清白無辜。鑒於有人證實霍納以前曾經犯過類似盜竊行為，地方法官不便草率處理此案，現已把此案提交巡迴審判庭審理。在審判過程中，霍納表現得異常激動，結論時竟然昏厥倒地而給抬出法庭。"

"哼，治安法庭提供的情況也就是這些，"福爾摩斯把報紙扔到一邊，若有所思地說。"我們現在要解決的問題是，從首飾盒中寶石被竊作為起點，到托特納姆法院路拾到的那隻鵝的嗉囊作為終點，把這一系列事件按順序理清。你看，華生，我們的小小推論，突然出現並非完全無罪這極重要的一方面了。這顆寶石目前在這兒，它來自那隻鵝，那隻鵝又來自亨利・貝克先生，也就是戴這頂破帽、還有我說得叫你感到厭煩的其他種種特徵的那位先生。我們現在要認真地去尋找他，並且弄清楚他在這件神秘小事件中扮演了甚麼角色。要做到這一點，我們首先要試用最簡單的辦法，無非就是在所有晚報上登載一則啟事。這個辦法若不成功，就要另想別的方法了。"

"啟事上說甚麼？"

"給我一支鉛筆和一張紙。就這樣寫：

'茲於古治街轉角處拾得鵝一隻和黑氈帽一頂。請
亨利・貝克先生今晚六時半到百加街 211 號 B 座聯繫，
以便領回失物。'

這樣寫既清楚又明瞭。"

"挺不賴。但他會看到這個啟事嗎？"

"他準會注意看報的，因為對一個窮人來說，這項損失真是
太大了。他明明是因為打碎了玻璃窗闖了禍，彼德森當時又走過
去，才嚇得不知所措，只顧逃跑了，但後來他一定感到後悔莫及，
痛惜因一時衝動而丟下了那隻鵝。另外，報上登出了他的名字他
一定會看到，因為認識他的人都會提醒他看報。彼德森，給你這
個，趕快把它送往廣告公司，讓他們刊登在今天的晚報上。"

"登在哪家報紙上呢，先生？"

"嗯，《環球報》啦，《星報》啦，《蓓爾美爾報》啦，《聖詹姆
斯宮報》啦，《新聞晚報》啦，《回聲報》啦，還有你想得到的甚麼
報，都登。"

"好吧，先生，可這顆寶石呢？"

"噢，對了，這顆寶石就先保存在我這兒。謝謝你。另外，彼
德森，你回來時買一隻鵝，送到我這裏來，因為我們要給貝克先
生準備一隻，取代你們全家現在正在大吃大嚼的那一隻。"

那位看門人走後，福爾摩斯拿起那顆寶石對着光線鑑賞。"真
是一顆絕妙的寶石！"他說，"你看，它多麼光彩四射啊！當然，
它又是罪惡的淵藪。每顆珍貴的寶石都是如此，它們是魔鬼最得
意的誘餌。在那些更大更古老的寶石上，每個刻面都可能意味着
一宗血腥罪行。這顆寶石問世以來還不到 20 年，它是在中國南

方廈門河岸上發現的。它的可貴之處在於蔚藍色而不是鮮紅色，可是它卻具有紅寶石的一切特點。它雖然流傳在世不久，卻已有一段不祥歷史。為了這顆 40 格令重的結晶碳石，人世間已經發生過兩宗謀殺案，一宗硫酸毀容報復案，一宗自殺案，還有數宗搶劫案。誰能想到一個如此美麗的小裝飾品，竟會是向絞刑架和大牢輸送罪犯的供應手段。我現在要把它鎖進我的保險櫃裏，並且給伯爵夫人寫封短箋，告訴她我們已尋獲這顆寶石。"

"你認為霍納這人無罪嗎？"

"這我還說不準。"

"那你認為另外那個人亨利·貝克跟這事有牽連嗎？"

"我認為亨利·貝克很可能絕對清白無辜。他決不會想到手裏那隻鵝，在價值上會比一隻用金鑄成的鵝還要貴重。我們那則啟事若有答覆，我就能用極其簡單的檢驗辦法來證明這一點。"

"在此之前，你就沒事可做了吧？"

"沒有了。"

"既然如此，那我繼續出診了。但我會在今晚你剛才說的時間回來，倒要看看這件錯綜複雜的事怎樣得到解決。"

"很樂意再見到你，華生。我七時吃晚飯，大概會有隻丘鷸。順便說一下，近來怪事頻繁出現，我也許該讓赫德森太太也檢查一下那隻丘鷸的嗉囊呢！"

有位患者耽誤了我一些時間，我又回到百加街時，已經過了六時半。我走近寓所，見到一個高大的男人，身穿一件鈕扣直扣到下巴底下的外衣，頭戴一頂蘇格蘭無邊軟帽，正等在屋外那片從梐窗裏射出來的半圓形亮光下。我來到門口，門正好打開，我們兩人便一起給引進福爾摩斯的房間。

"我猜您就是亨利‧貝克先生吧，"福爾摩斯一邊從扶手椅上站起來說，一邊立刻擺出一副和藹可親的神態迎接來客。"請坐在靠近壁爐那張椅上吧，貝克先生，今天晚上挺冷，我注意到您的血液循環系統適應夏季勝於冬季。哦，華生，你來得正是時候。貝克先生，這是您的帽吧？"

"是的，先生，是我的帽，沒錯。"

他是個身形高大，圓肩膀厚實，大頭，一張透着聰明樣子的寬臉，蓄着棕裏透灰的絡腮鬍子，前端尖尖翹起。鼻和兩頰略顯紅潤，手伸出時微微發抖。這些特徵使人不由得想起福爾摩斯對這人的推測。他那件黑禮服已經褪了色，鈕扣全都扣齊，領子豎起，瘦長的手腕從大衣袖口裏裸露出來，不見裏面有襯衣或襯袖。他說起話來慢慢的，斷斷續續，措詞嚴謹，總的來說給人留下一個時運不佳的文人學者印象。

"這兩樣東西在我們這兒保存好幾天了，"福爾摩斯說，"因為我們一直期待從尋物啟事上看到您的地址。我不明白您為甚麼沒登報呢？"

我們那位客人不好意思地笑笑。"我目前不像過去那麼富裕了，"他說。"我相信那夥襲擊我的流氓肯定把我的帽和鵝都搶走了。我也就不想徒勞無益地試圖再花錢找回它們了。"

"這倒也說得合情合理。順便說說，至於那隻鵝，我們不得不把它吃掉了。"

"吃掉了！"我們的來客不由得激動得從椅上欠起身來。

"是啊，我們若不那樣做，那隻鵝想必就會使誰都沒法享用了。不過，我認為那隻放在枱上的鵝跟您那隻在份量上差不多，也更新鮮，同樣會叫您滿意的。"

"哦，當然，當然！"貝克先生鬆口氣，答道。

"我們當然還保留了您那隻鵝的羽毛啦，爪啦，嗉囊啦甚麼的，所以您如果希望……"

那個人放聲哈哈大笑起來。"那些玩意倒是可以作為我這次遇險的紀念品，"他說，"除此之外，我看不出那隻鵝的支離碎片對我還有甚麼用處。先生，您如果允許的話，我還是把精力都放在我看到枱上那隻絕妙的肥鵝上吧。"

夏洛克·福爾摩斯機警地朝我瞥一眼，微微聳肩。

"那麼，您的帽和您的鵝在那兒，"他說。"順便問一聲，您能不能說說您是在哪兒弄到那隻鵝的？我對家禽飼養挺感興趣，很少見到再比您那隻養得更肥的鵝了。"

"當然可以，先生，"貝克站起來，把新拿的那隻鵝夾在腋下，說道，"我們有數個人常去博物館附近的阿爾法小酒店——因為我們白天都留在博物館裏，您明白嗎？今年我們那位好店主溫迪蓋特創辦了一個鵝俱樂部，考慮到我們每週向俱樂部交兩三個便士會費，便在聖誕節送給我們每人一隻鵝；我一向都是按時付錢，後來發生的事您都已知道了。我十分感謝您，先生，另外還請您多多原諒，因為我戴着這樣一頂蘇格蘭無邊軟帽既不適合我的年歲，也不適合我的身份。"他擺出一副令人可笑的自負神態，向我們兩人嚴肅地鞠一躬，就邁開大步走了出去。

"亨利·貝克先生的事到此就結束了，"福爾摩斯關上房門後說。"完全可以肯定他對這件事一無所知。華生，你餓了嗎？"

“不太餓。”

“那我建議我們乾脆把晚飯改為宵夜吧。我們現在該馬上順藤摸瓜，打鐵趁熱。”

“好，當然可以。”

這是一個寒冷的夜晚，所以我們穿上長大衣，頸項圍上厚圍巾。外面繁星點點，在無雲的空中閃爍着寒光。過往行人嘴裏吐出的呵氣猶如許多手槍射擊時的煙霧。我們的腳步發出清脆響亮的聲音，一路上我們經過倫敦民事律師公會、溫波爾街、哈利街，然後穿過威格莫爾街來到牛津大街。一刻鐘內我們便到達布盧姆斯伯里區內的阿爾法小酒館，它座落在通往霍爾伯恩區一條街的轉角處。福爾摩斯推開那家私營酒吧的門，向那位紅光滿面、繫着白圍裙的店老闆要兩杯啤酒。

“你的啤酒若能跟你的鵝一樣出色，就該是世間最好的啤酒了，”他說道。

“我的鵝？”店老闆似乎顯得有點驚訝。

“對，半小時前，我剛跟你們的鵝俱樂部那位亨利・貝克先生談過。”

“哦，我明白了。可是，先生，那些並不是我們養的鵝。”

“真的，那又是誰的呢？”

“哦，我是從科文特加登廣場一位推銷員那裏買了 24 隻。”

“真的，他們當中有些人我也認識。你是從哪位手中買來的？”

“他姓布雷肯里奇。”

“哦，我不認識他。好，老闆，祝你身體健康，生意興隆！再見。”

“我們現在去找布雷肯里奇先生，”我們兩人走出酒吧，外面天氣嚴寒，福爾摩斯扣上大衣鈕扣說。“記住，華生，我們這根鏈條儘管一端是一隻普普通通的鵝，另一端卻肯定是個會給判處七年勞役徒刑的人，除非我們能證明他無罪。可是我們的調查也可能證明他有罪。不管怎麼樣，反正我們抓到了一條被警方忽略了的調查線索；一定要趁這難得的機會追查下去，直到水落石出為止。現在我們往南快步前進！”

我們穿過霍爾伯恩區，轉入恩德爾街，接着又路過蜿蜒曲折的貧民區來到科文特加登廣場。一個較大攤位掛着布雷肯里奇的姓名招牌，檔主是個長着馬臉的男人，下巴削瘦，蓄着整齊的絡腮鬍子，正在幫助一個小員工收攤。

“晚安，今天晚上可真冷啊，”福爾摩斯說。

檔主點點頭，拿懷疑的目光打量一下我的同伴。

“看來你的鵝都賣光了，”福爾摩斯指着空蕩蕩的大理石櫃枱說。

“明天早晨，您要五百隻都會有貨。”

“不行，我現在就想要。”

“煤氣燈那邊的貨攤上還有數隻。”

“但別人介紹我到你這裏來買。”

“誰介紹的？”

“阿爾法酒吧老闆。”

“對，我給他送去了 24 隻。”

“那些鵝可真不錯。你是從哪兒進貨的？”

叫我大吃一驚的是，這一詢問竟使那位檔主勃然大怒。"哼，先生，"他揚起頭，雙手叉腰，說道，"你這是甚麼意思？有話就明說！"

"我說得夠明白了，很想知道你供給阿爾法酒吧的那些鵝是從誰哪裏進貨的？"

"但我不想告訴你，就這樣！"

"哦，那也沒甚麼關係，可我不明白你為何為這點小事大發脾氣？"

"大發脾氣！你要是也讓人這樣糾纏個沒完沒了，也會大發脾氣的。我花好價錢進好貨，這不就完了嗎？可你卻要問，'鵝哪兒去了？''你把鵝都賣給誰了？''你們這些鵝要賣多少錢？'你聽到別人對這些鵝這樣沒完沒了的嘮叨，也許還當牠們真是世間獨一無二的鵝了。"

"我可跟那些向你打聽的人都沒關係，"福爾摩斯漫不經心地說。"你若不肯告訴我，這個打賭也就算告吹了。就這樣吧。但我一向堅持我對家禽的判斷。我吃的那隻鵝是鄉下飼養的，為此願意下五鎊的賭注。"

"那你可就輸了你那五鎊，因為那隻鵝確實是城裏飼養的，"檔主斬釘截鐵地說。

"絕對不是。"

"我說就是。"

"我不信你的話。"

"你以為你對家禽的了解比我還強嗎？告訴你，我從小就做這一行了。不瞞你說，所有供應阿爾發酒吧那批鵝都是在城裏飼養的。”

“你別想説服我。”

“那你敢打賭嗎？”

“那只會叫你輸錢，因為我知道我是正確的。不過呢，我還是願意拿出一枚金幣跟你打這個賭，好教訓教訓你以後別再這樣固執己見。”

檔主格格冷笑兩三聲，説道：“比爾，拿賬本給我！”

一個男孩拿過來一個薄薄的小賬本和一個封面油膩膩的大賬本，把它們攤在吊燈下。

“好，過份自信先生，”檔主説，“剛才我還以為我的鵝都賣光了，可我在收攤前，你會發現我店裏還有一隻呢。看見這本小記事簿了嗎？”

“怎麽樣呢？”

“這是賣鵝給我的人名單。看見了嗎？嗯，這一頁上面是老鄉的，他們的姓名後面的數目字是總賬的頁碼，他們的賬都記在那個大本的總賬本上呢。好，你看見紅墨水寫的另一頁了嗎？這是一張城裏賣鵝給我的人名單。現在，你再看那第三個姓名，唸給我聽聽！”

“奧克肖特太太，布里克斯頓街 117 號，249 頁，”福爾摩斯唸道。

“不錯，現在再查看一下總賬本吧！”

福爾摩斯翻到指明的那一頁。“有了，‘奧克肖特太太，布里克斯頓街 117 號，雞蛋和家禽供應商。’”

“好，看看最後一筆賬是怎麽記的？”

"'12 月 22 日，24 隻鵝，每隻 7 先令 6 便士。'"

"不錯，再看看下面一行寫的甚麼？"

"'賣給阿爾法酒館溫迪蓋特先生，每隻 12 先令。'"

"你現在還有甚麼話可說？"

夏洛克・福爾摩斯顯出十分懊惱的樣子。他從衣袋裏掏出一個金鎊硬幣扔在大理石櫃枱上，帶着一種難以言傳的厭惡神情走開了。走出兩三步之後，他在路燈下面站住，用他那特有的默默高興的樣子微微發笑。

"你要是遇到一個留着那樣的絡腮鬍、衣袋裏揣着粉紅報的人，總可以用打賭的方式讓他吐露真情，"他說，"我敢說即使我拿出一百鎊放在他面前，那個人也不會像通過打賭那樣痛快地提供給我如此全面的情況。好了，華生，我想我們已經接近調查的尾聲。目前唯一要決定的是，我們今天晚上就去找奧克肖特太太呢，還是留待明天再去。聽那個陰陽怪氣的人的口吻，除了我們之外，明明還有別人也在急着了解這件事，那我該不該……"

他的說話聲突然被我們剛離開的那個攤位發出的一陣喧嘩聲打斷。我們回頭一看，只見一個獐頭鼠目的矮小男人，站在那盞搖搖晃晃的吊燈黃烘烘的光暈下，布雷肯里奇檔主擋在他的攤檔前，向那個畏畏縮縮的人狠狠地揮動拳頭。

"你和你的鵝真惹得我煩透了！"他喊道。"巴不得你們全見鬼去吧！你要是再胡言亂語糾纏我，我就放狗出來咬你。你去叫奧克肖特太太來，我會給她答覆，但這跟你又有甚麼關係？難道我的鵝是從你那兒買來的嗎？"

"不是，不過其中有一隻鵝是我的啊！"那個矮小男人唉聲嘆氣地說。

“那你找奧克肖特太太要去吧！”

“但她叫我來找你。”

“那你可以去找普魯士國王討要呢，我管不了。我已經聽夠了，給我滾開！”檔主惡狠狠地衝向前，那個問話人嚇得一溜煙跑掉，消失在黑暗裏。

“哈，這倒可以省得我們兩人去布里克斯頓街了，”福爾摩斯輕聲說，“快跟我來，我們看看從這個人身上可以查出點甚麼來。”我們便穿過那些在燈光照耀下，攤檔周圍閒逛三五成群的人。我的夥伴迅速趕上那個矮小男人，拍一下他的肩膀。那個人突然轉過身來，我在煤氣燈光下看得出他那張臉煞白得全無血色。

“你是誰？你要做甚麼？”他顫抖地問。

“對不起，”福爾摩斯和藹地說，“我剛才無意中聽見你跟那個檔主的對話。我想我倒能幫你點忙。”

“你？你是誰？這事你怎麼知道的？”

“我叫夏洛克·福爾摩斯。知道別人不知道的事是我份內事。”

“但你對這事又能知道些甚麼呢？”

“對不起，這事我全知道了。你是在急着尋找那數隻鵝，牠們是布里克斯頓街奧克肖特太太賣給布雷肯里奇檔主的，他又轉手賣給阿爾法酒館老闆溫迪蓋特，他呢，又把鵝轉到他的鵝俱樂部，而亨利·貝克是那個俱樂部的一名會員。”

“哎呀，老哥，您正是我想見到的人，”矮小男人哆哆嗦嗦地伸出雙手，大聲說道，“我簡直沒法向您解釋我對這事多麼感興趣！”

夏洛克・福爾摩斯叫住一輛路過的四輪馬車。“要是這樣的話，我們與其在這寒風颼颼的菜市場交談，倒不如找個舒適的房間聊聊，”他說。“不過，我們出發之前，請告尊姓大名。”

那個人猶豫了一下，答道：“我叫約翰・魯賓遜。”

“不，不，我問的是你的真實姓名，”福爾摩斯和藹地說，“用化名辦事，總是不太方便。”

那個陌生人蒼白的臉突然漲得通紅。“那好吧，”他說，“我的真名是詹姆士・賴德。”

“一點也不錯，大世界酒店的領班。請上車吧。我很快就會把你想知道的全部詳告。”

矮小男人站在那裏，來回打量我們兩人，眼神顯得又有點擔心又心存希望，一個人處於不知是凶是吉的境地時往往都會這樣。他上了馬車，我們在車上都沉默不語，那位新夥伴呼吸急促而微弱，兩手時而攥緊，時而放鬆，顯出他內心極度緊張。半小時後，我們回到了百加街，進入客廳。

“到家了！”我們魚貫走進屋，福爾摩斯歡欣地說。“在這樣糟糕的天氣裏，這爐火真叫人看得高興。賴德先生，你好像渾身挺冷似的，那就請坐在這張藤椅上吧。在解決你這件區區小事之前，讓我先換上拖鞋。好了，現在你是想知道那些鵝的情況吧？”

“是啊，老兄。”

“毋寧說是那一隻鵝吧。我料想你感興趣的那隻鵝是一隻白色的，尾巴上有一道黑斑。”

賴德激動得直發顫。“哦，老哥，”他喊道，“您能告訴我那隻鵝到哪兒去了嗎？"

"牠啊，來過這兒。"

"這兒？"

"對，確實是一隻曠古未聞的鵝。你對那隻鵝如此關懷，我一點也不感到奇怪。那隻鵝死後下了個蛋——人世間最美麗最明亮的小藍蛋。我把它珍藏在我的私人博物館裏了。"

我們那位客人搖搖晃晃地站起來，右手緊緊抓住壁爐台。福爾摩斯打開他的保險櫃，拿出那顆像寒星那樣光芒四射的藍寶石。賴德站在那裏，臉孔低垂，直瞪着那顆寶石，不知該認領呢，還是放棄好。

"玩的這齣把戲該結束了，賴德！"福爾摩斯平靜地說。"站穩些，賴德，要不然你就會跌進爐火裏去了。華生，扶他坐下！他還沒有足夠的膽量泰然自若地犯重罪。給他喝點白蘭地。好了，他看起來有點人的樣子了。他可真夠瘦小的，活像顆蝦米！"

那個人一時跌跌撞撞地差點摔倒，白蘭地使他的兩頰現出點血色；他又坐下來，驚恐不安地盯視着那譴責他的人。

"我差不多掌握了這事的各個環節，也有了可能需要的全部證據，因此也沒有甚麼太多的事需要你告訴我。不過，為了使這件案圓滿結束，還是要弄清楚一件事。賴德，莫卡伯爵夫人這顆藍寶石你聽說過嗎？"

"是凱瑟琳・古錫告訴我的！"他急促地輕聲答道。

"嗯，我明白，是伯爵夫人那位女僕。於是，如此唾手可得的大筆橫財對你的誘惑實在太大了，就跟那顆寶石以前引誘過比你本事更大的人一樣，可你使用的手法卻不太高明。在我看來，賴德，你這個人生性就是個很狡猾的大惡棍。你知道那個水管工人霍納曾經犯過類似的盜竊行為，因此懷疑便很容易落在他頭上。那你做了甚麼呢？你在夫人房間裏做了點手腳——聯同你的同黨古錫一起做的——你設法派霍納去夫人那個房間。然後，在他走後，你撬開那個首飾盒，緊接着就報警，說是發生了盜竊，警方便把那個不幸的人抓起來。隨後你……"

賴德突然撲通一聲跪倒在地毯上，抓住我朋友的雙膝。"看在上帝份上，饒了我吧！"他尖聲哀求道，"想想我的老爸！想想我的老媽！這會叫他們傷透了心的。我從沒做過壞事！我再也不敢了。我賭咒發誓。我可以把手按在聖經上發誓。噢，千萬別把我送上法庭！看在基督的份上，千萬別這樣！"

"坐回椅上去吧！"福爾摩斯嚴厲地說。"你現在倒知道畏畏縮縮地趴在地上求饒了，可你就沒想到那個可憐的霍納卻被誣告犯了一宗他根本不知情的罪名而受審。"

"我逃走，福爾摩斯先生。我逃離這個國家，先生。這樣一來，對霍納的控告就會給撤銷了。"

"哼！這個問題我們是要好好談談的。可現在先讓我聽聽這個把戲的第二幕真實情況。那顆寶石怎麼進了鵝的肚子，那隻鵝怎麼又到了菜市場？跟我說實話，這可是你能獲救的唯一希望了。"

賴德用舌頭舐舐他那乾裂的嘴唇。"我一定如實告訴您，"他說，"霍納被捕後，我覺得應該立刻帶着寶石逃走為妙，因為我不知道何時警方會想起搜查一下我和我的房間。可是酒店裏沒有一處安全的地方，我便假裝受人差遣出去辦事，跑到我姐姐家。

姐夫姓奧克肖特，住在布里克斯頓街，姐姐靠飼養家禽供應菜市場。一路上，我碰到的每一個人都像是警察或偵探，因此那天晚上儘管天氣十分寒冷，我到達布里克斯頓街時，已經汗流滿面。我姐姐問我發生了甚麼事，為何臉色那麼蒼白，但我只告訴她，酒店裏遺失寶石那件事弄得我心緒不靈。隨後我就到後院去抽煙斗，琢磨該怎麼辦才好。

"以前我有個叫莫茲利的朋友，他後來變壞墮落了，剛在潘頓威爾服刑期滿。有一天他碰到我，跟我談起偷竊的門徑，還有贓物怎樣脫手的辦法。我相信他不會出賣我，因為他有那麼一兩件犯法的事我一清二楚。我便決定到基爾伯恩他的住處去找他，把他當作知心人，透露這件事。他會教我怎樣把這顆寶石換成錢。但是，如何才能安全到達他那裏呢？我一想到從酒店來的一路上惶恐不安的痛苦心情，就感到也許隨時都會遭到逮捕和搜查，而那顆寶石就在我的馬甲衣袋裏。當時我正倚着牆，望着一群鵝在我腳下搖搖擺擺地走來走去。我突然心生一計，相信一定能瞞過世上最精明能幹的偵探。

"兩三個星期前，我姐姐跟我說過我可以挑一隻白鵝作為她送給我的聖誕節禮物，我知道我姐姐向來說話算數。我不如現在就拿走那隻鵝，把寶石藏在鵝的肚裏，帶到基爾伯恩去。後院裏有個小棚，我便從棚後面趕出一隻鵝，一隻大白鵝，尾巴上有一道黑斑。我抓住牠，張開牠的嘴，用手指頭盡力把寶石塞進牠的喉嚨，一直塞到手指能夠達到的地方。那隻鵝把寶石吞嚥下去了，我覺得寶石已經順着鵝的食道到了牠的嗉囊。可是那隻鵝拍打着翅膀拼命掙扎，我姐姐聞聲跑了出來，問我發生了甚麼事。

我轉身跟她說話那一剎那，那隻鵝從我手中掙脫，拍打着翅膀回到鵝群裏去了。

"'傑姆，你抓住那隻鵝在做甚麼？'她問道。

"'嗯，'我說，'你說過送我一隻過聖誕節，我在摸摸哪一隻最肥！'

"'我們早把準備送給你的那隻留在一邊了，我們叫牠"傑姆的鵝"，就是那邊那隻大白鵝。我們一共有 26 隻鵝，一隻送給你，一隻留給自己，24 隻要送到市場上去。'

"'謝謝你，麥琪，'我說，'如果對你來說都是一樣的話，我還是想要我剛才抓住的那隻鵝。'

"'留給你的那隻足有三磅重呢，'她說，'我們特意為你餵肥的。'

"'沒關係，我就要我抓的那隻。我打算現在就拿走牠，'我說。

"'噢，那就隨便吧，'她有點生氣地說，'你要的是哪一隻啊？'

"'那隻尾巴上有一道黑斑的白鵝，就在那群鵝裏面。'

"'那好吧，你去把牠宰了帶走吧。'

"於是我就照她說的做了，福爾摩斯先生，我隨即就把那隻鵝帶到基爾伯恩。我把我做的事都跟我那個夥伴說了，因為他是一個可以推心置腹相告這類事的人。他笑得喘不過氣來，我們就拿刀把鵝開了膛。可我一下子透心涼了，因為鵝肚裏根本沒有那顆寶石。我明白這一定是出了極糟糕的錯。我丟下鵝，急忙奔回我姐姐家，匆匆走進後院，可是那裏一隻鵝也沒有了。

"'麥琪，那些鵝哪兒去了？'我喊道。

"'已經送到經銷商那裏去了。'

"'哪一家？'

"'科文特加登廣場的布雷肯里奇。'

"'有沒有尾巴上有道黑斑的那隻？'我問道。'跟我挑的那隻一樣。'

"'有啊，傑姆，我養了兩隻尾巴上有道黑斑的鵝，連我都分不清哪隻是哪隻。'

"我當然明白這是怎麼一回事了，便盡快跑到布雷肯里奇檔主那裏，可他早就把那批鵝統統賣掉了，他說甚麼也不肯告訴我鵝究竟給賣到哪兒去了。兩位今天晚上也都聽到了。唉，他一直就那樣回答我。我姐姐認為我瘋了，我自己有時也這麼認為。可現在——我已經是一個帶有標記的竊賊，卻從來沒得到為此出賣自己人格的財富。上帝寬恕我吧！上帝寬恕我吧！"他雙手捂着臉，放聲大哭起來。

房間裏久久陷入寂靜，只能聽到賴德呼呼的喘氣聲和夏洛克·福爾摩斯的手指尖頗有節奏地叩打桌邊的聲音。隨後，我的朋友突然站起來，把門打開。

"滾出去！"他喊道。

"甚麼，先生！噢，上帝保佑您！"

"少廢話，快滾！"

無需再多說甚麼了。只聽見樓梯上一陣噔噔的腳步聲，接着是砰的一聲關門聲。隨即從街上傳來一陣爽快的奔跑聲。

"華生，"福爾摩斯一邊說，一邊伸手去拿他那個陶土製的煙斗。"我畢竟沒受警方聘用，也就沒必要非向他們提供他們不知道的案情不可了。霍納如果現在處於危險境地，那當然另當別論了。不過看來這個人不會再出庭作偽證控告他了，這件案也就會不了了之。我認為我這樣減輕了一項重罪，無非是在挽救一個人。這人從此不會再做壞事，他已經給嚇得魂飛魄散。現在若把他送進大牢，那他就會成為一名終身監禁的罪犯。再說，目前正是寬恕人的聖誕季節，我們何樂而不為呢。純屬偶然的機會使我們碰上了這個最為奇特的古怪問題，這樣解決也算是它本身應得的回報了。醫生，麻煩拉一下鈴，我們開始調查另一宗案吧，其中主要的特點還是一隻動物。"

6.

斑繩案

近八年來，我陸續記錄了我的好友夏洛克・福爾摩斯經辦的七十多宗案件，研究了他的破案方法；我粗略翻閱一遍這些案例記錄，發現其中悲劇性案例居多，也有一些是喜劇性的，絕大部份僅是離奇古怪而已，卻沒有一例是平淡無奇的，這是因為他工作與其說是為了獲得酬金，還不如說是出於對他那一行調查本領的愛好。他拒絕接辦任何調查起來，毫不離奇甚至毫不怪誕的案件。在這些形形色色的案件中，我記得有一件案更具異乎尋常的特色，那就是薩里郡斯托克・莫蘭鎮著名的羅伊洛特家族那宗案件。這事發生在我跟福爾摩斯交往的早期。當時我們兩人都是單身漢，在百加街合租一套寓所。我原本早就可以把這事記錄下來，可我當時做出了保守秘密的許諾，直到上個月我給予保證的那位女士不幸過早去世，這項約束才算解除。現在，這事也許該公諸於世了，因為我確實知道外界對格里姆斯比・羅伊洛特醫生的死因眾説紛紜，廣泛流傳的種種謠言使那件事變得比真實情況更加駭人聽聞。

事件發生在 1883 年 4 月初。一天清晨，我一覺醒來，發現夏洛克・福爾摩斯衣着整齊地站在我的牀邊。他通常是個愛睡懶覺的人，壁爐架上的時鐘顯示剛剛七時一刻。我有點詫異地朝他眨眨眼，也許還有點不大高興，因為我的生活習慣一向很有規律。

"真對不起，華生，叫醒了你，"他説，"今天一大早我們的命運都一樣，先是赫德森太太被敲門聲吵醒，她作為報復喚醒我，現在我又來叫醒老兄。"

"發生了甚麼事？起火了嗎？"

"沒有。來了一位委託人，像是一位年輕女郎，情緒相當激動，堅持非要見我不可。她目前正在客廳裏等着呢。年輕小姐如果大清早這個時間徘徊在城市街頭，又叫醒睡得香甜的人，我想她必定有十分緊急的事要找人商量。如果這是件挺有趣的案件，我確信你一定從一開始就願意關注，因此我考慮無論如何也要叫醒你，免得你失去這個機會。"

"老朋友，我當然不願意失去這個好機會。"

我平生最大的樂趣就是跟隨福爾摩斯進行專業調查工作，欣賞他迅速作出的推論，那種推論都是憑直覺快速作出來的，卻又一向基於邏輯。就這樣他一一解決了那些委託給他的疑難問題。我連忙穿上衣服，數分鐘後便準備就緒陪同我的朋友進入客廳。一位身穿黑衣服、戴着厚面紗的女郎剛才一直坐在窗前，一見我們進來，便站起來。

"早安，小姐，"福爾摩斯愉快地説。"我叫夏洛克・福爾摩斯，這位是我的好友兼同事華生醫生，你在他面前跟我談話，無需顧慮。我很高興赫德森太太想得很周到，已經把壁爐點着了。請靠近些火，我會叫人給你端來一杯熱咖啡，因為我注意到你渾身在發抖。"

"不是冷得發抖，"那位小姐低聲說，按照福爾摩斯的要求換了個座位。

"那又是為甚麼？"

"是因為恐懼，福爾摩斯先生，因為恐懼！"她一邊說，一邊揭開面紗，我們看得出她確實處於焦慮不安、讓人憐憫的狀態。她臉色灰白，十分憔悴，兩眼流露出被追逐的動物那種驚惶失措的神情。相貌和身材像 30 歲女人的模樣，可頭髮卻過早夾雜着數縷銀絲，表情萎靡不振。夏洛克・福爾摩斯迅速上下打量她一下。

"不必害怕，"他彎身拍拍她的前臂，撫慰道，"我們很快就會把事情處理好，這我可以保證。你是今天早晨乘火車來的吧？"

"這麼說，您認識我？"

"不認識，我注意到你右手手套裏露出半截回程票。你想必很早就動身了，到達火車站之前，還乘坐一輛雙輪輕便馬車在泥濘道路上趕過一段路程吧？"

那位女郎大吃一驚，目瞪口呆地望着我的夥伴。

"這並不神秘，親愛的小姐，"他微笑着說。"你的外衣左袖上有好幾處濺了泥。泥點都是新濺上去的，只有雙輪輕便馬車駛過泥濘道路才會這樣，而且你是坐在馬車夫左邊，才會濺到泥。"

"不管您是怎麼推理的，說得都對極了。"她說，"我今天早晨六時前就出門了，六時二十到達萊瑟海德，趕上了開往滑鐵盧的第一班火車。先生，我再也受不了這種緊張壓力，照這樣下去，我就會發瘋了。我求助無門——沒有真能幫助的人，除了一個真正關懷我的人，可是他，可憐的人，也沒有一點辦法。我聽說過您，福爾摩斯先生，我是從法林托希太太那裏聽說的，您曾經在她最需要幫助的時候援助過她。我是從她那兒打聽到您的地址的。噢，先生，您不認為也能幫助我，至少在那圍繞我的黑暗中，給我指出一線光明嗎？目前我不能酬謝您對我的幫助，不過一兩個月內我就會結婚，便可以控制自己的收入；那時候您至少會發現我不是個忘恩負義的人。"

福爾摩斯轉身走向他的書桌，打開抽屜上的鎖，取出一個案例小記事本，查閱一下。

"法林托希太太，"他說，"哦，是啊，我記起那宗案了，那是涉及乳白寶石冕狀頭飾的案件。華生，你那時大概還沒來呢。小姐，我只能說我願意像當初為你的朋友效勞那樣，也為你這事盡點力。至於酬勞呢，工作就是我的酬勞，以後你甚麼時候覺得合適，可以隨便支付我可能在調查這件事情上的費用。那現在就請把情況都告訴我們吧，好讓我們對這事有個判斷。"

"唉！"我們的來客答道，"我的處境可怕之處，在於我的恐懼十分模糊不清，心中猜疑的事在別人眼中，全像是微不足道的瑣碎小事。就連我那個最親近而且能夠給予幫助和指點的人，也把我告訴他的事看成是神經質女人的胡思亂想。他倒沒這樣說，可是我能從他安撫的話語和迴避的眼神中察覺出來。福爾摩斯先生，我聽說您能洞察人心裏的種種邪惡。請您告訴我，我在這危機四伏的情況下該怎麼辦？」

「我在認真聽着呢，小姐。」

「我叫海倫·斯托納，跟繼父住在一起。他是薩里郡西邊斯托克·莫蘭鎮的羅伊洛特家族最後一位倖存者，這個家族是英國最古老的撒克遜家族之一。」

福爾摩斯點點頭，說道：「這個姓氏我挺熟悉。」

「這個家族一度是英國最富有的家庭，土地佔地較廣，超出了本郡邊界，北至伯克郡，西至漢普郡。可是到了上世紀，由於四代子嗣都是生活放蕩、揮霍無度之輩，到了攝政時期，家業終於讓一個賭棍徹底敗掉，除了兩三畝地和那棟二百年歷史的古老宅邸外，都已蕩然無存，就連那座宅邸也已典押得差不多了。最後一位老爺在那裏過着落魄貴族貧困可悲的生活。但是，我的繼父就是這位老爺的獨生子，他意識到自己要適應新的處境，便從一個親戚那裏借到了一筆錢，這使他得到了一個醫學學位，隨後他便到加爾各答行醫，在那裏憑藉他醫術高明和堅強性格，業務十分發達。但是後來由於家裏不斷被盜，他在盛怒之下把那個印度管家毆打致死，差點給判處死刑，結果遭到了長期監禁。後來，他返回英國，變成了一個性格暴躁、失意潦倒的人。

「羅伊洛特醫生在印度時跟我母親結了婚，我母親當時是孟加拉炮兵司令斯托納少將的遺孀。我和我的姐姐茱莉婭是雙胞胎，母親再婚時，我們兩人才兩歲。母親相當有錢，每年不少於一千鎊收入。我們跟羅伊洛特醫生住在一起時，母親就立下遺囑，把全部財產遺贈給他，但是附加了一個條件，那就是我們姐妹兩人日後如果結婚，每年要撥給我們兩人一定數目的金錢。我們回到英國後不久，母親便不幸去世了——她是八年前在克魯附近一次火車事故中喪生的。母親去世後，羅伊洛特先生便放棄了在倫敦重新開業的意圖，帶我們一起回到斯托克·莫蘭鎮故居生活。母親遺留下的錢足夠支付我們的一切開銷，看來我們的幸福似乎毫無障礙。

"在這段時間裏，繼父的變化非常之大。我們的鄰居起初看到斯托克·莫蘭鎮的老宅中，又住了一位羅伊洛特家族的後裔都十分高興。可是他卻跟鄰居互不來往，整天留在自己的住房裏，深居簡出；不管碰到甚麼人，他都跟對方窮兇極惡地爭吵。這種近乎瘋狂的暴躁脾氣在這個家族的男人當中有遺傳性，我想他長期旅居在熱帶地區，更加重了他這種脾氣。一連串使人丟臉的爭吵接連發生，其中兩次是在治安法庭上結束的。結果他變了村鎮裏人人望而生畏的人，人們一見到他，無不敬而遠之，趕緊躲開，因為他是個力大無窮的壯漢，又有一個根本無法控制的暴戾脾氣。

"上星期，他把當地的鐵匠扔出橋邊上的矮檔牆，掉進河裏，最終還是由我賠償了我能湊到的一筆錢，才避免了另一件社會醜聞。他除了跟那些流浪的吉卜賽人來往之外，一個朋友也沒有。他跟那班吉卜賽人相處得非常融洽，允許他們在他那數畝象徵着家族產業、荊棘叢生的土地上紮營居住，他會到那些帳篷裏去作客，有時還跟他們一起出外流浪數週。他還特別寵愛一名記者送給他的印度動物，他現在養着一頭印度獵豹和一隻狒狒作為他的寵物，這兩隻動物在他的土地上自由地跑來跑去，村裏人就像害怕牠們的主人那樣怕牠們。

"您們通過我的敘述，不難想像我們姐妹兩人過着多麼不愉快的日子。家中沒有一個僕人做得久，我們兩人已經很長時間擔負起一切家務。我姐姐死時才 30 歲，可她跟我一樣早已有了白髮。"

"這麼說，你姐姐已經去世了？"

"她是兩年前去世的，我想跟您談的就是姐姐死亡的事。您能明白我剛才說的那種生活狀況，我們姐妹兩人幾乎見不到任何跟我們同年齡、同地位的人。幸虧我們有個姨媽——霍諾麗婭·韋斯法爾小姐，是我母親的姐姐，終生未嫁，住在哈羅市附近。我們只是偶爾允許去探望她。茱莉婭兩年前到她家去過聖誕節，遇到一位領半薪的海軍陸戰隊少校，跟他訂了婚。我姐姐回來後，繼父聽說了她的訂婚事，並沒表示反對；但是在預訂婚禮日子的前半個月發生了一件可怕的事，奪走了我唯一的同伴。"

夏洛克·福爾摩斯一直仰靠在椅背上，閉着兩眼，頭沉陷在一個軟墊裏，這時候他半睜開眼，瞥一下他的客人。

"請把細節說清楚一點。"他說。

"這太容易了，因為那段時期發生的每件事我都記憶猶新。我剛才說過宅邸很古老，如今只有一側住人。那側的臥室都在一樓，客廳在樓房中間。三間臥室連接在一起，第一間是羅伊洛特先生的，第二間是我姐姐的，第三間是我自己的。三間房間互不相通，房門都朝向一條共同通道。我說清楚了嗎？"

"挺清楚。"

"三個房間的窗戶都朝向外面的一塊草坪。發生命案那天晚上，羅伊洛特醫生很早就回自己的房間去了，可是我們知道他並沒睡覺，因為我姐姐被他習慣抽的那種印度雪茄濃烈的煙味燻得不太舒服。她就離開自己的房間，到我的房間坐一會，談起她即將舉行的婚禮。11時，她回自己的房間，走到門口時，她回過身來。

"'告訴我，海倫，'她說，'你在深夜聽見過有人吹口哨嗎？'

"'從來沒聽過，'我答道。

"'我想你睡覺時不可能吹口哨吧？'

"'當然不會，怎麼了？'

"'因為最近數天深夜裏，我總在三時左右聽到清晰、輕輕的口哨聲。我是睡不沉的人，那聲音就把我吵醒了。我弄不清那聲音是從哪兒來的——可能是來自隔壁房間，也可能是從草坪那邊傳過來的。我當時就該問問你是不是也聽見了。'

"'沒有，我沒聽見過。想必是那些在種植園裏可憐的吉卜賽人弄出的聲音吧。'

"'很可能是。可是如果是從草坪那邊傳來的，我奇怪你怎麼會沒聽見呢。'

"'哦，我睡得比你沉吧。'

"'好了，反正也沒多大關係，'她朝我笑笑，關上我的房門；沒多久，我聽到她的鑰匙在門鎖裏轉動的聲音。"

"真的，"福爾摩斯說，"晚上睡覺前鎖上門，這是不是你們一貫的習慣？"

"一向如此。"

"為甚麼？"

"我想我剛才說過了，醫生養了一頭印度獵豹和一隻狒狒。不鎖上門，我們感到不安呢。"

"倒也是。請接着説。"

"那天夜晚我睡不着，有一種模模糊糊的不祥預感。要知道，我們姐妹兩人是雙胞胎，我們之間的連繫多麼微妙。那天夜裏，狂風呼嘯，雨點劈劈啪啪打在窗上。在那嘈雜的風雨聲中，突然傳來一聲女人的驚恐狂叫。我聽出那是我姐姐的叫聲，就從牀上跳起來，披上一塊披肩，衝向走廊。我打開房門時，好像聽到一聲姐姐形容過的那種口哨，緊接着又聽到像是一堆金屬落下來的哐一聲。我沿着通道跑過去，姐姐的房門已經打開鎖，正在慢慢開啟呢。我驚恐地注視着那扇門，不知會從裏面走甚麼出來。借着走廊上的燈光，我看見姐姐出現在房門口，她那張臉蒼白如紙，滿佈恐懼的神情，雙手向前摸索着尋求援救，整個身體就像醉漢那樣搖晃。我急忙跑上前去，雙手摟住她，可她彷彿渾身無力，一下子跌倒在地。就像一個感受劇痛的人那樣，她在地上翻滾扭動，四肢可怕地抽搐。起初我以為她沒認出我，可我俯身要扶她起來時，她突然發出一陣我這一輩子也忘不了的淒厲喊聲：'噢，天哪！海倫，是一條繩！一條斑點繩！'她似乎還想説些甚麼，把手舉起來，指向醫生那個房間，可又一陣抽搐使她説不出話來了。我奔跑出去，大聲喊我的繼父；我看見他穿着睡袍正急忙從他的房間那邊趕過來。他趕到我姐姐身邊時，姐姐已經不省人事。儘管繼父給她灌了白蘭地，又派人到鎮上請來了醫生，可是一切努力都無濟於事，因為姐姐已經奄奄一息，嚥氣之前沒再甦醒過來。這就是我那親愛的姐姐悲慘的結局。"

"等一下，"福爾摩斯説，"你敢肯定聽到了口哨聲和金屬撞擊聲嗎？能發誓保證嗎？"

"本郡驗屍官在調查時也這樣問過我。我明明聽見了，很深印象，可是那天夜裏狂風暴雨，還有舊屋吱吱嘎嘎的響聲，我也有可能聽錯。"

"你姐姐當時還穿着白天穿的衣服嗎？"

"她已經換上了睡衣。右手有根燃過的火柴棍，左手握着一個火柴盒。"

"這說明出事時，她劃過火柴，向四周看過。這點很重要。驗屍官得出了甚麼結論？"

"他挺仔細地調查了這宗案，因為羅伊洛特醫生的品行，早已在郡裏臭名遠播，可是他還是沒能找出任何能説服人的致死原因。我做了證明，房門是從裏面上了鎖，窗戶都由帶有寬鐵柵的老式百葉窗護着，每天夜裏都關得密實。四面牆仔細敲過，都很牢固，地板也徹底檢查過，結果一樣。煙囱雖然挺寬，卻已用四個 U 形大馬釘攔住，從上面下不來人。因此，可以肯定我姐姐死時，房間裏只有她一個人。再説，她身上沒有留下任何暴力痕跡。"

"會不會是中了毒？"

"醫生為此做了檢驗，卻未能查出來。"

"那你認為你那不幸的姐姐是怎麼死的呢？"

"我認為她純粹是由於恐懼，神經受到震驚而死的，可是究竟是甚麼把她嚇得那樣，我卻不能想像。"

"當時種植園裏有吉卜賽人嗎？"

"有，那裏幾乎總有些吉卜賽人。"

"另外，她提到了繩——斑點繩，你推斷出那是甚麼意思嗎？"

"我有時想那只是一時神志不清的胡言亂語，有時又覺得她指的是一群人[11]，也許就是種植園裏那些吉卜賽人。他們有很多人頭上裹着斑點頭巾，我弄不明白她使用了這個怪形容詞，有沒有可能指的是這個。"

福爾摩斯搖搖頭，好像不滿意這個説法。

"問題很複雜，"他説，"請繼續説下去。"

"從那以後，兩年過去了，直到最近，我感到比以往越發孤單寂寞。一個月前，我認識多年的一個好朋友向我求婚。他叫阿米蒂奇——珀西·阿米蒂奇，是雷丁市近郊克蘭·沃特鎮上阿米蒂奇先生的二兒子。繼父對這件婚事沒表示不同意，我們便決定春季結婚。兩天前，我們的舊宅西側要修繕一下，我那間臥室的牆已經給打穿，因此我不得不搬到姐姐死在裏面的那間臥室去住，睡在她睡過的那張牀上。您倒想想看，昨天夜裏，我躺在她的牀上根本睡不着，回憶起她那可怕的遭遇，忽然在那寂靜的黑夜裏，聽到那曾經預告姐姐死亡來臨的輕輕口哨聲，不禁毛骨悚然。我跳起來，點亮燈，卻在房間裏甚麼也沒發現，我嚇得渾身哆嗦，不敢再上牀睡覺，於是就穿上衣服；天一亮，我便悄悄出門，在對面皇冠酒店租輛輕便馬車去萊瑟海德，今天清晨從那裏來到您這兒，拜訪的目的是想聽聽您的意見。"

"你這樣做很明智，"我的朋友説。"可你是否全都説給我聽了？"

"全都説了。"

"斯托納小姐，你沒有。你在袒護你的繼父呢。"

"呃，您這是甚麼意思？"

作為回答，福爾摩斯把來客放在膝上那隻手的黑花邊袖口褶邊滑上去，那白皙的手腕上露出五個青腫印，那是四個手指頭和大拇指的壓痕。

"你受過虐待，"福爾摩斯説。

那位女士一下子漲紅了臉，立刻捂住手腕，説："他是個壯老漢，也許不知道自己的力氣有多大。"

一陣長時間的沉默，福爾摩斯托着腮，凝視着壁爐裏劈啪作響的火焰。

"這事並不簡單，"他最後開口道，"在決定採取甚麼行動之前，我還需要了解更多細節。可是時間緊迫，我們如果今天就去斯托克‧莫蘭鎮，有沒有可能讓我們查看一下那三個房間而又不讓你繼父知曉？"

"巧得很，繼父説他今天要進城辦數件非常重要的事。今天一整天他都很可能不在家，這就對你們不會有甚麼干擾。我們家現在有個女管家，年紀大了，有點糊塗，我很容易就能叫她出去。"

"太好了，華生，你不反對走一趟吧？"

"決不反對。"

"那我們兩人都去。小姐，你還有甚麼事要辦嗎？"

"我既然已在城裏，倒真有一兩件事想去辦。可是我會乘 12 時那班火車回去，好在那邊及時迎接兩位。"

"我們一過中午就到。我本人也有點零碎事要去辦。你不在這兒吃點早餐嗎？"

"不了，我要走了。我把自己的煩惱告訴您兩位之後，心情好多了。我下午等着你們。"她拉下厚厚的面紗，就悄悄走出房間。

"華生，你認為這究竟是怎麼一回事？"福爾摩斯靠在椅背上問道。

"在我看來，這是一件十分陰險毒辣的事。"

"夠陰險毒辣的。"

"如果那位小姐說地板和牆都挺堅固，門窗和煙囪又鑽不進人，那她姐姐神秘死亡時，想必是獨自一人在房裏。"

"那麼，半夜哨聲是怎麼一回事呢？還有那個女子臨死前說的話又是甚麼意思？"

"這我倒也想不出來。"

"半夜哨聲啦，那群跟老醫生關係密切的吉卜賽人的存在啦，我們有理由相信那位老醫生存心阻止繼女的婚姻啦，女子臨死前提到的繩啦，最後還有海倫・斯托納小姐聽見哐一下的金屬撞擊聲，很可能是扣緊百葉窗的鐵條跌落原位，你把這些情況聯繫起來，我想就有充份理由相信我們沿着這些線索便可解開這個謎。"

"可是那些吉卜賽人當時做了些甚麼呢？"

"這我也不能想像。"

"我倒覺得這樣的推論存有不少漏洞。"

"我也有這種感覺。這正是我們要去斯托克・莫蘭鎮的理由。我想看看這些漏洞是否無法彌補呢，還是通過解釋可以給消除。真見鬼！"

我的夥伴這一聲叫喊，是因為我們的房門突然給撞開，一個彪形大漢堵在房門口。他那身裝束古古怪怪，使他既像個專業人員又像個農夫。他頭戴一頂黑色大禮帽，上身穿一件長燕尾服，腳穿着一雙帶綁腿的高筒靴，手上揮動着一根獵鞭。這人很高，帽擦到了門框上的橫樑，魁梧的身體幾乎堵住了門。那張寬臉曬得焦黑，滿佈皺紋，神情邪惡，兩隻兇光逼人的凹陷眼睛朝我們兩人來回怒視，再加上那細高的鷹鼻，使他活像像一頭老朽兇殘的猛禽。

"你們兩人誰是福爾摩斯？"那個鬼怪似的人問道。

"我就是，先生，不知您是哪位？"我的朋友平靜地說。

"我是格里姆斯比·羅伊洛特醫生，住在斯托克·莫蘭。"

"幸會，請坐！"福爾摩斯和藹地說。

"少跟我來這一套！我的繼女剛才來過你這兒。我一直在跟蹤她。她跟你說了甚麼？"

"今年這個季節還真有點冷啊，"福爾摩斯說。

"我問你她跟你說了甚麼？"那個老伯伯狂怒地喊道。

"可是我聽說番紅花會開得很好。"我的朋友繼續泰然自若地說。

"哼！你這是想敷衍我嗎？"來客揮舞起手中那根鞭子，向前邁一步說。"我知道你，你這個無賴！我早就聽說過你，你就是專愛搬弄是非的福爾摩斯！"

我的朋友微微一笑。

"你就是愛管閒事的福爾摩斯！"

我的朋友更加笑容可掬。

"你就是倫敦警局自命不凡的福爾摩斯！"

福爾摩斯格格笑出聲來。"你說的倒挺有趣，"他說，"請你出去，關好門，因為有股對流風。"

"我要把話説完才走。你要是膽敢管我的閒事，那我可對你不客氣！我知道斯托納小姐來過這兒——我一直在跟蹤她！我可不是好惹的！看這個！"他向前急走兩三步，奪起火鉗，用他那兩隻褐色大手把它拗彎了。"小心別讓我逮住你！"他咆哮道，把那根彎曲的火鉗摜在壁爐旁，大步走出房間。

"他倒挺和藹可親啊！"福爾摩斯笑着說。"我沒有他的魁梧體型，可是他若多留一會，我倒可以讓他看看，論手力我並不比他差。"他一邊説，一邊拿起那根火鉗，突然一用力，把火鉗又拗直了。

"真沒想到他居然如此無禮地把我混淆成官府偵探！這倒給我們的調查工作增添了興致；我只望我們那個小朋友別粗心大意，讓這個畜生跟蹤，吃到甚麼苦頭。華生，我們兩人現在吃早餐，然後我要去醫師學會，希望能從那裏弄到一些有助於我們調查這事的材料。"

福爾摩斯從醫師學會回來已經快午後一時了。他拿着一張藍紙，上面潦草地寫着一些筆記和數字。

"我查到了他那位已故妻子的遺囑，"他説，"為了弄清遺囑的確切意義，我不得不計算出有關投資目前的價值。那筆投資在那位女士去世時的每年進項，略低於一千鎊，可是現在由於農產品價格下跌，則不超過 750 鎊了。兩個女兒結婚時可以各拿 250 鎊，顯然兩個女兒若都結了婚，那個怪人的收入就少得可憐了。即使是一位小姐結了婚，那也會嚴重削弱他的財源。我今天上午做的沒白費，證實他確實有阻止兩個女子結婚的強烈動機。華生，現在情況十分緊急，尤其是那個老伯伯已經意識到我們要干預此事，所以你如果已經準備好，我們就租輛馬車去滑鐵盧車站。你最好帶上你那支左輪手槍。對付一位能把火鉗拗彎的先生，一支埃利二號手槍是解決爭端的最好工具了。那把槍再加上牙刷，大概就是我們需要帶的東西了。”

在滑鐵盧，我們正巧趕上一班開往萊瑟海德的火車，從那裏我們租了一輛雙輪輕便馬車，沿着可愛的薩里郡小道行駛了四、五里路。那天陽光明媚，空中飄浮着數朵白雲，樹木和路邊的樹籬剛剛綻出嫩綠的新枝。空氣中散發着令人心曠神怡的濕潤泥土氣息。就我來說，我至少覺得眼前春意盎然的景色，跟我們要去做的險惡調查形成奇特反差。我的夥伴坐在馬車前部，交叉着雙臂，帽子拉低遮住兩眼，下巴垂在胸前，顯然深深陷入了沉思。可是他忽然抬起頭來，拍拍我的肩膀，指着前方草地。

“看那邊！”他說。

那是一片樹木茂盛的園地，沿着平緩的斜坡向上延伸，在頂點形成一片密林。樹叢中矗立着一棟十分古老的宅邸，灰色山牆和高高的屋頂隱約可見。

“斯托克·莫蘭鎮吧？”他問道。

“是的，先生。格里姆斯比·羅伊洛特醫生的宅邸就在那邊，”馬車夫說。

“那邊有些房屋在進行修繕呢，”福爾摩斯說，“我們就是要去那裏。”

“村落在那邊，”馬車夫指着左邊遠處的一些屋頂，說，“你們如果想去羅伊洛特醫生家，順着這條路去更近；越過籬牆邊上的階梯，沿着地裏小道走過去就到了。看，那位小姐正在那條小道上走着呢。"

"我猜那位小姐就是斯托納小姐吧，"福爾摩斯把手遮在兩眼上方，說道，"好，我們就接受你的建議。"

我們下了車，付了車錢，馬車便嘎嘎地返回萊瑟海德。

我們登上籬牆邊上的階梯時，福爾摩斯說："我覺得讓那個人把我們兩人當作來這兒的建築師或是辦其他事的人也好，免得他四處散播流言蜚語。午安，斯托納小姐，你看我們說話算數吧。"

那位清早來過的委託人急忙跑過來迎接我們，臉上流露出高興的神情。"我一直焦急地等着你們到來，"她一邊跟我們熱情握手，一邊說。"一切順利。羅伊洛特醫生進城去了，傍晚之前不會回來。"

"我們已經榮幸地認識了醫生，"福爾摩斯三言兩語地說了說早上發生的事。斯托納小姐聽着聽着，整個臉連嘴唇都變得煞白。

"我的天！"她驚呼道，"這麼說，他一直在跟蹤我！"

"看來是這樣的。"

"他狡猾得真是叫我完全不知道甚麼時候不受他的威脅。他回來後會說甚麼呢？"

"他必定會設法保護自己。因為他可能發現有個比他更狡猾的人在監視他。今天夜裏你要提防他，把房門鎖上。他如果動粗，我們就把你送到哈羅市你姨媽的家裏去。現在我們要抓緊時間，請立刻帶我們去那數間要檢查的房間。"

這棟宅邸是灰石磚砌成的，石壁上佈滿了青苔，中央部份高高聳起，兩側是呈弧形的廂房，就像一對蟹鉗那樣向兩邊延伸。一側的房屋窗戶都已破碎，釘着木條，房頂也有部份塌陷，真是一幅破敗景象！屋中央部份稍微做了些修繕，右邊那排屋則比較新式。窗戶上有窗簾，煙囪冒出青煙，說明這邊是這家人居住之處。牆盡端那邊架了些棚架，石牆上有數處給鑿通了，可是我們去的時候卻沒見到工人的蹤影。福爾摩斯在那片馬馬虎虎修剪過的草坪上慢慢踱步，仔細檢查數扇窗戶的外部。

"我料想這間是你過去睡的那間臥室吧，中間是你姐姐那間，緊挨着主樓那間是羅伊洛特醫生的臥房吧？"

"正是。可是現在我睡在當中那間房裏。"

"我理解是因為房屋在修繕吧。順便說說，我注意到盡端那邊的牆，似乎沒必要急需修繕啊。"

"根本沒必要，我認為那只是讓我遷出自己那間房的藉口罷了。"

"啊！這倒是個想法。嗯，這狹窄的一側另一邊有條通道，三個房間的房門都朝向它，那裏面當然有窗戶吧。"

"有，不過窄小得很，連人都鑽不進去。"

"你們兩人夜裏睡覺時都鎖上門，不可能有人從那邊進入你們的房間。現在請你回到你的房間裏去，並且閂上百葉窗。"

斯托納小姐照吩咐做了。福爾摩斯認真檢查那扇敞着的窗戶，隨後想方設法打開百葉窗，卻怎麼也辦不到，就連插一把刀的裂縫都沒有。接着他又用放大鏡檢查鉸鏈，可是那鐵製的鉸鏈牢牢嵌入堅硬石牆。"嗯，"他有點困惑不解地搔着下巴，說，"我的推論肯定有些地方出了差錯，這扇百葉窗一旦閂上，就沒人能夠鑽進去。好吧，我們進屋看看有沒有甚麼可以說明問題的線索。"

一扇小旁門通向牆刷得雪白的通道。三間臥室的門都朝着這條通道。福爾摩斯不想檢查第三間臥室，我們便徑直走到第二間，這是斯托納小姐現在睡的那間臥室，也就是她那不幸的姐姐死在裏面的那一間。那是一間簡樸的小屋，天花板低，有一個開口式壁爐，完全按照鄉鎮舊式宅邸的樣式蓋的。房內一隅立着一個棕色大櫃，另一隅放着一張窄牀，牀上罩着白牀單，窗戶左側有個梳粧台，另有兩張藤椅，室內中央鋪着一塊威爾頓機織方地毯，房間裏的擺設僅此而已。室內四周的棕色櫟木的木板牆和鑲板上蛀孔斑斑，顯得十分陳舊而且褪了色，像是當年蓋這棟屋時的原樣。福爾摩斯拉過一張椅，默默坐在上面，兩眼四周上下打量，全神貫注地觀察室內每個細微地方。

最後他指着那條垂在牀邊上的粗鈴繩，問道：「這條拉鈴繩跟哪兒連接？」鈴繩頭的流蘇就在枕頭上面。

「連接管家的房間。」

「看起來它比房間裏別的東西要新一些。」

「是的，它才裝了一兩年時間。」

「我猜想是你姐姐要求裝的吧？」

「不是，我從沒聽說她用過。我們姐妹兩人想要甚麼，一向都是自己去拿。」

「是嗎？真是的，那就根本沒必要裝這麼一條漂亮的鈴繩了。對不起，我要花兩三分鐘查看一下地板。」說完他就趴在地上，手裏拿着放大鏡，輕快地前後匍匐移動，挺認真地察看地板之間的隙縫。接着他又以同樣方式察看一下護牆板。最後，他走到牀邊，盯視那張牀好長一段時間，順着牆上上下下來回打量。最後他抓住鈴繩，突然用力一拉。

"咦，是條假鈴繩，"他説。

"不響嗎？"

"不響，上面甚至沒接上線。這倒挺有趣！現在你可以看出繩一頭剛好繫在那個小小的通氣孔上面的鉤上。"

"多荒謬啊！我過去完全沒注意到。"

"太奇怪了！"福爾摩斯拉着那條繩，喃喃道。"這屋裏有那麼一兩處顯得挺怪。譬如説，那個蓋屋的人多麼愚蠢啊，竟把通氣孔通向另一間房，他原本可以花費同樣的工夫把通氣孔通向戶外啊！"

"這也是新安裝的，"那位小姐説。

"是跟那條鈴繩同時安裝嗎？"福爾摩斯問道。

"是同時，那一次還另有數處做了些小改動。"

"看來這些都是挺有趣的特徵——假鈴繩啦，通氣孔不通氣啦。斯托納小姐，請允許我們再到裏面那間房去查一下。"

羅伊洛特的房間比她兩個繼女的房間寬敞些，可是也佈置得同樣簡樸，一張摺疊牀，一個放滿書籍的木書架，上面排列的大都是技術書，牀邊放着一張扶手椅，靠牆還有一張普通木椅，另有一張小圓桌和一個挺大的鐵保險櫃，一眼能看到的就是這些擺設了。福爾摩斯慢慢繞一圈，極其敏鋭地逐一做一番檢查。

"這裏面放着甚麼？"他輕敲一下保險櫃，問道。

"我繼父的文件。"

"哦，你見過裏面的東西嗎？"

"好幾年前見過一次。我記得裏面都是文件。"

"打個比方，那裏面沒養貓嗎？"

"沒有，您這個想法多奇怪啊！"

"那你看看這個！"他拿起放在保險櫃上面的一小盤牛奶。

"沒有，我們家沒養貓，可是養了一隻狒狒和一頭獵豹。"

"哦，對了，一頭獵豹倒像隻大貓，可是用一小盤牛奶來餵獵豹，我敢說這哪兒夠啊！還有一點我要確定一下。"他說完就蹲在那張木椅前面非常仔細地檢查椅座。

"謝謝，這裏都檢查完了。"他站起來，把放大鏡放進上衣衣袋裏。"嘿！這兒還有件挺有意思的玩意！"

他發現那件挺有意思的東西是掛在牀頭上的一條打狗的鞭子。可是那根鞭子是捲起來的，而且上面還打了個結，使鞭繩有了一個圈。

"你說這是做甚麼用的，華生？"

"這是一條再普通不過的鞭子，可我卻不明白為何要紮個扣。"

"這就不太普通了吧，是不是？唉！這真是個萬惡的世界。一個聰明人若把自己的智慧用在犯罪上面，那可就再糟糕不過了。我想我在這兒已經看夠了，斯托納小姐，現在我們一起到草坪上去走走吧。"

我們離開調查現場時，我從沒見過我朋友的神情那麼嚴峻，眉頭那樣緊鎖。我們在草坪上來回散步，福爾摩斯陷入了沉思冥想，我和斯托納小姐都不想打斷他的思路。

最後他終於說道："斯托納小姐，現在至關重要的是你要在各方面絕對聽從我的吩咐。"

"行，我一定照辦。"

"情況十分嚴重，不容任何猶豫不決。你的性命就看你聽從不聽從了。"

"我向您保證，絕對聽您的安排。"

"首先，我和我的朋友今天夜晚要在你的房間裏過夜。"

斯托納小姐和我都目瞪口呆地望着他。

"對，必須這麼做。讓我解釋一下。那邊大概就是村落裏的旅館吧？"

"是的，那是皇冠旅館。"

"好極了，從那邊看到你那間房的窗戶吧？"

"當然看得見。"

"你的繼父一回來，你要謊稱頭痛，留在房間裏別出來。等你聽到他躺下睡覺後，你就打開房間的百葉窗，拉起窗戶搭扣，把燈放在窗口作為給我們的信號，然後你就帶上可能需要的東西回到你原來的房間裏去過夜。我毫不懷疑那裏儘管在修繕，過一夜總還是可以的。"

"嗯，當然可以。"

"別的事就由我們來處理。"

"可你們要做甚麼？"

"我們要在你那間臥室裏過夜，調查一下那種打擾過你的聲音是從哪兒來的。"

"福爾摩斯先生，我相信您已經打定了主意，"斯托納小姐把手放在我朋友的袖上，說道。

"也許是的。"

"那就可憐可憐我吧，告訴我，我姐姐是怎麼死的。"

"我倒寧願找到更確切的證據後再告訴你。"

"您至少可以告訴我她是不是突然受了驚嚇而死的，我這個看法是否正確？"

"不，我並不那麼認為。我認為可能有某種具體原因。現在，斯托納小姐，我和華生要走了，要是讓羅伊洛特醫生回來碰上，那我們就算白來了。再見，勇敢些，你若照我的囑咐去做，那就儘管放心，我們很快便會驅走那些威脅你的危險。"

夏洛克‧福爾摩斯和我在皇冠旅館，挺順利地訂了一間帶臥室和客廳的房。房間在上一層，我們從窗口可以清楚望到斯托克‧莫蘭鎮，那座宅邸臨街大門和住人的那側廂房。傍晚時份，我們看到羅伊洛特醫生乘馬車經過，他那魁梧身軀赫然聳現在趕車的瘦男孩身旁。男僕打開沉重的大鐵門時遇上點困難，我們聽到醫生嘶啞的怒吼聲，還看見他朝那個男僕揮舞拳頭。輕便馬車駛進大門；沒多久，我們便看到樹叢間亮出燈光，那個客廳點上了燈。

"華生，"我們兩人坐在夜幕漸漸降臨的黑暗裏，福爾摩斯說，"今天晚上我帶你來，心裏真有點不安，因為這事明顯會有危險。"

"我幫得上忙嗎？"

"有你在場可能幫到極大的忙。"

"那我當然要去。"

"真是太感謝你了。"

"你談到危險，想必你在那間房裏看到的比我要多。"

"沒有，我可能只稍微多做了些推斷。我想你跟我一樣看到了所有東西。"

"除了那條鈴繩外，我幾乎沒看到甚麼值得注意的東西，而且那條繩究竟有甚麼用場，不瞞你說，我還真想不出來。"

"你也看到了那個通氣孔吧？"

"看見了，可是我認為兩間房之間開個小洞也並不稀奇古怪，那個洞口小得連老鼠都鑽不過去。"

"我們兩人來斯托克・莫蘭鎮之前，我就知道會發現一個通氣孔。"

"親愛的福爾摩斯，怎麼會呢？"

"嗯，我確實那麼想的。你記得那位小姐告訴過我們她姐姐聞得到羅伊洛特醫生的雪茄煙味。那當然就是說那兩間房之間必定有個通口。那只能是很窄小的，要不然驗屍官在詢問時會提到的，因此我推斷是個通氣孔。"

"可那又能造成甚麼危害呢？"

"嗯，至少在時間上有着古怪的巧合。鑿了一個通氣孔啦，掛上一條鈴繩啦，睡在牀上的小姐的死啦，這難道叫你不感到奇怪嗎？"

"我還是想不出這三者之間有甚麼關聯。"

"你有沒有注意到那張牀有甚麼不大尋常的地方嗎？"

"沒有。"

"它是讓螺絲釘固定在地板上的。你以前見到過那樣固定的牀嗎？"

"從來沒見過。"

"那位小姐沒法移動她那張牀，牀總要跟通氣孔和繩保持在一定位置上，我們叫它繩吧，因為那明明不是用來做鈴繩的。"

"福爾摩斯，"我喊道，"我似乎隱隱約約領會了你暗示的意思。我們正好來得及阻止某種陰險可怕的罪行發生。"

"是夠陰險可怕的。一個醫生一旦誤入歧途，就會是最兇惡的罪犯。他既有膽量又有智慧。帕爾默和普里查德就是他們那一行的傑出人物。但是我認為這個人技高一籌，可是，華生，我相信我們比他還要更高明。不過在天亮之前，讓人擔心害怕的事還會不少，看在上帝份上，先讓我們靜靜抽袋煙，在這數小時裏想點叫人更愉快的事吧。"

大約夜晚九時左右，從樹叢中透過來的燈光熄滅了，宅邸裏一片漆黑。兩個小時慢慢過去了，時鐘正敲響 11 時的時候，我們的正前方驀地出現一盞孤燈明亮的光芒。

"那是發給我們的信號，"福爾摩斯跳起來說，"燈光是從當中那間房的窗戶亮出來的。"

我們兩人走出旅館時，福爾摩斯跟店老闆打了個招呼，說我們要去夜訪一個老朋友，很可能就在他那裏過夜。我們很快便來到一條漆黑的路上，一股涼颼颼的寒風吹在我們臉上，一柱昏黃燈光在我們前方閃爍，在這朦朧的夜色中引導我們去完成嚴峻的使命。

我們很容易就進入了那棟宅邸的院子，因為庭園的古老圍牆上有不少沒有修補的豁口。我們穿過樹叢，越過草坪，正準備鑽進窗戶，忽然從月桂樹叢中竄出一樣像是醜陋畸形的小孩模樣的東西，扭動着四肢縱身跳到草坪上，隨即飛快跑過草坪，消失在黑暗裏。

"老天！"我低聲説，"你看見了嗎？"

福爾摩斯也跟我一樣嚇了一跳。他緊張得用他那老虎鉗似的手緊緊抓住我的手腕，接着他輕聲笑了起來，朝我耳邊説聲悄悄話。

"真是絕妙的一家！是那隻狒狒！"

我已經忘了醫生喜歡養的怪寵物。還有一頭獵豹呢，我們隨時隨刻都可能發現牠趴在我們的肩膀上呢。我承認我學福爾摩斯那樣脱掉鞋鑽進臥室，心情才感到踏實些。我的夥伴輕輕關上百葉窗，把那盞燈挪到桌上，向四周掃視一眼。室內全都跟我們白天看見的一樣。他躡手躡腳地走到我身邊，把手圈成喇叭形，又在我耳邊説聲悄悄話，聲音低得叫我剛能聽清他説的意思，"如果出一點聲，我們的計劃就徹底失敗！"

我點點頭表示明白了。"我們兩人還要熄了燈，摸黑坐着。他會從通氣孔發現亮。"

我又點點頭。

"可千萬別睡着，這關係到你的性命。準備好手槍，我們也許用得着。我坐在牀邊，你坐在那張椅上。"

我掏出手槍，把它放在桌角上。

福爾摩斯隨身帶來了一根細長的藤條，把它放在身邊的牀上。牀旁邊他放了一盒火柴和一個蠟燭頭。然後他就熄滅了燈，我們兩人便坐在黑暗裏。

這次可怕的守夜叫我這一生怎能忘懷呢？我聽不見一點聲響，連喘氣聲也聽不見，可我知道我的夥伴睜着大眼就坐在離我數尺遠的地方，跟我一樣處於神經緊張的狀態。百葉窗擋住了外面微弱的亮光，我們徹底在黑漆漆的室內等待。外面偶爾傳來一聲貓頭鷹的叫喚，還有一次就在我們的窗戶下有一聲野貓似的長長嚎叫，這說明那頭獵豹確實在院子裏到處亂跑呢。我們還可以聽到遠處教堂深沉的鐘聲，每隔一刻鐘就敲響一次。那每一刻鐘顯得多麼漫長啊！鐘敲響十二時，一時，兩時，三時，我們還默默坐在那兒等待可能出現的任何情況。

突然間一瞬即逝的亮光從通氣孔那兒閃現出來。隨之而來的是一股煤油燃燒和金屬加熱發出的強烈氣味。隔壁房間裏有人點着了一盞遮光的提燈。我聽到一陣輕微的挪動聲，隨後一切又都靜下來，只是那股氣味越來越濃。我坐着側耳傾聽足足有半個小時。接着又突然聽到另一種聲音——非常柔和的輕微聲響，就像一個沸騰的水壺不斷發出的嘶嘶噴氣聲。我們剛一聽到這聲音，福爾摩斯就立刻從牀上一躍而起，劃着一根火柴，用藤條用力抽打那條鈴繩。

"華生，你看見了沒有？"他喊道，"看見了嗎？"

可是我卻甚麼也沒看見。福爾摩斯剛才劃火柴那時候，我倒是聽到了一陣低微清晰的口哨聲，可是突然那一閃亮，照花了我的兩眼，使我沒看清我朋友在拼命抽打的是甚麼東西。但是，我看得出他面色煞白，一臉恐懼和憎惡的神情。

他已經停止抽打，正抬頭注視着通氣孔。這時候，黑夜裏忽然爆發出我這輩子聽到的最嚇人的慘叫聲。叫聲越來越響，一種混着疼痛、恐懼和憤怒的可怕的尖聲哀嚎。據說，村鎮裏，甚至連遙遠的教區，人們都被這陣慘叫聲從睡夢中驚醒，這可真使我們毛骨悚然，我站在那裏望着福爾摩斯，他也望着我，一直到淒厲的嘶叫回聲最後消失，周圍恢復原來的寂靜時為止。

"這是怎麼一回事？"我氣喘吁吁地問道。

"這表明這事全都結束了，"福爾摩斯答道，"總的看來，這個結局也許是最好的了。拿着你的槍，我們到羅伊洛特醫生那間房裏去看看。"

他面帶嚴峻的神情，點着了燈，帶頭從通道朝醫生那間臥室走去。他敲了兩次門，裏面沒有一點反應。他便轉動門把，開門走進去，我緊隨在後，手裏握着扣起扳機的手槍。

出現在我們眼前的是一幅奇特景象。桌上放着一盞遮光的提燈，遮光板半開着，一道亮光照射在櫃門半開着的鐵保險櫃上。桌邊那張木椅上坐着羅伊洛特醫生，他身穿一件灰色睡袍，兩隻光腳踝在下面，腳伸在一雙土耳其式平底拖鞋裏。膝蓋上橫放着我們白天注意到的那根短柄長鞭子。他的下巴翹起，兩眼盯視着天花板上處的一角。額頭上繞着一條奇特的黃繩，上面有棕色斑點，那條繩似乎緊緊盤在他的頭上。我們走過去，他既沒吭聲也沒動。

"繩！斑點繩！"福爾摩斯低聲說。

我向前邁一步，那個古怪的頭飾開始蠕動起來；從他的頭髮裏豎起一條有鑽石型的頭、頸項鼓脹的毒蛇！

"這是一條沼澤地帶的蝰蛇！"福爾摩斯驚呼道，"印度最毒的蛇。人被牠咬後，十秒鐘之內便會喪命。真是惡有惡報，陰謀家掉進自己挖的陷坑，害人反害己。我們先把這條毒蛇弄回牠的窩裏去，就可以把斯托納小姐轉移到一個安全地帶，然後再通知當地警方這裏發生了甚麼事。"

他一邊說，一邊迅速從死者膝蓋上抽出那根鞭子，輕輕把活結甩過去套牢毒蛇頸項，把牠從那可怕的盤踞地拉起來，伸直手臂拉着牠，把牠扔進保險櫃，隨手關上鐵門。

這就是斯托克・莫蘭鎮羅伊洛特醫生死亡的真實情況。這篇敘述已經夠長了，至於我們後來怎樣把這可怕的經過告訴那位嚇壞了的小姐，我們陪她乘早車到哈羅市，交給她那好心腸的姨媽照顧啦，警方怎樣經過漫長的調查而得出結論，判定醫生是輕率地玩弄自己養的危險寵物時不慎喪生啦，等等等等，我就沒必要再敘述。案情中我還有點不太了解的地方，福爾摩斯在翌日回城的路上詳細給我解釋了。

"親愛的華生，我曾經得出一個完全錯誤的結論，"他說，"這表明根據不充份的資料進行推論是多麼的危險。那些吉卜賽人的存在，還有那位可憐的小姐使用了'繩'這個字，無疑是在說明她在劃亮火柴後驚恐瞥見到的東西，這些情況足以引導我跟蹤一條完全錯誤的線索。後來我弄清那種威脅到室內人的任何危險都不可能來自窗戶，也不可能來自房門，我便立刻重新考慮了想法，只有這一點可以說是我的成績。我剛才已經跟你說過，我的注意力馬上被那個通氣孔和那根掛在牀頭的鈴繩吸引住了。我一發現那根鈴繩是個煙幕，那張牀釘牢在地板上不能移動，這就引起我猜疑那根繩很可能是給甚麼鑽過小孔來到牀上的東西起個橋樑作用，我當即想到了蛇，又聯想到醫生養了一些印度動物，就覺得自己的思路完全對頭。只有受過東方式鍛煉的聰明而又冷酷的人，才會想到利用任何化學試驗都檢驗不出的毒物。從他的觀點來看，這種毒物又能立刻起作用也會大為有利。只有目光十分敏銳的驗屍官才能驗出毒牙咬的兩個小黑點。接着我又想到口哨聲。當然了，天沒亮之前，他就要把那條蛇召喚回去，免得讓受害人發現。他可能是利用我們看見過的那一小盤牛奶，訓練了那條蛇一聽到口哨便回到他那裏去。他會在他認為最合適的時候把蛇送過通氣孔，確信牠會順着繩爬到牀上。蛇也許會咬，也許不會咬牀上的人。女孩可能整整一週每天夜裏都倖免於難，卻遲早難逃此劫的。

"我還沒走進醫生的房間就已經得出了這個結論。檢查了他那張椅，使我明白了他為了伸手到通氣孔當然要常常站在椅上。再見到那個保險櫃啦，那盤牛奶啦，那條鞭子上的活結啦，就足以消除剩下的疑點了。斯托納小姐聽到那金屬的哐聲顯然是她繼父急急忙忙把那條毒蛇關進保險櫃後關上鐵櫃門的響聲。你知道，我一旦打定了主意，就要採取甚麼步驟來證明這件事。我一聽到那爬蟲動物發出的嘶嘶聲，這你無疑也聽到了，我就馬上點亮房間，猛烈抽打牠。"

"抽打的結果是把牠趕回了通氣孔。"

"不但如此，還使牠在另一頭向牠的主人反撲過去。我那數下子藤鞭抽得牠夠厲害，激起了毒蛇的本性，牠就對準看到的第一個人狠咬了一口。因此，我對格里姆斯比・羅伊洛特醫生的死亡無疑負有間接責任，可是憑良心說，我對此並不感到十分內疚。"

7.

紫銅欅

夏洛克・福爾摩斯把《每日電訊報》的廣告頁扔在一邊，說道："對為藝術而藝術的人來說，最大的樂趣往往是從最普通、最平凡的藝術表現形式中獲得。華生，你為我們經辦的那些案件辛辛苦苦做了小小記錄，我因從中發現你倒是掌握了這一真理而高興，而且我還要說，你偶爾添油加醋時，突出的並非是我出頭露面的許多 causes célèbres[12] 的偵破和聳人聽聞的審訊，而倒是那些情節本身可能平凡瑣細，卻給我留下了發揮空間，發揮那已成為我特殊本份的推理和邏輯綜合才能。"

我微笑着說："可是我還是沒能完全使自己擺脫，那種竭力反對過我在記錄中使用聳人聽聞手法的指控。"

"你大概確實有錯誤，"他一邊說，一邊用火鉗夾起一塊火紅的爐渣點着他那個櫻桃木長煙斗，通常他在爭論而不是在考慮問題時，習慣用這個煙斗替換那個陶製的。"你的錯誤也許在於試圖把每項記述都寫得生動活潑，而不是把你的任務局限在記述事物因果關係的嚴謹推理上——其實這才是事物唯一值得注意的特點。"

"在這件事上，我覺得自己對你還是相當公正，"我有點冷冰冰地說，因為我不止一次注意到我這位朋友，獨特的性格中有一種叫我很反感的、自以為是的因素。

"不，這既不是自私自利，也不是驕傲自滿，"他說，像慣常那樣，是在回答我的想法而不是我說的話。"我若要求公正對待我的本事，那是因為這種本事並非屬於個人，而是已經超越了我本人。犯罪的事常見，邏輯性則罕見。因此你該把重點放在邏輯上而不是在罪行上。你已經把本該是一套講授課程降低為一系列故事。"

那是早春一個寒冷清晨，我們兩人在貝加街那個老房間裏吃過早餐，各自坐在熊熊爐火的兩旁。戶外滾滾濃霧瀰漫在一排排暗褐色房屋之間，對面住宅的窗戶在那繚繞的黃色霧圈中，隱隱變得陰暗、模糊不清而不成形。我們點着的煤氣燈，燈光照在枱布上，照在閃亮的瓷器和金屬器皿上，因為早餐後的桌子還沒有收拾乾淨。夏洛克·福爾摩斯整個早晨都一直沉默地翻閱一系列報紙的廣告欄，最後他顯然放棄了查閱，帶點情緒地就我的文筆上的缺點教訓了我一頓。

他停頓一下，一邊坐着抽他的長煙斗，一邊盯視着爐火，又接着說："可是同時也不會有人指責你使用聳人聽聞的筆法，因為你感興趣的案件，其中一大部份根本就不是法律意義上的犯罪行為，例如我盡力幫助波希米亞國王那件小事啦，瑪麗·薩瑟蘭小姐的奇特經歷啦，那個跟歪嘴男人有關的問題啦，那個貴族單身漢的事件啦，這些都是法律範圍以外的事。但是，避免了聾人聽聞，我又擔心你記述得可能過於繁瑣細碎了。"

"結尾可能是這樣，"我答道，"可是我採用的手法卻既新穎別致又饒有趣味。"

"行了吧，親愛的老兄，大眾，那些不善於觀察的廣大公眾，幾乎不會從一個人的牙齒看出那是一名編織工，從一個左拇指看出那是一名排版工人，他們根本就不在乎分析和推理的細微差別！不過呢，你如果寫得過於繁瑣，我也不怪你，因為做大案的時代已經過去。如今的人，要麼至少是犯刑事罪的人，已經沒有以往那種冒險創新的精神。我自己這個小業務似乎也退化到了一家代辦處的地步，只能辦理替人尋找丟失的鉛筆啦，替寄宿學校的年輕女子出出主意啦，諸如此類的小事了。我想我的事業已經跌到了谷底。今天早上我收到的這封短信，看來正標誌着我的事業的最低點。看一下這個吧！"他把一封揉成一團的信扔給我。

這是昨天晚上從蒙塔克廣場寄來的，內容如下：

敬愛的福爾摩斯先生：

　　我非常希望能跟您商量我是否該應聘當家庭女教師這件事。如果方便的話，我明天十時半前來拜訪。

　　　　　　　　　　　　　　　薇奧萊特・亨特敬啟

"你認識這位小姐嗎？"我問道。

"不認識。"

“目前已經十時半了。”

“是啊，我敢肯定這是她在拉門鈴。”

“這事也許要比你想像的有趣。你記得那宗藍寶石事件一開始只是異想天開的念頭，後來卻演變成一場嚴肅的調查。這事也許會一樣。”

“嗯，但願如此！不過，我們的疑團很快就會給解開，因為我若沒弄錯的話，當事人已經來了。”

他正説着，房門開了，只見一位年輕小姐走進房來。她衣着簡樸，卻十分整潔，一張透着機靈樣子的臉，長着啄木鳥蛋那樣的雀斑，舉動敏捷，像個為人處世很有主見的女人。

“您大概會原諒我打擾你吧，”我的夥伴站起來迎接她，她説道，“我遇到了一件怪極了的事。我因為沒有父母或任何親屬可以請教，就想到您也許會好意指點我該怎麼辦。”

“請坐，亨特小姐，我很高興能為你效勞。”

我看得出福爾摩斯對這位來客的談吐舉止印象良好，他用敏鋭的目光打量她一番，便靜下心來，垂下眼皮，兩手的指尖相抵着，傾聽她講述。

“我在史潘斯‧芒羅上校家裏當了五年家庭教師，”她説，“但是兩個月前，上校奉命調到加拿大新斯科舍省哈利法克斯工作，他便帶着數個孩子去了美洲，我便失了業。我登報求職，也按報紙上的廣告去應徵，卻都沒有成功。最後我的點滴積蓄眼看着就要花光，我已經到了智窮計盡的地步。

“西區有一家叫做魏斯塔韋的著名家庭女教師介紹所，我每週去那裏一次，看看有沒有適合我的工作。魏斯塔韋是這家介紹所創辦人的姓氏，實際上是由斯托珀小姐管理。她坐在她那間小辦公室裏，求職的婦女在接待室裏等待，然後一個接一個地給喚進去；她查閱登記簿，看看有沒有適合她們的工作。

"嗯，上星期我又去那家小公司，給喚進那間小辦公室，可是我發現室內並非斯托珀小姐獨自一人，她身旁還坐着一個面帶笑容、很胖的男人，下巴疊起好幾層厚厚實實地垂在喉嚨前，鼻上架着一副眼鏡，仔細觀察每個進去求職的小姐。我進去的時候，他在座椅上為之一震，立刻轉身對斯托珀小姐說，'這位可以了，再好不過了。太好了！太好了！'他看起來十分激動，極其和藹可親地搓着雙手。他那種和氣的樣子叫人看着他感到挺愉快。

"'你是來找工作嗎，小姐？'他問道。

"'是的，先生。'

"'做家庭教師？'

"'對，先生。'

"'你要求多少薪金？'

"'我以前在芒羅上校家裏是每月 4 鎊。'

"'哎呀呀，太少了——真是少得可憐！'他一邊大聲說，一邊伸出兩隻胖手情緒激動地在空中揮動。'怎麼竟會有人出這麼一丁點薪金給這樣一位具有才華和魅力的女郎！'

"'我也許沒有您想像的那麼有才華，先生，'我說，'懂一點法文，懂一點德文，懂一點音樂和繪畫……'

"'嘖，嘖！'他大聲說，'這些都不是主要問題，關鍵在於你有沒有一位有教養的婦女那種舉止和風度。簡而言之，就是這麼一回事。你如果沒有，就不適合教育一個有朝一日會在國家的歷史上扮演重要角色的孩子。可是你如果有，那麼，哎呀，任何一位先生怎麼能叫你委屈地接受少於三位數的薪金呢？小姐，你若肯受僱於我，薪水會從一年一百鎊開始。'

"您可以想像，福爾摩斯先生，這樣的待遇對我這個一貧如洗的人來說簡直好得難以叫人相信！那位先生可能看出我臉上現出懷疑的表情，就打開錢包，取出一張鈔票。

"'這是我的一貫作風，'他說，愉快地笑着，笑得兩眼在他那滿佈皺紋的臉上都眯成了兩條亮縫，'一向預先支付一半薪水給我僱用的年輕小姐，好讓她們能應付旅費上的零星開支，添置數件服裝甚麼的。'

"我覺得我從沒遇到過這樣體貼人的僱主，因為我當時還欠着店主不少債呢。這筆預付的薪水倒會解決我的困難。然而，這整個洽談總叫我覺得有些不大自然，我在許諾之前還想多了解些情況。

"'請問您住在哪裏，先生？'我問道。

"'漢普郡紫銅櫸，可愛的鄉村地區，離溫切斯特五里路。真是一處最可愛的鄉村，親愛的小姐，並且還有一座最可愛的古老的村屋呢。'

"'我的工作是甚麼呢，先生？我很想知道自己做甚麼事。'

"'照顧一個小孩——一個剛六歲的可愛的小淘氣。你要是看見他用一隻拖鞋拍死蟑螂，啪噠！啪噠！啪噠！你還沒眨下眼，三隻已經死了！'他靠在椅背上，笑得兩眼又眯成了縫。

"孩子這樣取樂倒叫我有點吃驚，可他爸爸的笑聲卻又讓我覺得他也許是在說笑話。

"'那我唯一的職責就是照顧一個小孩？'我問道。

"'不，不，不，不是唯一的，不是唯一的，親愛的小姐，'他大聲說。'你的職務還有，我想你是通情達理的，聽從我太太可能會做出的小小的吩咐，那些吩咐如果對一位小姐來說可以得體地遵從的話。這沒有甚麼困難吧，是不是？'

"'我很樂意做點事幫你們。'

"'那太好了。比如說，衣着方面！我們是講究時尚的家庭；要知道，講究時尚，卻心地善良。我們如果要求你穿上我們可能會提供給你的衣服，你不會反對我們這種小小的癖好吧？'

"'不會，'我答道，可是對他說的話還真有點驚訝。

"'或者讓你坐在這兒，坐在那兒，你也不會反對吧？'

"'哦，不會的。'

"'或者讓你來我們家之前剪短頭髮呢？'

"我簡直不敢相信自己的耳朵。您也許注意到了，福爾摩斯先生，我的頭髮長得很密，有一種相當特殊的栗色光澤，頗為秀麗，我做夢也沒想到要如此隨便地把它犧牲掉！

"'這一點恐怕不大可能，'我說。他一直用他那雙小眼睛盯視着我，我說完後看得出一股陰影掠過他那張臉。

"'這一點恐怕還是相當重要的，'他說，'這是我太太的一個小小的癖好，女士的癖好；要知道，小姐，女士的癖好也必須顧及的。這麼說，你不肯剪短頭髮？'

"'不行，先生，我辦不到，'我堅決地答道。

"'好吧，那就算了，真怪可惜的，因為你在其他各方面都挺合適。斯托珀小姐，讓我再從別位女士當中挑挑吧。'

"那位女經理一直忙着處理自己的事，沒對我們兩人說過一句話，可這時她明顯露出很不耐煩的神情，瞥我一眼，使我不由得懷疑她是否因為我的拒絕而失掉一筆可觀的佣金。

"'你還願不願意把名字留在登記簿上？'她問道。

"'給我留下吧，斯托珀小姐。'

"'唉，你既然這樣拒絕了別人提供的最優厚的待遇，看來再登記上也沒用了。'她刻薄地説。'你很難指望我們再為你盡力找到這麼好的工作了。再見，亨特小姐！'她按一下桌上的鈴，我就由一名小男僕帶出去了。

"福爾摩斯先生，可是等我一回到家，看到食櫥裏幾乎空空如也，桌上還放着兩三張賬單，就覺得自己是不是做了件蠢事。這些人如果有些怪癖，期望別人聽從那種異乎尋常的要求，畢竟至少準備為自己這種古怪行為付錢啊，英國很少有家庭教師一年賺一百鎊。再説，我的頭髮對我又有甚麼用途呢？如今很多人都留短髮，覺得更時髦，我或許也該成為她們當中的一員。第二天，我傾向於認為自己大概是錯了。第三天，我肯定自己是做錯了事。我幾乎已經克制了自己的傲氣，想去介紹所打聽一下那個工作是否還空着；就在這時，我收到了那位先生寫來的一封親筆信。我把它帶來了，唸給您聽聽。

溫切斯特近郊紫銅櫸

親愛的亨特小姐：

　　承蒙斯托珀小姐把你的地址給了我，使我得以寫信徵詢你是否重新考慮過你的決定。我太太很盼望你能來，因為我對你的描述引起了她的好感。我們願意每一季度給你 30 鎊，也就是每年 120 鎊，以補償我們的癖好給你帶來的小小的不便。這些要求畢竟對你並非過於苛刻。我太太偏愛特別深的鐵藍色，希望你早晨在室內穿着這種顏色的服裝。你不用花錢添置新的，因為我們有這樣一套衣服，原是（現居美國費城的）我們親愛的女兒愛麗絲的，我認為你穿上一定很合身。再者，讓你坐在這裏或那裏，或者指定你怎樣消遣時光，這些要求也不至於叫你感到甚麼不便。至於你的頭髮，剪掉確實很可惜，尤其是我在短暫會見你時，就不由得大為讚賞你那頭美髮。可我恐怕還要堅持要求你剪短，我只希望增加的薪水也許能夠補償你的損失。至於照顧那個孩子的職責，那會是很輕鬆的。請務必前來，我會乘一輛雙輪輕便馬車到温切斯特接你。盼告搭乘的火車班次。

傑夫羅・魯卡斯爾敬啟

"福爾摩斯先生，這就是我剛收到的那封信的內容，我已經決定接受這個工作，可我想做出最終決定之前，要把整個這件事跟您說說，聽聽您的意見。"

"亨特小姐，你若已經打定了主意，那就這麼辦吧，"福爾摩斯微笑着說。

"可您為甚麼不勸我拒絕呢？"

"說老實話，我倒是不想看到自己的姊妹申請這樣一個職務。"

"為甚麼呢，福爾摩斯先生？"

"我目前沒有具體論據，說不上來。你自己也許已經有了甚麼看法吧？"

"我認為這只有一種可能的解釋。魯卡斯爾先生看起來是個很善良而溫厚的人。他夫人會不會是個瘋子，因此他希望把這事捂住，不讓人知道，以免她給送進瘋人院；為了不讓她的神經病發作，他便想方設法滿足她的怪要求。"

"這倒是一個說得過去的解釋，實際上，照目前的情況來看，真可能就是這樣。但是，無論如何，對一位年輕小姐來說，看來那並不是一戶好家庭。"

"可是那筆薪金，福爾摩斯先生，錢可給得不少啊！"

"對，當然，薪水是很高的——太高了！這正是叫我擔心的原因。他們可以花 40 鎊就能挑選一個家庭教師，憑甚麼要付給你一年 120 鎊呢？這背後必定隱藏着某種特殊緣故。"

"我想我把情況都告訴了您，以後萬一我需要您的幫助，您就明白這是怎麼一回事了。而且我覺得您是我的後盾，自己就會更勇敢。"

"哦，你可以帶着這種感覺前去。我向你保證，你這個小難題很可能是近數個月來我遇到的一件最有趣的事。這裏面有些特徵明明很怪。你如果感到沒把握或者感到危險……"

"危險？您預見到甚麼危險了嗎？"

福爾摩斯嚴肅地搖搖頭。"我們若能給危險下定義，那就不成其為危險了，"他說，"但是不論甚麼時候，白天也好，夜晚也好，打個電報給我，我就會幫助你。"

"這就足夠了，"她從椅上敏捷地站起來，臉上焦慮的神情一掃而光。"現在我可以安心地去漢普郡了。我會馬上寫信回覆魯卡斯爾先生，今天晚上就把我這可憐的頭髮剪短，明天便去溫切斯特。"她又對福爾摩斯說了數句感謝的話，向我們兩人道了晚安，便匆匆忙忙地走了。

我聽到她下樓的矯捷步伐，便說道："看來她至少是個能照顧好自己的女子。"

"她正需要這樣，"福爾摩斯一本正經地說，"要是很多天後聽不到她的消息，我就大錯特錯了。"

沒過多久我朋友這個預言就兌現了。半個多月來我時常在思索那件事，弄不清那位孤單的女子誤入了甚麼樣古怪的人生歧途。那筆異乎尋常的薪水啦，奇特的要求啦，輕微的職務啦，全都表明情況不大正常，那究竟是一種個人癖好呢，還是一個陰謀詭計；那個人究竟是一位慈善家呢，還是個惡棍，我都沒有能力做出判斷。至於福爾摩斯，我發現他經常坐在那裏皺着眉頭沉思半個多小時，可我一提起那件事，他就會一揚手表示不願意談。"論據！論據！論據！"他不耐煩地嚷道。"沒有黏土我做不出磚頭。"最後他總是自言自語說他絕對不會讓自己的姊妹接受這樣的工作。

終於在一天深夜裏我們接到一封電報。當時我正要上牀睡覺，福爾摩斯則準備安頓下來，着迷地做一個通宵化學試驗；往往是夜間我離開他時，他彎着腰在試管或曲頸瓶前面做化驗，次日清晨我下樓來吃早飯時，他還保持着那個姿勢呢。他打開那個黃信封，瞥一眼電報內容，就把它扔給我。

"查一下去布拉德肖的火車時間，"他說，又轉身做他的化學試驗。

電報內容簡短而緊急：

請於明天中午到溫切斯特黑天鵝酒店。務必前
來。我已經智窮計盡。

亨特敬啟

"你願意跟我一起去嗎？"福爾摩斯抬頭問道。

"願意。"

"那就查一下火車時間表吧！"

"九時半有一班車，"我一邊說，一邊查看要找的布拉德肖，"11時半到達溫切斯特。"

"這倒很合適。那我最好推遲一下我的丙酮分析吧，因為明天早晨也許我們的精神和體力都需要處於最佳狀態。"

翌日11時，我們已經順利地在前往英國舊都的途中。福爾摩斯一路上只埋頭翻閱晨報，可是一過漢普郡邊界，他便扔下報紙，欣賞起風景來了。這是一個理想的春天日子，淡藍的天空點綴着從西到東飄浮着的朵朵捲毛白雲，陽光燦爛，可還是有點令人爽快而振奮的涼風。在那整個鄉野，遠至環繞奧爾德肖特的綿延起伏的山巒，到處都有紅色和灰色的農舍小屋頂顯露在青翠新綠的葉叢中。

"多麼清新美麗的景色啊！"我來自煙霧瀰漫的百加街，不禁熱情地大聲讚嘆起來。

福爾摩斯卻嚴肅地搖搖頭。

"你知道嗎，華生，"他說，"我觀察事物總會跟自己探討的

問題聯繫起來，這是我的心靈該詛咒的一面。你是在欣賞那些星羅棋布的房舍，美麗的景色給你留下深刻印象，而我看到它們，心裏唯一的感覺卻是這些房舍互相之間疏遠隔離，會使那裏可能發生的犯罪行為得不到應有的懲罰。”

“我的天！”我驚呼道，“誰會想到把那些可愛的鄉村古老房屋跟犯罪聯繫起來呢？”

“它們一向叫我充滿某種程度的恐怖感覺，華生。根據我的經驗，我相信那些令人歡欣的美麗的鄉村與倫敦最底層惡劣的小巷相比，可能會發生更可怕的犯罪行為。”

“你讓我感到害怕！”

“可這是顯而易見的道理呢。在城市裏，公眾輿論的壓力能起到法律起不到的作用。沒有一條小巷會壞到連一個受虐待的孩童的哀叫聲或者一個醉漢的毆打聲，都引不起鄰居的同情或憤慨那種地步，況且司法機關離得很近，一旦有人提出控訴，就會馬上採取行動，犯罪離被告席只有一步之遙。但是，看看這些孤零零的屋，全都蓋在各自的田園裏，裏面住的人大都是愚昧可憐的老鄉，對法律了解得很少。想想看，這些地方可能年年都發生兇惡殘暴的行為和暗藏的罪惡，卻沒被人發覺。那位前來向我們求助的小姐如果住在溫切斯特，我就絕對不會為她擔憂。危險出在她住在五里以外的鄉村。不過，她本人目前明明還沒受到威脅。”

“沒有，她能到溫切斯特來跟我們見面，就說明她還能脫身跑出來！”

“對，她目前還有個人自由。”

“那究竟會是怎麼一回事呢？你能解釋嗎？”

"我曾經設想過七種不同的解釋，每種只適用於迄今我們所知道的事實情況。但是，只有得到那正等待我們的新信息，我們才能決定哪種設想正確。嗯，那邊是教堂塔樓，我們馬上就會聽到亨特小姐要告訴我們全部最新情況了。"

黑天鵝旅館在這條大道上是個有名的小旅館，距火車站不遠；我們在那裏找到了那位等待我們的女士。她已經在餐廳訂了一個雅座，午餐已經放好在桌上。

"你們來了我真高興，"她熱情地說。"太感謝兩位了；我真不知道該怎麼辦才好了。你們的指點十分寶貴。"

"那就告訴我們你遇到了甚麼麻煩？"

"我會的，我還要趕緊說，因為我答應魯卡斯爾先生三時以前回去。今天早晨我向他請假到城裏來，他並不知道我進城的目的。"

"那就按順序說說吧，"福爾摩斯把他那兩條瘦長的腿伸到火爐旁，靜下心來聽她說。

"首先，我要說，大體上我沒受到魯卡斯爾夫婦的虐待。這樣說對他們是公平的，可是我卻沒法理解他們，對他們總不放心。"

"你沒法理解他們甚麼呢？"

"他們為自己的行為所做的辯解。我說說所發生的事吧。我初到這裏，魯卡斯爾先生到車站接我，用他那輛雙輪輕便馬車接我到紫銅櫸。那裏像他說過的那樣，環境優美，屋本身並不美，是一幢粉刷成白色的四方形大屋，都讓潮濕和壞天氣侵蝕得斑駁，四周圍着空地，三面有樹林，另一面是個斜坡，一直伸展到南漢普頓公路，那條公路距離那棟屋的前門約百碼遠，彎彎曲曲地延伸。屋前面那塊地是屬於這屋的，而周圍的樹林則是薩瑟敦勳爵領地的部份防護林。那棟宅大門前種有一片紫銅欅樹叢，因此那裏就以紫銅欅命名。

"我那位僱主還像先前那樣和藹可親，駕車接我到家中。晚上把我介紹給他的夫人和孩子。福爾摩斯先生，我們在百加街您家裏猜測的情況並不符合事實。魯卡斯爾夫人沒有瘋，我發現她是位不言不語、臉色蒼白的夫人，比她丈夫年輕得多，我估計她最大 30 歲，而她的丈夫至少有 45 歲了。從他們的談話中我了解到他們兩人已經結婚大約七年了；他原是個鰥夫，跟前妻生下的唯一的女兒去了美國費城。魯卡斯爾私下告訴我他女兒離開他們是因為她對繼母有一種不合情理的反感情緒。由於那個女兒大概不會小於 20 歲，我完全可以想像她跟她爸年輕的妻子住在一起，處境想必不很舒服。

"我覺得魯卡斯爾夫人的面色和心靈都一樣蒼白。我對她既無好感也無惡感。她是個無足輕重的人。很容易就看出她全心全意熱愛她的丈夫和她的小兒子。她那雙淡灰眼睛不時地左顧右盼，一察覺到他們兩人有甚麼小小的需要，就趕緊搶先滿足他們兩個。魯卡斯爾先生對她也很好，只是方式上虛張聲勢些；大體上，他們像是一對幸福夫婦。但是，那位夫人卻私下有點憂愁，經常會陷入沉思，臉上現出十分悲傷的神情。我不止一次驚訝地發現她在落淚。我有時想這一定是她那個脾氣壞的孩子惹得她傷心，因為我從沒見過一個給寵得那樣壞的小朋友。他沒有同齡孩子那麼高，頭很大，顯得跟身軀很不相符，好像整天不是野性發作，就是板着面孔不高興。他唯一的消遣就是對那些比他弱小的動物施加酷刑。他在捕捉老鼠、鳥兒和昆蟲這方面所想出來的招數，表現出很了不起的才智。我不想再談這個孩子，福爾摩斯先生，真的，他跟我要談的事沒多大關係。”

“我對所有的細節都感興趣，”我的朋友說，“不管你覺得它們跟你有沒有關係。”

“我會盡量不漏掉任何重要細節。那棟大宅頓時叫我感到不愉快的事是僕人的外表和行為。家裏只有兩個僕人，一名男僕和他的老婆。男僕叫托勒，粗魯笨拙，頭髮灰白，蓄着連鬢鬍子，整天酒氣熏人。我有兩次跟他們在一起時，他醉得挺厲害，魯卡斯爾先生卻好像沒看見似的，滿不在乎。他的老婆很高挑，身強體壯，面目可憎，跟魯卡斯爾夫人一樣沉默寡言，卻遠不如她那樣和氣。他們兩個是一對最叫人討厭的夫妻。幸運的是我大部份時間都留在保育室和自己的房間裏，這兩間屋毗連，都在那間大宅的一個角落裏。

“我到紫銅櫸之後，頭兩天生活挺安靜；第三天，魯卡斯爾夫人吃過早餐後下樓來，跟她丈夫悄悄說了兩三句話。

“‘哦，對，對，’他轉身對我說，‘我們十分感謝你，亨特小姐，接受了我們的癖好把頭髮剪短了；我向你保證，這一點也沒損傷你的美貌容顏。現在我們要看看那套鐵藍色服裝合不合身，那套服裝就放在你房裏的牀上，你如果肯穿上它，我們夫婦都會非常感激的。’

“放在那裏等我穿的那套服裝的顏色特別暗藍，是用一種極好的嗶嘰料做的，可是一眼就能看出那是穿過的。我穿上它就像是量身定做的那樣合身，魯卡斯爾夫婦看見後都非常高興，甚至有點激動。他們在客廳裏等着我，那是一個很大的房間，佔據了那棟屋的整個前半部，有三扇落地窗，當中那扇窗的近旁放着一張椅背朝窗戶的椅。他們讓我坐在那張椅上，隨後魯卡斯爾先生便在房間另一頭來回踱步，開始給我說一連串我從沒聽過的很有趣的故事。你們想像不出他有多麼滑稽，我都笑累了。可是魯卡斯爾夫人卻顯然沒有甚麼幽默感，連笑都沒笑一笑，只是端坐在那裏，雙手放在膝上，臉上現出又憂鬱又焦慮的神情。大概過了一個小時，魯卡斯爾先生突然宣稱我該開始一天的工作，換掉衣服去保育室找小愛德華了。

"兩天之後，我又在完全相同的情況下照樣表演了一次：換上那套服裝，坐在那扇落地窗旁，聽我那位僱主說那些逗樂人的故事，他說得真是別人都模仿不出來，我不由得再次盡情大笑。隨後他遞給我一本黃封面的小說，把我的座椅向旁邊挪動一下，好讓我的身影不至於遮擋住那本書。他請我大聲唸給他聽。我就從某一章當中開始唸，唸了約十分鐘，正當我唸到一個句子的中間時，他忽然叫我停住，去更換衣服。

"您不難想像，福爾摩斯先生，我多麼難以理解這種離奇的表演究竟是甚麼意思。我注意到他們總是很小心謹慎地不讓我的臉面對窗戶，這就引起我極想看看我背後到底發生了甚麼事。一開始，這似乎是不可能的，可我很快便想出了一個妙法。我有一面小鏡碎了，我靈機一動，偷偷把一小片碎鏡藏在我的手帕裏。在又一次場合中，我在發笑時便把手巾舉到眼前，稍做調整就能看到背後的情況。坦率地說，我很失望，頭一眼甚麼也沒發現。

"頭一個印象至少是如此。可我再瞥一眼，卻看到一個男孩站在南漢普敦公路那邊，他身穿灰色衣服，蓄着絡腮鬍子，好像正朝我這個方向眺望呢。那條路是一條重要的公路，總有人來來往往。可是那個人卻斜倚在我們圍着空地的欄杆上，而且是在認真地觀望。我放低手帕，瞥一眼魯卡斯爾夫人，發現她正用最銳利的目光盯視着我呢。她甚麼也沒説，可我深信她猜到了我手中有塊鏡片，而且我也看到了背後的情景。她頓時站起來。

"'傑夫羅！'她説，'公路那邊有個沒規矩的人在盯着看亨特小姐呢！'

"'是不是你認識的人，亨特小姐？'他問道。

"'不是，我在這裏誰也不認識。'

"'老天！多麼沒禮貌！請轉身，揮手叫他走開！'

"'最好還是不答理他。'

"'不，不，那他就會常在這裏閒蕩。轉過身去，就這樣揚手叫他走開！'

"'我便按照吩咐做了，就在同時魯卡斯爾夫人放下了窗簾。這是一個星期以前的事，從那時起，我就沒再坐在那扇窗前了，沒再穿過那套藍裝，也沒再見到那個小子站在公路那邊了。"

"請接着説，"福爾摩斯説。"你説的事聽來將會挺有趣。"

"我擔心您會覺得我要説的事有點零散，互相之間沒有甚麼關聯。我第一天抵達紫銅櫸時，魯卡斯爾先生領我去廚房附近一小間外屋；走近那間小屋時，我聽到一根鐵鏈的啷聲和一頭挺大的動物走動聲。

"'從這兒往裏面看！'魯卡斯爾先生指着兩塊木板之間的隙縫，説。'多美的東西！'

"我從板縫往裏一看,只見黑暗中蜷伏着一個模糊的身軀和兩隻炯炯放光的眼睛。

"'不用害怕!'我的主人說,見我那副吃驚的樣子格格直笑。'那是卡羅,我的大猛犬,雖說是我的,其實只有我的男僕老托勒才管得住牠。我們每天只餵牠一次,不能餵得太多,這樣才能叫牠總有股狠勁。托勒每天晚上放牠出來。誰要是膽敢私自闖進我的家門,碰上牠那尖利的牙齒,那就只能求上帝保佑他了。看在上帝面上,晚上你可千萬別以任何藉口跨出這個門檻,那樣做可就不要命了!'

"這個警告並非隨便說說。過了兩夜,我在半夜二時左右,偶然從臥室朝窗外看看。那天夜裏月光皎潔,屋前的草坪銀光閃閃,明如白晝。我站在那裏,沉浸在美麗寧靜的夜色中,忽然間察覺有甚麼東西在紫銅櫸樹叢陰影下移動。牠一出現在月光下,我便看清那是甚麼了,原來是一隻像小牛般大的狗,全身棕黃,顎骨垂下來,黑嘴一張,骨骼龐大鼓出,慢慢穿越草坪,消失在另一邊陰影裏。這個不作聲的嚇人守衛真叫我心裏打了個寒噤,沒有一個竊賊會像牠那樣嚇壞我。

"現在我要告訴您一件特別怪的事。要知道,我是在倫敦剪短頭髮的,我把頭髮捲好放在我的衣箱底。一天夜裏,孩子上牀睡覺後,我開始欣賞臥房裏的擺飾,也重新整理一下我的零碎東西。房間裏有個舊衣櫃,上面兩個抽屜空着沒上鎖,下面一個鎖着,我把衣物裝滿那兩個抽屜,卻還有些東西沒處放。我當然由於不能使用那第三個抽屜而感到不悅。後來我驀地想到那也許是無意中鎖上的,我便拿出自己的一串鑰匙試着打開它,第一把鑰匙就正合適，鎖一下子便給打開了。抽屜裏只放着一樣東西，可我敢肯定你們一定猜不出那是甚麼。它竟是我那束頭髮！

"我拿起它來仔細察看，簡直跟我的頭髮特有的色澤完全一樣，密度也一樣。這種事根本不可能，我的頭髮怎麼會鎖在這個抽屜裏呢？我雙手發顫地打開自己那個衣箱，把裏面的東西翻出來，找出自己的頭髮。我把兩束頭髮平放在一起，我向你們保證它們完全一樣。這不是太離奇了嗎？我百思不得其解，琢磨不出這是甚麼意思。我把那束奇怪的頭髮又放回抽屜，後來也沒跟魯卡斯爾夫婦提起這事，因為我覺得打開別人鎖上的抽屜是不正當的。

"福爾摩斯先生，您也許已經發現我生來愛觀察事物吧。沒多久我的腦裏便對那間大宅的格局有了一個清晰的輪廓。一側的廂房看來根本沒人住。托勒夫婦住的下房前面有條通道，那裏有扇門直通那側的廂房，可是那扇門總是鎖着。有一天，我正上樓，碰見魯卡斯爾先生從那扇門走出來，手裏提着一串鑰匙，臉上的神情跟我平時常見的那個胖乎乎圓臉蛋上的愉快表情大不相同，使他儼然判若兩人。他因發怒而兩頰漲得通紅，眉頭緊鎖，激動得兩邊的太陽穴青筋畢露。他把門鎖上，從我身旁匆匆走過，一語未發，連看都沒看我一眼。

"這引起了我的好奇心。後來我帶着孩子在外面散步，便繞個圈，偷偷走到宅那一側，可以看到屋那部份的窗戶。那裏一行四扇窗，三扇非常骯髒，另一扇關着百葉窗。裏面顯然沒人住。我在那裏來回溜達，偶爾朝那邊瞥一眼。這時候，魯卡斯爾先生來到我面前，顯得跟往常一樣歡欣愉快。

"'啊！'他説，'我如果從你身旁一聲不響地走過去，請你千萬別以為我無禮，親愛的小姐，我剛才是忙着處理一些事。'

"我叫他放心，我並不介意。'順便問一下，'我説，'那邊好像有一整套房間空着，其中一間還關着百葉窗。'

"他顯得有些出乎意外，而且我覺得他聽了我的話有點吃驚。

"'攝影是我的一項愛好，'他答道，'那邊數間房是我洗相片的黑房。可是，哎呀，我們遇到了一位多麼細心的小姐啊！誰會相信呢？誰會相信呢？'他用一種開玩笑的口吻説，可他卻並非用打趣的目光望着我。我只看出一副懷疑和不滿的神情，絕不是在開玩笑。

"嗯，福爾摩斯先生，我自從明白那套房間有些我不該知道的事那一時刻起，就打算非查個明白不可。這不單純是出於好奇心，儘管我承認有這方面的因素，而更可以説是出於一種責任感，覺得識破那裏的隱秘，説不定是做了件好事。人們常談論女人的本能，或許正是女人這種本能使我有了那種感覺。不管怎麼説，這種感覺確實存在。我便特別留意任何可以進入那道禁門的機會。

"直到昨天我才遇到了這個機會。不瞞您説，除了魯卡斯爾先生外，托勒夫婦也常在那幾間廢棄的空房間裏忙着做些事。我有一次看見托勒抱着一個大黑布袋從那扇門裏出來。他近來一直酗酒，昨天晚上還喝得酩酊大醉，我上樓發現那扇門上插着鑰匙，這肯定是他遺漏在那兒了。魯卡斯爾夫婦那時都在樓下，那個孩子也跟他們在一起呢，我可有了一個難得的大好機會，便輕輕轉動鑰匙，打開門，悄悄進去。

"我面前有條小通道，沒貼牆紙，也沒鋪地毯，盡端轉彎處是個直角。轉過那個彎有三扇並排的門，第一和第三扇門敞着，裏面都是空房間，灰塵僕僕，陰陰沉沉，一間房間裏有兩扇窗，另一間只有一扇，窗戶上都積滿厚厚的塵土，夕陽光線只能微微透進來一點。當中那間的房門關着，門外擋着舊鐵牀的數根粗鐵槓，一頭用掛鎖鎖在牆上的一個環上，另一頭用粗繩捆住。那扇門也鎖着，鑰匙不在門上。堵住的門明明是跟外面關上百葉窗相一致的。可是從門底下的隙縫透出來的微弱亮光，使我明白房間裏並非黑漆漆。顯然室內有個天窗可以透進光線。我站在通道裏注視着那扇不祥的門，心裏奇怪那裏面隱藏着甚麼秘密。這時我忽然聽到室內有腳步聲，從房門底下的隙縫透出的微光我看出有個人影在裏面來回走動。這真使我心中驟然產生劇烈的莫名恐懼感。福爾摩斯先生，我神經一下子緊張得失去控制，轉身就跑，跑的時候像是有隻可怕的手在後面揪住我的衣裙，我跨過那扇門，撞在魯卡斯爾先生的懷裏，他正在門外等着我呢！

"'果然是你，'他微笑着說，'我看見門開着，心想準是你！'

"'哎呀，真把我嚇壞了！'我氣喘吁吁地說。

"'親愛的小姐！親愛的小姐！'——您想像不出他當時多麼親切，多麼體貼——'是甚麼把你嚇成這個樣子啊，親愛的小姐？'

"可他的聲音卻有點像是在哄騙。他裝得太過火了。我頓時警覺起來。

"'我走進空屋那邊，真夠傻的，'我答道，'可是在昏暗的光線下，那邊多荒涼多可怕啊！我給嚇得跑了出來。噢，那裏真是死氣沉沉，寂靜得可怕！'

"'就是這些嗎？'他問道，目光尖銳地看着我。

"'怎麼，那您怎麼想呢？'我問道。

"'你知道我為何鎖上這扇門嗎？'

"'不知道。'

"'就是不准閒人入內，你明白嗎？'他依然笑容可掬地說。

"'我要是早知道，肯定就……'

"'那好，你現在知道了！你要是膽敢再跨過這個門檻……'這時候他那種微笑頓時變成憤慨的獰笑，那張臉好似魔鬼的臉，兩隻兇眼瞪視着我，'我就把你扔給那隻大猛犬！'

"我當時真給嚇壞了，弄不清自己做了甚麼，想必是從他身邊飛快跑開，奔回自己的房間。我甚麼也記不起來了，渾身哆嗦地躺在牀上，隨後我就想到您了，福爾摩斯先生。如果沒人給我出出主意，我真是沒法再在那裏留下去了。我害怕那幢屋、那個男人、那個女人、那兩個僕人，甚至那個孩子，他們都叫我害怕。我要是能帶你們去那裏，那就好了。當然我也可以從那裏逃跑，可我的好奇心幾乎跟我的恐懼同樣強烈。我便很快做了決定，打個電報給您。我穿上大衣，戴上帽，走到約一里半開外的電報局，然後又回來，心裏踏實多了。可我走近大門時，忽然擔心那隻惡狗可能會給放了出來，但是我又記起那天夜裏托勒喝得爛醉不省人事，我知道家裏只有他管得住那頭野畜生，沒有人膽敢把牠放出來。我悄悄安全地回進家中，一想到很快就會見到你們，心裏高興得躺在牀上徹夜未眠。今天早晨我挺順利地請假來到了溫切斯特，不過要在下午三時以前趕回去，因為魯卡斯爾夫婦要出門作客，整個晚上都不在家，因此我要回去照顧孩子。現在我把經歷的事都說給您聽了，福爾摩斯先生，您要是能告訴我這究竟是怎麼一回事，那我可太高興了；關鍵在於我現在該怎麼辦？”

福爾摩斯和我着迷地聽完她說的這些怪事。我的朋友站起來在室內來回踱步，兩手插在袋裏，臉上現出極為嚴肅的神情。

“托勒現在還醉着沒醒嗎？”他問道。

“醉着呢，我聽他的老婆對魯卡斯爾夫人說她拿他一點辦法也沒有。”

“那好，魯卡斯爾夫婦今天晚上要出門，對不對？”

“對。”

“大宅裏有沒有一個地窖和一把不易打開的好鎖？”

“有個存酒的地窖。”

“我覺得你在整件事情上表現得像個勇敢機智的女孩，亨特小姐。你能不能再扮演一個角色？我要是不認為你是個很了不起的女士，就不會這樣要求你的。”

“我會盡量試試看。要我做甚麼呢？”

“我和我的朋友七時會到達紫銅櫸。魯卡斯爾夫婦那時已經出門不在家中，我希望托勒那時還醉得甚麼事也做不了。家裏只剩下托勒太太一個人，她也許會報警，可你如果能使她去一趟地下的酒窖，然後把她鎖在裏面，那就大大有利於我們的調查了。”

“這我會辦到，絕對沒問題。”

“太好了！那我們就可以徹底調查一下這件事。當然，只有一個說得通的解釋。你給僱到那裏是為了冒充一個人，而那個人正給鎖在那間空房裏呢。這是很明顯的。至於那個給囚禁起來的人是誰，我敢說就是魯卡斯爾先生的那個女兒愛麗絲，我如果沒記錯的話，據說她去了美洲。你被選中，肯定是因為你跟她在身高、身材和頭髮色澤上都很相像。她的頭髮可能是由於患了甚麼病而給剪掉了，所以你的頭髮也要犧牲掉。你發現了她那束頭髮純屬偶然。那個站在公路上觀望的小男孩無疑是她的好朋友——也可能是她的未婚夫——當然，你穿上她的服裝那麼像她，他每次看見你的時候，從你的歡笑和姿態都深信魯卡斯爾小姐挺幸福愉快，不再需要他關心。那隻惡犬每天夜裏都給放出來，是阻止他想跟愛麗絲接觸。這些都一清二楚了。這個事件最嚴重的一點是那個男孩的性格。"

"他跟這事又有甚麼關係？"我插嘴道。

"親愛的華生，你作為一名醫務人員，要了解一個孩子的傾向就要不斷研究他的父母才會得到領悟。你難道沒看出相反的研究也同樣有道理嗎？我經常從研究孩子入手，從而對他的父母的品格得到真正的認識。那個男孩的性格異常殘忍，只是為殘忍而殘忍，不管這種性格像我猜疑的那樣，是來自他那笑瞇瞇的父親呢，還是來自他的母親，反正這對他們控制的那個可憐的女子都肯定壞徵兆。"

"我相信您說的完全對，福爾摩斯先生，"我們那位委託人大聲說，"我回想起很多事，都使我確信您說到了重點。哦，我們別再耽擱，趕快去拯救那個女孩吧！"

"我們要小心謹慎，因為我們是在對付一個非常狡猾的人。七時之前我們辦不了甚麼事。一到七時，我們兩人就會跟你在一起，很快便能識破這個謎。"

我們恪守諾言，七時準時抵達紫銅櫸，把那輛雙輪輕便馬車停放在路旁一家小客棧那邊。那樹叢，還有它那在夕陽照耀下好似擦亮了的閃閃發光的紫黑葉，都使我們足以認出那個大宅，即使亨特小姐沒一直站在門口台階上等我們，也不要緊。

"你都安排妥當了嗎？"福爾摩斯問。

這時從樓下甚麼地方傳來了挺響的撞擊聲。"托勒太太給關在地窖裏了，"她說，"她丈夫躺在廚房地毯上鼾聲如雷地大睡呢。這是他的那串鑰匙，跟魯卡斯爾先生那串完全一樣。"

"你做得實在出色！"福爾摩斯大聲稱讚道，"現在你領路，我們很快就會見到這個陰謀的結局。"

我們走上樓梯，打開一扇門的鎖，沿着通道直奔亨特小姐所說的那扇給堵住的門前。福爾摩斯剪斷那根粗繩，挪開那數根橫擋着的鐵槓，然後試用數條鑰匙開門，可是都沒有成功。屋裏沒有一點動靜，福爾摩斯面對這種寂靜，臉色陰沉下來。

"我相信我們來得並不太遲啊！"他説。"我想，亨特小姐，你先避一避，我們兩個人最好先進去。現在，華生，用你的肩膀，看看我們兩人能不能把門撞開。"

那是一扇不牢靠的舊門，我們兩人一起一用力就把它撞開了。我們衝進去，裏面卻空無一人。室內除了一張簡陋的牀、一個小圓桌和一筐替換衣服外，別無他物。屋頂上的天窗是敞着的，可是裏面那個給囚禁的人卻沒影了。

"肯定有人做了手腳，"福爾摩斯説，"那個壞蛋大概已經猜到亨特小姐的意圖，搶先一步帶走了那個受害人。"

"怎麼帶走的呢？"

"從天窗。我們馬上就能弄明白他是怎麼做的，"他攀登到屋頂。"啊,對了,"他喊道,"這裏有個輕便的長梯靠在屋簷上,他肯定是這麼做的。"

"這不太可能,"亨特小姐說,"魯卡斯爾夫婦走的時候,這條梯不在那兒。"

"他又跑回來搬來的,我說過他是個狡猾的人。你聽樓梯上的腳步聲,如果不是他才怪呢。華生,我想你最好把槍準備好。"

他還沒說完,房門口就出現一個挺胖的粗魯男人,手裏拿着一根粗棒。亨特小姐一見到他就尖叫一聲,縮身靠在牆邊,夏洛克·福爾摩斯卻縱身向前,面對那個人。

"你這個惡棍,你的女兒在哪兒?"

那個胖子四周環視一下,抬頭看一眼那敞開的天窗。

"這個問題該我問你,"他尖聲嚷道,"你們這班盜賊!間諜和盜賊!可讓我逮住了你們,是不是?你們跑不了了。我會伺候各位!"他轉身噔噔地跑下樓梯。

"他去放出那隻惡犬!"亨特小姐喊道。

"我手裏有槍,"我說。

"最好把那扇前門關上,"福爾摩斯大聲說。我們便一起衝下樓梯,還沒走到前廳就聽見那隻惡犬的狂吠聲,接着傳來一聲痛苦的尖叫聲,隨後又是一陣聽起來嚇人的撕咬聲。一個滿臉通紅、上了年紀的人搖搖晃晃地從邊門走了出來。

"我的上帝!"他喊道。"有人放那隻狗出來了。我已經兩天沒餵牠了。快,快,要不就來不及了!"

福爾摩斯和我急忙衝出去,轉過房角,托勒緊跟在後。那條餓慌了的巨大畜生正用黑嘴緊緊咬住魯卡斯爾的喉嚨,他在地上痛苦地打滾，悽慘地尖叫。我跑上去，一槍把那隻狗的腦打開了花，牠倒下去，一嘴白牙還嵌在魯卡斯爾那胖頸項的皺褶裏呢。我們費了好大的力氣才把人和狗扯開，抬他進屋；他還活着，可是已經血肉模糊，傷勢不輕。我們把他放在客廳的沙發上，叫那個給嚇醒了的托勒趕快去通知魯卡斯爾夫人，我盡力減輕他的疼痛。我們圍着他忙，這時進來了一個瘦高的女人。

"托勒太太！"亨特小姐喊道。

"是我，小姐。魯卡斯爾先生回來時放了我出來，才上去找你們。唉，小姐，可惜你沒事先告訴我你的打算，否則我就會勸告你，別白操心！"

"哈！"福爾摩斯說，敏銳地望着她。"托勒太太明明對這事比誰都清楚了解。"

"對，先生，我確實了解，隨時準備說出我知道的情況。"

"那就請坐下，說給我們聽聽吧，因為我要承認這件事裏面確實還有數個地方我還不太明白。"

"我現在就給你們說明白，"她說，"我要是能早點從酒窖裏出來的話，早就可以這樣做了，"她說，"這事如果弄到治安法庭上去解決，你們要記住，我作為一個朋友，站在你們一邊，而且我也是愛麗絲小姐的知心朋友。

"愛麗絲小姐在家裏從來就沒快樂過。自從她爸爸再婚以來，小姐便一直鬱鬱不樂。她在家裏受到冷落，甚麼事都沒有發言權。在她還沒在一個朋友家中認識福勒先生之前，情況倒還不算太壞。據我所知，愛麗絲小姐根據母親的遺囑享有自己的權利。她不言不語，安靜忍讓，從沒提起過自己的權利，事事都交給魯卡斯爾老爺處理。她爸爸明白對她可以放心，可她一旦有了丈夫，那個男人肯定會要求她在法律範圍內應得的東西。所以她爸爸認為是該出面阻止的時候了。他就讓小姐在一份文件上簽名，聲明不管結婚與否，他都可以用她的錢。小姐不願意簽，老爺就沒完沒了地折磨她，弄得她後來得了腦炎，六個星期裏差點死了。後來小姐漸漸康復，卻已骨瘦如柴，並且把那頭美髮也剪掉了；可是那個男孩一點也沒變心，對她依然一片忠誠。"

"嗯，"福爾摩斯說，"謝謝你告訴了我們這些情況，讓我們明白了這件事。其餘的我也能推斷出來了。我猜想魯卡斯爾先生因此就採取了囚禁這個措施。"

"對，先生。"

"他從倫敦請來亨特小姐，好擺脫福勒先生那種叫人不愉快的糾纏。"

"是這樣，先生。"

"可是福勒先生是個執着的人，就像優秀的海員該做的那樣，封鎖了這幢屋。後來他碰到了你，用論證、金錢或別的方式說服了你，讓你相信你們兩人的利益是一致的。"

托勒太太開朗地說："福勒先生是個說話和氣、手頭慷慨的人。"

"他就這樣設法讓你的丈夫不缺酒喝，讓你一等主人出門就準備好一條梯。"

"您說得對，先生，就是這麼一回事。"

"我想我們方才把你鎖在地窖裏，真該向你道個歉，托勒太太，"福爾摩斯說，"因為你已經把我們困惑不解的事都解釋清楚了。現在，村裏的外科醫生和魯卡斯爾太太快要來了。華生，我想我們最好護送亨特小姐去溫切斯特，因為我覺得我們兩人目前在這裏的 locus standi[13] 頗成問題了。"

那座門前有紫銅櫸的不祥的大宅之謎就這樣解開了。魯卡斯爾先生雖然保住了一條命，卻變成了一個精神頹喪的人，只是在他那忠心耿耿的太太的護理下苟延殘喘。他們還跟那兩個老傭人住在一起，大概因為那對夫婦對魯卡斯爾老爺過去的底細知道得太多了，使魯卡斯爾先生很難辭退他們兩人。福勒先生和愛麗絲小姐出走後的第二天，便在南安普敦市申請特許證書結了婚。目前福勒先生在毛里求斯島擔任一個官職。至於薇奧萊特·亨特小姐，福爾摩斯叫我感到失望，因為她不再是他探討的一個問題的中心人物，他便不再對她感興趣了。現在亨特小姐是沃爾塞爾地區一間私立學校的校長。我相信她在教育工作上一定做出了成績。

完

註解

1 鮑斯韋爾 (1740-1795)，蘇格蘭作家，為著名文學家約翰遜的助手。

2 此處均指英尺英寸。以下類同。

3 約翰‧黑爾 (1844-1921)，19 世紀中葉到 20 世紀初英國著名喜劇演員。

4 瑪麗‧薩瑟蘭小姐是《身份案》中的人物。

5 拉丁文，意為大智若愚。

6 英國當鋪的傳統標誌。

7 均見《四簽名》一案。

8 法語，意思是四人一組。

9 法語，意思是"人是渺小的——著作才是一切。"

10 舒爾托那家人，指《四簽名》中的人物約翰‧舒爾托上校和他的兩個兒子。

11 原文 band 作"繩"解，亦可作"一群"解。

12 法語，著名案件。

13 拉丁文，出庭的權利，合法地位之意。